THE MIDNIGHT
MAYOR

THE MIDNIGHT
MAYOR

Or, The Inauguration of
Matthew Swift

KATE GRIFFIN

www.orbitbooks.net

Copyright © 2010 by Catherine Webb

All rights reserved. Except as permitted under the U.S. Copyright Act of 1976, no part of this publication may be reproduced, distributed, or transmitted in any form or by any means, or stored in a database or retrieval system, without the prior written permission of the publisher.

Orbit
Hachette Book Group
237 Park Avenue, New York, NY 10017
www.HachetteBookGroup.com

First US Edition: March 2010

Orbit is an imprint of Hachette Book Group. The Orbit name and logo are trademarks of Little, Brown Book Group Limited.

The characters and events in this book are fictitious. Any similarity to real persons, living or dead, is coincidental and not intended by the author.

Library of Congress Control Number: 2009935450

ISBN: 978-0-316-04123-2

10   9   8   7   6   5   4   3   2   1

Printed in the United States of America

THE MIDNIGHT
MAYOR

We be light, we be life, we be fire!
We slither blood blue burning, we sing neon rumbling, we dance heaven!
Come be me and be free.
Me be blue electric angel.

— Anonymous graffiti, Old Street

Don't give me all this hokum about the Midnight Mayor. You tell me
there's a man who is the chosen protector of the city? Who cannot die so
long as the idea of the city exists, who carries burnt into his flesh the mark
of the city and hears the dreams of the stones themselves? You seriously
want me to believe that the Midnight Mayor is real and out there in the
night keeping us safe from all the big nasties that are going to gobble us up,
then the first thing you should do is tell me what these nasties are that I need
so much protecting from.

— M. Swift, "The Midnight Mayor and Other Myths"—
Urban Magic Magazine, vol. 37, June 2003

Prelude: The Heavy Metal Spectres

In which a sorcerer is surprised to find himself cursed, burnt, branded, chased and condemned without any apparent reason and in the wrong pair of shoes.

The telephone rang.
  I answered.
  After that...
    ...it's complicated.

Pain.
  No room for anything else.
  Just pain.
  Time went by.
  Don't know how much. Watch fused to wrist; burnt. No clocks.
Mobile phone somewhere in my bag, but my bag wasn't on my shoulder. Wasn't near at hand. I raised my head. Drying blood crackled
like Velcro. I saw my feet. They were wearing someone else's shoes. It
took a minute to remember why.
  I raised my head a little higher.
  My bag was on the ground. It had fallen some distance away, spilling paint cans and old socks. Above it swung the telephone. A dribble
of blood was running down the receiver and splatting droplets onto
the ground. The blood was mine. There didn't seem to be any other
candidate.
  I put my head back down on the concrete, and closed my eyes.
  More time went by.
  It started to rain. Proper night-time rain, that sensed the wind chill
and wished it was snow. I found that my left arm, the one that hadn't
answered the phone, would obey basic commands. I said twitch, it
twitched. I said check for anything broken, and it checked. Nothing
was broken. Even the blood running down the back of my neck was

melodrama. There's two kinds of head wounds—the kind that look worse than they are, and the kind that kill you. Not dead; not again.

I let my left hand relax.

The wind was blowing the rain in at a 45-degree angle. In the gloom it was visible only as a sheet across the sodium-coloured streetlamp at the edge of this patch of concrete nothing. There was a drumming on the roofs and a rumbling in the gutters as three weeks of unswept dirt was washed into the grating. The rain was a blessing. We turned our shaking right hand up to the cool water and let it wash the blood off our fingers. Then, as it started to seep through my coat, shivering and the ache of deep-down cold began to replace the burning pain.

The decision to get out of the rain meant getting up.

Hercules didn't have anything on us; Muhammad Ali would have been impressed.

We got up.

Halfway there, my knee slipped on the wet concrete. My right hand hit the rough grain of the floor, and we nearly screamed.

The Terminator would have given up and gone to bed by now; the Knights Templar would have called it a day.

I got up. My world swam between blood-red and sapphire-blue. A dying streetlamp buzzed like a mosquito. Water had pooled in the plastic bubble that held the bulb, casting rippling shadows over the black-silver street. I staggered to the phone. My bag was a faded satchel made of plastic fibre pretending to be cotton. I picked it up and slung it over my shoulder. The phone swung uselessly on its cord. From the speaker it made the loneliest sound in the world:

Beeeeeeeeeeeppppp . . .

Wedged around the telephone itself, in the gap between machine and wall, were cards offering:

!!!SEXSEXSEXSEXSEX!!

Or:

PERKY PLAYFUL BLONDE

Or:

THINKING OF ENDING IT ALL? CALL THE SAMARITANS.

I had a scarf around my neck; I noticed one end was scorched. I pulled it tighter and tucked it inside my coat, an off-beige colour turning off-brown in the rain. Our head hurt. Our everywhere hurt, so many different parts demanding attention that it was hard to identify any single one. In my bag there was a first-aid kit, showing its wear. I found a bandage and wrapped it round my right hand. All I could see was blood, rain, and angry purple flesh puffed up so thick it was hard to tell where my palm ended and my fingers began. To hold the bandage in place, I pulled on a black fingerless glove. Pressure on the pain made it worse; but worse was good. Worse made the agony local, and meant we couldn't notice all the other parts of us that hurt.

I looked around.

I was in a garage. I knew this because, facing the street, a stained banner the colour of weak tea said: "CAR WASH AND SPARE PARTS". There were no other clues as to its function. Just a concrete floor exposed to the sky, four walls of corrugated iron, and a chain across the entrance. The telephone and a few discarded buckets were the only equipment I could see. Weeds were coming up between the cracks in the floor, and a sheet of torn plastic that might once have been a roof flapped in the wind.

A truck went by in the street outside. The sound of wheels through water always seems further off than it is. At this time of night, or morning, trucks were almost the only vehicles, delivering tomorrow's supermarket food to be stacked on the shelves behind yesterday's leftovers. Trucks; and the night buses, every passenger a suspect simply for being awake, every driver a lunatic who hears the call of fifth gear on every empty street.

Our head throbbed. I could feel each artery pulsing. We felt sick. I looked at the telephone receiver; then reached out, knuckles first, not trusting my fingertips to it. And would have touched it except that a sound—or the absence of a sound—held me back.

The *beeeeeeeeepppp* of the dialling tone stopped.

I drew my hand away instinctively. The phone hung limp as a dead squid. I listened. The sound of rain, the buzzing of a neon light about to pop. I stepped back a few paces, nursing my right hand, watching the telephone.

The sound of rain, the buzzing of a neon lamp, the swish of distant tyres...

What else?

We half closed our eyes, and listened.

Sound of rain, buzzing of neon, swish of tyres, scuttling of rats beneath the streets, scampering of the urban fox, king of the middle of the road, rustling of a pigeon in its overhead gutter; what else? Hum of mains voltage just on the edge of hearing, smell of rain, that incredible, clean smell that washes the dirt out of the air for just a few minutes, banging of a front door somewhere, crackling of a radio left on in the night, wailing of a car alarm, sing-song soaring of a siren, a long way off, distant *tumtetetumtetetumtete* of a goods train heading for Willesden Junction, and...and...

And there it was, right there on the edge; there was the strangeness.

It went:

Chi-chichi chi-chichi chi-chichi bumph bumph chi-chichi chi-chichi chi-chichi bumph bumph ...

I couldn't immediately work out what it was. Our ignorance frightened us. We wanted a weapon.

Chi-chichi chi-chichi chi-chichi went the sound. *Chi-chichi chi-chichi chi-chichi.* We didn't even have to close our eyes to hear it. Advancing, getting closer. *Chi-chichi chi-chichi* ...

The buzzing neon light gave up, popped and went out, shrivelling from sodium orange brightness to a blue shimmer in its core before darkness took it. It's easy to forget, in the city, how dark real darkness can be.

I started to walk. Climbed over the chain. Stepped out into the street.

There was someone at the far end, a few hundred yards off, smothered in shadows.

They were looking at me.

I turned in the other direction. If my shoes had been my own, I would have run.

I was in Willesden.

Christ.

Willesden is a nowhere-everywhere.

It isn't close enough to the centre of London to be inner city, nor far enough away to be suburb. It isn't posh enough to be well tended or have a single class of citizen, nor is it squalid enough to be dubbed "action zone" by a righteous local government bureaucrat. It doesn't have a unique ethnic character, but instead a mix of all sorts pile in from every corner, from tenth-generation Englishman dreaming of the south of France, to third-generation Afro-Caribbean who has never seen the equatorial sun. It sits astride a maze of transport links, buses, trains and canals, most of which are passing through to somewhere better. No one quite knows where Willesden begins or ends.

You can find anything you want in Willesden, so long as you don't go looking for it.

I would not have chosen to be in Willesden of my own accord. But we'd made a promise, and our promise had taken us here. Then a phone had rung in a garage and we'd answered it...

...and now there was something else on the streets tonight.

I could feel it.

Hear it.

A sound like an angry bee stuck in a jar, banging its head in regular and rapid rhythm on the glass.

Chi-chichi chi-chichi chi-chichi . . .

Cynics call it fate, romantics call it destiny, lawyers call it malign intent. No one uses the word "coincidence". I didn't. If you see vultures flying overhead and hear the distant sound of cannon, you don't call it coincidence, and in this city there were plenty of scavengers that could be lured out into the night, by the smell of blood. And our blood was a long way from merely human.

We thought of courage, we thought of fighting, we thought of running. Tonight, we concluded, was not a night for pride. Run.

I tried and couldn't. The shoes on my feet had been part of the promise too. But they were too big for me, and the two pairs of socks I wore to try and make up for it were soaked with rainwater. My right hand had been used as bait in a shark-fishing competition, my head had been sawn off for the trophy and reattached with a staple gun. And deep down we knew, though we didn't dare think about it, that these were probably just the superficial consequences of the night's work. There are more things you can catch from a telephone besides a burnt hand.

So I walked as fast as I could through the rain, head rising like a pigeon's to look ahead, then down to blink water from my eyes, then up again. Postbox, streetlights, falling rain, terraced houses, zebra crossing, with one of the flashing orange bubbles on its post smashed long ago. The lights were off in all the houses, except for the flickering of a TV to whose comforting nothings an old lady had fallen asleep this night like all the others. In someone's back garden, a cat shrieked with that unnatural sound that was either sex or death.

At a T-junction ahead a night bus stood; shadows sat in the bright whiteness of its windows. It was a short-route single-decker, the kind associated with old people out to collect their pension books, and empty beer cans rolling with each acceleration and brake. I couldn't see a number and didn't care. Four red walls and a set of wheels were all the protection I needed.

I picked up speed, half walking, half falling over the rhythm of my own feet, no longer caring if I was cold or wet, so long as I was somewhere that wasn't here. The road became lined with council flats, built from grey concrete streaked black in the rain. Lights shone from the communal doorways, and on the low wall separating the ground-floor flats from the street, some wit had written in tall white letters:

GIVE ME BACK MY HAT

I turned to follow the bus, in time to watch its brake lights disappear round a corner. Closer to, I saw the dim white light of a bus shelter, overhung by a plane tree. I went towards it, my shadow playing backwards and forwards like one cast on a sundial as I passed under the streetlamps.

There was someone at the bus shelter. Either I hadn't noticed him, or he'd just arrived.

There were also other, nastier possibilities. We tried to ignore them.

He sat on the narrow red bench, which was designed to be as uncomfortable as possible. His knees were wide apart as if someone had stuck a frisbee down his pants, his arms were folded across his chest to make it clear he didn't care about anything. He wore pale grey trousers three sizes too big, passed down by an elder brother moved on to better things, whose crotch began around the knees; a pair of black gloves like a motorbiker's gauntlets; sporty trainers adorned with rip-off logos; and a hoodie. The grey hood was drawn so low over his face I couldn't even see a protruding nose. It looked more like a cowl than a fashion accessory or, heaven forbid, protection against the weather. His head bounced gently to the rhythm playing from a pair of headphone cables that vanished into the interior of his tracksuit. The only sound that escaped them was a regular:

Chi-chichi chi-chichi chi-chichi . . .

Not an angry bee, but the bass rhythm of a song turned up too loud; tune, if there was one, lost to beat. Madness was no longer talking to yourself; technology had changed all that.

But this was something more.

On the top of the shelter someone had thrown a small plastic screwdriver and what looked like a child's left shoe, pretty pink turned dirty grey by the rain and the darkness. The single white lamp in the shelter was stained with dirty spots where a hundred insects had crawled inside it, and found it too hot for their wings to bear. A moth was the only survivor, fluttering impotently against the plastic cover.

The hoodie kept on bobbing to that invisible beat.

You don't ask strangers their business when waiting for the bus. Especially not in the small hours of the morning. I leant against the stop with its list of what was due when, and clutched at my burning hand.

Coincidence is usually mentioned only when something good happens. Whenever it's something bad, it's easier to blame someone, something. We don't like coincidence, though we were newer to this world than I. Inhabiting my flesh, being me as I was now us, we had quickly come to understand why so many sorcerers had died from lack of cynicism. I had been a naive sorcerer, and so I had died. We, who had been reborn in my flesh, were not about to make the same error. Too many people had heard of the blue electric angels for our new-found mortality to ever be safe.

Chi-chichi chi-chichi chi-chichi . . .

And because I didn't believe in coincidence, I raised my head from contemplation of the bus timetable, turned to the hoodie on the red plastic bench and said, "Hey, you got the time?"

He didn't move.

"Hey, mate, you got a light?"

He looked round, taking his time. He didn't need to rush; his kind never do. I stepped back, reaching instinctively with my bandaged fingers for the nearest light, the nearest whiff of mains power.

It'd have been nice, for once, to be surprised.

And "he" was an "it", and "it" had no face. It was a sack of clothes sitting on empty air, a pair of white headphones plugged into the floating nothing of his not-ears. The body of his clothes, bulked out so humanly, was held in shape by air, by an ignorance of gravity and a perversion of pressure, by floating shadow and drifting emptiness bundled together into a nothing-something in a tracksuit. He was an it, and it was a spectre.

Once, when I was a kid, I was taken to see a seer. His name was Khan. He read the future in the entrails of old shopping bags and the inter-weaving of vapour trails in the sky. He told me a lot of things, most of them sounding like they came out of a Christmas cracker; but finally he said "Yeah, man... you're like... you know... like gonna die."

I said something along the lines of "Yeah, I kinda figured that". Sorcerers do not have a long life expectancy, especially urban ones.

"Hey, dude, you totally don't get it!" he replied. "You're like... gonna die. It's after when it gets complicated."

At the time I thought he was being pretentiously metaphorical.

There are two ways to look at the gift of prophecy. Theory the first goes like this: prophet sees future = there is a predetermined path that the prophet is capable of perceiving = destiny = no free will = almighty God with a really sick sense of fun. Which is bad news if you're anyone lower than "pope" in the spiritual pecking order of life.

Theory the second: prophet sees future = ability to determine with an almost omnipotent degree of accuracy and skill the one most likely future from a whole host of determining factors, including human free will, random variables and continual and unexpected cock-up, what will happen next = omnipotence = God in mortal flesh. Khan didn't look like any sort of God to me, but as Mr Bakker

always said, sorcerers should keep an open mind. Just in case someone tried to hit it with a sledgehammer.

That was back in the good old days.

Back before Mr Bakker's stroke. Back before Mr Bakker resolved
not to die. Back before his shadow grew a pair of teeth and a taste
for blood. Back before the Tower killed the sorcerers of the city in
Mr Bakker's name. Back before his shadow killed me, one gloomy
night by the river, in its endless quest for life. Before the blue electric
angels, the battles and the vengeance and the life left behind in the
telephone wires.

Back before we came back into this mortal world.

No human can survive having their major organs ripped out by
the angry manifestation of a dying sorcerer's incarnated will. Or, for
that matter, by any other sharpened implement. And while my con-
tinued existence may argue against this medical truth, I was always
reminded when I looked in the mirror that once upon a time my eyes
had been brown. Not our burning electric blue.

Khan, in his own special, unhelpful way, had been right all along.

Imagine my embarrassment.

I ran.

See what we were capable of, when the situation called?

Our feet flapped and flopped on the wet pavement, our breath was
a puff of cloud lost in the rain. I'd never realised how ridiculous a man
can sound when running, all bouncing bag and thumping shoe, grace-
less and soaked. I crossed the empty street and was inside a council
estate in a matter of seconds that took an hour each to pass, rushing
past doors behind iron grates, and doors with children's pictures
doodled on them, and windows broken and windows cleaned and
doorsteps scrubbed and bicycles locked and bicycles smashed and
bins overturned and bins emptied and flowers tended and pots abandoned and council pledges made and council policies forgotten and
walls graffitied with all the rambling thoughts of the inhabitants...

C & J 4EVER

WHO DOESNT LIKE BULLET TRAINS THINK ABOUT IT

CALIPER BOY SMELLS

Şapkamı geri ver!

There was a play area in the middle of a forlorn patch of grass: two sad swings above "safe" tarmac that falling children could bounce on. A bike, its handlebar, wheels and seat ripped off, was chained to some railings.

Next to the bike, another spectre was waiting. At first I thought he was just some kid. But when he looked up, there was nothing inside that hood to stare with. And that nothing stared straight at me. He was dressed identically to the one at the bus stop; but nothing could have moved that fast, and the beat out of his headphones went *dumdumdumdumdumdumdumdum* with relentless cardiac monotony. For a moment we regarded each other, I too tired to look afraid, he too empty to look anything at all. Then he tilted his head back, and roared. It was the sound of old brakes about to fail, screeching a last scream on an icy road, of razored metal being scraped over a rusted surface, of a guitar string just as it snaps. I ducked and covered my ears, hoping to get below the sound. Around me it made each window pane hum and crack, and set the swings swinging in distress.

Spectres always hunt together, and it's easy to mistake a summons for a scream. I pushed my left ear into my shoulder and reached deep in my satchel until I found what I was looking for: a can of red spray paint. I shook it and, turning on the spot, drew around me a double red line. It spattered in the rain, and started to blur. I thought for a moment it wouldn't hold—but a double red line is a powerful enchantment, even in the worst of weathers, and as I completed the shape, its paint flashed brighter and settled, gleaming, into a solid state.

The summons stopped. Perhaps the spectre reasoned that sound wouldn't do much good against my ward on the ground. Perhaps it ran out of air from inside its floating chest. The physiognomy of a creature that isn't there is hard to study. I could hear the wailing of car alarms set off by the din; lights were coming on behind the area's newly cracked windows. Soon the whole estate would be up and buzzing, and then so would be the police, and then questions, about the dead and the almost dead and the should-be dead. We couldn't afford to waste time on such details.

The spectre moved towards me. He had no shadow and, apart from the *dumdumdumdumdumdumdum* of his headphones, made no sound as he approached.

Behind me was the *chi-chichi chi-chichi* of the creature at the bus stop and, somewhere against the car alarms, another rising bass line, of:

Boom boom boom boom-te-boom boom boom boom boom-te-boom

I squatted down inside my red circle and pressed my fingers into the ground, sniffing the air. I had none of the right equipment, nothing that could do more than slow down the pack. Just checking my bag had wasted twenty yards of their inexorable stride. The nearest spectre stopped, its toes scraping the edge of my double red line. Reaching with a gloved hand into the saggy kangaroo pocket of its grey jumper, it pulled out a flick knife. The knife was cheap black plastic with a silverish blade which revealed a series of notches at the hilt end that probably served no purpose, except to make an ugly weapon somehow "cool" by being that bit more ugly. The blade was no more than four inches long; but when four inches is two inches longer than the thickness of your wrist, size doesn't matter. We watched it, fascinated.

The spectre drew back the blade, held it up, and rammed it towards my face. As it passed through the air above the red lines it stuck, point-first, as if buried in thick foam; beneath it, the paint on the ground bubbled and hissed. Still the spectre kept up the pressure, pushing with both hands on the hilt. A little at a time, the blade began to move towards me.

Behind, a hiss-swipe through the air and the smell of burning plastic announced that the second spectre was doing the same with its knife. Coming out of a corner by the refuse bins was a third, heading towards me with a casual swagger. I knew it didn't need to run.

I dug my fingers deeper into the tarmac. It bent beneath them with the cold, crinkly texture of dry cereal, resisted, then parted. I pushed in my fingers, my wrist, then the lower arm, then in as far as my elbow, straining to delve through the mass of the earth. Still not deep enough. I cursed and bent lower, pressing my cheek to the ground and pushing my shoulder into the tarmac. It was faint and a long way off, but close enough now for my fingers to tingle with it, and most of all, I could smell it. Gas mains have always been built down deep; it's a sensible enough precaution.

I dragged my fingers out of the pavement, trailing loose chips of black tarmac. Wet dirt, grey, the colour of clay, clung to the length of my arm as I pulled myself free. When my fingertips finally came away, there was a broad tear in the earth, and the air above it wriggled like a desert mirage. The smell of gas is artificially pumped into it at the factory, a dry stink that makes itself known in every part of the nostrils and tickles at the back of the throat. I scrambled to my feet and let it rise around me, watched it spill out around my feet and ankles and, raising my hands, dragged more of it higher even as the red paint I had sprayed onto the ground began to melt, dribble, lose its shape. As the shimmering on the air spread around me, bringing tears to my eyes and making my lungs hurt, I reached into my satchel, digging deep for a much-used lighter that had never lit a cigarette. I slotted it into my bandaged right hand, drawing my coat up around my face and hunching my shoulders to present as small a target as possible.

When the ward broke, it did so fast. The third spectre, Mr *Boom boom boom boom-te-boom*, was still a few yards away. The paint bubbling at my feet gave way, turned black and peeled like dead skin off a corpse. *Chi-chichi chi-chichi chi-chichi* put his full weight on his blade,

making it jerk forwards and down in an arc meant for my neck. I
closed my eyes, and spun the wheel of the cigarette lighter.

I was aware of pain in the vicinity of my left collarbone, but it
wasn't the moment to care. Though my eyes were pressed tight,
the flash from the ignition burnt to the back of my retinas like a full
summer's sun. Even with my coat wrapped around me and all the
will I could spare focused on keeping the flames away, the heat dried
up every inch of my lungs, burnt the inside of my nose, turned my
tongue to leather, singed my eyebrows and caused black smoke to
dribble from my hair. It was the *thump-hiss* of all igniting gas stoves,
and it spread out around from me in a pool of shimmering leakage
from deep below the streets, a bright blue centre spitting out a circle
of yellow flame. Those windows close by that hadn't been broken by
the spectre's cry were now blasted inwards, shredding curtains, and
embedding glass in every wall. The bins lined up at the recycling
point were blasted open and their contents set instantly alight.

It faded quickly, leaving just a *hiss-whine* as the gas still trickling up
from the pavement burnt at my feet like a candle, smothered to a tiny
core by the falling rain. Every sound I still heard had to seep through
a background *whumph* in my ears; every sight seemed dimmer, full
of spinning whiteness that followed the movement of my eyeballs.
Steam rose in tropical illusion from my hair and coat. The soles of my
shoes, their laces charred, ripped away from the tarmac, leaving their
impression on the hot earth.

The spectres had been thrown back from the blast, and two of
them were still aflame. They staggered in the rain, trying to douse
the fires eating through their clothing, revealing the nothingness
beneath shreds of sleeve and blackened baggy trousers. Their headphones were still playing the relentless rhythms that marked out each
one. A blast that would have stopped an angry mammoth had barely
singed these creatures, and bought me not nearly as much time as I'd
wanted. I cursed from the bottom of my soul. Feet hissing as my hot
soles met the cold, rain-soaked tarmac, I ran.

I was two streets away before breathlessness and a burning in every muscle forced me to slow to an uneasy lope. My mind caught up with the rest of me, and reported another, new sensation—a hot, itchy dribble from just below my left shoulder. I kept walking, tugging my scarf and coat aside to see the problem, and found my shirt stained pink from a mixture of rainwater and blood. A spectre's knife, though wide of its target, had certainly found something. The bloody gash ran from just below my collarbone to deep beneath my left armpit. With each step I took it opened and shut like it was telling some obscene joke. Turning our face away, we pressed our bandaged hand over the injury, and smothered it from sight. Not too far behind, we heard the spectres' screams again and the crack of fractured glass. We tried to run, but only managed a few undignified paces before the pain throughout our limbs announced that death was preferable to haste.

A street corner brought me to a road lined with shops, the kind above which sat the owner's home, lights dimmed and curtains drawn. These were the strange, unlikely businesses driven from the centre of town years ago: discount stores selling nothing but plastic boxes and drying racks, hairdressers specialising in dreadlocks, wholesalers of Jamaican spice, cobblers who cut keys and sold raincoats as well, suspicious computer shops offering 5p-per-minute calls to Zambia. Strange, anorexic mannequins, creatures with waists as thick as my neck, stared out from bargain clothes shops, with scornful eyes. Inside a darkened pub, the bingo machine rippled all the colours of the rainbow, promising a £20 jackpot on only a £1 investment and the spinning of three cherries. From overflowing council bins spilt free newspapers, and takeaway boxes, their contents snuffled out by a prowling, falafel-addicted fox. Cars were only one a minute, and the traffic lights phased red-amber-green-amber-red at nothing except me and the rain.

I could hear...

...still a long way behind, but no denying what I could hear, I was past the point where imagination lied...

Dumdumdumdumdumdumdum

Chi-chichi chi-chichi chi-chichi

Boom boom boom boom-te-boom boom

Shhhshhhshhhshhha shhhshhhshhhshhha shhhshhhshhhshhha

Spectres always hunted in packs. Four or five was the average, but I'd read an article that reported as many as twelve in some cities.

I staggered down the street, snatching hot neon light from the streetlamps as I went, and bundling it into my clenched fists, bringing its comforting sodium glow close to my face and chest to wash away the fear and the cold, until my skin shone with orange-pink illumination. To my right, a primary school, gates locked, wall high and covered with anti-climb paint. A mosaic by the children, demonstrating that drugs were bad and superheroes were about family. A doctor's clinic, set back beyond sodden grass turned to mud, blinds drawn, a padlock sealed over the entrance. Launderette on my left, orange plastic chairs set in front of great, sleeping machines; vinyl store, rare enough now to be guaranteed a nerdy audience; locked metal door down to a snooker club; locked wooden door up to a discreet acupuncture clinic; shut post office selling kids' toys and birthday cards; pharmacy promising YOU a better body; billboards, advertising action movies with strutting heroes, and perfumes worn by women with an elegant naked back.

My own back might end up with a knife in it before the evening was out.

Shhhshhhshhhshhha shhhshhhshhhshhha shhhshhhshhh . . .

When I saw him, it was almost too late. He stepped out of the doorway without a sound, driving his knife up towards my ribs. We caught it by reflex, snatching his wrist and twisting. But all that twisted in response was an empty sleeve; there wasn't any flesh beneath it to hurt. And still the knife kept coming. I stepped aside — and realised the futility of all my usual responses. There was nothing to kick, no flesh to hurt, nothing to shock nor batter nor damage. I looked into the spectre's face. It rippled for a moment, then spat hot ash and black exhaust straight back at me. We covered our face, felt the ash burn our sleeves and thick dirt blacken our skin, tripped as we staggered back, half blinded by heat and dust, and sprawled useless in the gutter. Through rising tears, the spectre was a blur coming towards me. I raised my hands and, just this once, the pain helped, gave focus and determination to what must be done. The pavement ticked like metal expanding under a summer sun, cracked, and broke apart. Grey wires sprouted like ivy from the earth. I dragged them up, fuelling their growth with will and fear even as I crawled away from the gutter into the middle of the street. The wires grew, divided, rippled, grew again, wildlife photography speeded up a thousand times; they spread, and uncoiled a flower of barbs. I flung the wires up from beneath the spectre's feet and ordered them to dig deep into his feet, his legs, crawl up his ankles and wrap around his knees.

The spectre ignored them, his trousers tearing with a slow crunch as he kept on coming, revealing the nothing beneath. But his shoes were a harder proposition: the barbs caught deep and wound down into his trendy trainers, tangling with the shoelaces, which strained but did not tear with the spectre's uneven lurches towards me. I rolled onto my hands and knees, then got up on my feet; and once more the spectre, trapped by his feet, raised his head to scream, and I was bending beneath the sound and covering my ears, then running down the street at the sound of a thousand brakes locking against old metal casings.

A beggar sleeping in the door of a church looked up as I passed by, somewhere between running and falling. I snapped, "Get out of here!" and kept on going. He just stared. A light came on in a window overhead and a woman's voice shouted, "What the fuc..."

I skirted a small grassy rubbish dump that the council called a "community green space" and turned onto a road overhung by old trees. A maintenance truck was parked ahead, its orange platform raised up high to a broken streetlamp that one guy in a neon jacket was replacing, cold and miserable in the rain. I ran past it, and he ignored me, knowing better than to ask questions of bleeding strangers running through the night.

They were behind me; I didn't need to look to know. The pain below my collarbone that shock had kept off now began to make itself known. With every step I could feel my flesh open and close like the regular gulp of a goldfish. It was oddly electrifying, as if our body were not our own, but something we carried with us, and our distress someone else's that we experienced at a remove, like secondary smoking. Given time, that would change, and the thought of what was to come only weakened us further, made our stomach ripple. I saw a square of light off to my right, ignored it, then looked again, and could have laughed or cried.

The place was called "Qwickstop" in bright orange letters on a garish green background. Set out front of its lit-up window was a graveyard of unlikely vegetables and fruit, from the standard bruised apple to fossilised butternut squash, all overhung by a limp awning that dribbled unevenly onto the pavement. On the door a variety of signs advertised such a multitude of wonders, it was incredible that such a small shop could do so much—it was an off-licence, a ticket stop, a mobile phone top-up shop, a member of Neighbourhood Watch, an affiliate of Crimestoppers, an advertising centre for local messages and bulletins, a vendor of the *Evening Standard*, a vendor of the *Willesden Enquirer*, a profferer of fair trade and halal products and finally, most important and stuck up in flashing LEDs in the window, it was open twenty-four hours a day, seven days a week.

I staggered inside this place of miracles.

There was a man behind the counter, listening to a local pirate station broadcasting in Urdu. He had a salt-and-pepper moustache with its own ecosystem, a bald patch as sterile and reflective as the moon, and a darkish skin, like wax that had dried unevenly across his scalp. He looked at me and decided I was trouble. I smiled as nicely as I could and wiped some of the soot and dust off my face with the corner of my soggy sleeve. He smiled back, like the expression had been sewn into his skin. Struggling to breathe normally, I staggered over to a large glass-fronted refrigerator and pulled out four bottles of the cheapest beer I could find. With my prize I hobbled back to the counter and said, "Pack of fags, please."

"What kind, sir?" he asked. Always be polite to possible murderers: that was the twenty-four-hour-shopping philosophy.

"Cheapest you've got. And the strongest painkillers in the shop."

The least expensive pack of cigarettes was £5.99. On the back it had a picture of a blackened pair of cancerous lungs. The painkillers' selling point seemed to be how luminously green and futuristic they were, rather than their chemical content.

"And your Sellotape," I said.

"What?"

"Sellotape." A roll of the stuff sat by the till, in a plastic device for easy tearing off.

"This isn't for sale, sir."

I leant across the counter. The action set my neck on fire and made my hip tremble. "I'll give you twenty quid for the Sellotape."

He answered on instinct. When an offer that good comes along, even the innocent suspect a con. "I'm sorry sir, it's . . ."

"If you do not give us the Sellotape," we said through gritted teeth, "you will die. The only question will be whether *they* kill you, or *we* do."

He looked into our eyes. Once upon a time my eyes had been the same darkish brown as my hair. That had been then. They were now the bright blue of a summer sky, and reflective like the eyes of a cat. He pushed the Sellotape across the counter. I pulled out my wallet, and saw that a line of blood had run down my arm and over my fingers. I counted out forty pounds in stained notes, pushed them towards him, scooped up my beer, cigarettes, drugs and Sellotape, and staggered back out into the night. Behind me, he dialled 999. Forty quid doesn't buy you much these days.

What I needed now was a quiet place to work. I found a narrow alley, that had been transformed into the local recycling station. I sat on top of the plastic jaw of a wheelie-bin and prised the lid off each beer bottle. We took a swig from one, just to make sure it was all right, then up-ended each bottle and let the contents dribble away. It wouldn't be long before the spectres smelt it, even in the rain. I set down the emptied bottles and from the cigarette packet I slid out four white sheaths, carefully lighting each one. The flame flickered and spat in the rain, but these things were designed to catch in any weather, and soon gave a dull glow. I dropped a cigarette into each bottle, watching the smoke fill it. The Sellotape I put in my jacket pocket, the end sticking out ready to be peeled and drawn like a gunslinger's pistol. Then I waited.

I didn't have to wait long.

Dumdumdumdumdumdumdum

Chi-chichi chi-chichi chi-chichi chi-chi

Shhshhshhhshha shhhshhhshhhshha shhhshhhshh

Boom boom boom boom-te-boom boom

They came all at once, two from one side, two from the other. It's only in movies that you get attacked by one person at a time. I gasped between the pain and the shimmering sapphire burning over my eyes, *our* burning sapphire fire, just waiting for me to let it out, "Hello, sunshines."

The clothes of two were ragged black tissues draped over empty air, every part the traditional haunting ghosts, except for the headphones. A third had tears down the lower parts of his trousers, great gashes in the shoes on his feet. I slid down from the wheelie-bin as they approached, picking up the nearest beer bottle and giving it a gentle shake, feeling the suction of the air dragged in to feed the dull flame of the cigarette.

I picked the spectre who looked least battered, its grey tracksuit still intact, its head bobbing along to a muffled beat, and staggered up to it.

"Hey man," I intoned, "like, *respect.*"

Any magician can tell you words have power.

Any urban sorcerer can tell you the greatest language of power is whatever the other bugger happens to speak.

So as I spoke, the spectre, recognising the beginning of a binding spell, drew back a moment askance, and perhaps, in that non-brain behind that not-face drifting beneath its grey hood, realised what was about to happen. Much too late. We were too angry for repentance now. I drove the open lip of the smoking beer bottle straight into the middle of that empty void, stuck into that thick nothingness like it was a spear and this was war. I think it tried to scream, but the sound was sucked straight into the smoky glass; it raised its hands and clawed at the air, too late, much, *much* too late, whined and whistled as the essence of its not-being got sucked down into the interior of the beer bottle, and wriggled and writhed. The grey hood on its head began to droop as the non-skull supporting it collapsed and shrivelled inside my glass prison, then the shoulders drooped away, the torso began to flop and flap in the wet wind, the gloves dropped away from wrists too loose to support them, the arms withered down to flat nothings, the trousers dropped from the top and collapsed, the shoes seemed to shrink into themselves.

In a second, barely one second, there was nothing more than a pile of flopping grey clothes on the floor. I stuck my thumb over the mouth of the beer bottle, glancing inside it. The cigarette was still burning bright, as it would burn now for ten thousand years unless some idiot went and smashed it; in the smoke of its interior eddying shapes spun back and forth in indignant distress like an miniature ocean storm caught inside a bottle with its model ship.

The other spectres were nothing if not taken aback. I slapped a seal of Sellotape over the mouth of the bottle and picked up another, flourishing it at them. "Come on!" I said. "You want to spend the next ten thousand years stuck at the bottom of the Dumpster?"

They hesitated. "Come on!" we shouted. "If you think that shadows and gloom can really harm us, then do what you will! We have no
reason to spare you the consequence!"

Our voice echoed, a muffled whisper in the rain. The remaining
spectres began to back away. We laughed, shook the beer bottle
with its trapped nothing inside, watched the smoke twist and billow
beneath the Sellotape seal, watched the orange cigarette flare angry
crimson, and roared after them, *"Come on!"*

Then they were gone.

Even nothingness, it seems, knows how to keep itself alive.

We stood in the rain on a pavement stained with beer and overflowing with litter, not sure if we were going to laugh, cry, or both. In
the event, we did nothing; for all our blustering, we were not about to
chase after the spectres and finish the job. They knew how to recognise
danger when they saw it. At my feet, a sopping tracksuit lay flopped like
the rotting guts from a soothsayer's ritual, turning black in the rain.

I picked up the bottle I'd pressed into the spectre's face, pressed my
ear against the side, and listened. Imagination playing tricks? From
within the glass I thought, perhaps, just perhaps, I could hear...

Boom boom boom boom-te-boom boom

I shook the bottle for extra good measure, and slapped a half—cen-
timetre thickness of Sellotape over its smoky lips. As I did, I noticed
blood had seeped through the bandages on my right hand, and was
dribbling into the sticky recesses of my sleeve. The thought that I
needed help made us want to cry, like a shameful child.

I went in search of a night bus from nowhere-everywhere to somewhere else.

We figured we'd work out where on the way.

The bus was a double-decker that advertised itself as being able to
seat 36 passengers in the lower saloon, 48 in the upper saloon, and
23 standing. It made no reference to whether you could get a drink in
the "saloon", or if there'd be a man playing the piano.

There were two passengers on the bottom deck, three on the upper. The driver, when I got on, said, "Jesus!"

We pressed our hand over the slash below our collarbone. "What?" we snapped.

"You OK, mate?"

"No," we replied. "You going somewhere or not?"

"I can call..."

"No."

He shrugged. Night-bus drivers learn not to take too keen an interest. "Sure. Whatever."

I had a travelcard. Druids say there is no greater wand of power than a unicorn's horn given willingly to the supplicant. In the city, there is no greater wand of power than a Zone 1–6 travelcard. It is freedom to go anywhere and see anything, and all it costs is a large chunk of your income. Then again, a unicorn's horn usually involved quests and battling ancient demons, so the changing times weren't all bad. I pressed my travelcard to the reader, which beeped appreciatively; the driver had the good manners not to look surprised. I half fell up the stairs, and sat down heavily in the back row. The back of the top deck is the naughty seat, where the kids sit to curse and swear when school gets let out. The floor was sticky with spilt beer and scattered with a liberal handful of greasy thin chips made of 40 per cent potato. Yesterday's half-read paper lay on every third bench, the sudoku finished, the corners torn.

I knew if I lay down across the back seats, I'd never get up again. I shuffled into the darkest, dimmest corner, pressed my head against the cold of the glass, and watched my blue-eyed, grey-faced reflection watch the street as it passed by in a pulse of rippling streetlights and illuminated ads. I fumbled painkillers out of their packet and swallowed them with the last mouthful of spit I could muster, pressed my fingers harder against the folds of my bleeding chest, and watched.

At the very front of the bus, a young couple, probably not out of their teens, sat hand in hand, politely not kissing each other and desperate in their discreet silence to do so. On the seat above the stair, where you can watch all the passengers come and go, sat a guy with close-shaven hair revealing the white lines of a dozen scars on his skull. Fresh stitches were sewn into his neck, where a short and well-placed knife had tried for the jugular vein. A scorpion was tattooed onto his temple, and beneath the sleeves of his denim jacket protruded the ends of a dozen more tattoos besides. We wanted to ask if the scorpion had hurt when the needles went into his temple, who'd saved his life with the stitches in the neck and why so many scars on such a young face. Tattoos in that quantity meant jailbird.

Lights rose and fell across the rain-obscured blur of our vision. A cemetery rolled by, darkness behind closed, sombre walls. Empty wet football pitches for the local amateur team, floodlights still on, endless railway lines over which slow goods trains creaked and clattered on their night-time journeys; depots and working yards and goods yards and storage yards and open spaces for broken-down cars and, taller than the local council blocks, piles of shattered metal and torn-up engines. We were heading towards the sprawl of White City, where flyovers vied with tower blocks and the BBC as to which could be uglier. It's easy to get lost in White City: shallow streets of identical, anonymous houses merge beneath a roaring motorway; great shopping malls squat above video shops and haberdashers specialising in the sari; council estates leer down at genteel terraced backstreets where media executives plot to steal their neighbour's precious parking space. North and south play cunning, curving tricks on the unwary traveller, and navigation by a sense of style is nearly impossible. They give White City its own edgy magic, that ebbs and flows with uneasy irregularity, daring you to tap into a thick fist of here, only to have it vanish into a silken vapour two streets away. It was a magic of brick and neon, of solid and insubstantial matter mingling, as if life had forgotten how to make the distinction.

White City.

Whites.

And whether we liked it or not, there was blood seeping into our clothes, and I needed help.

So, since the bus was headed in that direction anyway, I went in search of the Long White City clan.

I do not know how the Long White City clan came to be founded. To find the answer to that would require a history of graffiti that I never came to grips with, since it is in the nature of the art that no one keeps an official log except the police, and they don't like to talk about it much.

What I do know is that sometime in the late 1960s, it was observed by those who bother to keep track of such things that a mutual collective of painters and magicians were coming together in the area of London known as White City, and between them practising a new and interesting form of magic. It was the Whites, more than any other group, who pioneered research into the new symbols of magic that were emerging with the urban evolution of the craft. The pentangle star was rejected in favour of the red "stop" octagon as a symbol of power; mystic runes in the Viking style were swept away in favour of the scrawled loop of silver paint plastered across an open wall. It was discovered that it was cheaper to paint a gargoyle protector than to commission one in marble, and that they served roughly the same end; it was realised that the image of a great eye painted at the end of Platform 14 of Clapham Junction station was a scrying tool of infinitely more value than your traditional bowl of silver water, and that nothing bound as effectively as a double red parking line burnt chemically into the earth. It was realised that those who found magic in the words and pictures drawn in the night would be better off as a whole if they stuck together.

So the Whites came into existence, as a rag-tag formation of egoists, magicians, artists and all-purpose mystic dabblers, donating to a common union. I have some time for their methods, since only a fool denies the power of what they do, but generally my interest has been elsewhere.

The development of a new "mega-mall" in White City forced the majority of the clan to seek housing somewhere else. A war with the Tower, which at one time was the single most powerful mystic body in the city, drove them underground into the old tunnels of the Kingsway Telephone Exchange. That had been in Mr Bakker's day; the bad old days of living shadows, dead sorcerers and broken promises. It was a war that had killed me before I even knew it had started. When we had come back, I and us, we and me, together in the same flesh, we fought back. Mr Bakker had died. So had his shadow. So had . . .

. . . others.

Mortals died so easily.

The ending of the war brought the Whites above ground again, albeit in smaller numbers than before. That the war ended and they survived had more than a little to do with us; we hoped they'd remember that tonight.

I looked for the signs.

An empty spray-paint can tossed onto the top of a bus shelter.

A painted elephant on the side of a house, playing a large trombone whose nose pointed further south.

A wall with four windows added onto it and a front door, from which a child with a red balloon peeked towards the nearest bus stop.

I changed buses.

A message scratched into the glass window of the bus—END OF THE LINE.

Not one from the Whites; they knew that such a message could be a threat, as well as an instruction. I ignored it.

A rat on the side of a green telephone router box, holding in its painted claws a tin of peanut butter, a knife dripping with a compromising yellow blob of the stuff, tip pointed towards the west.

I stayed on the bus.

A post standing up taller than the houses, laden with CCTV cameras, onto which a single white hand mark had been pressed in indelible paint. Another white hand a few doors down, and then more, getting more regular in succession until a school wall covered in a thousand multicoloured hand prints, of which only one was white, a single finger extended and pointing towards a door.

I got off the bus.

My head was the inside of a tumble-dryer, my throat the pipe for hot air. Someone was feeding old socks bound together with static in and out of me through the tear in my chest. My hands were the burning wires through which electric current flowed, my knees were the wobbly suspension springs on which the whole rumbling construction churned.

There was a door between an organic health food shop selling pink crystal lamps in its dark windows and a betting shop selling poor odds on bad investments. There was no name above it, no sign beside it. Just a solid metal door locked shut in a row of padlocked shops. A tiger was painted on it, leaping out of the framework with jaws gaping and eyes wild with fury. I stared at it, it stared at me, frozen for ever in its leap. It's easy to think that the eyes of a painting are staring just at you. In this case, they were.

I hammered on the door.

There was no answer.

I hammered harder.

Above me, a window slid back and a voice called out in the melodramatic whispered-shout of all good neighbours out to disturb the peace, "Who's there?"

I stepped back onto the pavement to see the speaker better, but could only see the shadowed silhouette of a woman against a wash of white neon.

"I'm here for Vera!" I called back in the same quiet-loud call of the night-time streets.

"Who?"

"I'm Swift! Matthew Swift!"

"So?"

"I need help!"

"I don't know you!"

"Tell Vera it's Swift!"

"Fuck off!"

Our stomach was a vat in which old bones were dissolved for glue. Each cell of blood in our body had grown little centipede legs that tickled and crawled along the inside of our veins.

I said again, "I need help."

"Go to the fucking police!"

"I'm a sorcerer..."

"Yeah, right."

So we looked up at her and said, "We are the angels. Help me."

And the darkness in the window hesitated. We raised our hand towards her and let the blood trickle between our fingers, and as it flowed, it wriggled and wormed, coherent rivers of red breaking away into fat liquid maggots on our skin that writhed and hissed off each other, burning cold blue electricity over our flesh. "We are..." we called through gritted teeth, as the light of our blood turned our face electric blue, "...we are the blue electric angels. Please—help me."

The woman in the window said, "Crap."

The door opened.

We went inside.

The door led to steps, the steps led to a basement.

The basement was a club. The walls were painted with dancing people, most of whom were wearing very little clothing.

They were frozen on every wall and across every counter,

stretched out over every pillar and rippling up onto the ceiling. The place stank of paint, magic, beer, smoke and sweat. A few hours earlier, these pictures would have danced with all the rest; the floor was stained with a thousand prints set in paint of high heel, trainer, loafer, boot, sandal and every kind of shoe that knew how to party. Some of the marks were still wet, and as we walked, our shoes—not our shoes, no, not quite—left blue footprints across the floor. Up was trying to be down, colour was trying to be sound, sound was trying to be sense, all things playing tricks, the painkillers nothing more than a cobweb through which the pain slashed.

The bouncer who met me at the bottom of the stairs had skin turned almost purple with the weight of tattoos on it. Unlike the tattoos of the jailbird on the bus, these stank of raw, sweaty power burnt into the skin. He looked me over in the half-gloom of the silent, stinking club floor and said, "This way."

I followed him without a word behind the bar to another metal door guarded this time by a furious polar bear whose fanged teeth dribbled silver saliva that rolled as I watched down his flat frozen skin, and whose eyes never left mine. The door led into a corridor whose walking space was 80 per cent empty beer bottle. White strip lighting hummed and buzzed irritatingly overhead. The corridor led to an office, all leather sofa and important desk, cluttered with empty coffee mugs and more abandoned bottles. The bouncer pointed at the sofa and said, "There," and I obeyed, sticking my legs up over one arm and my head back over the other. More painkillers. From where I lay I could see a brass-covered coffee machine, a photo of some minor celebrity whose name I couldn't remember, and a monolith-sized chunk of concrete. I didn't need to smell the power coming from it to guess what it was—magicians of every generation have always collected artefacts of power. I wondered how much the Whites had paid, or if they'd paid at all. Pieces of the Berlin Wall fetched a good price, these days, and for good reasons, although very few people appreciated what they really were.

There were pieces of slogans still visible on the wall. A remnant of:

— ISTIAN LIEBE FAMK —

Or:

GEBEN SIE MIR MEINEN HU —

Or a sad half-remnant of the CND logo, framed in flowers.

I crawled to the end of the sofa, unable to resist my curiosity despite the fire cha-chaing up my nervous system and the ice weighing the rest down. I reached out to touch the concrete, brushed my fingers over a dozen layers of bright paint, tasted... grey dust in the mouth, empty tightness in the belly, neon popping in the ears, crashing delight at the back of the neck, burning heaviness at the ends of the fingers, blue sadness behind the eyes—mostly just sadness, so deep and big you could fall for ever and never even notice you were heading down. The man who owned this particular artefact didn't need spells to protect him. A whiff of this magic and grown assassins would just sigh away.

I drew my fingers away. I heard the door open behind me in the sense that when he spoke, I was not surprised; but I did not listen to the sound until he actually said: "You like it?"

We didn't take our eyes from the concrete.

"Yes."

"Four and a half thousand euros. You believe that? Four and a half fucking thousand euros for a piece of concrete with some paint on. Best buy I ever made. Drink?"

Wrenching my eyes away was like turning away from the dying man who's just asked you for help. I looked at the man who'd entered the room. He was young, trying to look older than he was by cutting his hair so thin it bordered on the bald, growing grizzle but no beard and wearing carefully aged and scuffed black leather. He leant on the end of his desk with the casual air of a guy who's seen everything and, while impressed by nothing, is still prepared to be amused by it. We disliked him instinctively.

I said, "I need Vera."

"You're Swift, right?"

"Yes. I need to see Vera."

"She's kinda busy at five in the morning, you know? How can I help?" His smile was like the spinning mirrored whiteness of the disco ball.

"You can get me Vera."

"You look sorta crappy, gotta tell you."

"Help me. I need... I need a doctor. I need Vera."

"I thought that Matthew Swift was like, you know, tough."

"I'm not tough," I replied through gritted teeth. "I'm lucky. I'm so lucky that I can be killed by a shadow on the streets and come back without a scar on my skin. I'm so damn lucky that when I hear a telephone ring, I have to answer it and it's always for me, always. I'm so lucky I can be attacked by a pack of spectres and walk away with all my limbs attached. I'm so lucky that I am we and we are me, and I've gotta tell you, we could rip your eyes out and feed them to you right now and forget in the morning that we were even here. You think you're that lucky? Now get me Vera!"

He made the telephone call while I watched.

It went:

"Hey, yeah, sorry about the time, it's... yeah, before you... just listen... no, I've got this guy here... says his name is Swift... what? Uh... blue. Bright blue. Yeah. No, pretty bad way. Like... you know... blood. Sure. Sure. Yeah, sure thing. No, I'll... yeah... I'll let him know."

That was it.

Her name was Vera.

She was the almost properly elected head of the Whites. Almost properly, because it was generally agreed that if there was an election, she'd win, so what was the point of testing it?

She owed me.

She owed *us*.

She was one of the only people in London who knew that when the death certificate said I'd died, it hadn't gone into enough of the details.

The clock on the wall said 5.45 a.m. when she turned up. She was wearing a big puffer coat twice the width and nearly all the height of her small body, and having a bad hair day. A pair of bright green leather boots vanished inside the silver iceberg of her coat, and a pair of pink mittens covered her fingers. She took one look at me and said, "Jesus, you look shit."

I said, "I've been attacked."

"Know who did it?"

"No."

"Kill them?"

"Got one of them in a beer bottle," I replied.

"You kidding me."

"No," I said, and then, because it *was* 5.45 a.m. and we hadn't slept for far, far too long, and every part of us hurt and bled and ached and was burnt and dirty and stuck to its own clothes with dribbling blood, we started to laugh.

They bundled me into a car. It was a surprisingly boring car, for the head of the Whites—a trundling little Volkswagen with the charisma of a dry blister. Vera drove, rushing to beat the early morning traffic as we raced through deserted streets.

I said, "I need a safe place. Just a safe place where we can recover…"

"It's fine, I know."

"I need a doctor…"

"It's being sorted."

". . . someone who won't report to the police . . . no records . . ."

"I know, I know. It's being taken care of."

Pink neon lights rising, falling, rising, falling. The rain had eased off into drizzle. The streets were a perfect black mirror reflecting every detail of the lights above. Office lights left on for the night glowed empty white squares on the dark sides of the buildings, men in blue caps were drawing back the gates of the Underground stations. The wheels of Vera's speeding car threw up great sheets of water from the blocked drains in the sides of the street, spattering dirty brown stains onto the clean windows of the passing shops. In the kitchen windows of the early stirrers, lights were starting to come on, women in thick dressing gowns and furry slippers turning on the kettles, men shivering in their pyjamas scuttling for the heating. The first post vans of the day were rumbling through the streets, to deliver recorded packages and special parcels to the lucky few who merited their attention; outside the hotels, the international tourists going to catch the first flights of the day hurried to waiting taxis. We wanted to sleep; but by now we were too tired to stop our thoughts.

White City became Shepherd's Bush, a big roundabout leading to everywhere and anywhere, on which sat a large, long-dead barometer, or thermometer, or whatever it had been designed as before the money ran out. Some time, a thousand years ago, there was probably a shepherd who had a bush on this roundabout. Now there were subways and traffic lights and purple-brown hotels with mirrored square windows to admire it all from.

Shepherd's Bush became Bayswater, Bayswater rapidly became posh — big houses fit for a king and his servants, divided up into apartments fit for barons and their heirs, great trees hundreds of years old whose bare branches drooped twiny fingers between the yellow streetlamps. We followed the course of the Central Line running beneath the street and, as we drove, I could feel the whispered magics of the city changing, growing from that early-morning lull into a rushing, buzzing, humming rise as the city began to wake up for another day, hear it pushing inside my chest and running through my blood, a burst of energy that I didn't want and couldn't use but, even then, made me smile. Bayswater became Paddington, a maze of streets too tight for the uses they were put to, in which seedy hotels where you paid by the hour mingled with the mansions of the great and the squats of the passers-by. Those few mansions that had fallen victim to the war had been replaced with council apartments, but they were few and far between, and polite mews between grand, whitewashed houses still peeked their cobbled noses out into the paving stones.

The sun wasn't yet up. All of London seems surprised, when winter comes, how little sun there is—day crawls its embarrassed way into existence sometime between seven-thirty and eight, when most of the city is underground or too zonked to notice, and then waves its goodbyes around the 3.30 meetings, when most of the city is too busy working to realise the day has gone. Winter seems to last for ever, if it is measured by the staying power of the sun.

Vera parked in a residential bay in front of a white house on a neat white street of houses that could only have been in Paddington. She unbuckled her seat belt and got out of the car. I unbuckled mine, put my hand on the door handle and found it slipped off, leaving an ugly swipe of blood. Vera opened the door on my side and helped me out. My legs were a long way off, and somewhere between me and them there was a satellite delay. She slung my arm over her shoulders and walked me like a granddad up the stairs to the black front door of the white building, groped in her pocket for a set of keys, found one, opened the door. The corridor inside was all echoing tile and bare walls. A lift the size of a fat man's coffin was at the far end. It climbed upwards like it resented the service, discharged us onto the third floor. Another black door, another set of keys. An apartment, furnished in plywood and polyester straight from Ikea, no pictures on the wall, nothing to mark it out as individual except on the inside of the door, where someone with a spray can had painted a giant picture of a lollipop lady, hat drawn down over her eyes, sign turned to "stop". The Whites understand how to paint a good protective ward.

There was a sitting room that was also a kitchen, a bathroom with barely room enough to fit the bath, and a bedroom, mattress without any sheets. Vera didn't bother to offer any, but deposited me straight down on the bed. There were thin net curtains across the window that filtered out the shape of the streetlamps outside while letting in all their yellow light, that stretched great shadows across the floor and up the wall.

I stammered, "Doctor..."

She said gently, "There's one coming."

I nodded, then let my head fall back on the mattress and closed my eyes, not bothering to peel away my ragged clothes.

"Jesus, Matthew," muttered Vera. "What the hell happened?"

"Attacked," I stumbled. "Attacked. A phone rang and I answered and... and it burnt me. I hit my head. A phone rang and... then creatures came. They came for us. It rang for *us*. I just need a safe place..."

"I'll put the kettle on," she said.

Or perhaps we imagined it.

We closed our eyes.

Dawn was grey and sullen.

Whoever was pulling the watch off my wrist did so by the light of a lamp by my bedside. The plastic made a sound like velcro as it peeled away from my flesh. I opened my eyes. Vera stood at the end of the bed, drinking a mug of coffee. On the mug someone had written "I ♥ London" in large pink letters. With her duffle coat off, underneath I saw that Vera was still wearing pyjamas and a dressing gown. We felt the sudden and odd urge to cry.

Seeing our eyes open, Vera said, "Go."

It turned out not to be directed at me.

A sudden searing agony indicated that the target audience had done as commanded, and ripped, like a plaster from flesh, the burnt remnants of the watch from my wrist. A thousand pinpricks of blood welled to the surface, and we looked away, sickened at the sight.

"Cool," said a voice by my left ear.

I risked a glance at its owner.

The creature of torment who had pulled my watch free was roughly the same height as her stethoscope would be, if it was unwrapped to its full length. She had a round, cheerful face, short dark hair that somehow managed to be both straight and bouncy at the same time, and a casually merry attitude towards my distress that marked her out immediately as a member of the medical profession. I half-recognised her. She said, "Have you been getting into shit or *what*?"

"I know you," I breathed.

"Really? You know, that happens to me a lot."

She opened a bag. There were things in there that only a genius with no moral compass could have invented. She pulled out a syringe. Perspective plays tricks on things that are going to happen to you: a three-inch syringe when it's intended for someone else's arteries is just a three-inch syringe. When it's coming for you, it's a foot long and gleaming.

"What are you doing?" I asked.

Vera answered. "This is Dr Seah. You can trust her."

"You can't..." I began.

Dr Seah knew the sound of a refusal when she heard one, and knew that the only way to get round these things, was to ignore them before they could become admissible in court. She slid the needle into the skin of my exposed elbow vein without a sound, and pushed. We half imagined we'd see our arteries pop as whatever was in there rushed into our body; they didn't. "Hold," said Dr Seah briskly, putting a piece of cotton wool over the entry point. Vera held it.

"What did you give us?" we whispered.

"It'll help with the pain. Well...in a way. *Well*, put it like this—you're less likely to remember the pain afterwards, which is sort of like the same thing if you're not too hung up on semantics, right?"

"There's...I was attacked," I said. "I was attacked, they found me, I picked up the phone and then they came for me, they found me before, they might find me, I need to stay, to be..."

"You're as safe as you're going to be here," answered Vera. "If they find you here, they'll find you anywhere, and at least then they can throttle you quickly with your own body parts before you bleed to death."

Drugs straight into the vein. I found it hard to raise my head, heard my own words as if they were being hummed through water, felt my lips, huge and someone else's, flopping fat as I tried to speak.

Fingers that had been trained how to heal on plastic dolls that couldn't scream poked the slash down from my collarbone. "You're a lucky guy," said Dr Seah at last. "Long and shallow. Looks bad, but from a medical point of view, completely nah."

"Yeah," I croaked. "I'm just lucky."

"Ever had morphine?"

"They gave it to me once. It made me feel sick."

"Yeah, I know, crazy like that, isn't it? Hey, Vera, can I ask you to put some more water on the boil?"

"You need it for cleaning?" asked Vera with the enthusiasm of someone already anticipating the gratitude.

"Cuppa tea," was the reply.

As answers went, this was disappointing for the almost properly elected head of the Whites, who strutted from the room with the cool manner of someone far too sensible not to be of use, but who was not used to menial.

Dr Seah waited until she was gone, then leant in close. "Well, what do you want, good news or shiny news?"

Since we weren't entirely sure what "shiny" news was, we went for the good news first. "You'll live," she said.

"Terrific," I mumbled with a tongue made from sodden sponge.

"Want to know the shiny part?"

"Sure."

"Apart from this"—fingers of steel prodded the slash down my chest, a thousand miles away from my watching brain—"you're OK. You're going to need stitches, and while it'd be just so sexy to put you under for that, you kinda need anaesthesiologists and guys with the paddles and you know, things that go 'ping' to do a general anaesthetic, so I'm going to do it on local, and it's going to hurt like ten kinds of buggery. There's a few odd burns here or there, but they'll just make you look ugly for a while and I figure, hell, you're a big guy, you can handle it. The cut on the back of your head is nasty, but keep it clean and tidy and the worst thing that'll happen is a bit of premature grey and a few banged-up brain cells. The only thing I'm not totally zoomy on is this."

It took a while to realise she was holding up the beetroot lump of my right hand.

"Uh?"

"I mean, I totally get that you've been electrocuted in the last few hours, like, *totally*. And you know, like I said, if life was shiny I'd have you wired to a heart monitor right now in case anything went pop."

"Heard of bedside manner?" I growled.

"Sure," she said briskly. "But I figure, you know, fuck it. But see, there's this."

She raised my hand closer to my face so I could see. At first I didn't understand the problem; the beetroot looked slightly better cooked and less raw than it had a few hours ago, and some of the swelling even seemed to be on the retreat. Then it occurred to me: even in bad cases, electrocution rarely causes bleeding.

The blood, then, that had stained my right sleeve had come from something else. The something, almost lost in the folds of my puffed-up skin, was a thin red cross, carved with a scalpel into the palm of my hand.

We squeaked, "What did you do to us?!"

"Who, me? I didn't do this!"

"We didn't...it isn't..."

"You're telling me you didn't notice that someone's played Christian symbolism with your hand?" she asked. "You know, if you're into self-harm then, seriously, don't."

"We did not do this, this was not there before...until...there was nothing there until we answered the phone!"

"Yeah. Now, while every case is, like, unique, I gotta tell you, electrocution by telephone leading to the appearance of a cross carved in the palm of the victim's hand is unusual *even* for central London. You seriously have no idea how it got there?"

I hadn't said that. I didn't want to think about that. "Hide it," we whispered. "Do what you have to do. Please."

"Why do you want...?"

"Just do it! Please!"

Dr Seah hesitated, and for a moment there was something on her face that shouldn't have been there, deep, and serious, and a little bit sad, a sinking of features that were built to smile. Then she shrugged, beamed, showing bright white teeth in a face the colour of hot chocolate on a summer's night, and said, "Like, whatever."

She bandaged up my right hand. Whatever drug she'd shot into our veins was now playing games with the ceiling, pushing it slowly up and letting it fall again so low that it almost bumped our nose. We had never felt so degraded. But the drug helped keep us calm, keep us still and made our feelings of rage seem more like a distant story, in which I would tell a childish me, sitting on my lap, of a man who'd been given a drug and who was in pain, in a land far, far away.

We do not handle pain bravely. When she started on the stitches, we looked the other way, and as the needle slid into flesh, we pushed our face into the pillow to hide the tears. Not so much of pain, but at the thought of pain, at the idea of what might be there, but which wasn't actually except in the churnings of our imagination, worse than any truth. I bit our lip and recited ancient pointless things: song lyrics, shopping lists, bus routes, road junctions, declining verbs in exotic languages, anything to keep our thoughts away from our flesh and wandering in some mundane cage of artificial words and numbers.

Sleep, when it was all done, came easily. Real pain became a foggy memory, a comforting teddy bear that we held to our side like an old and familiar friend.

We slept.

When I woke, it was dark outside. The streetlamp outside the window could have glowed at any hour, but the sounds gave a more precise time. I could hear the distant swish of traffic, too heavy for the deepest part of the night, and from the far end of the street, the sound of a pub, which with each opening and closing of the door turned out gossip and music onto the street in a slow, fading roll. With my eyes fixed upon the slow curve of passing car headlights across the ceiling, I had no more desire to sleep; but neither did I feel the need to get up. So I lay on the bare mattress, stained with smudges of my blood that turned our stomach to look at, and assessed. My right hand was an igloo all in cotton wrapping, my left shoulder and a good part of my chest a shirt-load of bandages. The back of my scalp had been cleaned of blood and disinfected, but the rest of me still bore much of the stain of the previous night, my skin feeling two inches thicker than its natural depth. My tongue was a stiff leather slab in my mouth, my stomach a shrivelled hollow.

These discomforts were at first almost interesting novelties, but rapidly became an itching fury until at last, with a hiss of frustration, I swung my legs over the side of the bed.

On the bedside table were two bottles, one containing pills, the other liquid. A note said, "←THIS one for the pain, →THIS one to clean injuries. Seriously, don't get them confused. M. Seah."

There weren't any other instructions. She gave me more credit for intelligence than I felt I merited.

I looked for my belongings. I was still in my trousers and socks, but my shoes—or rather, not my shoes, merely the shoes I'd been wearing—had been put at the end of the bed along with my coat. My jumper and shirt were nowhere to be seen, nor was my satchel. I staggered from the bedroom into the blinding light of the living room next door, where Vera sat on a dust-covered sofa, eating prawn crackers from a plastic bag and watching TV. She didn't hear me enter, and as I tried to think of something to say I watched a dozen faces that the audience seemed to think I ought to know, learning how to sing and dance operatic numbers on ice while judges, who again I was supposed to recognise, hurled abuse at the weeping celebrities.

When I spoke, I was as surprised as Vera. I said, "Thank you."

She jumped, spilling prawn crackers across the sofa, then stood up, pretending it hadn't happened and glaring as if she dared me to say a word. "Yeah, sure. Hi. You're up, then."

"Thank you," I repeated.

"Gotcha. And you're welcome, I think. You look sorta crap." She'd been trying to find something nicer to say.

"Is there a bathroom?"

"Yeah. You need fingers like a safe-breaker to get the hot water to work, and there's no soap, but there's a bathroom."

"Thanks."

"You don't have to say anything."

"I know. Thank you for that too."

"Get on before I get all slushy. You want food?"

"Yes."

"Good. Dr Seah said you were to drink at least two litres of water when you got up, to make up for the stuff you lost when you were attacked... Matthew?"

"Yes?"

"About being attacked. We should probably talk. Get cleaned up first. I'll stick something in the microwave."

Vera had told no lies about the bathroom. The tap was sensitive to the lightest touch; a breath was the difference between arctic death and fiery combustion. When the neighbour two doors down turned on their shower, the water pressure dropped to a sulky trickle; when they turned it off, it exploded in scalding steam.

I struggled to clean myself with my left hand while keeping both my right hand and most of the bandaging out of harm's way. I dressed in suspiciously stained towels that smelt of fresh detergent and, poking my head round the door, said, "What happened to my clothes?"

"Disgusting," Vera's voice floated back. "A few more days and they'd have started talking. Men have no idea how hard it is to get blood out of clothes, and frankly, it's not worth my time."

"Say, no clothes?"

"I left some stuff under the counter. It's too big for you, but so's your shoes."

It wasn't yet the right time to explain about the shoes. I thanked her and rummaged around until I found the clothes she was talking about. In them I felt like an escapee from a children's cartoon, all cuff and trailing trouser leg, but at least they were clean.

Food was reheated Chinese takeaway. It was a meal designed to cause stomach cramps. We had never tasted such divinity and, when we thought Vera wasn't looking, ran our finger round the edge of the plate and licked sauce off our fingers. Vera was silent throughout the meal. She waited until a second after my plate had touched the table to say: "So. Attacked."

I rolled my shoulder and felt the tightness of my stitches as the muscles stretched beneath my collarbone; I flexed my fingers and felt the taut hotness of that bright red cross carved into my skin, burning beneath the bandages. Not an unpleasant burning. Drugs and fire kept it interesting, alive, rather than the pure pain that dumbs all else.

"What do you want to know?" I asked.

She went straight in with the priorities. "Will your attacker come here?"

"I don't know."

"Do you think they're capable of coming here?"

"Maybe."

"Do they know about your connection with me?"

"I don't know."

"Am I or any of my people at risk for helping you?"

"I don't know. Maybe."

"All right. What do you know?"

I thought about it long and hard. "Nothing," I said finally. "Absolutely nothing."

"I think I deserve more than that."

"I swear—nothing. I don't know who, I don't know why, I don't even know how. I know that a phone rang, I answered, and the next thing the sky was doing backflips. I know that some time after that, a pack of spectres came hunting and will probably not come looking for me again."

"Why not?"

"I caught one. They know that I know how. Spectres aren't stupid."

"You 'caught' a spectre?"

I suppose I should have been flattered by the flat disbelief in Vera's voice. It wasn't that she thought I was a liar. She just knew enough about spectres.

"In a beer bottle," I added for technical clarification.

"Really. Can I see this beer bottle?"

"It's in my bag."

She vanished into the bedroom and reappeared a second later with my satchel held out at the end of her arm as if it might start to tick.

She put it at my feet. I opened it up and pulled out the beer bottle. The cigarette still burnt sullen inside.

Vera took the bottle gingerly between her fingertips.

I said, "Listen to it."

She obeyed, holding it up to her ear. I saw her eyes widen. "Christ," she muttered. "You captured a ghost that's into heavy metal."

I took it back from her, put it reverentially on the table between us. "Yeah—don't open it in a hurry," I said. "Spectres aren't known for their humour."

"Why a beer bottle?"

"Why put a genie in a lamp?" I asked.

"Don't give me the whole metaphor bollocks. I asked a simple technical question."

"And got a simple technical answer. You use the container most appropriate. A lamp is a precious thing that grants illumination. A beer bottle is...well...not. I hate to get all sociopolitical on you..."

"Please don't."

"...but there's something to the theory that you can drown anything at the bottom of a beer bottle. Even if there *isn't* something to the theory, enough people believe it so that there is."

"Deep."

"You asked."

"I was being funny *and* sarcastic. I can do both." She sighed, eyes not leaving the bottle. "Spectres aren't stupid," she said at length. "And they don't go around attacking without reason either. You think they went after you specifically?"

"Yes."

"Why?"

"Because I don't believe in coincidence. The telephone rang and..."

"Yeah, what's up with you and the telephone? I would have thought, what with, you know, you being you...blue electric angels, gods of the telephone, song in the wire, fire, light, life, static interference with knobs on made flesh, Swift and the angels and so on and so forth — and now you're scowling?"

"It was a trap," we muttered; and saying it, we realised we were angry. "It was a trap designed specifically for *us*. We hear a telephone ring on an empty road in the middle of the night and we'll answer it, we'd always answer it, and it would always find us. We are...it's part of what we are. Someone *used* the telephone to target us. The telephone rang and of course we answered. Then they attacked us down the telephone, and sent spectres to finish us off."

"Who 'they'?"

"I don't know."

"Why you?"

"I don't know."

"Which you?" Her voice didn't change as she asked the question. Nor did her eyes leave the bottle to observe our face, which was full of surprise.

"I suppose..." I mumbled. "It doesn't matter."

"Doesn't matter to *you*," she corrected. "You'll end up dead regardless of which you 'they' were after. But it might matter to 'them'. Some guy wants to blaze electric fire across the sky, then there's no point just attacking Matthew Swift, but there'd sure be some credit to the notion of going after the blue electric angels. On the other hand, if some girl is pissed off that Matthew Swift ditched her at a party, then, sure, she might try and hurt him, and the blue electric angels will get caught in the crossfire. Just because you happen to be both entities inhabiting the same brain and the same body, it doesn't mean other people are going to respect the difference. So the question is...did whoever sent the spectres and dialled the telephone want to hurt Matthew Swift, or the electric angels? Or both at once, since you are now, technically, the same?"

"A question we'll ask," we replied, "when we meet 'them'."

Silence. Then Vera said, "Why are your shoes too big?"

"It's complicated. I was looking for someone."

"And that meant you had to wear big shoes?"

"This pair helped, yes."

"Who were you looking for?"

"Just a kid."

"You think he attacked you?"

"No. He wouldn't know how. Summoning spectres, attacking through a telephone, these things are complicated."

"Yeah," sighed Vera. "That's the thing, isn't it? We're not talking any nitwit doing these things to you. If you'd asked me a few years ago, I'd have said 'sorcerer' hands down. Summoning the monsters, sending fire down the phones—it all stinks of serious magic. But the sorcerers are either dead or mad, except you, and you're hardly the purest example of the kind. Which leads to the question, who or *what* else could be after you?"

"The old sorcerers are dead," I replied. "Doesn't mean new ones can't take their places."

"You taught any newbies how to summon spectres lately?"

I shook my head.

"See? It takes clout and experience to do these things. Some random sparking kid isn't going to hack it. Who's this kid you were looking for anyway?"

"Just a kid."

"Is that it?"

"Pretty much. I made a promise that I'd help—he's nothing special."

"OK. You should know."

Silence a while. I felt groggy again, fat on food and sluggish from the warmth. My skin tingled in a warning of imminent pins and needles. I hugged my knees to my chest, put my chin on them and watched the shadow of the bare trees outside moving across the glow of the streetlights. "What time is it?" I asked.

"Nineish. You slept deep."

"I am grateful..."

"Matthew?"

There was something in her voice. It was a high breath that had rolled out despite itself, a push all at once through a clamped-up throat. I looked round, to find her eyes fixed on the ceiling. "Matthew," she said again, firmer, getting control. "Matthew Matthew Matthew," she added with a sigh.

"Vera?"

"You believe in coincidence, Matthew? You believe...things like this are unconnected?"

"No."

"No," she said at last. "Me neither."

I waited for something more, but by now her gaze was locked, fascinated, upon the ceiling and there was no turning it away. I said, "I'll be gone in the morning."

"You think that's smart?"

"The doctor gave me painkillers."

"I think she may have mentioned something about taking it easy too."

"Someone attacked us," we replied. "We *are* going to find them."

"Sure," she sighed, rubbing the back of her neck with one pale hand. "'Course you are. Sure."

She turned the TV back on. There was something more that she'd wanted to say, but she didn't seem to have the inclination to say it any more, and I was too tired to press her.

I went back to bed.

A telephone woke us. It wasn't ringing. But we knew the instant we were awake that there was a telephone conversation happening nearby. We could feel the tingle of its energy up and down the length of our spine. Still dark outside; probably only a few hours had elapsed.

Through the bedroom door I could hear Vera's voice, a series of mumbled sounds and shapes on the air. I rolled stiffly out of bed, padded to the door, listened. I don't know why I listened. Curiosity may have killed the cat, but paranoia was what tied it up in a sack and buried it in wet concrete.

I heard Vera say, "Yeah. Yeah, I know. Didn't tell him yet. He's in a bad way...Look, I know how it seems, but I don't believe that he... no, don't do that. No. It's just his word for it, and the spectre in the bottle. You ever see him summon a spectre, it sound like his style? Don't give me that bollocks. For Christ's sake, I don't believe that for a minute—look, the guy seems genuinely freaked, I don't think this is the right time to...yeah. Yeah, I know. Look, I'll...if you must. But they won't like it. You say that, you haven't met them yet. I swear to God, if there wasn't a fucking sorcerer still in that skin, they'd have ripped the city apart just for kicks. No, that doesn't mean...yeah. I understand. You know where to go? OK then. Bye."

She hung up.

I slunk back deeper into the shadow of my room, and heard her footsteps approaching the door. Quickly, instinctively, like a child about to be caught reading in the dark, we rolled back into bed, putting our back to the door and forcing ourself to take slow, steady breaths, in through the nose, out through the mouth. A spike of light spilled over us and up the opposite wall as Vera opened the door, looked in, then closed it again. We counted to ten and sat back up, looking round at the empty neon-washed gloom. Paranoia seems more reasonable when you've got twelve stitches in your side. I looked around for my bag and coat, not necessarily with the intent of leaving, not yet; just to have the comfort of them there, with their supplies. My coat was drooped over the end of the bed. Some kindly pair of fingers had even stitched the slash in its fabric back together with bright red thread. My shoes, two sizes too big, were by the bedroom door. On a chair lay a huge green jumper with a saggy hood and a kangaroo pocket; I pulled it on, dragged my coat on over it and looked for my bag.

It was next door, with Vera. So was my watch, although with

the blood burnt to the strap it wasn't such a loss. I checked my coat pocket for supplies. A few receipts for sandwiches, a couple of old crisp packets, a piece of string. Merlin himself couldn't have made anything of this, not even a decent hand of cat's cradle. I sat on the edge of the bed and reached for my shoes.

The doorbell pinged. It played the first few bars of "Oranges and Lemons" before Vera got to the intercom. She moved fast, not wanting me disturbed; mumbled into the speaker. "Yeah—I'll let you right up."

I did up my shoelaces, fumbling uselessly with my right hand and struggling to get any kind of grace or coordination with my left. I walked to the window, looked down into the street. Two sleek black cars were parked clumsily in the middle of the road, all shadowed glass and hungry, growling engine. A man was leaning against one of them. At first I thought he was a preacher, with a big black hat and a black featureless coat beneath which protruded a pair of black leather shoes. No dog collar, though, and the languid angle of his body and the fold of his arms were too young and cocksure for a priest.

Then he looked up, and he was looking at us. We drew back instinctively from the window, knowing rationally there was no way he had seen us, and knowing honestly that he had.

From the next room, I heard a tapping on the apartment door and the chain being drawn back. Paranoia is not good at finding solutions. I looked round the room, searching for the mains sockets, and quickly flicked on every one regardless of whether there was a plug to use in it. If in doubt, a sorcerer's first line of defence is mains voltage, and I wanted there to be plenty around.

Vera's voice from next door, speaking to more voices. "Asleep... Look, is this necessary? I mean, I know that...no, no, I'll do it."

The bedroom door eased open. Vera stood in the light. "Matthew?" she called gently towards the bed.

"I'm here," I said. "I'm up."

"Yes," she murmured, looking me over. "There's some people here I think you should talk to."

"Who are they?"

"They might be able to help."

"Who are they?"

"Aldermen."

Aldermen.

I loathe the Aldermen. Not the fluffy, cocktail-sausage-and-champagne aldermen, they weren't the problem. The other Aldermen. The ones who only come out at night. Protectors of the city. The ones who do whatever it is that is necessary for the city to be safe; and right there was the problem. Sometimes "necessary" didn't mean "right".

I am scared of the Aldermen.

And the problem about Aldermen was that they never came out for the little things.

There were three of them, but none of them. On the surface they looked like escapees from the English Civil War, all big hats and black coats with fat black buttons. When the coats came off, the truth underneath was no better: pinstriped grey suits, silver ties and bright pink shirts designed to suggest the wearer's uniqueness, and which every fashionable young suit wore to work. There were little, little hints as to their nature, once you bothered to look; one had on his right fist a collection of rings, one of which was burnt with the symbol of the twin keys. Pinned above a silk handkerchief sticking out of an old-fashioned waistcoat pocket, another had a small badge of a red dragon holding a shield. A third had the two red crosses, the smaller one etched into the upper left-hand corner of its larger twin, that were stamped on the emblem of the Corporation of London. Secret societies are extra-thrilling when you can feel the smugness of wearing them on your sleeve and still not being noticed.

They looked at me, we looked at them. I got the feeling they weren't happy either.

Then one said, "So which are you?"

Vera rolled her eyes. The Alderman who'd spoken was young, male, and destined to rule the world. He had dark blond hair, slightly curled, a face just bordering on deeply tanned; bright blue eyes, a hint of freckle and a set of teeth you could have carved a piano with. If I hated Aldermen on basic principle, I hated *him* on direct observation.

"It's not that simple..." began Vera, and I realised that she was also afraid. It takes a lot to frighten Vera.

"Of course it's not," said the middle man. He was older, with a little lined face from which boomed a great rolling voice, and neat precise hands. When he smiled, his every feature crinkled gnomicly, and so great were the welcoming good manners in his voice and every other aspect of his presence that I automatically didn't believe them. "Mr Swift," he said, "I am Mr Earle."

He held out a hand only a few veins thicker than a sheet of paper. I shook it. "Mr Kemsley"—the young man with the teeth—"and Ms Anissina." Ms Anissina was a woman in her mid-thirties, wearing clothes for a bright twenty-something and a hardened face fit for a dying warlord. Everything else about her was a frozen blank, neither hostile nor friendly, happy nor sad, lively nor subdued: just stone in a suit. Either she was a woman of hidden depths, or there was nothing beneath that marble surface to hide.

"I gather you've been injured; would you like to sit?"

I nodded, considering there was nothing to be gained from feigning a strength I obviously lacked. The one sofa had only space on it for three good friends. They left it all to me, and dispersed themselves casually around the room, just far enough apart to make it impossible to look at more than one Alderman at a time.

Mr Earle took up position by the window. I thought of sniper rifles and bright lights. He said, "Mr Swift, first may I offer my regrets that you have clearly been a victim of some violence."

The words were the flat intonations of a busy priest, with three burials left to do before sunset and a migraine coming on. I said nothing. He didn't care.

"How much are you aware of the remit of our duties, Mr Swift?"

"You're the Aldermen," I replied flatly. "A formation of like-minded individuals of a magical inclining whose responsibility is to 'protect the city', whatever that means."

"Yes—you hit upon an ambiguity there."

I shrugged.

"You are broadly correct. There is more to our mandate than a loose 'protect the city' and, naturally, more than simply 'like-minded individuals' in our exclusive choice of membership; but I don't need to bore you with these details."

I shrugged again, feeling skin stretch around the stitches, pain dribble down my spine. "I'm guessing you're not here because you're worried about my health."

"Alas, that is not our main concern. I am sure you also understand our authority," added Mr Earle, finding a point and sharpening it.

"I understand," I replied, "that for nearly a thousand years there have been Aldermen watching over London, and that sooner or later anyone who opposes their will, dies. I know you serve the Midnight Mayor, who, if he exists, is the sacred protector of the city stones and whose heart beats in time to the rhythms of city life and so on and so forth."

"You don't believe in the Midnight Mayor?" he asked. "Interesting."

"Is that what you meant by 'authority'?"

"If you regard authority as merely being might, then yes. We could argue semantics all day, but I think you have the essential details. Well then, with all this in mind, perhaps I can ask you some questions. Where were you last night, Mr Swift, between one and three a.m.?"

I stared at him in surprise, which threatened to turn to anger. "Being stabbed by spectres," I replied.

"But *where*, Mr Swift?"

"Willesden."

"What were you doing in Willesden?"

"I told you. Being stabbed."

"Mr Swift..." He sighed, then asked, "Is this your watch?"

He held up a sad, burnt piece of fabric and metal, 99p from a vendor on the street, with a faded Mickey Mouse behind the frozen hands. I didn't ask how he'd got it, didn't blame Vera for giving it to him. "Yes," I said.

"I assume it was damaged during this...encounter with the spectres?"

"It stopped when I was attacked, yes."

"At two twenty-five in the morning?"

"I wasn't paying much attention to the time."

"No, no, of course not. No, naturally, why should you?" On the edge of something else, he asked, "Would you like a cup of tea?"

"No, thank you."

"Are you sure? Vera, my darling, a cup of tea?"

"I'll put the kettle on," growled Vera.

I could feel electricity buzzing through the walls, taste it on the air. A twitch of my fingers and I could wrap myself in it, send spinning mains lightning through the room, cranked up with all the will of a sorcerer's magic to the point where flesh would pop. I said, "Maybe I would like tea."

"Tea all round," sighed Vera.

"Coffee for me," said Mr Kemsley. "Decaf, if you've got it."

The head of the Whites, one of the largest organisations of magicians, painters and warlocks to burrow beneath the streets of London, smiled through her gritted teeth, and turned on the kettle.

"I don't suppose anyone saw this encounter in Willesden?" asked Mr Earle.

"A large number of people, I suspect. But they wouldn't know what to make of it."

"Anyone...of alternative inclining?"

"I'm guessing you're not referring to sex, biology or morals?"

"Forgive me, Mr Swift, but in my line of work it can pay to be careful in one's choice of language."

"You can ask whoever attacked me. They'll know what happened."

"Ah, yes. And I suppose you have no idea *who* attacked you?"

"No."

"You didn't see his face? Or speak to him?"

"No. It was all done by remote. Mr Earle?"

"Mr Swift?"

"Why do you care?"

Mr Kemsley almost snorted. Our eyes flashed to him and for a moment, he met our gaze, and cringed away from it.

Mr Earle said, carelessly, "Oh, you understand how it is, Mr Swift. After the business with Bakker and the Tower, sorcerers are in short supply. And sorcerers with...if you'll forgive me saying it...such a casual attitude as yours towards death, resurrection and the telephonic system cause us understandable concern, whenever anything bad befalls them."

"So you're just here because you care," I said, letting the sarcasm show.

"Something like that."

"Mr Earle?" we sighed, rubbing the bridge of our nose.

"Yes, Mr Swift?"

We looked up. He saw our eyes. Not just Mr Swift. My attitude towards the telephones had never been casual. "Mr Earle," we said, "why do you keep referring to our attacker as 'he'?"

He was good; but if he'd been brilliant, the question wouldn't have slowed him down. It did now. "I suppose it must be my natural socio-cultural gender bias. Forgive me, my dear," he added, nodding to Ms Anissina, whose face remained empty, and Vera, who scowled.

My bag was at the foot of the coffee table. The bottle with the spectre in it was on the end. There were three lights in the room, small bulbs churning out bright whiteness from the ceiling. I had my coat and shoes on. Mr Earle guessed what I was thinking. It didn't take much effort.

"You don't like Aldermen, do you, Mr Swift?"

"No," I replied.

"Why, may I ask?"

"You only come out for the big things."

"I don't understand..."

"When the peasants revolted in the reign of Richard II, the Aldermen came out to send the nightmares let loose by the fear of destruction back to sleep. When bubonic plague went through the streets, the Aldermen came out to stop the dead from walking. When the Fire of London gutted the city, the Aldermen made sure to save the precious treasures from the flames: the ravens in the tower, the London Stone — the altar supposed to have been laid by Brutus at the heart of the city, the heart of the damn country. When the bombs fell in the Blitz, the Aldermen were the ones who kept the things unearthed in the rubble from getting up and walking."

"And...you seem to regard this in a negative light?"

"When the plague rats came to the city, the Aldermen made sure the dead didn't walk. But they didn't lift a finger to stop the dead from dying."

"Ah — I see."

"You are the protectors of the *stones*, Mr Earle, of the memory and the riches and the buildings of the city. You do not protect the people. So I've got to ask again — why are we having this conversation?"

Silence in the room, except for the slow bubbling of the kettle. Mr Kemsley shifted his weight against the wall. Ms Anissina took a slow, quiet breath. Mr Earle smiled. Skulls smile, and in the grave, Mr Earle will grin for ever at a joke only he could understand.

"I respect your honesty," he said at last. This is something liars say. "You've been frank with me, I'll be frank with you. Quite regardless of your personal condition, our concern is larger than the mere trifle of whether you live or die again. We couldn't care less if you were attacked or who attacked you, except that there are...matters at work which require our involvement. And you, Mr Swift, seem to be currently sitting in the middle of them."

"What matters?"

"I do not think I need trouble you by reporting them."

"You already are troubling me."

"Then I shall be brief to save us all further inconvenience. I believe you when you say you were attacked last night. I believe that you were hurt, I believe that you were afraid; all these things are empirically obvious. I believe that there are very few powers in this city, if not on this earth, which could make creatures such as the blue electric angels either hurt or afraid. I believe that the Midnight Mayor is one of them. I believe you attacked the Midnight Mayor. I believe you killed him."

Strangely, we have never in our life been accused of killing a man.

I stared at Mr Earle and saw nothing but serious honesty in his little lined face. I looked at Ms Anissina and saw ice, I looked at Mr Kemsley and saw fire. I half-turned my head, looked at Vera and saw . . . for a moment, not Vera. Not quite: in the blinking of an eye, something else was standing where she should have been. Blink again, and there was Vera, face as empty as the mugs in her hand.

I looked back at Mr Earle and said, "You are totally shitting me."

"I am quite serious," he replied primly. "End of the line."

A threat, as well as a statement.

"Why would I kill the Midnight Mayor?" I asked. "I don't even believe he exists."

"Come now," he chided. "That's a poor argument. You know the Old Bag Lady exists, you've met the Beggar King, you understand that Lady Neon stalks the lamplit streets and Fat Rat scuttles in the Underground. You of all . . . creatures . . . should know that the Midnight Mayor is real."

"No," I replied. "Besides, even if he were real, the Midnight Mayor can't just die."

"Of course not! The Midnight Mayor is an idea, a concept, a drifting title, a name that happens to carry with it some considerable power. No, no, no, the Midnight Mayor isn't dead. Merely the man who happened to be him. There's another Midnight Mayor out there, somewhere in the city, waiting to wake up and taste the carbon monoxide. Even you can't kill an idea."

Three faces carved with a pickaxe from old rough marble looked at me from around the room. I rubbed my aching shoulder, tried to shake the bumble-bees from my ears. "Exactly how did you reach the conclusion that I did this, if this has even been done?" I asked, trying not to look at my bag and the spectre-filled beer bottle.

"Well," sighed Mr Earle, "apart from the obvious qualifications — I mean as regarding your capacity to kill, which is well established, and your abilities when it comes to this matter — there's a great deal of circumstance."

"Circumstance? Is that it?"

"I did say a great deal," he chided.

"It'd better be monumental," I snapped.

He ticked it off on his fingers. "One:" he intoned, "your clear hatred for the Aldermen and by implication, our chief, the Midnight Mayor..."

"If you believe he exists," I added.

"Who quite clearly exists, who was my friend and boss and who died last night face down in his own bodily fluids. Two: the manner of the Mayor's death..."

"Which was?"

"Stinking of sorcery," he replied. "Three: files left in the Mayor's office in which you were, I am sorry to report, the star. Four: your own injuries, most likely inflicted by the Mayor during your encounter. Five: circumstances around the city of London suggesting activities of the kind it takes a sorcerer or worse to inflict — you are, I think, still the only sorcerer in town?"

"Doesn't mean that other sorcerers aren't coming in from outside, or finding their abilities," I retorted. "Life is magic; sooner or later there'll always be someone new who works this out. What kind of 'activities', and why do you care?"

He didn't answer. Perhaps he was just scared of losing count. "Six: your watch."

"My watch?"

"Your watch," he replied. "Stopped at 2.25 when it was hit by what I'm guessing was a wallop of magical energy."

"Yes—and?"

"And by the coroner's report, the Mayor died at 2.26."

Silence.

There's no such thing as coincidence. At least there's no such thing when it's bad news. Everyone needs something to blame.

I said, "It wasn't me."

"You've killed before."

"I've killed the shadow that killed me! I've killed a walking corpse with paper stuffed down his throat! We have *never*..."

"You killed Robert James Bakker. Your teacher, your mentor, your—"

"Robert Bakker was the fuel that kept a walking shadow feeding on blood and death for two years! Robert Bakker was the man whose shadow ripped out my fucking throat and killed my apprentice, who..."

"You're not human, Matthew Swift. To be blunt about it. You're not human."

We stood up slowly. "We are human," we replied. "We have all the apparatus of humanity and more. We were *made* by humans. You mortals pour your thoughts, feelings, stories, knowledge, everything you have, you pour it into the phone lines and sooner or later, it had to live. We are everything that you are and more. We did not kill your Midnight Mayor."

Silence again. Then Mr Kemsley said, "I don't believe a word of it."

Mr Earle said nothing. Lips the colour of old slushed snow pursed beneath a pencil-sharpener nose.

Vera said, moving towards me calmly, "If the old Mayor is dead, who's the new Mayor? Is it done by appointment or what?"

No one felt inclined to answer.

We put our head on one side and looked at Mr Earle. His fingers twitched at his side. "No," he said finally. "Either way, it's not going to work."

It's not very easy to kill a sorcerer with magic, since nine times out of ten the sorcerer in question will be so hyped up on the stuff that they won't even notice you're trying. It's very easy to kill a sorcerer with bullets. We die like everyone else — most of the time.

I knew this. I'd been reminded the second Ms Anissina's hand went into her coat pocket. Which is why I pushed my bandaged hand up to the ceiling and curled my fingers around the lights, snuffing them out of existence before she had a chance to fire.

The good news was that Ms Anissina was, at the end of the day, an Alderman, trained in use of magic, not firearms. She fired anyway: blinding whiteness in a room of adjusting eyes. I heard something go, very quietly, *ah*. It wasn't me. It was a sound somewhere between surprise and being stung by a nettle. Then Mr Kemsley's hands were at my throat, and his fingers, once he bothered to stretch them, weren't just mortal flesh; they sprouted aluminium, unfolded metal armour from between the tiny curved lines of his fingerprints, sharp and cold and harsh and unremitting, and above all else, conductive.

I fell back beneath his weight, letting him push me, throwing him off balance, overborne by his own momentum, and as I fell, reached out towards the nearest socket and grabbed for its power. Electric fire snaked through the air to my fingertips, obedient to command, and with a fistful of lightning I slammed my fist into the side of his head, hurling him across my body and over towards the opposite wall.

The light of the electricity gave Ms Anissina a glimmer to see by; she was the black shadow raising the gun. So I hurled the stolen brightness of the snuffed lights at her face, a blinding sphere the size of a football containing the illumination of the whole room in a bundle. She turned her head away, covering her eyes, and the gun fired again, flashing a starlight explosion from the end of the barrel and poking a hole in the ceiling.

I crawled back onto my feet, scooped up my bag from the floor and fumbled in the darkness round the back of the sofa. As my eyes began to adjust to the yellow light from the streetlamps and the blue glow of the electricity spun around my fist, a claw closed round the back of my neck. Five fingers had sprouted five painted black metal claws; skin had turned silver and weakness had turned to a vicelike strength that threatened to pop my spine out from beneath my skin. No one should have that kind of strength, but Mr Earle wasn't just anyone. He pulled my head back so I could see the ceiling, and my back arched and bent to follow. In the light of the streetlamps and spitting electric flame I could see his face, and as I watched, the silverish metal covering of his skin was spreading even there, covering his lips, eyelids, spilling into his ears. His tongue flickered between his lips, and it was a thin red rolling fork; his breath was so hot it rippled the air and sucked moisture from my eyes, his eyes were bulbous, fishlike, burning white fire inside, and as he bent my head back even further, so far I thought it would break, I saw that the little pin on his lapel, the red cross of the Corporation of London, was glowing. Interesting, that. Very rarely do items of personal fashion glow, even under magical circumstances, unless they have something to do with events more than just bad taste.

Then Mr Earle raised his other hand, and it was a claw, and the curved tips of his spiked fingers were looking for the sockets of my eyes. I tried to reach up with electric fingertips, but his grip was so strong and so low that I nearly overbalanced and fell with the action. His lips rippled; not just human emotion, but an animal rippling.

Then Vera said, "Ah, shit."

He looked round.

I did my best to look, and saw, in the very corner of my eye, Vera, standing with kettle in hand, an irritated expression on her face and blood running out of a neat, bullet-sized hole in her chest. Then she smiled.

Not blood.

Paint.

And her skin was shining a bit too brightly, a reflective, acrylic glow, and her hair was dribbling down her back, melting and running down her face like eyeliner in the rain, and her face was melting, draining pale pinkness into her clothes, which wobbled and bubbled and fused into each other, and when she smiled, liquid white plastic sloshed over her running lips. Mr Earle and I stared at this shrivelling liquid thing in silence, both too surprised to say or do anything. Then Vera raised the kettle, little finger dropping off in a thick splat of pink as she did, and with what was left of her melting hand, swung it firmly into the side of Mr Earle's face.

He crumpled without a sound, and I fell on top of him, balance completely gone. In a moment I had scrambled free again. But he had merely fallen, nothing more, and as I staggered up, a fist curled round my foot and a pair of burning eyes looked up into my own. Thin red blood was trickling over the silver skin of his face. Acting on instinct, good education and pure adrenalin, I bent down and grabbed the glowing badge pinned to the front of his jacket. It was cool to the touch. He grinned as my fingers closed over it, revealing that forked little tongue, and white teeth grown to little fangs, and for a moment I doubted my own logic. But then his grin turned to something else, darker and more afraid, as I tore badge, lapel and silk away from his chest in a crackling heave, sparks flickering off my skin as my concentration lapsed and electricity stolen from the mains earthed itself around me.

The silver on his face immediately began to retreat, melting into his skin as fast as it had grown, and the blood, that had been a trickle, started to gush thick, gloopy rivulets into his hair. To my left, Vera was nothing more than a melted snowman of spreading paint, a sad lump of expanding coloured liquid pooling on the floor. I dragged my foot free of Earle's suddenly weakened grip and ran for the door. The lollipop lady painted on the inside had her back turned to me, one hand held up towards an invisible truck on the other side. I pulled the door open without thinking about it, ran out into the corridor, slipping Earle's now dull badge into my pocket, and walked into the fist of the fourth Alderman, the one who I'd seen waiting by the car. It wasn't a particularly hard punch, and he wasn't sure what to do with it after it had landed, but it sent us staggering back against the wall and automatically we threw our hands up, snarling our anger and unleashing a blast of electricity, dragging it out from the walls and the ceiling to slam firmly into the Alderman's chest. The shock picked him off his feet and slammed him back against the banister, which hissed and crackled as electricity earthed down the metal railings.

Then I was running again, tripping on the stairs and fumbling in the half-dark for support and guidance. The front door was open, the black cars of the Aldermen humming outside. I looked for a back way out, couldn't find one, and hammered on the door of a ground-floor flat until a serious-looking gentleman with an important beard and a tartan dressing gown opened it. "Can I . . ." he began.

I kicked the door open before he could finish the sentence, marched straight into the flat, down a corridor lined with pictures of dead fish and serious ancestors, sometimes in the same frame, found a kitchen, the window too small and blocked by an extractor fan, then a bedroom, in which a woman wearing far too little lace, designed for someone twenty years younger and five stone lighter, started screaming. It was none of my business. There was a window at the back of the bedroom; I opened it. It looked out onto a small cobbled mews, full of recycling bins, Dumpsters and impossibly angled parking spaces. I crawled out of the window and pulled it shut behind me. The woman just kept on screaming, as if I had the energy or the interest.

There was only one way out of the mews, into a street of expensive cars and not enough space to keep them in. No sign of the Aldermen, no sound of sirens. I ran to the end of the street, where I came to a network of zebra crossings and traffic lights, over which black taxis and delivery trucks swooshed in busy indifference. Here I slowed, skulking along the gloomy edge of a private garden square, and, sticking to the shadows at first, started to walk. A walking man never causes as much interest as a running man, and can sometimes get places faster. My head hurt, pounding from the inside out, against my skull. I walked with the confident, businesslike lollop of your good Londoner. Even if you've no idea where you're going, you have to *look* like you do. It's what keeps the locals different from the strangers.

I was in Bayswater. A tiny place in a big city, all things considered, but with its own unique character compressed between broad streets. If you didn't look too hard, it was an upper-class part of town, all grand houses in white terraces. Pay a little more attention, and the wandering eye would notice the broken window against the tatty tea-stained cloth hung up for a curtain; a dozen doorbells on a single house; the council flat housing an old lady, wedged between the restored mansions with their knocked-through basement. There's no place in London that's ever just *one* thing. I passed graffiti in a dozen languages; alongside the long flowing curves of Arabic script, all kinds of names and doodles.

RIDAMMI IL CAPPELLO

Or:

SUPPORT THE FRENCH REVOLUTION

Or:

SuPaSTARz

And other slogans and messages, meaningless except for the one person who knew already what the meaning was. There was something that made us uneasy about the secret scratched paintwork sprawled across the bare walls, or slapped onto the side of postboxes. Wizards had long known the value of leaving their marks in their regular haunts, back from when the first druid thought it might be interesting to carve a star into the bark of a tree and see if it started to burn. I thought about Mr Earle. Aldermen only ever came out for the big things.

The seeming dignity of Bayswater began to deteriorate into the endlessly changing buildings on the Edgware Road. Office blocks and underground car parks; palm trees in fake terracotta pots outside sliding glass doors; coffee shops; and all things Arabic. Every other sign was in swirling, elegant Arabic script, running right to left above the left-to-right English translation. Giant windows full of carpets, shisha pipes and overstuffed furniture; cars swooshing down the busy street; men in silk suits, walking ahead of women holding brown-eyed kids whose noses they dabbed with tissues from a gilt-trimmed box. Edgware Road believed in consumerism and cash. There were people, cars, CCTV cameras, restaurants and clubs, and shops that stayed open till 2 a.m. to serve Turkish delight and flat bread.

More to the point, there was the Tube.

There are two Edgware Road stations. Getting from one to the other involves taking a train four stops and changing. Getting from one to the other by foot involves walking under a small motorway. I went to the larger of the two, tapping in with my travelcard and staggering down the steps onto the first platform that took my fancy. Direction was an irrelevance. I slumped on a bench, holding my burning hand to my chest and fumbling in my pocket for painkillers. There was a vending machine selling a bottle of volcanically pure, organically treated, beloved, chilled and pampered water for £2.50, or a cardboard pack of sugar-laced, chemically treated fruit juice for 60p. I slurped blackcurrant-flavoured stickiness through a straw and swallowed the painkillers, then kicked another vending machine until it gave me chocolate.

A train pulled up on the opposite platform. It claimed to be going to Barking, but on its arrival it just sat there, chugging and clunking and not bothering to close its doors. The few passengers sat in silence and didn't seem surprised.

Above my bench the board announced an eastbound Circle Line train was coming, but didn't tell me when. If London Underground isn't telling you when the next train is due, you can usually assume it's bad news. I slurped more fruity sugar and waited. On the far side of the track, an enterprising graffiti artist with no fear of electrocution had written:

GEEF ME MIJN HOED TERUG

My thoughts, which had been left behind when the rest of me decided to run, had finally slipped back into the hollow comfort of my brain. Now they were setting up shop, putting out their wares and asking for a health and safety assessment.

Earle had said: the Midnight Mayor.

Which was alarming enough in itself, but then he'd gone further: the Midnight Mayor is dead.

And the Aldermen thought we'd killed him.

Which, while not true, was still justification for our execution.

And we *had* been attacked at 2.25 a.m., and they said that the Mayor had died at 2.26 a.m., and what was the use of their lying about it?

Even if the Mayor was real.

Even if the Mayor was dead?

I caught the Circle Line from Edgware Road to Baker Street; at Baker Street, changed to the Bakerloo Line for Oxford Circus; and from there took the Central Line, towards Bank and the City of London. The old city; the Golden Mile. The hunting ground of the Aldermen, and home of the Midnight Mayor.

Part 1: The Midnight Mayor

In which the nature of telephones is discussed, a connection made, a curse exposed and a title transferred to an unsuspecting inheritor.

This is the story of the Mayors of London.

Once a year on a usually cold and often drizzling November morning, a heavy carriage of tasteless gold and plump velvet is wheeled out from its resting place in the Guildhall, at the heart of the Corporation of London, the oldest borough of the city. It's dusted off, given a pair of footmen in white tights and a driver with a big hat, and sent to collect the Lord Mayor of London. In bright red robes and a ridiculous chain of office, this individual will then ride through the centre of town, swear a number of oaths, shake a lot of hands and generally celebrate and make merry for the good of the city. Ludgate Circus and Fleet Street are shut down for his procession; likewise Cheapside, London Wall and Bank are sealed off, cars out and policemen in, along with the tourists and onlookers who come to see the parade. Giant floats of distorted gaseous proportion, dancing bands and singing dancers, jugglers and hot dog vendors take to the streets and generally a fine if slightly pompous time is had by all. As the sun goes down, the Lord Mayor boards a boat on the Thames, between Blackfriars and Waterloo Bridge, and from anchored barges in the middle of the river fireworks are set off, funded by the big financial firms of the city. Champagne is drunk by dignitaries onboard, and the onlookers, as soon as the last boom has died away above the Oxo Tower, are quick to seek out the hidden pubs in the alleys between Fleet Street and Farringdon Road, or behind the National Theatre, Gabriel's Wharf and Southwark. And so the day is partied away quite nicely thank you and, for another year, the people forget that the Lord Mayor exists.

In the intervening time, the Lord Mayor of London fulfils his duties, promoting the financial district of the city, and making deals with names like KPMG, Merrill Lynch, Price Waterhouse Coopers and other megaliths lurking within their glass towers. He attends meetings with Governors, Committees, Secretaries, Aldermen; he shakes no less than a hundred new hands a week, goes abroad on expenses to promote the wonders of London, snarls quietly at the Greater London Authority and *its* Mayor, who regard the Corporation of London as something of a historical blip in the history of local councils, and perhaps in his vainer moments remembers that Magna Carta permits him, technically, to ban the Queen from visiting the city within the old London walls. He opens museums, attends parties, networks on behalf of the city and every now and then is invited to a wedding at St Paul's or tea at the Palace and all things considered, has a good time and does an OK thing.

So a year passes; so another Lord Mayor is chosen by the arcane reasonings of the Guildhall and Corporation staff, with no small interest expressed by the great financial giants of the city.

It is only after the Lord Mayor is in bed that the Midnight Mayor comes onto the streets. He too, like his daylight counterpart, must have his procession. Crawling out of the shadows, he carries around his neck the great black key of his office, an iron monster that once used to lock the gates of the wall of London. In his hand he carries a black staff whose thumping upon the cobbled stones can call rioters to order, on his back he wears a black cloak sewn together out of soot and the shrouds of the plague victims. When he walks past St Paul's Cathedral, they say the statues turn to watch him go. When he stands by the Monument, the great golden flame on its head flickers and spins with burning fire. When he processes around the old wall of London, the shadows follow him wherever he goes. He too, like the Lord Mayor, has his duties. Like the ravens in the Tower, the London Stone, even the river itself, he protects the city, watches over it and keeps it safe from...who knows what? It is in the nature of his duty that we never find out what he has protected us from, since to keep us safe, he ensured that it never happened. Some theorists say that he isn't a man at all, but a creature grown out of stones, a statue come alive from old cobbles and river mud. Others say it's just a title, *just* a title as if titles didn't have power, passed down from one old scrounger to another, generation after generation. Some say that the Midnight Mayor is a man, whose soul has become so consumed by the city that he often forgets he has feet at all, but sees with the eyes of the pigeons and breathes the thick fumes of the double-decker bus and finds in them ambrosia. The Aldermen are his servants — not the mundane, attend-a-few-parties, shake-a-few-hands aldermen of the Lord Mayor, but the other Aldermen, the hat-wearing, gun-toting arseholes of the magical community. And so while the city sleeps, the Midnight Mayor wanders, keeping us safe from all the nasties at the door.

That is, if you believe a word of it. Which under normal conditions, I didn't.

But these were interesting times.

All of which left me with two major problems:

1. What could possibly be so bad that even the Midnight Mayor (if he was real) took an interest?
2. What could possibly be so bad that the Midnight Mayor was killed by it?

My watch had stopped at 2.25 a.m. and the Mayor died at 2.26. I wanted to find out why.

Mr Earle had said "by the coroner's report".

Say what you will for the Aldermen, they were bureaucratic to an extreme. Of course they'd have a coroner's report on the death of their boss, the Midnight Mayor, *of course* they would. A coroner's report and a receipt for the funeral, if there was anything left to bury, and all of it tax deductible, thanking you kindly.

And in the Corporation of London, I had a fairly good idea where to find a coroner.

Just west of Moorgate and south of Old Street is a great grey vastness where a lot of bombs once fell. Street names reveal more about the city's past than any lingering hints from architecture or archaeology: London Wall (where the old city defences ran), Bishopsgate (the gate for the bishops), Cheapside (a shopping street), Poultry (a street where chickens were driven to market), and so on. The name of this area is the Barbican, referring to another gateway into the old city of London; and, as any magician, tourist or lost wanderer will tell you, it is a space-time vortex, all in gritty concrete.

Someone had clearly intended it to be a self-contained utopia, and in many ways, this was what it was. At its heart lay a shallow, slightly scummy lake in which the occasional optimistic heron sometimes waded, and from which there extended a maze of flats, cafés, restaurants, theatres, cinemas, conference halls, art galleries, schools, churches, gyms, libraries and gardens, connected to each other by walkways, bridges and tunnels, and mystic yellow lines that invariably led to the roof, even if they claimed to be leading you towards the underground car parks. A music school squatted behind a theatre whose billboards advertised Japanese mime artists and Cuban street bands, a piece of the city's old Roman wall crumbled mutely in a private garden for local residents, and on every other balcony dangled half-dead geraniums in flowerpots, maintained to the lowest standard the council could tolerate. A single, slightly grungy food and supplies shop loitered beneath a flight of slippery stairs, and among the high towers and tiled walkways, mini-tornados swished and tugged, and tore at even the best-tended haircuts. And because this was a place that had everything for an artistic, well-ordered, middle-class life, it also had the equipment for a quiet, tidy death, so that, wedged on one corner at the end of a bridge across a street some thirty feet below was the coroner's office.

Quite how the local residents felt about this was hard to judge. Our suspected conclusion was that they simply regarded it in the same way the average punter regarded a beggar: seen, noted, and then carefully, politely and deliberately ignored and forgotten. In many ways, it was hard to believe the sign declaring "coroner" wasn't a malign trick, pasted up by some local wit with a morbid sense of humour.

So, the wind dragging at my coat, and my right hand throbbing inside its bandage, I walked up to the small blue door tucked away round the side of the Barbican, and rang the bell.

Nothing happened.

I rang again.

A security guard appeared behind the wire-meshed glass. He looked like so many guards in the city: mid- to late forties, tightly cut hair turning greyish, dark uniform, black radio, shiny shoes, skin the colour of deep-roasted coffee. He opened the door, but didn't stand aside for me. When you look like the Michelin man on a famine diet, trust is not so easy to inspire.

"You looking for someone?" he asked.

I looked him up and down. He seemed like a principled man, the last thing I needed to see.

"Was a body brought here last night," I asked, "sometime after two in the morning?"

"I'd have to check the records. You family?"

"Yes" was the easy answer, but it led inevitably to the question "what name are you looking for?". I had no idea. In all the confusion, I only knew of the Midnight Mayor as the Midnight Mayor, nothing more specific.

"No," I said.

"Can I ask why you're interested?"

"Journalist" was the next most obvious answer, but unlikely to make me any friends. "Police" would require identification, "friend" would be politely told to go home. We said, "Someone attacked us

last night, a minute before the man in your mortuary died. We don't
know of any connection, but other people think there is one and
until we find out what it is and why this man died, we are going to
be hunted and assaulted and quite possibly die, and however hideous
this world is, we would not for all the fire in the wire die and leave it.
Please—will you let me see the body?"

The security man blinked at me. "What?" he said numbly.

"I only need a few minutes."

"You what?"

So much for the power of honesty.

"You could call your colleague," I added.

"I don't have a colleague…" he mumbled, and realised his mistake.
I reached forward and grabbed the back of his neck with my right
hand, pushed the palm of my left into the gap between his eyebrows
and squeezed. The magic of sleep was easy at this hour, the night so
quiet, footsteps so loud and lonely; the people of the city were either
in their deepest dreams or wide awake, burning up with loneliness
and imagination as shadows and sounds twisted into alien forms,
untouched by the blanket of daylight bustle. The guard himself was
a night owl; the streets in darkness thrilled him, walking down the
middle of a road whose traffic by day would be at a standstill, eating kebabs from suspicious shops at three in the morning, watching
the secret people of the streets, the cleaners, painters, repairmen,
engineers, delivery men, graveyard shift and junior night-time nurses
scuttling between the shadows. But he was also bored in his little
office above it all, with nothing but the buzzing of the electric lamp
to keep him occupied, and with his heart leaping at the sound of a
truck swishing down a distant street.

It was easy, easier than I'd expected, to send him to sleep, and fill
his dreams with the colour of yellow neon, and the sound of lonely
footsteps in the night. A simple spell.

Harder, in fact, to position him behind his desk, dragging him into
the uncomfortable tight space and propping him upright in his chair.

I turned off all but the desktop lamps and locked the door behind me, from the inside. Then I went in search of the body of the Midnight Mayor.

Death, as an idea, appals us.

As an experience, I cannot say I recommend it. The mind forgets pain, the physical sensation of pain. It doesn't forget terror.

Down a flight of stairs and into a room smelling of disinfectant and nothing else. I'd half expected rows of stainless steel cupboards, each one labelled with the name of the correct inhabitant, but there was no such thing. Above the mortuary floor of scrubbed grey tile, each member-guest had their own refrigerated coffin. I looked at the name tags pinned to the end of each metal slab and remembered again that I had no idea what the name of the Midnight Mayor was, if he had a name to begin with. So I started pulling the lids off the coffins. The women I ignored, because Mr Earle had called him "he"; and I was grateful for the chance to halve the number of empty faces I had to see: Mr Braithwaite with three lines carved in his chest like a bunch of flowers opening up towards his shoulders; Mr Wang, bile and vomit still clinging with a yellow rumpled thickness to his pouting lips; and, finally, Mr Nair.

We knew it was Mr Nair the second we saw the body, if body is what it was. It should have appalled us, but the flesh of Mr Nair was nothing more than the slabs of meat hanging from the butcher's hook, hardly a thing human any more. His skin hadn't been sliced off, but sliced *into*, a thousand, ten thousand times, with a tiny, thin blade that made the skin stand up from the flesh in little white tufts, like snowy mountain ridges seen from the window of a passing plane. The muscles exposed below looked like something out of a medical textbook, all fibre, but grey now, blood tumbled out of them so they looked for all the world like stringy chicken meat, or pork that had been boiled first and then sandpapered down. Every inch of his body had suffered from this effect, so extensive I thought it might have been a disease, if

I hadn't known better. Beneath the black clinging threads of his hair, the scalp was a churned-up mess of sliced skin and flesh; the cuts went inside his belly button and beneath his fingernails, going *under* the thin nail though it seemed not even slightly disturbed.

In films, the people with a moral compass throw up at these sorts of things. I didn't. There was nothing there, no human left. Just dry organic matter. It would have been like being sick at the sight of tofu. I pulled the lid back over the thing that had once pushed air out from between lips and so declared by its vibrations and humming, "I am Mr Nair", and went in search of personal belongings. They were in a box, each one bagged and wrapped neatly at the back of the coroner's office. I sat in a big revolving chair designed to give you good posture, and went through his things.

No staff, chain or cloak of office. So much for fairy-tale stories.

All his clothes were drenched in blood, every inch turned red. Not a cut on them. Nair's fate had befallen him either while he was naked, or regardless of the things he wore. No keys; I wondered if the Aldermen had taken them. No spray cans, no mystic arte-facts—travel-cards, obscure tickets, penknife, albino pigeon feathers or tail of rat—nothing I would have naturally identified as useful to a magician in their trade. Perhaps the Midnight Mayor was above such things. There was a mobile phone, which didn't turn on. A bloody fingerprint was pressed onto the screen, and scorch marks stained the otherwise shining, futuristic polish of the little machine. I put it to one side and pulled out Mr Nair's wallet.

A driving licence declared that this was the property of Nair, Anu; born 07-08-53, United Kingdom; resident at 137A New Court, Lincoln's Inn, London. The face that stared sombrely out at me from the licence photo had warm chocolate skin, protruding cheekbones and a tiny mouth, beneath straight, cropped greying hair. I tried to imagine it as belonging to a Midnight Mayor, and failed. I flicked through the rest of the wallet. A single credit card given by a bank whose name I couldn't even recognise, but which was pleased to give an Exclusive Gold Membership to Nair, A., and which seemed the heart and soul of his finances. No loyalty cards to any shops or super-markets—perhaps this was a man who didn't do his own shopping. No money either, no receipts, no video or library cards or any of the usual detritus of human existence that tended to pile up inside a wal-let. There was only one business card. I read the name with a sinking feeling that went right down through my belly and into my knees: D.B. Sinclair. Plus a telephone number.

Dudley Sinclair. "Concerned citizens." A man who made the older Orson Welles look trim and cockney. I respected him in the same way I respected the jaws of a lion—from a very long way off. He had been of use to me, in bringing down Bakker and the Tower. I had been of immense use to him. In retrospect, he'd done two parts filing to my ten parts bleeding. But that just made him all the smarter. He knew how to get others to do his dirty work.

I put the wallet to one side.

There was a police report, short, brisk, badly spelt but to the point. It announced that at 2.20 a.m. residents of Raleigh Court, North Kilburn, had called 999 to report almost every misdemeanour happening in their vicinity that could be reported. Windows were smashed, gas was leaking, electricity was going haywire, phones were ringing, TVs were smoking, water was boiling unbidden: the whole shaboom. By the time the police were headed that way, more reports were coming in, of screaming and a fight between two heavily armed men. By the time the police arrived, there was nothing to show but angry sleepless residents, a lot of broken glass, the wailing of car alarms, and a single, skinless body lying face-down in the night.

Not quite skinless.

The coroner's report corrected the error. The skin hadn't been removed. It had been cut, somewhere between ten thousand and twenty thousand times, by a blade no thicker than a piece of paper.

Obviously *not* a piece of paper, the coroner added, because the death was fairly quick—shock leading to cardiac failure—and it takes a long time to administer ten to twenty thousand paper cuts across every inch of flesh. Some kind of chemical compound, perhaps, or...

...or something like that.

Reading the report, I was grateful for a moment to the Aldermen. They had got the body taken to *this* mortuary to be examined by *their* coroner. I had assumed that the Midnight Mayor would have died in the City, the traditional prowling ground of the Aldermen. I'd been wrong. I'd got lucky. He'd died in Kilburn.

North Kilburn, to be exact. Willesden is a nowhere everywhere, and Kilburn is a somewhere inside that nowhere.

It was a connection I wished the Aldermen hadn't made.

I took the wallet and the sim card out of Nair's phone, left everything else. Lincoln's Inn was the nearest destination I could think of, but what were the odds that someone wasn't watching Mr Nair's house? Police, Alderman — killer? A braver man might have seen this as a good thing: confrontation and an early night. But we could think of only a very, very few creatures walking upon the earth with the mystic firepower at their disposal to cut a man's skin beneath the nail, while leaving the nail itself intact. All of them frightened us.

So I went looking for Raleigh Court, North Kilburn.

There was an internet café lurking on the Goswell Road, between a launderette and an all-purpose purveyor of rotting vegetables and cheap biscuits. It was open twenty-four hours, and as in most such places, the computers had been padlocked to the desks and the desks bolted to the floor. A young man reading an A-level textbook and sitting with his feet up on the office desk took a couple of quid with an expression of apathy and gave me a computer for an hour. There were only two other people in the café: one was a woman with prunelike skin and a giant weave of orange fabric on her head, using the internet telephone to talk to somewhere far, far away where the sun was still shining; the other, a pasty-skinned man, had chosen the furthest computer in the darkest corner for what could only, at this hour, be crime or porn.

I sat in the middle of the row of whining machines, proud of my nothing-to-hide, and looked up Raleigh Court. My A–Z covered the Kilburn area, but for specific details, you can't beat the internet. I found it, a beige blob in the middle of yellow grid streets, and, because no one can know everything, interrogated the machine a little more on how to get there. No Tube trains, but the night buses from the centre of the city understand their basic role — to carry those too drunk to walk, to the most obscure corners of suburbia quickly, cheaply and with no questions asked.

Then, because I'm rarely online, I checked my email.

!!PILLSPILLSPILLSPILLS!!
(From: twodollarpill@wonderdrug.com)
We need to talk. (From: Oda77@gmail.co.uk)
Re: ♂✌︎♱☜ ☞☜ ♋♒♌☺ ☞☼ ♇♒❀ (From: Unknown)

I deleted "PILLSPILLSPILLS" on automatic. If we had been in a more malign mood, and less tired, we might have replied with something obscene or cursed the computer from which the message was sent.

"We need to talk" from Oda77 was short and to the point. It said:

Sorcerer—
The Midnight Mayor is dead, the ravens are dead, the Stone is gone, the Wall is cursed, the city is damned — if you believe the ramblings of the wicked. I'll find you.
Oda

I wrote a reply:

Oda—
I'm damned too. I'll find you. Tell no one, otherwise they'll kill me before you get the chance.
Matthew

I wasn't in a hurry to meet Oda. Psychopathic fanatic magician-murderers with a penchant for dentistry and corrupted Christian theology were not high on my list of confidantes. She'd promised on a number of occasions to kill me, by grace of being a sorcerer, and especially to kill us by grace of being an abomination crawled from the nether reaches of the telephone lines into mortal flesh. God was her excuse, guns were her weapons, and the second I stopped being useful to her and her dentistry-crazed cult, the Order, would be the day I got to meet both. She had helped me only because she feared my enemies more than she hated me.

Besides, the last person who'd helped me . . .

. . . the last person . . .

Had been Vera.

Melted into a puddle of paint.

Hadn't even stopped to think.

Too much to do. Too damned. Too . . . too much too.

Hadn't even stopped.

Angry.

Sick and angry. Blink and here we are, looking back with a pair of bright blue eyes colder than the iceberg that hit the *Titanic*. On fire with frost. Angry. Attacked, burnt, attacked, hurt, attacked, fled, attacked, attacked, attacked, gunning for us, gunning for me, gunning for my . . . for people who stopped to help.

Angry.

Didn't know what to do about it, except doing itself. So I kept on doing while we clenched and cramped and twisted in rage.

I kept on at the computer.

The last message was obviously bad news. A sensible user would have deleted it and been done. We didn't. Maybe it was the arrogance from using an internet café, where the computer about to be infected by bad mail wasn't our own; maybe it was curiosity; maybe it was inspiration; maybe it was none of these things. Whatever it was, we, in full knowledge that it wouldn't be good, opened the message.

It said:

END OF THE LINE.

The screen went black.

I swore.

A white pinprick appeared at the very centre of the screen and started to grow. As it grew, it became a white circle, then the white circle grew a black circle within it, that expanded from the centre to fill almost its entire form, then the black circle grew white teeth within it, and the blackness wasn't just a blackness, it was a void, a great falling void that span off for ever into...

...everything, nothing, senseless perfection, freedom, death, entrapment, jubilation, emptiness, pick one, pick everything, all at once—

—and then the blackness was filling the screen and it wasn't just in the screen, it was crawling out of the screen, cracking and popping and bursting as the white jaw with its endless open gullet stretched out of the screen, dripping writhing worms of hissing static like saliva from its fanged teeth, straining towards my face and roaring the high background whine of a cooling fan about to burst, a hungry computer virus with jaws open for the skull of a mortal—

—then I pulled the plug.

It vanished. Glass fell with a splatter onto the desk and over my trousers, black smoke rolled in eye-watering sickly sweetness from the gutted interior of the screen. I flapped ineffectually at the smoke, coughing and blinking tears from my eyes, pushing myself away from the desk even as the young man with the A-level textbook stood up and began to shout in three different languages, all of them obscene.

Then he saw our face, and fell silent.

I walked away. No one tried to follow me.

It took two night buses to get where I wanted to go. It was faster than the one-every-three-minute bus routes of the day, despite the fifteen-minute wait, the bus swishing through empty streets, their natures lost beneath a haze of sodium glow. I breathed in the deep, heavy warm air of the buses, smelling sticky beer and old chips. The familiar weight of it comforted me, washed out some of the fatigue from my bones: an elixir almost as good as sleep.

The bus crossed Euston Road at Tottenham Court Road, skirted the southern edge of Regent's Park and headed towards Marylebone, into little neat streets untouched by chain stores, selling mostly fish and chips, Italian wine and cheese.

Raleigh Court was a nice name for a bad idea. It hadn't been so much built as slotted together out of old grey cereal boxes pretending to be flats. They were stacked one on top of the other in four flat tombstones around a dead place of concrete and garages with locked doors and no room for cars, just tall enough to block out the sun, though not high enough to see anything but each other. It was a bad place to die, an anonymous, forgotten hole. The air hummed with mobile phones and a tight, pressed-in magic, a magic of black shadows and little rattling things in the night, the kind of power that lent itself to the summoning of rats and invocation of ghosts, to the forbidden enchantments of naughty men who thought of life as just a trick of perspective. It was easy, in this place at 4 a.m., to slip past the police tape and the slumbering copper on duty. The tarmac ate up the sound of my footsteps; the neon bent away from my passing, willing to oblige a grey friend in a gloomy time. It was a place that looked after its own, frightened strangers away.

Signs of battle were scarred on the buildings inside the police cordon. Windows were taped up with dustbin bags, the broken glass either blown inside or already swept away. Scorch marks had burst up from between the gaps in the paving slabs where the gas had ignited, to send blackness crawling a few storeys up the overlooking walls. Electricity cables had been crudely strapped back together; phone lines dangled off the sides of buildings, awaiting repair. The metal shutters of garages were twisted and bent, and rubbish bags split open and blasted flat. A bomb hadn't exploded here. A bomb had been blasted out of the ground on a volcanic plume of gas, risen up to the height of a man's invoking hands, and spawned a dozen little scuttling offspring that ran to each corner of the court and exploded.

The whole calamity would be in one of those police reports that D. B. Sinclair and his "concerned citizens" filed carefully under "T" for "Things" at the back of a locked filing cabinet in the vehicle-licensing centre a day before a bonfire got accidentally out of control. Dudley Sinclair and his friends were *very* good at losing information that they didn't want to be found. Bureaucracy seems so innocent until it eats you up; but then this mess was pure embarrassment and mayhem written in sparkling mystic letters. Someone had to have seen it.

As it happened, someone had. I found a half-eaten kebab in the spilt litter billowing over the cobbles and, a bit below, a thrown-away end of pizza, nibbled to tatters except for the crusts. The guilty kebab shop was only round the corner, twenty-four hours a day of pulverised cardboard cooked on a spike. I bought two kebabs: one for me, one for my witness. Then I went back to Raleigh Court and sat down on the charred, wobbling remains of a bench, ate my kebab and left the second one open, salad and all, on the ground at my feet.

My witness had clearly been freaked by the night's activities; he came out reluctantly, not at his usual jaunty trot. I waited patiently, wiping ketchup and suspicious white goo from my chin, stuffing a tattered grey watery vegetable into my mouth that the shopkeeper had claimed was lettuce. We liked all foods, even the kinds that didn't like us, and at four in the morning, kebab in a bun is food the gods would eat.

My witness snuffled closer. I held my hand out to him, fingers stained in dubious sauce, and cooed, "Hello, come to Uncle Matthew. Come talk to us."

He was the size of a small dog; not too small to yap infuriatingly, not large enough to bark with any great power. His fur in the lamplight was dark orange heading for auburn, his nose a black wetness with a pair of whiskers sticking out above jaws that looked fit for biting arms off. His tail might once have been bushy, but wars with others of his kind, plus feral cats and traffic, had left it a tatty stump. Personal hygiene was not high among his priorities, and he stank of wet mud, old oils and frustrated alpha-male animal. He looked up at us, we looked at him. He started to eat the kebab at our feet, and we patted him gently on the head.

There's a long tradition of magicians keeping pet familiars. Once upon a time, an owl or wolf was the companion of choice; but magic, above all else, has to move with the times. For as long as I could remember, you couldn't do much better than to find yourself a fox.

I scratched the creature behind its ears and said, "Mind if I call you Mr Fox?"

It wasn't an imaginative name, but he didn't object.

I let him eat the kebab. He was not an underfed animal, and clearly choosy enough in his diet to avoid the limp salad. When he was done, I patted the wobbly planks of the bench where I sat, and he leapt up, regarding me curiously. I kept stroking the rough, sticky fur on the top of his head, all matted together with slime from the rubbish bins, and dried blood. After a while, my fingers were used to the texture, and the more relaxed my companion grew, the easier it was to . . .

meat scraped off plate brown sauce sharp sharp on tongue air rot growing and smell of

Overhead, a pigeon flapped in the darkness. I could feel the claws of the rats in the drains beneath me, their noses itching with mine. I kept on stroking the fox, which nuzzled its damp nose into my ribs, and I got a taste of . . .

exhaust from bus car motorbike scooter van truck lorry settled always settled background brown stench fog on the streets invisible fog weighing down air
    lavatory freshener window left open chemical bite in lungs
        detergent bubbling in drainpipe
           shower gel soaps at overflow
              rubber boots on tarmac floor
                old blood
                  new blood

"Come on, Mr Fox," we crooned. "Show us what you smelt last night."

taste of scraped-out meat fats and drippings thin meaty blood from frozen meat chicken fluids pale and left on the plate sunflower oil in soggy chips tossed aside peas turning brown yesterday's mash black mould growing on the top maggot maggot in the bins maggot in the meat maggot sleepy in the cold always maggot worming into the meat fat white body pop

"Come on, Mr Fox," we heard a voice say that might have been ours. "Come on, come on..."

smell of blood. fresh. nothing ever fresh fresh blood fresh fresh clean fresh clean blood on dirty floor swept by spinning water wheels that turned the dirt into prettier circles on the dirty concrete fresh clean blood hot

A thousand miles away, at the end of the badly receiving telephone line: "Come on, Mr Fox..."

human blood not scared not human fear thunder lightning rare things not human common human common car truck lorry bus motorbike scooter human common

human blood — not common

fear stench of blood, silver lance to smell, eyes widen, brain weep, human blood and

Here it came. We could smell the memories, see the stench of it in our eyes, hear the hum of smell in our ears, here it came, all that my precious witness, his fur covered in dirt, had seen...

human man standing in night. looking something somewhere eyes turned upwards doesn't see me in the darkness doesn't care don't fear human human is ... burning bright warm red fire. smell rat. rats are watching too rats down below smell stinking rat rat dead in jaws rats down below are watching human too pigeons up above feathers stuck in teeth pigeons are watching too and we watch the human because ...

...human who is not human ...

...flesh hiding flesh like you

smells of ... alcohol mixed with smell of flowers (FLOWERS!), silks softened by soaps black leather rubbed with varnish suit caressed with steam hair swept with oil face pampered with cream smells of lighter smoke still city but somewhere the cars

do not go so much of contained shut away contained of leather seats and interior of
car solid weighty hot heavy shakes door handle sweat sweat running down spine
sweat on head sweat fear listen! listen heart listen! smell fear! eat fear!

"Good Mr Fox, good Mr Fox..."

A thousand miles away, a hand stroking the head of a fox was
wired to a brain that might possibly have been our own, and we smelt
the fear on Nair, along with expensive aftershave and oiled hair, we
smelt terror and heard the beating of his heart and whispered, "What
else, Mr Fox, good Mr Fox, come on... what else? Show me what you
smelt."

flesh hiding flesh. human who is not just human smells like...

someone else!

runrunrunrun thick night deep

someone else someone else and he smells of

of...

"What, Mr Fox? Show me!"

of nothing. there is a creature standing there smells of nothing. empty nothing
that moves like a living thing and a living thing reacts to it, is afraid of it but it has
no smell. it is not living cannot be living has no heart has no blood has no smell but
it is human eyes see human eyes see legs arms head

"What else?!"

eyes see legs arms head hair nose mouth skin

"What does he look like?"

no smell. human that smells of oiled hair makes sound at human that smells of
nothing sound sound is roar sound is scream sound is shouting sound is thunder
sound is smell of burning run but do not run the rats are running! rats are running
and pigeons are flying get away get away fire and burning and shouting and want
to run want to run nowhere to run rats underground pigeons above and smell of
burning and screaming and heart and terror and fear and

And it's only Nair's fear...

...we can only smell Nair's fear...

no smell no smell no smell raises hands and has no smell and human screams and
no smell raises arms and human screams screams screams screams and we smell

We smell . . .

blood fresh blood human blood blood on nose blood on concrete blood in dirt

We see . . .

human human on floor less human less human screams less human meat screams screams screams and

And there was something in his hand?

plastic electric plastic

What was in Nair's hand?

flesh splitting, flesh splitting, face splitting eyes splitting blood human blood scream face flesh scream

Something in his hand, held up to his ear—

not ear not ear broken flesh scream blood

I knew what it was. Recognised it, even through the confusion of the fox's memories, saw the little plastic shape, saw the shattered remains of Nair's lips

blood blood blood blood blood fear

speaking into it, and recognised it, saw the shattered bloody flesh that was Nair speaking with his dying breath into a mobile phone.

Dead.

Just like that. We looked, me, us and the fox, through the terri-fied haze of its memories, and saw the body of Nair, torn meat inside a neat black silk suit, lying in his own blood, mobile phone the last thing the bloody criss-cross remains of his fingers were going to touch. And then, because the fox had looked, finally, the fox dared to look, we looked up at the man who had killed A. Nair, the Midnight Mayor.

And the fox was right. He was absolutely right. We saw a man, dressed in a neat pinstripe suit utterly untouched by the flames still burning in the rubbish bins, by the glass spilt across the floor, by the swinging electric cables and the spitting remains of electric lightning, by the fallen aerials and shattered metal shutters, by the torn bricks and broken paving stones; not a scratch on him. He wore a suit, the crease impeccable all the way down from his waist to his ankle; a pair of black leather shoes that clacked neatly with every step, a pinstripe jacket done up over a white shirt, the collar ironed and unstained. A white silk handkerchief stuck up from his jacket pocket, his thin dark hair was swept back, not a fibre out of place, from a high pale forehead and on his face was a look...

no smell

...a look that a busy plumber might give to a boiler that's been giving him more trouble than it's worth and has now been fixed; the conquering contempt of an expert who has proven his worth to a dumb machine.

And he had no smell. To the fox, watching this, Nair had stank from the moment he entered of expensive cleaning products and shaving lotions, of terror and fear. His shoes had smelt, his clothes had smelt, every part of him offering a different tone to the medley. But the man who had killed him, the *thing* that had killed him, which looked like a man in a pinstripe suit, who now stood over him utterly uncaring for either his triumph or the pity of the dead, had no smell. Not a part of him smelt, not even of cleanliness. He was a walking blank on the fox's recollection, even the dirt on his shoes. His heart made no sound; nor was there any proof, except that he had just killed a living man, that *this* man lived at all.

And then he looked at the fox. And the terror that swept through every nerve of the creature nearly knocked us from the seat, the strength of it, the absolute animal certainty that it was run or die. And we ran, us and the fox, we ran through the night with every hair standing up down the length of our back, ran until our paws ached and our spine groaned and our head was a dead weight looking down to the ground and we could smell nothing but our own fears and ran and ran and ran.

Terror broke the spell. Our fear, his fear, we weren't making the distinction. The fox was a trembling curl of fur beside us; and we weren't much better, every inch shaking from the shared experience of the creature's thoughts. Our head hurt, our body hurt, our paws still hurt, although we had none, and above all, and slicing through it to an agony pitch, our right hand blazed furiously inside its bandage and when we turned our hand over to look, pulling the black mitten away from the wad of cotton rolled over our skin, we saw blood was seeping through.

I fumbled in my bag for painkillers, took three in a single gulp, cooed empty noises at the trembling fox. I tried to pick coherent images out of the confusion of the fox's thoughts: focus on Nair, focus on his killer. I wondered how unamused the Aldermen might feel about being offered up an urban scavenger as a reliable witness for the claim "not me, guv, I didn't do it".

Still, it was something that I had seen the face of the man who killed Nair. If I had been frightened of him before, whoever he was, this no-smell in a suit, now I was rightly terrified. You do not walk the earth without a heartbeat and a smell, unless you were not designed for that particular promenade. And sooner or later, whether we liked it or not, we were constrained by the laws of earthly things, even if it, he, whatever it was, was not.

I patted the fox, taking comfort from the warmth of his body and the consistency of his companionship. The fox shuffled closer to me, and I stroked him some more. "There, Mr Fox," we sighed, and then, because we couldn't think of anything reassuring, added, "There, Mr Fox."

We sat there a long while, and might have sat there longer if it wasn't for the burning in our hand. The fox trembled and whimpered by us, and in time, a trembling became a breathing, a breathing a gentle sleep, and he began to forget the things he had seen. We didn't.

We had to . . .

. . . do something.

We just didn't know what.

A telephone had rung.

I'd answered.

Spectres had come.

The Aldermen had come.

The Midnight Mayor had died.

And as he'd died, at the hands of a whatever-it-was that could flay the flesh off a man without even touching him, who killed with ten thousand paper cuts, he'd used his mobile phone.

I reached into my bag. I had Nair's sim card, pried from the back of his phone. It didn't *look* damaged, but then what could you tell from a piece of plastic and silicon? I put it in my coat pocket, pushed the remnants of my kebab over to the little fox, and stood up.

Not much more I could do.

Dawn and sunset in winter both happen when you're not looking. You can see the beginnings of daylight, the shimmerings of dusk, the bending of the shadows; but the actual moment when the sun hits the horizon in either direction is lost behind buildings or in a moment of distracted conversation. Blink, and you miss it. The earth spins too fast to wait for your attention.

We sat on a bench on Primrose Hill and watched the sunrise.

There was frost in the grass that would be gone by the time the morning joggers reached us, and a deadness in the trees that the warmth of day would turn to cold billowing. Get away from a road in London, only a few hundred yards, and the rest of the city sounds a thousand miles off, like a distant gust of wind against a castle wall. Darkness, turned yellow-orange-pink from the glow of a thousand thousand streetlights, sprawled away as far as the eye could see. Landmarks, lit up all the colours of technology — the London Eye a distant purple blob, Big Ben in orange, the Gherkin in greens and blacks, the NatWest Tower with a square of vivid dark scarlet on its tip, Canary Wharf all in silver, thin cloud and steam curling off its top where its little red light flashes to warn away the planes. St Pancras, a gothic spike with a light blue arch stretching out into a sidewinder's paradise of silver railway snakes; the three towers of the Barbican, the lit-up column of the BT Tower, the spread-out rooftops of Soho and

Great Portland Street; the sideways-on slab of Centre Point, where not so long ago good people and bad people and the majority halfway in between had died in a fight on the topmost floor. That had been the night that the Tower fell, that Bakker fell, that Dana Mikeda…

…dead Dana Mikeda who'd died too fast for me to say sorry…

…that had been Centre Point. We turned our eyes from it.

The stop-start artery of Euston Road, carrying flicker-flash headlights from east and west; the slow slope of the North Downs along the edge of sight, a line of darker darkness against the sky where the streetlamps ended and real night, solid, frightening night that crushed imagination down to a pinpoint of darkness and left no space for stretched-out shadows on the street, marked the beginning of the end of the city.

Sunrise was a point of pale greyness at the eastern edge of the darkness, starting over the mouth of the Thames and spreading inwards towards the city. It wasn't a line of light, more the casting of a shadowy haze over the thickness of the gloom, the sun's upper edge nothing more than a tiny shimmer of distorted whiteness lost in the haze of the early morning clouds. No one part of the city lightened more than another, but by even degrees, black streets became fragmented, revealed themselves to be thick greynesses pierced by other roads, or changes in buildings, or unevenness in style, and then greyness became sullen blue that picked out the difference between a satellite dish and an air-conditioning vent, pointed out the rooftop apparatus of the buildings in the centre of town, raised up chimneys and revealed roof tiles facing the sky. Then came texture on the tiles; and the brightness of the streetlamps began to diminish, became merely the reflection of starlight on water, rather than the stars themselves, then vanished as the lamps began to flicker and whir out, a few bulbs at a time.

With each turn of my head to scan the city, more streets were in darkness and light all at once, the night-time lamps being replaced by the cold washing pallor of the day, that brightened further now in the east, spread blueness up towards the sky, filling in between the grey puffs of the retreating night clouds, and hinted, maybe hinted, at a bright white-silver sunlight on the horizon that came in sideways at the streets, burst out from behind the haze a dozen times only to fade away coldly, as if embarrassed by its own attempts, before finally making that great bold leap and declaring to every eye that dared to look, GET UP YOU LAZY BASTARDS! and pulling great thin shadows from end to end of every street.

This being winter, and this being London, by the time the sun was properly up, the shops were already open and doing busy trade.

I went to get Nair's sim card unlocked.

Tottenham Court Road was a strip of overpriced not-quite-illegality slammed into the heaving retail heart of London. The offices of Euston Road lay to the north, the great sprawl of University College and its teaching hospital dominated every grand building to the east, the restaurant-crammed backstreets of Fitzrovia ran behind squares and reconstructed Georgian terraces to the west, and to the south was Oxford Street, shopping hub of the city. And like all good shopping hubs, both it and Tottenham Court Road had learnt two important commercial lessons:

1. Looks aren't everything, location is.
2. If someone wants it, sell it.

What people wanted who went to Tottenham Court Road was electronics and electronic junk, with a side order of bedsteads and coffee.

As a result, computer shops selling the latest ultra-shiny, zappy-zoomy model for a mere grand or a contract on your granny's soul were crammed into a mixture of ancient buildings and concrete slabs, wedged together with the all the tact of rush-hour commuters piling onto the last train before a strike began. Speakers next to hi-fi next to games next to stereos next to furniture next to TVs next to mobile phones next to futons next to DVDs: this was the order of the street, competing for the know-it-all market that came for its slightly seedy but within-the-law shopping experience.

Almost within the law.

Go a few streets back from Tottenham Court Road, and the haziness of just what the law meant led to the other kind of electronics shop. The kind where you didn't buy an ink cartridge for your printer at £25 a throw, you bought an ink bottle and a very strong hypodermic needle for £5, and let's not ask too many questions about the patent. Where the windows were full of hard drives on special offer, wiped clean, one careful owner. Where, if you knew the right place to go and didn't mind paying cash, a sim card from a stranger's phone might be reactivated into a new handset, and all its secrets revealed.

Not quite illegal.

Not *quite*.

The legal system has always been a little behind the times.

The shop I chose was run by two men, one with no hair and the other with so much he'd stuck it in a woven balloon, carrying the colours of the Ethiopian flag and large enough to refashion as a decent-sized skirt. I gave him Nair's sim card and told him what I wanted.

He didn't ask questions, I didn't ask questions.

"Yeah, man, yeah, come back in like, twenty-four hours. Fifty quid, yeah, and twenty for the set?"

"A hundred and twenty and I'll come back in two hours."

Around Tottenham Court Road there are a thousand different places waiting to be waited in, at no great cost. The University of London Union offered services including free toilets, if you knew where to look, a gym if you felt in a guilty mood and hadn't found religion, a variety of pubs, and above all, cafés where no one would bother a guy who looked lived in and where the feeble coffee came in at an OK price. I found a gloomy corner behind a bank of snooker tables, and curled up to go to sleep.

It wasn't proper sleep; but the time passed faster than the crawl of normal senses, and my thoughts ran the hip-hop patterns of a brain that has switched off all higher functions, and sees without being able to look.

Then a woman said, "Mind?"

I was awake without any consciousness of having been asleep; but she had come out of nowhere and her voice was nothing but drifting sound on the air. A finger, bright pink skin underneath, dark chocolate on top, stabbed out towards an empty sandwich wrapper someone had left on an armchair next to me. She said again, "Mind if I...?"

"Sure," I mumbled, a default response to polite confusion.

The woman picked up the sandwich wrapper by one careful corner, and dumped it in a bright blue rubbish bag. She was a cleaner. She wore dull grey overalls and had parked a cart nearby, laden with plastic bottles and brushes. Her black hair was done in plaits wound so tightly to the curve of her skull that the fuzzy hair in between each row looked like it was rising to a carved ridge. Her eyes were two perfect brown ovals set in a face that was itself almost a perfect oval, except for the wide protrusion of her nose.

There was something about her—a quality that I couldn't quite seize upon.

I said, "Hello."

She glanced over to me, surprised, maybe even a little amused, by this hung-over mature student passed out behind the snooker tables. "Hi," she said. "Sorry to bother you."

"It's no problem," I said. "Thank you."

"What?"

"For the..." I gestured meekly at the blue bin bag, and the chair where the sandwich wrapper had sat.

She shrugged. "It's just a job." For a moment, she smiled. It was the weakest little smile I had ever seen, a twitch around a child's lips after it's fallen and hurt its knee, but is trying to be brave. We stared in wonder and opened our mouth to say something; but she was already gone, pootling round the room picking up old fallen beer bottles and tossed-aside Coke tins.

And that was it: moment passed. To get up and follow her would have turned us from two polite strangers to a stalker and his prey. I stayed where I was, watching her until she went out of sight.

There was something . . . important . . .

that I just couldn't figure.

Maybe later.

A hundred and twenty pounds bought me a flowery handset designed for ladies who liked shopping and which we nearly rejected out of hand, with Nair's sim card lodged in its plastic depths.

"It works?" I asked.

"Hey, yeah man, like, sure."

I handed over the cash. My wallet was getting light. If there had been any perks of my relationship with Mr Sinclair, it had been a post office box in Mount Pleasant full of ten-pound notes that I reluctantly dipped into when the desire for a soft bed became too strong.

I left the shop before testing the phone, and found a patch of wall in an alley, with a small play area facing it and an angry declaration of:

ODDAWAJCIE MI MOJ KAPELUSZ

written in three-foot-high white letters. Polish: a relatively new language come to the city.

The phone took for ever to power up. The first thing it did on settling down was send me a text message welcoming me to my new network and inviting me to enjoy many of the wonderful benefits I hadn't yet signed up to. I deleted this and went thumbing through the details of Nair's sim card. There wasn't much. No one had sent him a text message, and he had sent only one, to another mobile phone, a couple of nights ago.

I read it with a sinking heart. It said:

Find Swift.

That was all. Nair was clearly not a man of many words, but when he picked them, he really did.

His phone book was a little more busy. I recognised some of the names: Earle, who had received the one text message ever sent from this phone; Kemsley; Anissina. There were others, which I saw with sinking heart. Sinclair; a few Whites, including Vera; and—of course—Bakker.

Robert James Bakker.

I guessed Nair hadn't bothered to delete the names of the dead from his phone. I told myself I shouldn't be surprised, that only a few months ago in London, if you didn't have dealings with Bakker, you didn't deal in magic at all. We felt sick.

One other number caught my interest. It was simply "Black Cab", and a standard 0800 dialling code. I looked at it long and hard. Lots of people had numbers for cab companies on their phones, for that decadent day when, out late, a little tipsy and too far from the bus or Tube, their will, and then their wallets, would break and they'd splurge on a private cab home. But though the black cab was the most common taxi in London, this wasn't just a cab number. This was Black Cab.

I filed this thought away at the back of my mind under "S" for "Stuff", to worry about another day.

Then I checked Nair's call record. There was only one incoming, from Earle, a few nights ago, which didn't tell me anything I couldn't have guessed. There was also only one outgoing. It was registered at 2.25 a.m., the night that the phone had rung, and I'd answered.

I called the number, my heart a lump of muscle weighing down my chest.

An old-fashioned ring at the end of the dialling signal, as if a bell actually was being hit with a hammer, rather than a sound effect. Maybe just a very good sound effect. *Tingalingalingalingalinga . . .*

Then a voice answered, with a very, very careful "Yeah?"

I said, "I want to get my car washed."

"Sure, we can do that. Just bring it up here any time."

"How much do you charge?"

"£7 for a standard wash, £15 for a full clean, insides, out, with varnish. That takes about twenty-five minutes."

"And I can just bring it along any time?"

"Sure. We're open eight till ten."

"And where are you, exactly?"

"Willesden — near Dudden Hill Lane?"

"Yes," I sighed, "I know Dudden Hill Lane. Thanks. I'll find you."

"You sure?"

"I'm sure. I've been there before."

"OK, cheers."

"Bye."

"Bye!"

I hung up.

Well . . .

shit.

Time passed.

A lot of time.

People walked by and I stayed still.

I think I might have laughed a bit, and then stopped laughing, and then laughed again.

We wanted to cry.

Well . . .

shit.

                          *   *   *

runrunrunrunrunrunrunrunrunrunrunrun
    Just stop it.
    runrunrunrunrunrun
    Stop it. I'm smarter than this. We're more than this. Just stop it.
    runrunrunrun
    Better?
    Thank you.
    What next?
    Answers. I didn't really care who gave them.

I found a public phone, hit it until it obeyed, and dialled the number
on Nair's phone labelled "Earle".
    It was an 0207 landline number, somewhere in the middle of the
city. I didn't want to use the mobile, just in case the Aldermen were
the kind of magicians who understood that technology and magic
really, really wanted to be friends.
    The phone was answered almost instantly, but not by Mr Earle. A
nervous, young male voice that stammered on every hard consonant and
stuttered on the rest said: "H-Harlun and Phelps, how may I help you?"
    I said, "I'm looking for Mr Earle."
    "I'm sorry, M-Mister Earle isn't here right now, c-can I take a mes-
sage?"
    "I guess so. Tell Mr Earle that Mr Swift called. Tell him—and you
need to get this right—tell him I think I know who the new Midnight
Mayor is. Tell him I've seen the face of the man who killed Nair. Tell
him he has no smell. You got all that?"
    "Th-th-that you're Mr Swift calling for Mr Earle, you know who
the Mayor is, you know who k-k-killed N-Nair and he has no smell. Is
that Nair who has n-n-no smell or Mr Earle?"
    "Neither," I replied, and hung up.

*   *   *

I had an idea, and it was so bad, in so many ways, who the new Midnight Mayor was.

You can't kill an idea, a title. Not that easily. Nair might have died, skin torn to a thousand kinds of clinging shreds by ten thousand paper cuts, but the Midnight Mayor, the legend and the story, the protector of the city, doesn't die like that. Doesn't die at all, while there's a city left to protect. Just the man dies — just Nair. The title moved on somewhere else, and where there's an idea, there's always power lagging along behind, even if it doesn't like to brag about it.

My hand hurt. My head hurt too, but not with the same hot sharpness of my hand. It cut away all other sense, burnt beneath the bandages for attention.

I thought: *make me a shadow on the wall. Let me be secret, safe. Let it be just a bad idea.*

We mustered our strength, and went towards Lincoln's Inn.

Lawyers.

Hundreds and hundreds of lawyers.

I approached Lincoln's Inn from the south, through a tight grey alley wedged between a barber's shop and a shop selling barristers' wigs and judges' robes. I hugged close to the walls and the gloom, sheltering from the brightness of the winter sun, and watched the people around me.

Quite how the legal profession merited offices and apartments inside one of London's most desirable pieces of land was beyond me. Great courtyards of grand old houses, and modern replicas of the same, with high chimney stacks and thick oak doors, gazed out onto deep, lush flower beds and grass mown into spacious, do-not-walk-here rectangles. Cobbles ran beneath tall, many-paned windows behind which were bookshelves filled with leather-bound tomes, oil paintings of long-dead judges, desks exploding with papers and of course, hard at work or in a sombre-faced meeting, lawyers.

At the lodge gate, uniformed wardens monitored all traffic; beneath an arching fountain, gardeners in rugged shoes planted spring bulbs; inside the great red Gothic belly of the central hall, a lunchtime concert was under way; besides the remains of a medieval church, all pillars and dark echoing staircases worn smooth by centuries of shoes, the tourist guides explained the myths and wonders of this ancient place to awe-struck onlookers. Weaving busily between it all were, of course, more lawyers.

They dressed nearly the same; the women, all young, in tight suits that forced them to walk from the knees, not the hips, and strutting on sensible heels—not too gaudy, but high enough to give them the same stature as the men. The men, mostly young or middle-aged, dressed in matching dark suits, with only the pinkness of their shirts or the stripiness of their ties marking out one individual from another. The youngest wheeled great trolleys stacked with boxes stuffed with paper; the oldest strode along in big coats worn over a watch chain, and drove cars ten years too young for them. Outsiders were mostly the occasional student taking a cut-through to the library, all baggy trousers and bad hair, or a TV scout for the latest docu-drama surveying the Inns of Court in search of "authentic" historical London.

The air smelt of mown grass, and time. Time with a paper-thin edge. There were ghosts playing in Lincoln's Inn, trailing their fingers along the edges of the old stones, sticking their noses into the shrapnel holes from a fallen bomb, climbing trees taller than the spire of the church or peaked roof of the hall, just waiting for the sun to go down.

Name plaques on the doors announced the occasional private residence among what were almost entirely lawyers' chambers: here and there Lord and Lady So-And-So, or Major-General X, who lived three doors down from Sir Somethingorother and the charming Dame Thingamajig. You didn't *buy* a property in Lincoln's Inn;

money wasn't the point. Time and tradition were the names of the game. And on that count, it made perfect sense that the Midnight Mayor had found his niche within these walls.

Bright winter sunshine makes most places beautiful. The Inn looked like English good manners made out of ancient brick and weathered stone, all golden reflections, and thin shade lost in the glare. Lurking in the shadows, I had to remind myself that, chances were, there might be nasties hiding behind the windows, and not just the legal kind.

I pulled my coat tighter around my shoulders. Any good private detective out of any good American thriller will tell you that an old, plain anorak is a city's camouflage paint. Any good sorcerer will tell you that they're not just right, they're two incantations short of invisibility.

I stepped out into the sunlight, and strode towards the door of 137A New Court with the brisk pace of an Important Person with an Important Place to Be, and who, as such, shouldn't be noticed because frankly, it's none of your business. There was no police tape, no policeman. By the entrance to the staircase I'd been looking for, a white wooden board, lettered in black, listed everyone who worked or lived there. I climbed two flights of echoing stairs, clinging with my bandaged hand to a black iron banister, feeling its coldness even through the layers of wool and cotton and blood. On the top floor the staircase led to a door bearing the number 137A in brass; on the wall beside it, a plaque repeated the fact that here lived A. Nair Esq. I looked back down the stairwell, saw no one following; I also saw no place to hide. Fumbling in my satchel for a ring of blank keys, I found one best suited to fit the lock, slid it in and caressed it, murmuring to it until the metal of the key hissed into the shape of the barrel; turned; opened the door.

A moose was staring at me.

What kind of man sticks the antlered stuffed head of a moose to the wall by his front door? Was it supposed to be a coat rack? Perhaps a psychiatrist could derive some meaning from this.

A small burglar alarm started to beep a warning. I walked briskly over to it, flicked back the plastic panel over the keypad, and slammed my fist, crackling with stolen electricity, into the grid of numbers. The alarm spat black smoke and died.

I looked round the apartment.

It surprised me how much personality had been imposed on such a cream-washed place. The moose was not the only creature to have made its rendezvous with destiny on these walls. Keeping it company was a polar bear, mouth open to roar; also a couple of stags, a reindeer with wide glass eyes, a falcon ready to fly. And of course, at the far end, a fox. I looked at this creature a long while. Its fur was clean, dark orange, with a white band running below its jaw. Its head seemed tiny compared to the great antlers and outstretched wings of its neighbours, and its jaw was locked tight, as if holding in that last breath that would have allowed it to die. We couldn't look away, and felt . . . sad. As I left the hall, the fox's empty stare watched our back.

The kitchen was all terracotta tile, stainless steel and fresh herbs. The bedroom was 90 per cent book to 10 per cent bed, the texts were serious tomes, on law, history, geography, London. The bathroom was white plaster and stone, not a mark nor shaven hair to show for any inhabitant. Even the toothbrush looked new, and a great oval mirror bore not a spatter of toothpaste.

There wasn't a TV in the living room; just more books and a computer, the screen smashed, the base scorched black. The glass had fallen outwards, away from the screen in a circle on the floor, as if it had been smashed from the inside.

End of the line.

On the walls were portraits, in outsize carved and gilded frames: dead grandees with a hand absently held out to touch the globe; plumed great ladies, seated against vast gardens; dour-faced dowagers below a portrait of their husband in full-dress uniform. The ugliest object was a figure representing one of the dragons of the Corporation of London—a squat, terrier-sized beast in dull silver,

with a red forked tongue curling out of its fanged mouth, that sat up
holding in its claws the white shield and twin red crosses of the city.
Seen close, the wildness of the eyes and smallness of the wings gave
the dragon a comical, circus-act look. It proved to be hollow plastic,
which echoed faintly when struck.

This little monster sat by a great brute of a desk, all dark mahog-
any and green leather trimmings, that smelt almost overwhelmingly
of thin polish and thick, reflective varnish. Behind the desk lurked
a leather chair, built to dwarf any man who sat in it. Only one of
the desk drawers was locked. I stroked it carefully, breathing gentle
words into the barrel of the lock and twisting until it snapped open.

There were files inside, proper paper files in manila folders,
embossed with the dragons and the shield of the Corporation of London. I flicked through them, and was disappointed by how mundane
the majority were. Reports on exhaust emissions within the central,
inner and greater areas of London. Details of the maintenance on
the Thames Barrier; reports on roadworks near Waterloo Bridge,
notes on the progress of the water mains replacement project. I went
through them all with increasing frustration; we wanted to find something magical, something definitive, something that linked, once and
for all, Nair to the Midnight Mayor and if necessary, the Midnight
Mayor to us.

When I found it, I nearly went straight past it in my haste and
irritation, and had to flick back to make sure I'd seen it right. Inside a
folder just like any other, buried halfway down the pile, was my life
on paper.

I pulled it out, spread it across the desk and looked with rising
disbelief at the thick, chalky sheets before me. Every detail of my
existence — my mum, my gran, who liked to talk to the pigeons; my
childhood, my first encounters with urban magic, my teacher Mr
Bakker, my apprenticeship, my years as a not very interesting sorcerer, my time spent travelling, my death, our resurrection — everything was there, from former lovers to the average size of my annual

gas bill. Lists of friends I hadn't seen for years, who I hadn't dare see, to whom I hadn't known how to explain anything, whom I hadn't dared put in danger; of extended family I'd never really spoken to, of ex-girlfriends who'd attended my funeral, with their new husband and brand new babies left at home for the sake of good manners...

Pictures! Where had they got so many pictures? Mum up to her elbows in rubber gloves and dodgy plumbing; Gran waddling down the street in her slippers, the rats all watching her from the grid above the drains, the pigeons from the gutters on the roofs. School photos from back when my eyes were brown, not blue, and I was just starting to grow adult teeth; CCTV shots; the place where I'd died, all blood and torn clothes and of course, most important, no body, just bloody fingerprints on the dangling receiver of the public telephone. A photo of when we came back, wearing someone else's clothes too big for us, sitting alone on a bench in the middle of the night, then up to our armpits in the internal organs of a litterbug sent to find us, which we had destroyed. We were looking straight at the camera but I swear, we knew, we had not had our photo taken that night, there had been no one there to do it!

On the very last page was a neat typewritten page of A4. It said:

It is our final opinion that the fusion of the sorcerer Swift and the entities commonly known as the blue electric angels during their shared time in the telephone wires, has resulted in the creation of a highly unstable entity in the waking world. The Swift–angel creature, while appearing almost entirely human, is at its core a combination of a traumatised dead sorcerer and infantile living fire, neither of which is fully equipped to handle living as two separate entities, let alone one fused mind.

While we should perhaps be grateful that, to this date, the Swift–angel creature has not caused any more damage to the city, we should not assume that this happy state will last long. The Order claim to be capable of dispatching the Swift–angel fusion, but it would be wise to make our own preparations for the inevitable conflict the existence of such a creature in our city will cause.

Right at the bottom of the page, a neat, small hand had added: *Swift has the shoes.*

There wasn't any explanation.

I looked down at my shoes.

Not my shoes.

The shoes I wore, sure. The shoes I had been wearing, yes. But they weren't my shoes; I hadn't gone out and bought them. I'd taken them from someone else's house, put them on with a very precise purpose and gone for a walk.

Swift has the shoes.

I put the file back in the desk. We spun a few spins of the huge chair, feeling its greased bearings slide smoothly over each other. We rocked back and looked at the ceiling; we leant forward and looked at the floor. I put my shoes up on the leather-topped desk and examined them. Red and black, with a hint of gold stripe. Tasteless, flashy, expensive. They puffed every time I walked on them, little pockets of air being sucked in through tiny bellows to give that extra-springy experience. If they'd been two sizes smaller, I might have appreciated what they were about. They made my feet sweat in the two pairs of socks I had to wear. We spun a few more spins. I flexed the fingers of my right hand. Flesh gaped open, then closed, in my palm. Electrocution didn't do that for a guy. It took something more. Supposition took fact's bloody hand for the dance, and cha-chaed round the room. The plastic dragon rolled its tongue rudely at some invisible playground rival.

I spun a few more spins.

Why shoes?

Not my shoes. Just the shoes I was wearing.

I stood up and let them carry me a few idle paces round the room. Then a few paces more. They seemed as uncertain about what to do next as we were. On my second circuit beneath the stony-faced portraits of dead white men, I met the eyes of the little plastic dragon again.

I sat down on the edge of the desk. There was a portrait behind the mad-eyed dragon, all white whisker and tight waistcoat. A man in his late sixties, staring out disdainfully at all onlookers, a window behind him implausibly overlooking the Tower of London. One arm held some sort of yappy dog, whose misproportioned features suggested an animal incapable of holding still, especially for an artist. The other rested on the window sill, palm turned upwards, fingers pointing out to the city behind. I looked closer. I leant right in until my nose almost touched the rough canvas. There was a mark on the man's hand. It was thin, almost lost in the gloomy shadows of the portrait, a tiny stroke of red across the wrinkled gloom of his flesh. It looked like someone had taken a scalpel and carefully carved a shallow red cross into his skin—no, two shallow red crosses. One was smaller than the other, nestling in the top left-hand corner that the first cross made. The cut looked fresh, no pale scar tissue, but neither was there a bandage and I couldn't imagine the whiskered old man being in a hurry to make a big deal of his injuries. I looked back at the plastic dragon with the mad eyes, at the shield it held in its grip. A white shield with two red crosses on it, one smaller than the other, a sword more than a cross, painted into the upper left-hand corner of its big brother.

I sat cross-legged on Nair's desk and went through the inevitable. I pulled the black mitten off my right hand and bit and tugged at the knot of the bandage until it came free. I unwound the white cotton, feeling fibres sticking and breaking against the bloody mess of my skin, and with almost no surprise and a good deal of regret, looked at the palm of my hand.

Two red crosses, one smaller than the other, had been carved very carefully by a Catholic graffiti artist into my skin.

I changed the bandage, set fire to the older, bloodier rags, and threw the ashes into the nearest bin. I pulled my glove back over my fist, threw cold water over my face and walked from Nair's apartment as casually and calmly as if I was a gasman, come to take the reading.

We walked. Where didn't concern us, and why didn't even feature. We walked because we could walk. We walked through Lincoln's Inn and down towards Middle Temple, through grand courtyards and tucked-away alleys, until we came to the Embankment. We walked along by the river, smelling it, watching the high tide rub against the old black stones, west until we came to Cleopatra's Needle. The smell of greasy hot dog in a paper bag stopped us. We bought one with extra ketchup and, goo dribbling down our chin, kept on walking. We climbed the steps onto Hungerford Bridge, crossed it, trains rumbling noisily alongside, the river churning peacefully below. I stood in the middle of the bridge and turned my face towards the east and breathed in the smell of water, salt, seagulls and tourist boats. At the end of the bridge sat a beggar, huddled over in the cold, wrapped in jumper and duvet both turned the colour of the thin London dirt that billowed in dry winds. I gave him a couple of quid and got a dirty look from a couple waiting for the lift down to the street. We ignored them and trotted down the stairs to the flat square stones of the South Bank.

It was already past lunchtime, but the restaurants beneath the Royal Festival Hall, all shining glass disguising uninspired interior, were heaving. Jugglers competed with ice cream vans parked opposite the skaters who spun and twisted in the uneven concrete ups and downs around the pillars of the Hayward Gallery and National Theatre. I watched them for a while. Kids, average age maybe sixteen. Hoods and thick gloves against the cold, baggy jeans, greens and blues and blacks and dark reds, sports logos and battered old wooden skateboards with the edges splintered off. There wasn't much room for impressive stunts—a few stairs, a few slopes, a few drains—but that didn't stop them from throwing themselves at everything that got in their way, people included, while whooping at some achievement only they who knew the secrets of skateboarding could appreciate. Behind them, the walls were so thick with graffiti that the council had given up, determining that this was art, not vandalism. Great splashes of colour thrown over each other again and again until the shadowed depths of the place looked like a psychedelic grammar lesson—words spelt to a careful level of comprehension, so only those in the know would understand—bubble letters of silver, their meaning lost to the detail of their drawing, and here or there, smaller notes along the usual lines of "B IS COUL" or "7JS B 4EVER" and other mystic warnings.

The wall being taken, some graffiti artists had moved on to the pillars, spinning paint round the concrete columns to make snakes, or poisoned twisted ivy, or biting barbed wire, or even, in one case, to say from the ceiling down to the floor in bold white letters:

GIVE ME BACK MY HAT

I looked at this a long while, wondering. It seemed like a strange sentiment to go spraying up on any piece of concrete, let alone a pillar beneath Waterloo Bridge.

We kept on walking. Books for sale at stalls under the bridge; outside the theatre, modern art, or twisted bits of concrete depending on your point of view; one busker on the Jamaican drums outside a TV studio, others playing Beethoven outside Gabriel's Wharf. Oxo Tower, all orange brick and iron banister; grotty concrete flats in the city's best location, glass fronts looking into open offices where meetings were being held to talk about magazines, covers, content, pictures and staff. Blackfriars Bridges—all three of them, if you counted the row of stubby pillars in the middle of the river, across which no road ran. Tate Modern (more art/twisted concrete), Globe Theatre, restaurants, Southwark Bridge, offices, black reflective glass over a broad stretch of water between bridges, looking out towards a building site and Cannon Street, a forgotten station; the rattling of trains overhead, the rumbling of buses crossing Southwark Bridge. Pubs, restaurants, cafés, cobbled streets, hotels, men holding beer and women chatting in silly shoes; buskers again, jugglers, fire eaters, ranters with their loudspeakers worrying that you haven't met God yet and now is the time, the smell of curry powder, the smell of chips. Little lost newsagents selling everything you'd expect, at double the price; the Golden Hinde, an extra "e" added on for historical authenticity, a ship built for short people next to a shop selling almost nothing but pirate hats and plastic swords; Southwark Cathedral, where in summer all the shoppers at Borough Market sat outside to eat smoked salmon and heart-stopping chocolate cake.

London Bridge.

A grotty bridge, if all truth be told, grizzled concrete and fierce traffic. By night, it was beautiful, lights directed along its length in the colours of the rainbow. From its pavements you could see all the things a tourist might want to see. To the west, the London Eye, Charing Cross station, the BT Tower and Centre Point. To the east, Tower Bridge, the Tower, Butler's Wharf, HMS *Belfast* and City Hall, which would always and for ever be known by Londoners after its inaugural mayor as Ken's Bollock.

We stood on London Bridge and faced the wind and let it wash the pain out of our bones. Here, we felt safe.

I looked towards the Tower of London, and thought without words. Wind and walking were all I needed.

A voice said, "Midnight Mayor."

My voice.

I tried it again, a few more times, rolled it over for size. "Midnight Mayor."

Repetition didn't make it seem any more a good thing, so I shut up.

I kept on walking.

*   *   *

Full circle.

I hadn't known I was going there, but when I arrived, I knew with absolute certainty that it was the right idea.

The Museum of London sat at the southern extremity of the Barbican. Its white tiles and grey, rounded walls gave it the superficial appearance of a boil-in-the-bag toilet that had got too big for its own plumbing and burst up from street level in a grimy eruption of clay tiling and half-swept dust. Strangers to the city always had a hard time finding it, since the main entrance wasn't at street level at all, but a storey above it in that network of ramps and walkways that made up the space-time vortex that was the Barbican Centre. Even if you found, at street level, any sign to mark its presence, the idea seemed too absurd that a city council might casually dump a museum beside a roundabout so overshadowed by buildings that to people who worked there, sunlight had become nothing more than a wistful fantasy.

That was good; that meant the inside was peaceful, without the nattering of children to disturb us. Those who had made it inside either knew its secrets already, and were there to wonder and appreciate anew, or were so surprised to discover this well of knowledge that even the most easily bored were silent with respect.

I wandered through the history of London, not paying much attention. I'd been here before, and what I was looking for was very specific.

I found it, sitting on a little stool beside a large display, lit up in shimmering orange and red, of the Great Fire of London. It was snoring, very quietly, very professionally; the snoring that could be dismissed as "heavy breath" at a moment's notice. I poked it with my toe and said, "Excuse me?"

The snoring stopped. Set within a squashed red face, a pair of almost spherical eyes opened, drifted up to the ceiling and round the walls, and settled on me.

"Uh?" The sound was pumped out by a pair of lungs inside a great bulbous chest inside a security guard's black uniform.

"You work here?" I asked.

"Sure, yeah, sure…What?" The security guard resettled himself on his stool. It looked designed to be as hard to sleep on as possible, but he'd pulled it off. "Jesus!" he muttered, as consciousness caught up with the rest of him. "Can I help you?"

I beamed.

"You lost?" he asked.

"No, don't think so."

"You sure?"

"Not unless we're going metaphysical."

"Jesus!" he added, as the rest of consciousness slammed into the forefront of his brain like a TGV without the brakes. "Right, yeah, fuck, Jesus! I mean…"

"I'm sure you didn't mean it to come out like that," I said.

"Sorry. I've got this medical thing…"

"I can tell."

"I'm fine now."

"Sure. I need to have a nose round your archives."

"Uh, right, yeah, sure. You'll be wanting to go talk to the lady at reception, she can get you an appointment…"

"Not those archives. I'm looking for some information, the kind you don't find in many libraries, or even on the internet."

His eyes narrowed. "What kind of information?"

"I'm trying to find out a few things about a guy called the Midnight Mayor."

"Oh," he groaned, stretching his short arms, whose hands ended in red, clubbed fingertips. "Not the Lord Mayor?"

"No. The Midnight Mayor. The museum seemed like a sensible place to start."

"Safer to ask about the Lord Mayor. We've got his coach somewhere, very swish, very shiny."

"The Midnight Mayor. I'm absolutely certain."

His face saddened. "Well, if you're sure..."

"I am."

"...just remember that I warned you, OK? Health and safety and stuff."

"Sure."

He stood up. "You'd better come with me."

His name was Frank. He had a hard accent coming out of a chubby mouth and said he was from Lambeth. He also said he didn't like trouble.

"Smart to ask the security guy," he added, as we rambled through the quiet, dark halls of the museum. "Twenty years in this place, you pick up a few things, and don't get so fussed as the historians. They give keys to the security guards that they'd never give to the archaeologists. Can't trust these academic types not to lose them somewhere."

"I know. That's why I asked."

"Oh," he sighed, jangling his keys absently as we picked our way through a line of panels showing the Blitzed-out ruins of the city. "You're one of them, aren't you?"

"One of what?"

"The guys in the know. No one asks about the Midnight Mayor who isn't already in too deep for the lifejacket to do any good. What are you? Magician, warlock, petty wizard with a thing for the big time?"

"None of those," I answered, as he unlocked a door behind a display dedicated to the Docklands Redevelopment and led me from the gloom of the museum halls into a white, neon-lit corridor. "But you're in the right sort of area."

His shoes snapped loudly on the concrete floor. Mine puffed and wheezed. He spun the keys round and round, jangling on their chain, and grunted at each door he opened. "'Course," he went on, "none of my business. I just look after the museum, see? I don't dabble."

Another door, heavy, black and metal; a room of dead paper and cold dry air. He shooed me in and closed the door behind us. The room had no windows, just vents and dull strip lighting that failed to illuminate between the long stacks of shelves dividing up the floor.

"Smart not to ask too many questions," he announced, marching down the rows of files. "You never know who'll come knocking. I just point them in the right direction, see? That's all that I can do — just the doorman, just keep an eye out."

Another door at the end of the room. Two locks, and a keypad on the side. "Where are we going?" I asked.

"Thing is," he sighed, as the locks turned and the door opened, "you're the second guy this week to come asking about the Midnight Mayor."

I stopped dead above a flight of metal stairs headed into darkness. "Who else?" I asked. "Who else came looking?"

"Hey — none of my business, remember?"

"Please. I want to know."

"Knowing's nothing unless you've got the qualification on your CV," he sighed. "I know the whole fucking history of London but can I get a decent job? Fuck it."

"A man in a suit," we blurted. "Was it a man in a pinstripe suit? Thin dark hair, slicked back, dark suit, light shirt, shiny shoes? There'd be . . . he wouldn't have smelt of anything. No smell."

He waved down the dark staircase. "Hey, I didn't say anything, OK? You want to know about the Midnight Mayor, it's your own damn business. I don't dabble, see? It's the best way to get by, because otherwise, if you're just a guy, you know, just doing your thing, that sorta thing would send you crazy."

I looked at the stairs descending into blackness. "The answers are down there?"

"You wanna know about the Midnight Mayor?"

"Yes."

"You gotta get in deeper. Sign these."

He handed me a couple of sheets of paper on a clipboard. I read them over in the gloomy light. "What's this?" I asked, as their meaning utterly failed to sink in.

"Legal waivers."

"What?"

"You want to find out about the Midnight Mayor, and you do it on museum premises, then I need your written consent not to hold the museum liable for any damage that may happen to you."

"'Damage'?"

"Not my business. You gonna sign? Can't give you answers unless you sign."

"Does it have to be in blood?" we asked, curious.

"What? No, Jesus! You've got one fucking twisted head on your shoulders." He handed me a biro. I read, and signed. He snatched pen and paper back from me and gestured down the dark stairs. "Great knowing you, good luck in your research, give me a mention in the credits, right? Byeeeee!"

"What about..." we began.

He slammed the door.

We stood on a staircase painted black in a black corridor leading down to unending blackness, with any light switches that might have illuminated the blackness probably having been painted black.

We swore.

I let out a long patient breath, pressed the palms of my hands together, as much to calm myself as anything else, then opened them up. Light, the shimmering pinkish-sodium glow of the streets, rippled between my fingers. I let it fold out of my skin, taking warmth with it, pressed it into a bubble and threw it up above my head. Our shadow stretched down to a black door at the end of the black staircase. We walked down carefully, trailing our fingers along the cold walls. I could taste something on the air, old and slippery. It smelt of fishmonger, of thin fog and old forgotten things. It set my stomach turning, made the hairs on the back of my neck stand on end, made my little sodium glow twist and shimmer above me in shared unease. I reached the door at the bottom of the stair, and pushed it open. Not locked. Beyond it was a room. In the middle of the room was a cauldron, placed squarely beneath a single overhanging, metal-shaded lamp.

I said, "You are taking the mick."

I was talking to the cauldron; but the voice that answered me came from a woman.

She was in her mid- to late thirties, had a haircut that reduced her blonde hair to straight shoulder-length discipline, and wore sensible leather pumps and a neat woollen jumper. She came out of the endless shadows so suddenly that despite her smiling, friendly face I started away from her. Putting her hand, with its short, tidy nails, around my shoulder, she said, "Cup of tea?"

I looked at the contents of the black iron cauldron. A dozen sad, drained tea bags were floating on the surface. I said, "Oh, you have got to be taking the piss!"

"You disrespectin' us?" demanded another voice. I looked up and saw another woman's face, younger, not out of her teens, hair dyed black and bright purple, face drilled with metal rings, in her ears, her lips, her cheeks, her tongue, her eyebrows, her nose.

"Erm..." I mumbled.

"Biscuit?" A third voice, a third woman. This one had steel-silver hair, a cream blouse with gold buttons done all the way up to her drooping chin, a dark blue tartanesque suit and an expression of mild reproach. She held a small plate of assorted biscuits, neatly arranged.

"Um...thank you." We never say no to free food.

"You can dunk, you know," added the old woman, and to prove her point, selected a digestive from her plate, and dipped it in the bubbling black cauldron.

"You know, this isn't how I imagined the Museum's archives department..."

"Huh!" grunted the young woman.

"Oh, dear," sighed the middle-aged woman.

The old woman looked at me like I was a persistent fly circling closer to the sticky paper.

"...but I mean I'd heard stories, wouldn't have come if I hadn't heard stories..."

"Of course you have."

"...and I suppose in a way, it makes sense..."

"Well, *duh*."

"Maybe we can help, dear."

"Another biscuit?"

I looked at them. Three ladies in a room beneath a museum, with a cauldron full of tea. There are certain things that never change. Call them Fates, Muses, Furies, Prophets, Seers or just three twisted biddies with a caffeine fixation, the magic of three women and a cauldron will never fade, even when the cauldron is full of PG Tips.

So I bowed, opening my arms wide in a gesture of peace, and said, "Ladies."

The young one said, "Fucker!" It would have been nice to call her the Maid. I doubted I could.

The middle-aged one said, "So nice to meet a polite young man!" It would have been appropriate to call her the Mother, but I wasn't sure how she'd take it.

"Society is on the down!" concluded the old woman. We wanted to call her the Hag, and were smart enough to steer clear of the idea.

But whatever we called them, we could recognise them for what they were. Three women with a cauldron—that meant power, ancient and old power, and old power meant old traditions, and that meant rules, and rules usually meant risk, since 90 per cent of the time rules are invented to stop something, that could be bad, from being even worse.

Then the Maid said, "He's a fucking sorcerer. Jeezus."

Then the Mother, patting me nicely on the shoulder, said, "They're the blue electric angels."

Then the Hag, putting the biscuits down, leant straight over to me and grabbed my bandaged hand. She jerked it towards her and I, still seeing just old woman — forgetting the rules — staggered straight into her grip and half fell at her feet. Turning my hand every which way, she dug her sharp fingers into the bandages until we nearly screamed.

"He's the Midnight Mayor," she said. She leant up close, steel-coloured eyes beneath silver hair that didn't even twitch with her moving. "That's what you wanted to know, isn't it?" I looked into her perfect false teeth made of plastic, smelt tea on her breath and ancient, ancient magic in the dull thick cut of her jacket, and heard her say, "You're the Midnight Mayor. Say it until it becomes natural, say it until you believe it. You're the Midnight Mayor, sorcerer. Electric angel. Isn't that what you needed to hear? That bit of info's a freebie, take it or leave it."

She squeezed one last time on our bloody hand and let go. We flopped against the edge of the cauldron, cradling our hand and hunched around the pain until our eyes were no longer full of blue electric fire, biting our tongue to force away everything but staying in control.

"He doesn't look much like a Midnight Mayor," sighed the Mother.

"You look kinda a dork, mate," concurred the Maid.

The Hag grunted, picked up the biscuits and set about carefully nibbling around the sticky centre of a jammy dodger, saving the best for last.

I dragged us back onto our feet, leaning heavily on the edge of the cauldron. "I don't suppose you've got a cup?" I asked at last.

"Of course!"

A mug proclaiming *"I really love Mum"* was handed to me from the darkness beyond the cauldron. I dipped it in the bubbling liquid.

"Tea, sugar?" asked the Mother.

I shook my head, reached for my satchel, seized a handful of painkillers, drowned them in tea. For a liquid boiled in a cauldron that probably hadn't seen daylight for two thousand years, the tea wasn't half bad. They waited for me to drink, draining down the whole mug and putting it carefully aside. I wiped my mouth on my sleeve. On my right hand I felt the burning brand ache and stick to the bandages.

"I'm guessing," I said at last, "that there are rules. I'm guessing it'll be something like 'you can have three questions' and I want to make it absolutely clear right now that I do not believe that rhetorical flourishes or prompting statements qualify as a direct question."

"Hey—you flunked out too," said the Maid, with what I guessed was the nearest to understanding I was going to get from her.

"While you're broadly correct, my pet," sighed the Mother, "'three questions' is so old-fashioned. This is the age of modern educational initiatives!"

"That's a very unhelpful answer," I said, "since it doesn't really answer anything, while still leaving the option open for me to make a pig's ear of this whole procedure and blow one of my questions on something banal like 'duh, so are there more than three questions, then?'—which isn't, by the way, a question!"

"Sharp, aren't you?" The Hag spoke from the corner of her mouth, something either a smile or a grimace. "But which one of you is sharp?"

"Please," I growled. "Let's establish this right now. I am we and we are me. We are the same thought and the same life and the same flesh, and frankly I would have thought that you, of all entities to wander out of the back reaches of mythical implausibility, would respect this."

"But it's not healthy!" replied the Hag. "A mortal and a god sharing the same flesh?"

"You know, this isn't why we're here. I can get abuse pretty much wherever."

"Yeah," sighed the Maid, "but I bet a tenner I can make you cry in half a minute."

"That's the problem, isn't it?" added the Mother, slurping tea.

"Did you hurt your little handywandy?" crooned the Hag.

I pinched the bridge of my nose. "All right," I said. "Let's play this game. Statement: I am the Midnight Mayor."

"Yes," said the Mother.

"Don't give the fucker a freebie. *Christ!*" exclaimed the Maid.

"Sorry, dearest," muttered the Mother, with every sign of genuine contrition.

"Statement:" I tried again. "I became Midnight Mayor when Nair died."

Three stony faces stared back at me. I didn't need an answer to know I was right. "Statement: when Nair died, he made a telephone call. He breathed his dying breath into the wires and with his dying breath went the idea, the title, the power, the brand, everything that makes up Midnight Mayor. But it couldn't stay as signals in the wire; the Midnight Mayor needs to be flesh and blood. So it went in search of a phone to ring and it found us. It was *always* going to find us. It is our nature."

"Isn't it nice to see that youth can still reason?" sighed the Hag.

"Statement: the Aldermen think I killed Nair because, let's face it, if we'd known what he was about to do to us, we probably would have. Because they don't understand what we are; they don't understand why we are alive. Because... because they don't know who else to blame. Because Nair was killed by a man who basically flayed him alive while Nair was still in his clothes, peeled away the skin *under* his nails without even trimming them down, and that, *that* isn't just sorcery. That's the kind of magic that makes the moon think twice about its orbital path. That's...that's the kind of magic that people don't want to understand, don't want to know about, because it makes them tiny.

"Statement: fact! Nair died and I was hit by a curse out of the telephone! One Midnight Mayor is dead and another walks, because you can't kill a brand on the hand, not while there's a city that made it.

"Fact! The man who killed Nair had no smell, and men—mortal walking, breathing men—always smell.

"Question:"

"*Finally*," groaned the Maid.

"Yes, dear?"

"Well?"

"Question:" I licked my dry lips, tasting of peeled skin and tea. "Who or what killed Nair?"

There was a long silence. Finally the Maid said, "Shucks. You ain't gonna live long, sunshine."

"Well, now, you see, that's an interesting one," murmured the Mother.

"If you care about these things," snapped the Hag.

"But you're three ladies with a cauldron," we said, managing another bow. "You'd know without needing to care."

"Hey, sunshine!" snapped the Maid. "It wasn't a fucking man! You said it like—blokes what breathe and piss and eat don't fucking not smell."

"And of course the question is," added the Mother thoughtfully, "did the man kill the Mayor, or the man's maker?"

"He'll be after you now," concluded the Hag. "It doesn't matter whose skin it is, it's the brand on the hand. You could be any little wormy maggot crawling up from the biscuit plate and he'd still come to squish you down. Thought about running away?"

I bit my lip, pulled my hand tighter into my chest. "All right," I muttered. "OK. Cryptic I can deal with. Sure. Whatever. Statement: you said...the man or his maker."

"That's conversation skills he's got there," chuckled the Hag.

"Statement: ergo—the man who killed Nair wasn't in fact a man. Something else. The possibilities are endless!"

"Pity you've only got so much time, then, isn't it?"

I wiped my forehead with my sleeve. I felt hot. The stitches in my chest ached and throbbed, my hand burnt. The world seemed a mirage away. I stammered, "Question: in Nair's house there was a file, and in the file there was a note, and the note said, 'Swift has the shoes.' What does this mean?"

"Trendy pair of trainers," said the Maid appreciatively, nodding at my feet.

"Very clever of him to notice, really," added the Mother.

"You're wearing the boy's shoes," concluded the Hag. "Or didn't you think it would be important?"

I looked down at my shoes. "These?"

"Was that a . . ."

"No, no, it wasn't a question. It was more . . . thinking aloud. It would be fair to allow me to get a little clarification before I blow my next question."

"Fair!" laughed the Maid.

"Well . . ." sighed the Mother.

"Huh!" grunted the Hag.

"It would be moving with the times . . ." I added. "Education being what it is."

"I got an A at Art."

"All right then."

"Clarify away."

"Statement: these shoes"—I twitched my toes inside the flashy trainers—"aren't mine. I took them from a boy's room in Wembley. They belong to a kid called Mo. I was using them to find him, for his mum's sake. He's been missing. He's got nothing to do with magic, as far as I can tell, and she certainly hasn't. Just a favour for a friend. But—still statement—the Mayor's files mentioned these shoes. Nair thought they were important. So here's my clarification question: was Nair also looking for the kid who owned these shoes?"

To which, simply and flatly, the Hag said, "Yes."

We wanted out. We knew it with a sudden and absolute certainty. We wanted a ticket to somewhere foggy, a nice thick green haze to get ourselves lost in, deep tunnels and obedient lights. We wanted out and down and gone, it was nothing to do with us, none of this was anything to do with us and we weren't prepared to die for it.

So I said: "Question: what the bloody hell is going on?"

The three women exchanged looks.

"Is that fair?" asked the Mother.

"Kinda *total* disrespect!" added the Maid. "I like your balls, bozo!"

"It's not about fair," retorted the Hag. "If it was about fair, none of this would happen."

I raised a polite hand. "Answer, please?"

The Hag sighed, and put down the small plate of biscuits. She moved carefully round the side of the cauldron towards me. So did the others. Tough guys aren't supposed to be intimidated by ladies. I guess I wasn't so tough. She looked us in the eye and said, "City's damned."

"Beg pardon?"

"Damned. Cursed. Buggered. Totally and utterly fucked, to use the crude vernacular. It's going to burn. It's going to sink. It's going to crash and splinter and shatter and everything will be dust. Pick one. The ravens are dead. The Stone is broken. The Wall is defaced. The Midnight Mayor is killed and his replacement"—a chuckle like the last gasp of a throttled chicken—"didn't even know he was in the job. Cursed. Damned. Run away, little electric angels. Run, if you can."

They were next to me, around me, behind me. Three little ladies who'd been around ever since the first village midwife decided to ask her friends round for a hot cup of something on a foggy Sunday evening, back in the days when the magic came from the earth and the sky, rather than the tarmac and the neon. We were tiny to them. I was afraid.

"What do you mean, damned?" I stammered. "What do you mean, the ravens are dead, the Stone is broken? Why are these things happening? What kind of total tit goes around making *us* Midnight Mayor? I don't even believe in the Midnight fucking Mayor! What the bloody hell is going on?!"

A hand whose fingers were all bone and false nails grasped the back of my neck. The Hag leant in so close I could hear her breath, feel it tickling my eardrum. When she spoke, it was with the whisper of the treacherous lover. She said:

"'Give me back my hat.'"

Then, without a word of apology or flicker of embarrassment, she pushed me face-first into the cauldron of boiling tea.

In times of uncertainty, someone has to take charge.

Her name was Judith.

It was her fingers at my throat, looking for a pulse, that woke me up.

Time had passed, without bothering to tell me about it.

The sky was the colour of an old bruise, the sunlight a washed-out yellow reflecting off the topmost windows.

Judith wore a puffy green sleeveless jacket, a matching jumper, sensible boots and a badge. The badge said, "Judith". In the top-left corner it added, "Here To Help".

She said, "Mister? Hey — you OK?"

I considered this difficult question. With my left hand I felt at my face. It didn't feel burnt. A little tender, perhaps, but hardly scalded by boiling tea. I sniffed my fingertips. A faint lingering odour of PG Tips and digestive biscuit? I ran my hand through my hair until I encountered grains, then a grainy surface which announced itself as the ground. I dug my fingers into the surface on which I lay. Dirty, gritty, damp sand parted beneath my fingertips. I looked at Judith. Her face was concern hiding confusion with just a hint of suspicion thrown in for good measure. I looked to my right, and saw offices clinging so close to the river's edge that there wasn't space for a rat to scuttle. I looked towards my feet and saw the blue-black waters of the sunset river gnawing at my toes. I looked to my left and saw Tower Bridge. I groaned and let my head flop back on the dirty low-tide sand.

"Bollocks," I said.

"Hey, mister, you all right, like?"

I turned to look closer at the woman kneeling beside me. Behind, safe on the higher reaches of an embankment, a small crowd of interested passers-by and tourists had gathered to watch this curious scene at the water's edge; some though were already drifting away, disappointed that I wasn't a corpse. Behind *them* stood the low thick walls of the Tower of London.

I looked back at Judith, Here To Help.

I said, "Bollocks buggery bollocks."

"You're welcome," she replied.

I sat up slowly, just in case anything was broken or dislodged. Nothing. Even the stitches in my chest were a comforting ache, a reminder of normality. I looked at my right hand. The bandages, stained a faint tea-brown, were still spun tight. From my new height I could see past my toes, to where the slow waters of the Thames were quietly, secretly edging their way up towards the stone face of the embankment. They'd already washed away the worst of the low-tide debris, plastic bags and old Coke cans. And with it, they'd washed away a message, written carefully at my feet by an extended finger-tip. All that remained was:

ACK MY HAT

I looked at Judith. "This sounds strange, but I don't suppose you saw three mad women with a cauldron of boiling tea pass by this way?"

"No," she replied. The polite voice of reasonable people scared of exciting the madman.

"Flash of light? Puff of smoke? Erm..." I tried to find a polite way of describing the symptoms of spontaneous teleportation without using the dreaded "teleportation" word. I failed. I slumped back into the sand. What kind of mystic kept a spatial vortex at the bottom of their cauldrons of tea anyway?

"Have you called the police?"

"No," she replied. Then casually, "Did you jump?"

Her eyes flickered to Tower Bridge. I shook my head. "No. Pushed. Don't call the police."

I staggered up. The rolling waters of the river didn't wash like the sea, but crawled, by imperceptible advancement. The long straight lines of the "A" filled with foam.

CK MY HAT

I thought about the three women and their cauldron. I looked up at the Tower of London. I looked down at Judith.

I said, "Listen to me. This is very important. I need to know about the ravens in the Tower."

I had to see it to believe it. I bought an overpriced ticket like all the good tourists who waddled in orderly queues between the barriers guiding you this way to that tower, that way to the crown jewels. The battlemented walls shut out all the city's traffic noise, creating within the old courtyards of the Tower an eerie stillness. The air smelt of rain to come. A few yards from the executioner's block, left out as something macabre to please the children, was a chained-off patch of grass. A small sign announced in four different languages that there were nine ravens in the tower, named after Norse gods, and legend held that should ever the ravens leave the Tower of London, then the city would be doomed. Cursed, damned, fire, water, crumble, crash: pick one, pick them all.

Even if the legend was a lie, time and belief gives everything power.

Next to that was a sign saying, **Please Do Not Feed The Birds**.

The grass was empty.

I took Judith, Here To Help by the arm—customer sales assistant, Tower of London, and incidentally the only person who knew first aid and had the guts to try it on floating bodies—and said calmly, "If you do not show me the ravens, I will throw myself off Tower Bridge and this time the tide will be high and you won't be able to save me, capisce?"

She was at heart a kind woman. She wasn't about to say no to a guy she thought had tried to commit suicide.

Below one of the towers in the wall, in a deep whitewashed room that hummed with ventilation fans and poor plumbing, were nine neat little coffins laid out on a neat little table. Inside each coffin was a black-feathered dead bird.

Judith said, "They just died. A few days ago. All of them—just died. We thought maybe poison but they hadn't been fed by anyone except...and there'll be an autopsy but they all just...we're getting replacement birds, flown in special, secret like, because we don't want the tourists to know, but they just...they all just died."

We reached out, appalled, fascinated, and touched a feather.

"You mustn't!" she hissed. "I'll be in enough trouble already!"

We drew back our hand, hypnotised by the unblinking black eyes staring back at us from the little coffins.

"Was there...a message?" I stammered. "The night they died, a message...something written on a wall? Left on a phone? Something you didn't expect to see?"

She licked her lips. "You didn't try to off yourself, did you?"

"No, I was pushed into a cauldron of tea and woke up here, and..." we laughed, "there's no such thing as coincidence. Not in my line of work. Was there a message?"

Nine black eyes looking up from the sides of nine black heads on nine dead feathered bodies. Judith nodded, sucking in air. "There was something painted up on one of the walls. We washed it off. Don't know how they got it there, not easy, you know, it is a castle! It said... someone wrote, 'give me back my hat'. In big white letters up on the wall where the ravens liked to sit. Just 'give me back my hat'...Who pushed you?"

"Three ladies. With a cauldron, like I said. I've got to go."

"Go where?"

"Anywhere," we replied. "Anywhere that isn't here. Judith, thanks for all your help, and now take a traveller's good advice, and get out of the city. Get out *now*."

"Why?"

"Because it's true," I answered. "All of it. The ravens in the Tower are dead. That's a curse, that's damnation. Someone is out to destroy the city and I have no idea who it is." I chuckled, "Which is terrific, because I'm the one who is supposed to stop them! So run. Because I have no idea how I'm going to do it."

I don't know if she took my advice.

There were other things we had to know.

I nearly ran to Cannon Street station, an iron shed in a street one block up from the river's edge. Opposite its square mouth was a sports shop, a small plaque nailed to the door. The plaque said: "Within these walls is the London Stone, an ancient Roman altar from which all the distances in Britain were measured. It is said that should the London Stone ever be destroyed, the city will be cursed."

I went inside the shop. A young man with curly blond hair and a Northern tinge to his voice came up to me and tried to sell me a pair of running shoes for more money than I lived on in a month. We took him by the shoulders so hard he flinched, stared straight into his eyes and said, "We have to see the London Stone."

"Um," he mumbled.

"Show us!"

"Uh..."

"*Show us!*"

"It's gone," he stammered.

"Gone where?"

"Someone, um, someone, um, hit it and..."

"Where is it?"

"Broken."

"When?"

"A few days ago."

"The London Stone is broken?"

"Um..."

"Was there a message? Something written? On the walls, on the windows, was there a message?"

He pointed at a window. "On the..."

I hissed in frustration, let him go, pushing him back harder than I'd meant into a pile of badminton rackets, and stormed from the shop. The front had a number of metal shutters that could roll down over the windows. One of them was already closed in preparation for the evening. On it, someone had written in tall white letters:

GIVE ME B

We thumped it so hard our knuckles bled.

I ran through the London streets, not caring now about my own aching limbs. I was flying on rush-hour magic, the buzz of neon propelling me along with the swish of my trailing coat lightening the weight of my body, feeding on the raw hum of the city streets. Rush hour was a good time for sorcerers, when the streets shimmered with life, so much life pumped up into the air, just waiting to be tapped. Our shoes—that weren't our shoes—puffed and huffed as we ran, feeling our way by the shape of the paving stones, smelling our way by the thickness of the traffic fumes, guided by the numbers on the buses, weaving through the commuters on the streets like the deer that had once danced here through the forest. It was the same magic; the same enchantment.

The nearest piece of the London Wall I knew of was tucked down to the south of the Barbican, amidst bright tall offices and renovated stone guildhalls. Its red crumbled stones had been incorporated into an excavated garden where the bank workers and clerks of the city ate their sandwiches, all shiny fountain and well-tended geraniums. As I caught sight of the Wall I thought for a naive moment that it would be all right, saw clean stones, well loved, standing along one side of this little dip full of greenery. Then as I descended the wooden steps to the garden, by the light of the windows all above, I could see more of the Wall, and we laughed, cried, shouted, bit our lip, all and none and everything at once.

On the ancient Roman stones of the Wall of London, someone had written, of course someone had written:

GIVE ME BACK MY HAT

I slumped on a bench beneath the wall, and let the pain of my aching body reassert itself over the heady rush of streetside magics. I found my left hand unconsciously rubbing at the sticky bandages of my right. I peeled off my mitten, then unwrapped the tea-stained cotton. Beneath, drawn across my skin, were the two thin crosses, one lodged in the corner of the other, bright red, still a little tender, but otherwise sealed into my flesh, like an old friend left over from my mum's womb.

We were the Midnight Mayor. Guardian protector of the city. And now the ravens in the Tower were dead; the London Stone was broken; the Wall of London cursed like all the rest. The ancient, blessed, and secret things that had always protected the city. And now someone had destroyed them, defaced them, cursed them, damned them.

Cursed, damned, doomed, burnt, drowned, crushed, crumbled, cracked, fallen, faded, split, splintered — pick one, pick them all.

None of our business.

Not our problem.

What were we supposed to do about it?

I looked down at my shoes.

Swift has the shoes.

GIVE ME BACK MY HAT
END OF THE LINE

I am the Midnight Mayor.

Say it a few times until you get used to the idea.

My city.

I put my head in my hands, squeezed back against the aching in my skull. It didn't make it better. I raised my head to the orange-black sky, saw the flickering lights of a passing plane, turned down to the earth at my feet, the shoes that weren't my own, looked up at the wall. The ancient wall, protector of the city, magic and history all muddled up in one and I saw it again, what I should have seen before, plastered in great white letters:

GIVE ME BACK MY HAT

I reached into my satchel. I pulled out the phone with Nair's sim card in it. I thumbed it on.

I dialled the number for Dudley Sinclair.

Just because I didn't trust him didn't mean he couldn't be useful.

A while passed before a voice answered. It was surly, with a slight lisp. "Yeah? Who's this?"

I said, "This is Matthew Swift. I need to speak to Sinclair."

Silence for a second—the kind of second it takes to recognise a name, dislike it, and muster a polite reply. "OK. Hold on."

I held on. This involved hearing tunes by the Beatles played on what sounded like a reed nose-flute. I held on a little longer, drumming my fingers. It's hard to stay psyched up for anything in the face of a nose-flute rendition of "While My Guitar Gently Weeps". We nearly hung up.

When Sinclair spoke, his voice boomed out so loud and sudden that I nearly dropped the handset. "Matthew! So good to hear from you! How are you keeping?"

"Mr Sinclair," I said. "I think you should know that someone has cursed the city."

Not a beat, not a moment. "Really, dear boy?" he intoned. "How tedious of them. Any idea who?"

"No. But the ravens in the Tower are dead, and the London Stone is broken, and the Wall of London has been painted on in big white paint, and the Midnight Mayor was flayed alive without ever actually being touched, by a man who has no smell and is therefore probably not a man. Someone is systematically destroying all the magical defences that the city has."

"What a pain," sighed Sinclair. "And you have no idea who might be indulging in this scheme?"

"No."

"Pity. I suppose this means that all sorts of nasties are going to get out onto the streets and start tormenting the innocent. Well, so much for the Christmas bonus."

"Mr Sinclair, there's something else I think you should know."

"Of course, dear boy, of course, you know I always enjoy our mutually beneficial working arrangements!"

"Mr Sinclair," I said, taking a deep breath, "I am the Midnight Mayor."

"Really? Good grief, when did that happen?"

"About the same moment that the last Midnight Mayor expired down the telephone."

"Oh, I see. How...unexpected. Yes, really, that is...that is most unusual and rather remarkable. I suppose it must have come as something of a surprise to you too?"

"I'm a little freaked, yes."

"Well, naturally, yes, of course, yes, you would be! But naturally. Yes..." His voice trailed off. "You know, Matthew, I am very rarely surprised by much I hear these days, and I must admit, in a spirit of frankness and free exchange, your phone call and this somewhat remarkable information concerning your current mythical status is undeniably different. Are you absolutely sure of all this?"

"Yes."

"Including being the Midnight..."

"Yes. It makes a sickening sense. Mr Sinclair—I think I might need your help."

"Well, naturally, anything for you, dear boy, naturally, naturally!"

"I've seen the face of the ... the creature that killed Nair."

"Creature? Not a man, then, a creature?"

"Yes."

"And you say you saw him?"

"Yes."

"Remarkable! Yes, that is a remarkable thing, I must admit, I was wondering how you might have ..."

"There was a fox that saw the whole thing. We shared a kebab and a few reminiscences. Mr Sinclair — the creature that killed Nair didn't even touch him. I've never seen anything like it. And we have no reason to believe that, if it killed Nair for being Mayor, then it won't do exactly the same to us, and we don't know if we can stop it."

Silence, a long while. I have almost never known Sinclair to be silent.

"All right," he said at last. "Let's meet."

Purpose.

Purpose meant reason.

Reason meant thought.

Thoughts meant ...

...*dead men not humans just meat dead meat on the slab dead Midnight Mayor ten thousand paper cuts not even touched dead meat lost of all faces and nature and just* ...

Stop it.

...*dead ravens GIVE ME BACK MY HAT dead ravens broken stones shattered wards broken protections GIVE ME BACK MY HAT end of the line end of the line make me a shadow on the wall no smell no smell just killed him dead meat and the fox hid no smell end of the line end of the line I am Midnight Mayor Midnight Mayor dead on a slab kill an idea kill an idea kill a city kill a city idea ward protection something coming make me a shadow* ...

We didn't like thoughts.

We tried to muffle them in our walking.

Walking meant rhythm.

Fleet Street. Pinstriped trousers, perfect silk suits, swished-back hair, black leather briefcases. Lawyers and bankers, the common, rich men of the city. Did these men smell? Hard to tell in the exhaust from the buses, the coffee from the open doors, cakes and the smell of yeast from the expensive bakeries, perfect drenched cleanliness from the cafés, stiff cleaning powders from the dry-cleaners. Did their hearts beat, did they breathe, did their throats draw in and out inside the collar of their shirts? To look was to stop walking too fast, to walk slow was to think, to walk slow was to be noticed, and who knew who would be watching? And we saw endless blotchy anonymous faces blurred into pinkish-grey passing shadows moving in and out of the streetlamp glows, sharp polished leather shoes snapping on the paving stones, white shirts and crisp ties, and what colour had the tie of Nair's killer been? We couldn't remember, it had been smell and terror and sense and blood. Ten thousand little deaths all at once, every one stinging sharper than the finest razor on the flesh, all at once, ten thousand little deaths from a face . . . just a face in a pinstripe suit. And it didn't get much more pinstriped than Fleet Street.

This was *my* city.

Royal Courts of Justice. News crews, knobbly stone spikes and bright white lights. Aldwych. St Clement's Church, ringing out "Oranges and Lemons" above the tree-shaded bus stops, the London School of Economics, all chips, ring-binders and scuttling shoes, a bank, the BBC, statues of big ladies holding burning torches, the Indian embassy, swastikas and curly lettering in stone — and did that kid over there in the hood have a face? Cafés and theatres. Bright lights that drove away shadow and imagination. Cheap sandwiches, packed bus stops. We could taste the magic on the air, bright, hot, red, like strong curry settling over our stomach, filling our veins, pushing us further forward, giving us courage. We couldn't imagine these lights ever going out, no harm here, too many people, too much brightness, too much we could use.

Drury Lane, one show that had run for ever, one show that would die in a week, five different kinds of restaurant and one warehouse piled full of furniture that no one would ever sit on, and everyone would always admire. I went for the backstreets, wiggling round the back of Covent Garden, watching my back, running my fingers over the railings, round the streetlamps, over the walls, listening with much more than ears, staying smart. I did two whole circuits of Covent Garden before I finally chose to go inside, looping the loop round the back of St Paul's Church, its yard shut up for the evening, round the cobbled street that threaded its quiet way south of Long Acre, back towards Bow Street, into the Royal Opera House. Glass, steel, marbled pillar and thick red carpet. I rode bright new escalators up past a glasshouse laden with candle-lit restaurant tables. In the bar I ordered a packet of peanuts, a big glass of orange juice and rights to the darkest, tightest corner there was. It cost the price of a small dowry, but we were not in the mood to complain. There we sat and watched.

Theatre-goers in London's West End are unique unto themselves. Opera-goers are a step beyond. Women in big throat-clutcher necklaces, fat silver brooches pinned above their silk-clad breasts; jackets that looked like shawls, coats that wished they were cloaks left over from some forgotten era when the top hat was still sexy, handbags on gold chains, fine-rimmed spectacles balanced on the end of ski-slope noses. For the men, suit and tie was still the norm, but even here they'd raised the bar. Walking penguins complete with silk handkerchief from a waistcoat pocket bustled against 100 per cent tartan sleeves, who in turn shuffled round with murmurs of "excuse me, excuse me, yes, thank you, excuse me" in suits of sweetcorn yellow and navy blue, to suggest that while they were dressed up for the evening, it was a casual thing that had cost great time and expense in becoming so.

Very few people stood out from this silken medley; I feared I was one of them. There were also an American couple, all big bum bags and open necks; a cluster of Japanese tourists who nodded and bobbed at everything they saw; and a pair of students whose big hair and carefully slashed jeans cried out "arty type". Whoever had said in the guidebooks that the bum bag was a sensible device against theft had lied; no single item of dressware ever invented cried out "mug me" more than a pouch of zip-up plastic suspended by your groin.

I huddled deeper into the shadows of my corner. There was magic here, expectation, secrets, trickery, illusion, they were the business of the place and that I could use. People were more willing to sink into a spell, more willing not to notice, and both these things could keep me safe. I wrapped myself in the stuff, dragged thick blankets of shadow over me, spun distraction and expectation into the air and let every eye that glanced across my corner see nothing more than a shape in a shadow and then forget and move on to more important things. I drank my orange juice and ate my peanuts: opera house special, coated in spices and roasted in a Mediterranean sun.

Dudley Sinclair arrived three minutes before the curtain went up. He wore full evening dress complete with semi-cloak draped off his great round shoulders; his paunch was warping within the straitjacket waistcoat he'd somehow welded around himself. He wasn't alone. I recognised Charlie, his usual companion, PA, secretary, assistant, whatever. I smelt Charlie, even in the bustle of the room: the rolling treacle smell of shapeshifters who'd spent too much time as a rat.

They didn't bother to look for me, and I didn't bother to introduce myself. I sat and watched and waited, looking to see if they'd brought anyone else. If they had, "anyone" was doing a good job of blending in. The bell rang as a final warning, the crowds sloshed through the open doors to the auditorium. Sinclair went with them, Charlie remained by the door. I waited until he was the last person there; then since he was, and since I was, he saw me.

He gestured impatiently. I finished my drink and walked towards him; he handed me a ticket. "Paranoid," he snapped.

"Stabbed and burnt," I explained, gesturing vaguely at my battered skin.

Charlie merely grunted.

Sinclair had got a box. We felt instantly uncomfortable, locked away in a little upholstered cabin with this great fat man and his friend. I had always imagined that when the revolution began and the guillotine went up, people who had their own private boxes at the opera would be the first for the chop.

I sat uneasily in my chair, shuffling it closer to the wall, wanting to get my back against something more solid. Sinclair said, "Matthew! So glad you could make it! Do you like opera?"

"Not sure," I mumbled. "Never seen any."

"Well then, this *will* be an experience. A chance to enlighten the uninitiated. Champagne?"

There was a picnic hamper set on a small folding table in front of us. We began to understand the point of boxes after all. I said, "I'd better not drink," as we took a sandwich. We *never* say no to food. I'm always a little surprised to see our reflection looking so thin.

"You look tense."

I shot him a sour look. "Lincoln was assassinated in a theatre."

"But at least the assassin was caught, no? Matthew! You are in a dreadful way, aren't you? You should relax a little. I'm sure all this business with the city being damned and you being responsible will be sorted out without too much fuss, and when it's all over, you'll look back and laugh and say, 'thank goodness that's over, what an anecdote for the pub'. Now sit back...and enjoy one of man's greatest art forms."

We tried our best.

Man's greatest art form, if that's what it was, involved a cast and chorus of approximately forty people dressed in anything from tight tights and a clinging top to Viennese ballgowns of the kind that required you to turn sideways to get through any door. We regretted that we understood so much of it. The music of itself seemed beautiful, even moving, but we couldn't reconcile ourself to the lyrics, which much of the time seemed to revolve around bickering over who sent who what letter.

I did my best, letting the spell roll over me, trying to wash out all the thoughts of fear and confusion. We had always loved a good story, and I wanted, just for a moment, or a lot of very long moments, as the show turned out to be, to feel safe, and forget to think with words.

Sounds and music helped take the trembling away, helped hold us still, if only for a while. We let it. Sinclair had probably planned it that way. He was smart, when it came to things like that.

At the interval, gins and tonics were brought to the door by a soft-footed man to whom Sinclair tipped a fiver. Charlie gave me a glass. I said, "I'm on painkillers, I'd better not."

"Never mind," replied Sinclair merrily, and before we could object he had taken the glass back from us and handed it without a glance to Charlie. Charlie downed it in one, like it was vodka.

The second half didn't do much to resolve the crises of the first, but seemed to forget about them and carry on in its own strange way with a new story, involving a fool and a priest. All things were eventually sorted, courtesy of two stabbings and a bout of consumption that, for all it killed the woman who sang about it, didn't seem to get in the way of her vocal control. At the end of each good bit, the audience stood and went as wild as an operatic audience could. We leant on the edge of the box, chin rested on our hands, and watched, fascinated. We had never before encountered the full bizarre, hypnotising strangeness of opera, never imagined it would be so bright and big and loud, and just so much *so*.

When it was done, the audience cheered and the cast bowed for a brief eternity.

Sinclair clapped nicely and didn't cheer.

"Rather crude," he muttered. "Not the finest work."

Charlie just smiled. It was the smile of a man who'd sat through more opera than the eardrums could take, losing the ability to hear all frequencies in the soprano range, but not missing them one bit.

We drifted out into the departing crowd. It was lateish, that odd hour of the night when it's justifiable to go to bed, but somehow it's not honourable. Covent Garden was yellow washes of light and buzzing arcades, open doors and clattering chairs, tinkling music and strumming buskers; still alive, still heaving, despite the biting cold and settling fog, visible as a haze over the streetlamps.

"You won't say no to a little supper, will you?" said Sinclair, as Charlie carefully wrapped another layer of coat around his boss.

"Supper would be good."

"Excellent! I know a little place..."

The little place was a restaurant tucked into the tight dark streets between Covent Garden and the Strand, where long ago Dickens had feared every shadow, and thieves had lurked in alleyways now filled with hissing vents and rotting chips. It was the kind of restaurant that you could only go to if you knew about it. There was no menu on the door, no sign above, no indication in the brown-stained windows that, within this plain black door that could have been any stagehands' exit, here was a place to eat. The sense of unease, which the music had largely suppressed, returned to us.

Inside the door, taking Sinclair's coat and hanging it up behind great red curtains, was a man in a top hat and white gloves. We stared at him in amazement. He looked at us with barely hidden distaste and said, "May I take your coat, sir?"

I shook my head numbly. "I'd rather keep it."

"Of course, sir."

There were a pair of escalators, clad in bronze. One started as we approached, then carried us up a narrow stairwell lined with mirrors, also in bronze, that projected our warped faces at us to infinity. At the top of the stair was more red curtain, swished back by more white gloves, and an interior of dim lighting, copper and bronze, everywhere everything glimmering with twisted faded reflection. I was relieved to see other diners at the tables, and hear the low burble of good—mannered, wine-fed gossip. We were led to a circular table in the middle of the room, with three chairs already in place. We weren't given a menu; I guessed it was bad manners to ask.

"It's a very modern style," offered Sinclair to my look of bewilderment. "The chef here likes to experiment with some interesting ideas...not really my thing, of course, but interesting, nonetheless. An experience."

He knew us well.

I smiled, nudging a piece of cutlery in front of me that looked like it had escaped from an eye surgeon's trolley.

"So," said Sinclair calmly, "you're the Midnight Mayor."

"Yup."

"And how is that working out for you, Matthew?"

"Not too well."

"No, no, of course, no. It is of course none of my business and I wouldn't want to give the wrong impression, naturally, naturally, but as a friend I can't help but notice that you look a little pale."

"Yes."

"May I, in fact, make a great leap of judgement, and forgive me if I go astray here, but were you not, indeed, not planning on becoming the Midnight Mayor? It doesn't seem like the kind of career path you would choose."

"I didn't," I snapped. "The phone rang and I answered and next thing I know, whack. Some arsehole has gone transferring titles down the telephone line and I've got a hand like a boiled beetroot and four angry spectres after me."

"Spectres?"

"Four of them."

"How unfortunate. I take it the encounter didn't end too badly?"

"I got one in a beer bottle," I replied. "The others scarpered. At the time I thought they were sent by the same person who attacked me down the telephone. But now I think about it . . . they weren't sent to attack *me*, they were out looking for the Midnight Mayor. Drawn to it. You can't have that kind of transference of power without some sort of hitch."

"Spectres . . ." murmured Sinclair, "are unusual in this city."

"Yes."

Drink arrived—some kind of deep purple goo in a cocktail glass. Sinclair sniffed it and winced. "Yes," he murmured. "Well, experimental cookery. I believe that it's supposed somehow to complement the dishes, react with tannins or proteins or some such scientific curiosity. I won't be offended if you don't drink it, Matthew. Had you met Nair?"

He knew who the last Midnight Mayor was. Concerned citizens make it their business to know these things.

"No."

"Interesting."

I said nothing.

"You know, traditionally, the Midnight Mayor is . . . shall we call it a role? A duty, perhaps, a responsibility, something a bit more than a title. Passed on by the *will* of the previous incumbent to a chosen, well-trained and appointed successor. Usually an Alderman. Nair was an Alderman, before he was Midnight Mayor. It has been the way for generations. So why, dear boy, *why* do you suppose you have ended up with this . . . remarkable predicament?"

"I don't know."

"There must be a *reason*. Mystic powers, metaphysical forces, fate, destiny, choice, and so on and so forth. No such thing as coincidence, not in your particular, special line of work."

A plate of . . . something was brought before us. It looked like mashed intestine garnished with thistles. I poked it nervously with the end of a thing that might have been a fork. I had a feeling the dim light was meant to disguise the full horror of the food. I closed my eyes, we speared a mouthful, and ate it.

Could have been worse.

Out of the corner of my eye, I saw Charlie sniffing it uneasily. Sinclair tucked in, napkin folded over his collar.

"I assume you've done your research, that the city really is damned—not that I doubt it for a minute. I mean, we've all heard the rumours, naturally, all seen a few signs and generally agreed that when the Midnight Mayor—I mean Nair—is brutally murdered then things are inclining towards the dubious, if you follow me. You must have seen a few things, asked a few questions—one does not reach these conclusions lightly!"

I said, "'Give me back my hat.'"

"I beg your pardon?"

"'Give me back my hat.'"

"Did you have a hat, or is this a metaphor the elaborate nature of which currently evades my higher faculties?"

"It's everywhere. The words, the phrase. I didn't notice before, didn't look. But now I've started looking, and it's everywhere. On the pillars below Waterloo Bridge, on the walls in Willesden, above the dead ravens in the Tower, on the shutters of the shop where the London Stone should have stood, on the Wall of London. Give me back my hat."

"You are suggesting that this quaint request is somehow linked to your predicament?"

"Yes."

"How?"

"I don't know. But wherever bad things happen, there it is. The ravens in the Tower are dead, the London Stone is broken, the writing is on the Wall. These things have always been protectors. Keeping out the bad things in the night."

"What 'bad things'?"

"I have no idea. If I knew that, then odds are the bad things wouldn't have been kept out to begin with."

"I see your point."

"But as you said—spectres aren't common in London. And they did come looking for me, when I answered the phone. You destroy the defences, kill the ravens, who knows what will come out from beneath the paving stones? Someone deliberately did that, killed the ravens, killed Nair. It can only be bad news."

"And now you're in the middle of it," murmured Sinclair, more to himself than me, prodding a puddle of lumpy goo on his plate that might have been food. "How . . . controversial."

"Yes."

"And the odds are, Nair *chose* you."

"Yes. Odds are."

"Now why do you think he'd do that?"

I hesitated.

"You must have dedicated some thought to the question."

"I saw the face of the creature that killed him. That killed Nair."

"Oh? And what did he look like?"

"Just a guy in a suit. Pinstripe suit, ironed, clean. Slicked-back hair. Just . . . just a guy in a suit. He didn't even *touch* him, and there was so much blood and Nair was just . . . meat and bones by the time he was finished. I'd never seen . . . we'd never imagined it was . . . we will not die like that."

Sinclair leant forward, folding his chubby fingers together. "Ah. I think I understand."

"He had no smell. The fox saw it all, and we asked the fox, and the fox smelt nothing. The creature that killed Nair wasn't human. A guy in a suit and he wasn't human. Nair wouldn't have died if he wasn't Midnight Mayor. That's the reasoning, isn't it? You get a brand on the hand, protector of the city: come gobble me up all ye nasties. Come hunt for me, spectres and shadows. We will *not* die like that!"

"You don't know what it was? The thing that killed Nair?"

I shook my head. "No."

"But he looked like a man."

"Yes."

"But wasn't."

"No."

"I see. That could be problematic." Sinclair sighed, rolled back in his chair. Waiters drifted in, took away the plates. They had class — enough class not to ask how the meal was, but just to take it that you'd never eaten anything like it.

Finally, with a great huff that puffed out his red cheeks, Sinclair said, "Tell me about your shoes."

He asked it so casually, so distantly, that for a moment I didn't even notice the question. "What?"

"Your shoes."

"Why do you want to know about them?"

"They're hardly your style, Matthew, and that interests me."

"Give me credit," I snapped.

He smiled, little neat teeth in a round mouth. "Come, now, Matthew, come. You know that I take an interest in these things. The instant I heard that Nair had been killed, I thought 'trouble'. Then the ravens died, then the Stone was broken, and I thought 'how tedious, someone is out to destroy the protectors of the city'; and it seemed, in light of all these facts, a sensible, yes indeed, a most sensible precaution to do a little research. Naturally I checked up on you. Who else, I thought, who else can really muster the kind of supernatural clout to do these things? Who else could have killed Nair? Who else might be mad enough to try it?"

Our fingers tightened on the cutlery. "You know us better," we snarled.

"Yes, perhaps I do. Perhaps that was where the Aldermen made their mistake. I know about the Aldermen, Matthew. We have... mutual connections, in times of crisis. This is a time of crisis. But I'm sure you've noticed that. I know about the file in Nair's desk. It says, 'Swift has the shoes'. Now what exactly does this mean?"

I looked down at my shoes, then back up at him. I said: "I thought it was nothing."

"Well, that's what we thought about the graffiti, and now look where we are. Spectres in the streets. Let's assume for a moment that nothing is something and feel proud of ourselves for a grasp of the quantum, shall we? Tell me about your shoes. They're clearly not yours. While I would never judge your fashion sense..."

I snorted.

"...trendy red and black trainers several sizes too big for you are hardly what I would expect. Nair said, 'Swift has the shoes'. Why would that interest him so much? Why would he make you the Midnight Mayor?"

So, I told him.

*   *   *

First Interlude: The Sorcerer's Shoes
In which the story of a pair of trainers is recounted over dinner.

I said: "The shoes aren't mine. They belong to a kid. His name is Mo. Actually, his name is Michael Patrick Hall, but you can't be cool and be called Michael unless you've been to prison. So everyone calls him Mo. I've never met him. But that's really the point."

It happened without bothering to explain itself.

I was in Hoxton, the street market. I can't remember why. It can be hard, coming back. There are things, rituals, routines, that I had taken for granted. Not any more.

Anyway. Hoxton. The word is "trendy", but I don't know if it can be rightly applied. It's a mishmash. Great rows of terraced houses with new paint, next to boarded-up windows. Council estates rotting from the inside out, mould and crumbling dust dripping with water from broken pipes down the walls. New apartment blocks, all bright paint, fresh brick and steel; art galleries tucked in behind the local boozer, yoga centres nestling in between the old rip-off robbed-radio garages. Tandoori and chippy, Chinese takeaway and halal kebabs, kosher bakeries and low squatting greengrocers selling strange growths that might be vegetables. Clubs hidden away underground, the door just a door by day, a purple-lit cavern at night, guarded by big men in black. Social clubs where no one cares about the smoking laws, snooker tables underneath low neon lights; leisure centres, where every shoe squeaks on old varnished floors. Hoxton is a bit of everything, all at once, a low old grandpa squinting at the scuttling kids. There's magic in Hoxton, if you know where to look for it; enough to start a fire, although you'll never quite know what will catch.

There was a chippy in the street market. I went there one night, for no good reason. Because we smelt vinegar on the air and cannot resist fish and chips. It was late, maybe elevenish, the shops shut up, the usual left-over debris of the market billowing in the street. Broken splattered fruits, empty cardboard boxes, torn-up plastic bags. The guy serving up the chips was called Kishan, an Indian name, though he was as white and freckled as dirty snow. He had dreadlocks and dyed black hair, and an earring that wasn't just a piercing—it was a great round gaping hole, the size of a ten-pence piece, pushed out of his lobe by a plastic hoop. We were fascinated and appalled by it. I did my best not to stare.

I had plaice and chips and sat at a table in the window. Everything about the place was plastic, and just two squeaks short of sterile.

I had been there about half an hour when Kishan said, "Closing up, now."

I shrugged, and ate up faster.

"Hey, mate, you getting back OK?" he asked.

This is not something I usually get asked. Men don't ask other men if they're getting home OK, they just assume that beneath the frail, weak exterior lurks a muscle-building kung fu master fearless of ever being mugged. I said, "I'm fine, thanks."

He was uneasy, we realised. His eyes kept dancing from us to the window and back again. "Yeah," he muttered. "Sure."

I followed his gaze out of the window, but saw nothing but the slow rumpling billow of the litter in the streets. We finished the last chips, wiped our hands on the edge of the greasy paper, stood up.

"Hey, are you sure everything's OK?" I asked.

He looked at me sideways and said, "Yeah. Fine. Yeah. Just fine."

These things don't take much translating.

"Well, OK," I said. "'Night."

And we walked out of the chippy.

There's a phrase—curiosity killed the cat.

We are very curious. The world, this *living* world is so full of incident, strangeness, experience, event, happening so busy and so fast, that it's a wonder you mortals don't go mad. But you learn how to shut it out, to perceive only that which is relevant to you. You say things like—curiosity killed the cat. So very sensible. Such an unforgivable waste.

We are curious and, like I said, I didn't have much better to do.

We walked about fifty yards, then looked back. The street was bare. I turned up the collar of my coat feeling for those little enchantments sewn into the lining. Then I walked back. There was a doorway between a chemist and a bakery where I snuggled myself out of the wind. Waiting is an innately boring process. In the old days, men who watched and waited would smoke a cigarette, for something to do. We'd read detective books, devoured the films. Philip Marlowe, loitering in some handy bookshop opposite the staked-out joint, would find a girl with blonde hair, and glasses that transformed her when they came off, and they'd drink bourbon and talk about nothing in particular and everything, without it needing to be said.

That was there; this was Hoxton.

When it started, it was a smell. We thought there was an open drain somewhere, the wind carrying the sharp stench of it. Not turn-your-stomach sewage; it was too precise a bite. It went in via the tear ducts, then wriggled down the nose, and by the time it had drifted into pockets in your lungs and writhed down your gullet there was little sense left for the stomach to be repulsed by.

Then came the sound.

It was like plasters being peeled off hairy skin, all crackles and splats and slow ripping of a thousand tiny needles. It was like thick oil being poured out of a can from a great height, a long way off. I saw the lights go out in the chippy on the other side of the street, the shutters go down. Kishan came outside, and there was dread in his eyes, looking down the street, straight over me like I wasn't there, and now fear on his face, in every part of him. He had seen this before, I realised, smelt this before. In the chippy, he had been trying to warn me, get me away, and I hadn't gone. Now he stood in the street, frozen with a familiar fear that was no less for being a regular occur-rence. I followed his stare, and realised *why*.

The thing was yellow-white, with a surface ooze of thick olive-brown that sloshed out from its surface skin and trickled slowly down it like water off a fountain. It had no recognisable shape, but crawled up from a drain in the middle of the street in great splats, from a warping bubble of a body which extended limbs like a jellyfish extends its tendrils. It was a squid out of water, liquid but not so: its surface gleamed with slime but its innards were a viscous mass that split and parted and re-formed as it rose up between the grates like it was made of hot rubber. It had no eyes, no ears, no organs at all that I could see, but moved like a great slobbering amoeba down the street, trailing oil and grease. A snail-squid-amoeba-rubber thing, crawling up from underneath our feet, squeezing up from the sewers. I could give it a name; a simple name for a simple thing. It was a saturate.

Kishan stood in the street staring at it, jaw half-open, dribble pooling in one corner of his mouth. The thing was still gathering its dripping mass out of the drain thirty yards away. I walked briskly up to Kishan, poked him firmly in the shoulder and said, "Oi. You."

His head turned to look at me, his eyes stayed fixed. I poked him harder. "Oi. Sunshine."

His eyes flickered to me. "You," we snapped. "Run."

His body was smarter than his brain.

He ran.

We looked back at the beige-white thing crawling up from the drains. A puddle of yellow oil was building around its base, trickling out across the tarmac to lubricate the mass of not-flesh that composed the creature's not-body. I turned my fingers up towards the nearest lamp, snatched a bundle of pinkish light from it and cast it over the creature's head. It didn't care. Oblivious of me and my doings, it just kept dragging itself up. Now the size of a dog, now the size of a wolf, now the size of a tuna fish, now the size of a small car, the great mass of its dripping body rose from the drain, a pool of goo spreading around its spilling rolls of fat.

By my stolen light, I could see its body in more detail. Beneath the oil that flowed out of its skin, things moved within it. Half an old yellow chip burst to the surface for a second and then sunk back down; a torn condom slid down its flesh and spilt into the expanding puddle of oil at its base; a lost, broken and gouged teaspoon surfaced briefly at the top of its spilt bubble-body, and then sank back down into the churning flesh. We drew more light from another streetlamp, dragging it down close, fascinated by this strange, inhuman stench-splat growing upon the street, the size of a small car, the size of a large car, the size of a small truck...

Its flesh, if you could call it such, was held together by friction and hair. Not hair of its own, we realised, but human hair, webbed and matted and foul, spun over every part of it like a net, sometimes in thick dirty clusters, sometimes in sticky strands of every colour. It rose up in front of us, liquid fat flowing off and then rising from within, a constantly moving fountain of grease and oil; and now it was almost as wide as the street. And the smell! Its stink knocked us backwards, made our eyes water and our head spin. Now it was almost a storey high, a great wobbling blancmange, and the oil spilling off it had rolled almost as far as my feet, running down the gutters and then filling the centre of the street.

I stared up at it, and it seemed to look back at us, a sort of head-bubble twisting at the summit of its rolling form. There was a good reason why the magicians of the city feared the saturate: the grease-monster, the oil-devil, the demon of fat poured down the drain, of tallow and cookery grime, of burnt-up crispy bits and congealed animal liquids poured down the plughole. It was disgusting, foul, vile, an abomination and, just perhaps, a bit beautiful. Life is magic, and this thing of fat and tallow was so clearly alive.

Alive, and not a little angry.

We laughed, not because there was anything funny, but to have seen this sight. Then we tossed the stolen neon back to its tubes, and retreated a few paces from the bubbling oil at our feet. I threw my satchel to one side and looked for the nearest likely weapons.

And the saturate was shaking itself now, sending splatters of grease and dried fat onto the walls, pulling itself out of the drains with one last great *shloooop* and rolling forwards in its own liquid.

I looked round at the window of the chippy, threw my arm and my will at it and shattered the glass with a thought. Reaching past, I found the warm, familiar hum of gas in the mains: heat and fire to burn the fat. I dragged at it, pulling faster than I had planned, sucking out the smell and rippling it upon the air until the street was a mirage of twisted neon and competing stenches. Adrenalin kept us moving, backing away from the advancing tide of yellow-brown oil dribbling over the pavement and the tower of fat rippling in its wake.

My plan was easy; so very easy. We were going to burn it.

I spun the gas around me, let it fill and hiss and shimmer against the flesh of the rolling white saturate-slug. I pushed a tendril of it up towards the pink tube of a neon light—all I needed was a spark, just one and that would be it, so long saturate, goodnight and good luck with your next coagulation...

...and someone muttered, "OhJesusohGod."

I looked around and saw what I should have seen before: a woman, standing with her back pressed against the wall of a cobbler's shop, handbag draped in the crook of her elbow, high-heeled shoes and pasty face, staring up at the saturate with the frozen terror of a squirrel in front of a cement truck. There was oil around her feet, staining her shoes, sliding along the pavement like meltwater over sand.

For a moment, just a moment, holding on to the gas, the spark, woven tight into the palm of our hand, we thought about doing it anyway.

Then I crushed out the spark, let go of the gas, let it spill upwards from the street and roll in thick smelly shimmers towards the open air, stopped the spillage from the chip shop and turned my attention towards the woman. She was only a few yards from the main body of the saturate as it rumbled at slug's-crawl down the street; in a few moments more, she'd be lost behind it. Yellow fat and white drool ran down the walls beside her, shaken off the main body of the beast, and splattered on her black shoulder jacket. I shouted, "Move, woman!"

She didn't move, couldn't move, just saw rolling flesh as high now as a bus, stubby white limbs sprouting and shrinking back into the flesh like a hedgehog uncertain about growing spines.

"Move!" we screamed.

I looked up at the saturate, and it was so close now, so close, it didn't need to grow a mouth or teeth or jaws, it just needed to keep coming and that was it, death by drowning, drowning by fat. It would suck me up and crush me and the only question would be whether it was suffocation or broken bones that stopped our heart.

She was going to die like that too.

I ran. My feet slipped and went out beneath me the second I hit the oil; I crawled back up, human hair tangling between my fingers, warmish brown goo seeping through my trousers, sticking to my knees. I reached the pavement, staggered to my feet, and grabbed the frozen woman by the shoulders. The saturate was only a few feet away, it filled the world, the smell worse here than ever, making it hard to breathe.

I shook her, and she looked at me, jaw moving in silent prayer.

"Run," I hissed.

She didn't move.

We slapped her, not particularly hard, across the cheek. She blinked, once. I put my slippery hand into hers, and felt it slide straight out again. I grabbed her by the sleeve.

"Run!"

She jerked, started to move. I dragged her towards the end of the street; and it was right behind us. I could feel a dollop of white flesh dribble down the back of my neck as a limb reached out for us, shedding matter as it went.

At the end of the street was a park, dark and shut up for the night. I pushed the woman off the pavement into the street and shouted, "Get out! Move!"

She staggered back towards the park, half slipped and kept on staring, just staring at the thing coming after us.

No time to bother, too late, much, much too late. We turned to the saturate, thought again of fire, saw the fat and oil dribbling down our fingers and gave up on the idea as a bad one. We raised our head towards the rolling jelly-thing, vile, repulsive, amazing, and I said, "Veolia!"

It kept on coming.

Words have power. You just had to pick the right words. In the good old days, this involved a lot of Latin and some very fruity intonation. These days, the words were different, new, bright, and in this case, plastered on the sides of most refuse collection carts in London.

I raised my hands to the sky and called out, shouted into the air, "Veolia, Accord, Kiggen, ECT, Onyx, ELWA, in accordance with

Hackney Borough Council, you are contracted to collect, remove and recycle household refuse and waste..."

Still it kept coming.

"...all commercial and household refuse and waste produced within the boundaries laid down within Hackney Borough, Veolia, Accord, Onyx, I invoke you..."

Not ten yards away, it drew tendrils of dripping fat that crawled out towards me.

I screamed to the heavens, spread my fingers wide and prayed for magic, miracles and a speedy demise, "Geesink Norba collecting and recycling waste and refuse for you!"

And from somewhere behind the creature, there was the diesel-thumping roar of an engine coming to life.

I staggered back from the creature, slipped in oil, crawled towards the hypnotised woman, grabbed her by the sleeve. The roar behind the creature turned into the steady *thudathudathudathuda* of a badly tuned, unloved engine. It filled the street, echoed off the houses; and with it there was light now, a spinning yellow madness that flashed on-off-on-off too fast to see, an epileptic nightmare, reflecting like a sick sun off the walls. A great white limb of grease descended towards us and I pushed the woman out of the way, skidded to one side. It hit us across our back, we felt our teeth jar, our spine try to hide in our stomach, we felt fat dribble down our back and saw great dollops of it splatter onto the ground beside us. The blow had knocked us flat; on our belly we crawled towards the park, grass and dirt suddenly seeming the cleanest thing in the world. Slime was running down our hair and pooling in our ears. The yellow flashing light in the street cast twisted shadows all around.

"Geesink Norba," I whispered. "Geesink Norba, Geesink Norba, by the terms and conditions of contract to remove all commercial and household waste within the borough, Geesink..."

The roar became a rattling battle cry; with it, there came another sound. It said:

"Please stand clear. Vehicle reversing. Please stand clear. Vehicle reversing."

I reached the grass, rolled onto my back, looked down the street I'd crawled from and saw the saturate start to turn, infinitely slow, currents and counter-currents spinning within its great belly as it began to think about the thing that was behind it. The woman was fallen a few feet from me. I turned to her and hissed, "Cover your head."

She obeyed, and I curled up as tight as I could, arms over my skull.

I saw the saturate contort and twist as the flashing yellow light and mechanised voice came closer. I saw it seem to contract downwards and expand outwards, as if it was somehow going to leap. I heard, *"Please stand clear. Vehicle reversing,"* saw flashing yellow madness, heard wheels sloshing through oil, engine thundering, heard a sucking sound like the whole ocean being pulled down a very small plughole, heard a great grinding as of metal jaws, and whispered, "Veolia, Accord, Geesink Norba, Onyx, rubbish collected on your scheduled day..."

And something hit the saturate. It hit it smack in the middle, punched a hole straight through its belly and out the other side, a great darkness that seemed to suck everything in, and the darkness had teeth, heaven help the ignorant, the darkness had teeth made of aluminium and steel, silver flashing teeth that crunched down on all that fat and swallowed it whole into some forsaken black gullet, sucked it all in with a roar of diesel and pumped out black smoke in its place, until the saturate was half its size, a quarter, just rivers of white fat pouring into that darkness, sinking deeper and deeper until with a final splatter...

There was just oil and grease spilling across the road. Inanimate liquid, dribbling from the jaws of the beast that had sucked the life from it. Little blobs dripped from the branches of the trees like smelly snow. I got to my feet and looked at the thing that had killed the saturate.

It was a dustbin truck. Its sides were black, not through paint, but time and use. Burnt-black, charred-black, dirt-black, coal-black, every kind of black there could be, all spattered and scratched and scorched onto its flesh. The welding that held it together was brown chipped rust that shed breadcrumbs of reddish copper onto the ground as it drove; its wheels were the height of a large child; its light, spinning on a roof of twisted, crooked metal, was yellow, too bright and too fast to look at. I shielded my eyes, and saw in the dull remnant of my vision a man get out of the driver's cabin, a whole man's height above the pavement, and walk carefully round to the back of the truck. He knelt down beside it, reached under the back wheel, and twisted something. A great gout of black smoke burst from a pipe in the top of the truck's roof, and slowly, two metal vault doors began to ease shut over the open back of the truck, sliding down over silver teeth gleaming in the reflected light and dripping white fat. They came together with the clang of the doors of Fort Knox. The dustbin man looked up.

His eyes were two blown light bulbs, the little twisted wires gleaming in their sockets. His skin was the same charred blackness as his truck; his hair, which had one time been dreadlocks, was now just living blacknesses, writhing and twisting around his face with the mess of insect life and vermin that crawled from it. When he exhaled, the same black smoke of his vehicle rolled across his silverish lips, and as he walked, his green-yellow neon jacket shimmered and flashed, almost drowning out all other perception. I flinched back from the brightness of it as he approached, three-inch boot heels clanging on the ground, tangled old string tying together their ruptured leather and soles of melted rubber. He was coming straight towards me, impassive, face drained of all feeling. I turned to the woman and hissed, "Do you have a tenner?"

She was a whimpering huddle on the ground. "Uh?"

"A tenner, a tenner! Your purse!"

I covered my eyes with my arms against the brilliance of his jacket; but I could hear him, smell him only a few inches away: the rank odour of an old bin left out in the summer sun. Numbed, the woman tried to open her purse. I felt movement beside me, saw his hand gloved in thick red leather that oozed ancient blood between the old stitches, as if the fabric itself could bleed. The woman held up a ten-pound note. I grabbed it, turned and, keeping my head bowed against the neon dazzle, pushed it into his outstretched palm.

For a second, the dustbin man just stood there. I knew he was staring at me, but couldn't raise my eyes to see. Then he closed his fingers around the ten-pound note, which began to wilt, shrivel, and stain with smudged darkness as he slipped it into his trouser pocket. As stately and careful as he had come, he turned, dreadlocks writhing around his head, and walked away.

We stayed frozen in place for...I do not know how long.

The engine roared again in the dustbin truck, the wheels turned. I smelt black smoke and the lingering odour of rot. Then it drove away, oil dribbling off its wheels as it sped up the street, yellow light fading until, at the far end, it turned, and vanished from my sight.

Drained, we sank to our knees on the grass, pressed our head into it and trembled.

A hand brushed our shoulder. A voice said, "Um..."

We looked slowly up. "This," I said, "is a really bad time."

"You OK?"

I looked round me. Oil was dribbling into the drains, and a greasy trail stretched all the way up the street to the drain, that damned drain, outside the chippy.

"Curiosity killed the cat," I said, and pressed my head back into the grass and felt grateful for how clean the dirt was.

Her name was Loren.

Her world-view had just been shattered, but she was dealing with it the most sensible way she could; by dealing with other things first.

She said, "You owe me a tenner."

I said, "What?"

"A tenner."

"Are you seriously telling me, that having just saved your life from a monster made out of grease and fat crawled up from the nether reaches of the sewers, you want *me* to give *you* a tenner?"

"When you put it like that . . . it's just tenners aren't easy."

"It was give the guy a tenner, or be consumed by a supernatural dustbin truck."

There was silence. Fat dripped and pooled slowly around us.

"So why couldn't you give him a tenner?"

"Because I dropped my bloody bag while trying to save your bloody life."

"Sorry. It's all a little . . . you know."

She flapped. We seethed.

Finally she said, "The thing . . ."

Here it came.

"Yes?"

"You know, I always said to myself, if I go mad, I'll like, you know, go with it? Because I figure if you're mad then you can't really do anything about it so you might as well just . . . It was a monster, wasn't it?"

We wiped a dribble of fat off our nose. "That depends."

"On what?"

"Your point of view. In the sense that it would have crushed the life out of you and you would have drowned in a sea of animal fats and other remains, yes, it was a monster. But it meant you no harm. You just happened to be there."

"You killed it."

"No."

"I saw you, you spoke those words, magic words."

"Brand names."

"What?"

"Brand names. Waste collection companies. Geesink Norba, Accord, Onyx — they collect rubbish in the city."

"But . . . you spoke their names and . . ."

"I spoke words that, unless you pay close attention to these things, have no meaning. People don't pay attention to the rubbish men; they cross over to the other side of the street to avoid them. Geesink Norba...they are sounds on the air. Meaningless, unless you know how to look. I invoked an idea."

"What do you mean, 'invoked'?"

"Summoned. Commanded. Requested for the cost of a ten-pound note."

"You're some sort of wizard?"

"Some sort, yes."

"So there's magic? And wizards? And monsters?"

"Yes."

"In Hoxton?"

"Well, yes."

"Oh. And the thing that came? The dustbin truck?"

I tried my best. "There are...things in this world, made up of other things—ideas—that are given life just by the nature of that idea, by the nature of living, life making magic, magic coming out of the most ordinary, trivial bits of life. Like...like when you speak into the telephone and your words are life and passion and feeling and they're in the wires and sooner or later the wires will come alive or else they'd burst, with all that thought and emotion in them...or like a dustbin truck, just one dustbin truck because we have no idea how much waste a city can produce, just one tidying up afterwards, asking nothing but a tenner at Christmas and your council tax, anonymous faces picking up anonymous crap that no one wants to pay any attention to and sooner or later you ignore so much, you turn your face away so much, don't want to think about it so much that...even that gets life. Do you see? Furious, passionate life, waiting to be seen, cleaning up afterwards, struggling out of the shadows. And where there's life, any life, anything that..."

I saw her face. She was crying.

"I'm sorry."

"It's a bit..." she mumbled, waving her hands uselessly. "It's just...
uh..."

I said, "My name's Matthew."

"Loren," she whimpered.

"Where do you live, Loren?"

She flapped a hand in a general direction.

"Near?" I asked.

She nodded.

"With a shower and a lot of soap?"

She nodded again.

"Good. Let me take you home."

It was a council block a few streets back from the canal. On the
ground floor there were grey metal shutters nailed over the windows,
and bars across the front doors. The windows on the higher floors
had little balconies with dead flowers withering on them. The stairwell smelt of piss, the lifts were scarred on the inside with who knew
what mad burning. She lived on the fifth floor. The lights were on in
the flat to her left, and as we went by, the door was opened and a man
in a white skullcap leant out.

"Loren!" he exclaimed. "He's gone out again; I'm sorry." Then his
eyes fell over us, and his look turned to one of brief disgust followed
by forced concern. "Are you all right? What happened?"

"Fine," she mumbled, red puffy eyes and a swollen puffy voice.
"Thank you, fine."

There were three locks on her door. She fumbled with the keys,
dropped them, picked them up again, unlocked the door. A narrow
corridor, occupied 99 per cent by a black sports bike, all pumps and
shallowness; a single bulb swinging from a low ceiling, lampshade
long since lost. She waved me towards a kitchen the size of a cock-
roach's cupboard and said, "You can help yourself to whatever you
want."

I looked at an array of empty pizza boxes and used tea bags.

She headed into the bathroom. As the shower went on, the boiler above the sink started rattling and roaring, shaking so hard I thought it would pull itself free from the wall. I made do with rubbing my hands on an old dishcloth and my face with some kitchen towel, until I just felt thinly slimy, rather than all-over glooped. From the kitchen window, I could see Hackney, low lights and uneven streets, council estates and long, Victorian-lamp-lit terraces, stretching away.

Loren emerged from the shower, disappeared into the bedroom. Her voice drifted to me: "You can use it, if you want."

I wandered from the kitchen into a small living room, containing a single brown sofa and sunflower wallpaper that had never been a good idea, even before it started to peel. There were shoes every-where — men's shoes, and boys', strewn in boxes and around every wall, and dirty clothes, tracksuits and baggy jumpers, messy old plates and fallen library books with catchy titles like *Pass GCSE IT in 28 Days!* and *Foundation French for Dummies*.

A door opposite the living room had, among a collection of post-ers featuring everything from dinosaurs to heaving models with extra-heaving bosoms, a sign written in big red letters — KEEP OUT. A boy then — a teenage boy.

"Take some of Mo's clothes! Towel's under the sink." Loren's voice carried from the bedroom.

Clearly Mo was not in residence. I opened the KEEP OUT door, and was hit by the smell of tomato ketchup and hair gel. I rummaged through the wardrobe until I found a T-shirt and a pair of trousers, both too big for me. Whoever, wherever Mo's father was, he had clearly evolved from another breed of men.

The shower was at once the most pleasurable and most disgust-ing experience of our life. The water kept drifting from hot to cold, and only scalding hot and the application of half a bar of soap could remove the grease that wanted to cling to every part of our skin. Our hair was like raw slices of chicken in our slipping fingertips, and bubbles of white fat spun in the stained old plughole.

I changed into Mo's clothes. In the kitchen Loren was wearing pyjamas, a dressing gown, and fluffy pink slippers. She leant pale-faced by the sink, cradling a hot mug of tea between her hands and looking at nothing. I raised my grease-spattered clothes. "Uh..."

"Just stick them in the washing machine, OK?"

I turned the machine up hot, threw in powder and watched it go. We do not understand why people who watch the workings of the washing machine are mocked. Meditation classes and serene chants have nothing on the slow turning of socks in soapy water.

She gave me a mug of tea and said, "Sorry, I don't have any..."

"Thank you. This is fine."

I felt I should say something more. "Look, I can just go, once..."

"Are you human?"

The question caught us off guard. "What?"

"Are you human?" she asked.

"Yes." Mostly.

"Oh. Then, I mean, what happens now? Like in films, and on TV, there's rules, like amnesia and stuff. I mean, is there...?"

"No. I'm sorry."

"OK. Uh, I can't afford counselling; so, if you could just..."

"I can go," I said.

She gave up, seemed to shrink into her dressing gown, became, for a second, aged. I wondered how old she was: a young voice from a lined face, dark hair greying at the edges. "Look," she said, "you seem like a nice guy. I mean, you saved my life, so I figure, you can't be all shit, unless this is some cunning plan of yours to be like a rapist or something, in which case I figure...

"I mean, what I'm saying is that I get up at six-thirty every morning to go to work and come back at six-thirty every evening and make pasta for supper and watch the telly and go to bed at ten-thirty and on the weekends I clean up and see some mates and my kid is... and you know, sometimes there's guys and that's nice and I get support from the council and there's like so much fucking paperwork you would not believe and it's just...it's ordinary, get it? Five hours ago, it was just..."

"Ordinary?" I suggested.

"Just tell me it was a coincidence. A thing came up from the sewers, and it was just luck, right?"

"Yes," I replied. "Bad luck, to be exact, but still just luck. There was no reason for you to be there, no reason for it to be there. It just happened. Sometimes things do just happen."

"You don't sound like you believe that."

I shrugged. "I guess sooner or later the rationale is, I just happen to be crossing the road when a car comes and knocks me down, and he's only there and I'm only there for a world of reasons an infinity apart and because it was going to happen to someone, so why not me?"

"Why were you there?"

"We wanted fish and chips."

"How come you can do things?"

"It's just a point of view. I'm a sorcerer. It's just a way of seeing things differently. That's all."

"Sorcerer."

"Yup."

"Like, big beards and stuff."

"Times have changed. You can always tell you're being sold a bad product if it comes attached to a pentangle star. New times — new magics. Different symbols."

"Symbols? Like spells?"

"Sort of."

"Show me."

"You don't want to —"

"Show me!"

So I did. I got a piece of paper and drew a sign of power, a protective ward. She looked at it, unimpressed. "It's the Underground sign."

"Yes."

"Oh, God. You are a whack-job."

"You're not listening. Life *is* magic. Ideas, symbols, words, meanings. New meanings, new words. In the old days if you wanted to banish a demon you invoked the powers of the winds, north and south. These days, you summon Geesink Norba. In the old days, a wizard would call on silver moonlight to guide them through a monster's lair. These days, we summon sodium light and a neon glow, and the monster's lair tends to have a trendy postcode and pay council tax."

"You make it sound..."

"Ordinary?"

"Boring."

"It's not boring. Keep away from it."

And she looked at me, at us, she looked us in the eye, and wasn't scared. She took our hand. Clean fingers, dry from soap. She said, "Do you have a home?"

"Not really."

"Why not?"

"I lost certain things."

"Where do you live?"

"I move around."

"Do you have a job?"

"Sometimes. It's not very glamorous."

"Do you pay income tax?"

"No. I did, though, before...I did pay tax."

"What's your favourite food?"

We licked our lips. "Too many choices."

"Where did you last go on holiday?"

Hard to remember. A world ago, a different meaning. "Istanbul."

"What's your favourite colour?"

"Blue."

"Worst bus route."

"91, Crouch End to Trafalgar Square. It gets stuck up at Euston, crawls round King's Cross, takes for ever—faster to walk."

"Favourite..." she drawled, "...favourite ice cream flavour."

"Too many choices."

"Everyone has a favourite flavour."

"Strawberry. Although it depends on how sunny it is."

"All-time best memory."

"Living," we said instinctively, and was surprised to hear our own words.

"Tad tossy," she replied.

"There's a story."

"Worst memory."

"Dying," I said.

"And you're not smiling."

"No."

"You know what—not going there."

"Probably for the best."

"Matthew," she said firmly, "will you stay here tonight?"

She slept in the bed; I slept on the floor.

She didn't sleep. At three in the morning she got up and pronounced, "Buggerit."

We watched TV, wrapped in duvets. You haven't seen bad until you've seen 3 a.m. TV. It made *EastEnders* look like class. At 3.30 a.m. she put on a DVD. It was some kind of fluffy romantic thing, that baffled and bemused us in equal measure. At 4.00 a.m., without ever planning on it, Loren fell asleep at just the right angle to trap my legs and sever blood supply to my left arm. I didn't move. It wouldn't have been right.

The boy got the girl, the girl got the boy, they sailed away beneath the Golden Gate Bridge as fireworks went off in the background. I thumbed the DVD player off with the remote control, watched a bit more telly, and eventually, even we fell asleep as the first touch of sunlight slid through the window in the smallest hours of the morning.

*   *   *

My friends are dead. That, or they think I'm dead. But most of them are dead. They died. They were killed; murdered. Just like me. The annihilation of everyone who stood in the path of Robert Bakker and his shadow.

Dana Mikeda helped us and died. My apprentice, grumbling, to-the-point Dana Mikeda who had stood over my grave when I died and helped me when we returned and for her pains, her neck had been torn apart by the shadow of Robert Bakker. An act of spite; pure spite. Vera helped us, and her body is paint on the floor, a bullet spinning in the colours. I say sorcerer and people are afraid; we say blue electric angels, and people run from us as though we were vengeance and fire sent upon them for their sins. Why should we care for their failures?

Dead friends dead for me.

We still do not, to this day, understand why I gave Loren my mobile number.

I left after breakfast. She had work to do, was already late. Work is routine, routine is ordinary, and there is always some salvation to be found in the ordinary.

There was some passing time.

A few weeks.

She called me once, in the middle of the night, crying. She was hearing sounds, strange sounds. I came round. The kid's bedroom was empty again, but she didn't speak about that. The sound turned out to be from a mouse. I don't know how it had got in, but the thing was in the kitchen, confused, rattling around trying to find its way out. I crooned pretty sounds at it until it came out from where it was hiding behind the washing machine, stroked its tiny back, not as long as my thumb, let it run into the palm of my hand and told it firmly that here was not the place to be. Then I went away again. Ordinary routine; get up, go to work. Safety in ordinary. Nothing needs to be said or done that isn't...

...ordinary.

Then one day—only a few days ago, it seems longer—she rang me.

She said, "My son has gone."

His name is Mo. He is seventeen years old—just the wrong age to be almost anything. He dropped out of school, wants to be a stuntman. Drives fast motorbikes, none of which are ever his own.

His room is a biological warfare strike zone.

His shoes are two sizes too big for me.

She said, "My son has gone. Please—the police have looked and can't find anything. His friends have gone. It's been four days. He's been gone before, but not four days. And there was...things have been...please."

Mothers are the last people you should ask about their seventeen-year-old sons.

The police said he was a kid heading for trouble. Some graffiti, some vandalism, some "anti-social behaviour". ASBO kid. All hood and attitude, proud to be against the law, proud just to be against. And there was something else—his friends were missing too. Kids he'd met not at school, but at a club, she didn't know what kind of club it was. Somewhere in North London, a club where the kids went. Or maybe the kidz. You can't be cool and spell well at the same time.

Never ask a mother about their kids.

Far more sensible to ask their shoes.

It's a lie that women care more than men about their shoes. Women may buy more pairs, to match up with this or that outfit, or to serve this or that purpose, but they do it easily, with a casual statement of "I'm going to buy some shoes now".

Men, when they buy shoes, invest body and soul in the effort. This is not just a pair of shoes — this is *the pair of shoes*, the one and only; they have to be perfect, they have to be right.

Mo was a kid who liked his shoes. Every six months he seemed to have invested what little money he had in a new pair, sometimes Nike, sometimes Adidas, never anything in between, always the right brand, at the right time. This month, gold with blue stripes was in; this month, and black and white football boots, spikes sticking out of the soles, were the only things to have.

"What's the most recent pair?"

Loren pointed at a pair of red and black trainers, all sponge and wheeze. I tried them on for size. Too big. I put on some more socks, tried them again, shifted round until my weight was right.

"What are you going to do?" she asked.

"Go for a wander."

"Can you find him?"

"Dunno. I'll do my best."

"If you find him . . . don't say anything, will you? It'll only make it worse if you say something."

She gave me a photo. It's in my bag. The kid is ugly. He has a big head made bigger by having shaven off his hair. His jaw alone could demolish an old wall; his mouth is too small for the length of chin that surrounds it.

I left my shoes with Loren, a promise that I'd come back, and walked out of the door with the kid's shoes on my feet.

It is surprisingly hard to scry by footware. It requires a submergence of will, an utter belief that your feet know where they're going. Sometimes magicians learn how to do this by literally blinding themselves, tying rags over their eyes so that they have to trust entirely in the direction their body takes them, and never question, never doubt, that this is where they have to be. The problem about that is that a pair of shoes, while it may remember where it wants to go, is less likely than a brain to stop at a red light.

You need just enough awareness to stay alive, to stay smart, but not so much that you ever take control. Never question, never doubt. Just take a deep breath, and start walking.

So that's what I did. Let the door to Loren's flat click shut behind me, and started walking. I was lucky — there was only one way in and out of the flats, and that gave me momentum, got me going in the right direction without having to think about it. I walked out of that council block behind the canal, to the end of the street and kept on walking, past fenced-off football fields, past empty grass greens, past a Costcutters and a grand new development built up from the remnants of a warehouse; and my walk wasn't my own.

I was *swaggering*. I was swinging my hips and bouncing at the knees, I was walking to an invisible hip-hop beat and only a second of awareness short of gesturing in the inexplicable, untold language of all wannabe bros out to be cool. That was good — now I knew that I was swaggering, it gave me a way in. If the spell was ever broken, a good swagger, and the shoes could take over again, recognise a familiar step, find the key to the magic.

So I swaggered, past old schools with portable cabins in the playing fields to make room for big classes pressed into a small space, past a swimming pool smelling even on the outside of thick chlorine, past little roundabouts which every driver swept across, careless of the rules of the road, past clamped vehicles and old broken telephone boxes. There was a bus stop, request; and seeing it I started to run, a strange, sideways lope, that made me feel like I had rickets. You can't be cool and run for a bus; but I did, and got on it, knowing with absolute certainty that this was the right thing to do.

I swaggered to the back of the bus, the bottom deck, and sat myself in the darkest, hottest corner, knees stuck out, one foot propped up on the seat in front of me, hands draped out across the back of the bus like it was a throne and me the king. It's easier if your whole body speaks the same language as your shoes; it's another way to keep the spell.

At Old Street, my feet jerked towards the door and I followed, head bopping to a beat that even I couldn't hear. I ambled down a long curved ramp, past several beggars, and didn't give them a single penny. I would have—*we* would have—but not these shoes; they moved too fast, too cool, they weren't going to stop.

It was late—rush hour dribbling to an end. I bounded down the escalator, elbowing passengers out of my way, swaggered onto the northbound platform, found a bench, sat on it, legs stretched out to occupy two seats with one movement, waited. The shoes hated waiting, tapped and fidgeted, but it was the Northern Line—waiting was what you did.

Train to King's Cross; there we changed, going west to Baker Street; there we got out, and bought some kind of pasty that burnt through the paper that held it, ate it, crumbs across the seats, and rode the Jubilee Line north to Dollis Hill.

Dollis Hill. The area round the station felt not so much built as dropped down in a game of Monopoly. White houses too small for the floors they contained, streets too narrow for the cars that crawled through them.

Tired. It is tiring, sharing the journeys of a stranger. Late, now, late and no supper. I forced myself to walk like a human being when I came to the first pizza parlour that was open, ordered food, devoured it. It was past eleven when I finished, and my feet in my borrowed shoes felt like soggy prunes.

I walked again. Swaggered to get back into the feel of it, bobbed my head, twisted my hips, let the rhythm of the movement restore my confidence. We walked...miles. I don't know how many. There were...things. Strangenesses. We would come to places and just stop and stare, and our feet would itch and we would see things, that... that made us uneasy.

A length of wall beside a quiet pub, where drunken youth should have sat, guffawing at passers-by and scaring the old ladies, and where now there was nothing. Just shadow and empty beer cans.

A skater park beneath a railway bridge, the wooden slopes empty, and on the walls, old graffiti.

Δοσ μον πισο το Καπελο μου

Or:

ΗΜΓ ΓΜΟ 2

Or:

FREE PALESTINE

There should have been something more. A "Mo was 'ere" wouldn't have gone amiss. There was . . . a strangeness. A bite in the air, like the distant taste of the street from inside the tree-sheltered stretches of an urban cemetery. A sense of something that should have been, but wasn't any more.

So we kept on walking, our swagger losing some of its confidence as the hours rolled by and all the places where there should have been something — the pub showing the football, the empty skater park, the closed off-licence, the houses with their lights turned down — there was nothing.

And then a telephone rang.

It was the small hours of the morning by then, and we were still walking, just walking and walking and the shoes wanted to go further, but a telephone rang, somewhere near Dudden Hill Lane.

And it was . . .

. . . of course we were going to answer but . . .

. . . it is our nature . . .

I had no reason.

We just had to.

*   *   *

"Well. You know the rest.

A telephone rang in Willesden, between Dollis Hill and Dudden Hill Lane. It rang at 2.25 in the morning, and I, despite having Mo's shoes on my feet, I went and answered it. I answered the telephone and after that...

...I guess my priorities changed.

I thought he was just some missing kid. We had no reason to think of it as anything else. I went looking for him in order to help a friend. Then the phone rang and we answered and all this began: the Midnight Mayor, the spectres, the dead ravens, the broken Stone, Nair, Vera, the Aldermen. It all happened and we were caught in it and didn't think, didn't stop to think that Loren would be...

...didn't stop.

I think that's all I can really say on the matter."

*   *   *

I finished talking.

Sinclair was eating something that looked like a miniature version of Table Mountain, carved out of yellow goo and black grain. He took a careful sliver, and ate it. He put his fork down. He dabbed at his round lips with the end of a napkin. Charlie's food sat uneaten on the plate in front of him. We scraped something that might have been gravy on the end of our fork, and licked. The restaurant was emptier, people gone on to a sexy midnight time, or maybe just to bed, only a few tables still inhabited in the gloom.

At last he said, "Well..." And then stopped. Then tried again. "Well, what times you have been living. You know, saturates are..."

"Rare. Yes. I know."

"Saturates and spectres."

"Both rare."

"And you seem to walk into both—unfortunate, so very unfortunate."

"We're rare too."

He smiled, a knife-thin flash of teeth in a great stretch of mouth. "So," he said at last, "what do you propose to do about all this?"

I hesitated. "Well, there's some choices."

"Such as, Matthew, such as?"

"One—run away."

"A somewhat ignoble suggestion, perhaps, in light of your otherwise gentlemanly conduct so far."

"Two—find the creature that killed Nair."

"That would make some sense."

"No it wouldn't. If it could flay him alive without trying I have no reason to believe it wouldn't do the same to me. It would be madness. Pointless. Suicide by pinstripe suit. Besides, I have every confidence that if I stick around long enough, trouble and abuse can find me out just fine on their own terms. Which leaves option three—find the kid."

"You're not interested in this...this curious writing on the wall? This 'give me back my hat'?"

"I am interested. But I don't know what I can do about it. If Nair was looking for Mo, then he must be more important than I thought. He said—Swift has the shoes. Their only use is finding the kid. Nair was killed only a few miles from where I was when I let the shoes carry me walkies. And we promised...I promised to help her. Loren. What else can I do?"

"So you're going to, as it were, carry on as normal? Continue doing what you were doing, regardless of the fact that you are now Midnight Mayor, last defender of the city, protector of the magicians and midnight magics of the streets, saviour and general all-purpose valorous champion and so on and so forth?"

"Yes. Pretty much."

"I imagine the Aldermen won't be entirely pleased about that."

"That's why I wanted to talk to you. I don't want the Aldermen involved. I don't want anything to do with them. I know you have ... connections."

Sinclair sighed, long and low. "Yes," he said at last. "I have connections. It is my business, my pension, if you will, to have connections. To keep a keen interest on matters such as these — tiresome though it can be. But you have to understand, Matthew, having connections is about much, much more than being a messenger boy. I can inform the Aldermen that you are the Midnight Mayor, ask them to help you or, if you really feel it is necessary, to leave you alone. Of course I can do this, of course.

"But then how will they feel about me, who let you walk away into an almost certain — as certain as these things can be for yourself — almost certain death, without clarifying what is going on, what the brand on your hand means, what *must* happen for the good of all? It is a fine balance, keeping my connections. Sooner or later you have to make some sacrifices."

It wasn't just the way he said it.

We reached for the nearest knife.

"Bang," said a voice. "Bang."

It was a woman's voice. It was accompanied by a woman's hand. The hand went round my neck, fingers under my chin, pulling it back. The other hand was somewhere nearby. Probably at the other end of the gun pressed into my skull. We recognised the voice.

"Bang," she said.

"Oda," we whispered. "We wondered."

That's the problem with psycho religious nutcases. They're never there when you need them. And when you could really do without, they decide to crash the party. Oda had never been a social animal.

Sinclair stood up, pulled the napkin from his throat and folded it up neatly in front of his plate. "I am honestly sorry about all this," he intoned. "But while I trust you, Matthew, to come round eventually and do the right thing, or at the very least, the thing that needs to be done, there is no guarantee I can offer in heaven or earth that *they* won't take the first option you happened to suggest, and just run. Fire and light and freedom and life, isn't that how it goes? Terror and love of life, so big and so bright that you think you'll drown in it? Too big and too bright to ever let go. I am sorry, Matthew, that for their sake this has to happen."

I tried to turn my head; Oda's fingers pinched into my throat, her arm pressed against my windpipe. She leant in close, so close her breath drifted over my eyes, and whispered again, "Bang." I could just see the blackness of the gun out of the corner of my eye; you can't outrun bullets. The other guests in the restaurant didn't seem to be paying any attention, were bent over scrupulously studying their dishes, not looking up, the buzz of good-mannered chit-chat continuing in the gloom. A waiter came over, laid down the bill in a leather case by Sinclair's plate.

"If you kill us," we hissed, "what will happen then to the Midnight Mayor?"

"You pose an interesting and pertinent academic question," exclaimed Sinclair. "One that, in truth, I have never really considered until now. No doubt the brand will move on to some other unfortunate, who will no doubt be as confused as you were to discover themselves so cursed. Or blessed, I suppose, depending on your point of view. Traditionally the Midnight Mayor could control these matters, command them before he died—but then, I don't think you really know how, do you? You have no idea what it really *is* to be the Midnight Mayor, because as I believe you yourself have suggested, you don't even believe he exists. Thankfully," he exclaimed, flicking open the leather case with the bill and glancing down the list, "there are concerned citizens willing to consider this possibility in further analytical depth that I, alas, in my ignorance, cannot."

He turned his head. I couldn't see what he was looking at, who he was smiling at; there were just shadows, noise in the corner of my vision. But I could guess. Charlie was on his feet as well, reaching into his pocket for something, a slim black box from which came a slim silver needle attached to a very small glass tube.

We snarled, "Keep away!"

"Bang," whispered Oda in our ear. "Bang three to the chest two the head. Bang, bang."

"Oda," I whimpered. "Please, Oda, this isn't..."

She didn't care. Or if she did, I couldn't tell.

There was some sort of drug behind the needle.

It had my name on it.

Lights out. Goodnight and good luck with your next coagulation...

...sweet dreams my sweet...

End of the line...

Darkness.

Part 2: All Roads Lead to Kilburn

In which a pair of shoes gets to complete its journey, a plot is discovered and the death of cities gets dust on his suit.

Her name was Oda. I didn't know her last name, and it was more than possible that she didn't either. She believed in magic, the same way the Pope believed in Satan. Vera had always called her psycho-bitch. It wasn't far wrong. I knew she killed magicians. I hadn't thought she'd do it to me.

And the Lord said — let there be light.

And lo it came to pass that the nine-volt battery was invented, shoved into a torch, stuffed into the right hand of a woman and shone in our eyes.

We kicked out instinctively. Our foot hit the torch, sent it flying back, struck the hand that held it, knocked it to one side. It occurred to us that we had to be lying down, and lo, that also came to pass. We rolled to one side, tried to get up, found our eyes were full of water and our stomach full of grit, crawled onto our hands and knees and verily the Lord God smote us with the butt of a 9 mm pistol swung by a woman known mostly, of course, as psycho-bitch.

There was a lot less light.

There was a bit of time. There was some blood. Mine, I guessed. It seemed the norm.

I was aware of hands pulling at mine. I turned my head and saw somewhere on the other side of the equator my right hand, stretched out on a dirt floor popping with weeds. Someone was pulling off my glove, unwrapping the bandage. A lot of light was being shone on my hand. I twitched my fingers and a boot — big, black, with straps instead of laces, in case you hadn't got the idea — pressed down on my wrist hard enough for us to cry out, turn away, losing sight of the scrabbling at my palm.

We felt the bandages peel away. We heard a voice, male, mutter, "Fuck shit."

The pressure on my arm relaxed.

Faces crowded in to look closer at my hand. I recognised some of them. Earle, Kemsley, Anissina and, behind them, others, more men and women dressed in preacher's black, peering in with a collection of torches and rifles, examining me and my damned hand. Oda. A face almost as dark as her close-cropped hair. She had the damn gun pointed at my face, not in an offensive way, but casually, as if it had just happened to flop there from the end of her trigger-pulling fingers. She looked at the brand on my hand and there was nothing there but contempt.

"You're in trouble, sorcerer," she said.

I tried to speak. My voice was trapped somewhere behind a great warty toad that had taken up residence at the entry to my lungs, inspecting each molecule of air one at a time on their way up and down.

Earle's face appeared upside down over mine. I was lying on my back in dirt and weeds. I could taste . . . magic of a sort, but different. Distant, shut away. He said, "How did you get this?"

He meant our hand.

I licked my lips and croaked, "Nair."

"Nair what?"

"He did it. He gave it to me."

"No."

"He did."

"He would *never* have let you be Midnight Mayor. How did you get this?"

"The phone rang. I answered."

"Tell me the truth!"

"I am."

"He is." Oda's voice, calm and level.

Earle's face flashed with anger. "You have nothing to do with this," he spat. "You and your people are not involved."

"I was invited here for a reason," replied Oda calmly. "The Order was invited here for a reason. I know the sorcerer. He's telling the truth."

"What makes you sure?"

"I know him."

"Is that it?"

"Yes. That's it."

"That's *nothing*," snapped Earle. "The Midnight Mayor is an Alderman, that's how it's done. It passes from one Alderman to another, has done for hundreds of years, never moves outside the circle. No one outside would understand what's necessary, what is *needful* to be done. Nair would not have chosen this creature!"

A toe prodded the side of my head. It wasn't meant to be a hard kick, not particularly, but it was my brain and it was a tough leather shoe and I wasn't at my best. I could hear the thump of it roll like the sea in my ears, feel the soft tissue of my brain bounce nervously against the sides of my skull.

Kemsley said, "What happens if we kill him?"

I said, "End of the line." We laughed, let it roll up the desert of our throat. "End of the line!" we cackled, "End of the line!"

"Get him up."

Earle had authority. A pair of arms helped get me up. I slouched in them for all I was worth, making their lives hard, from spite mostly. Grass and trees, dead leaves and black twigs. We were in a park somewhere, a big park, couldn't even hear the traffic. Trimmed hedges and neat rectangles of mud that might one day hold flowers. Smart, to take an urban sorcerer to a park. Things were harder here.

Earle's face looked scalded, anger turning him livid pink. He prowled up and down in front of me; I didn't bother to watch, but counted the beats of my heart, matching them to each turn he made.

"Sinclair thinks he's telling the truth," said Oda at last. "He's good at being right."

"What do you care?" snapped Kemsley.

"I am thinking of the sorcerer's use," she replied. "I have no love for his kind, and find this situation as ugly as you do. But let's not deny how useful he can be."

We raised our head, grinned at her, tasted blood on our lips. "She's thinking about *it*," we said. "She's scared too—scared mortal, little scared human, seen a man turned to meat, seen a human reduced to raw flesh, so scared—"

Someone without a sense of humour kicked us behind our knees. We cried out and sank forwards. Our hand was aching and burning, the red crosses carved into our skin smarting in the cold air.

"These things," hissed Kemsley, "can't be allowed to desecrate the Mayor!"

"Which things?" we demanded. "Do you mean me? I am us and we are me, we are me and I am us." Then we laughed, and turned our face back to Oda. "It's all right to be scared," we hissed. "The fox was scared, so why shouldn't you be?"

"What's he saying?" snapped Earle, to Oda, not to me.

She shook her head. "Not *him*," she replied. "*Them*."

"No," I snapped. "Me. I think you're scared too. You're all scared. Because here's what it boils down to—you kill me, someone else will become Midnight Mayor. Maybe one of you. And then what will you do? Go and find the thing that killed Nair? Go stand in front of it just like Nair did and have the skin carved away from your bones by a piece of paper? Go turn from walking human with a brand in the hand, to dead meat with no skin left on your bones? Isn't that what you're thinking?"

"You assume we think you're innocent," snapped Earle.

"You know I didn't kill Nair. You're an arrogant arsehole, but even you, *even* you will have had time now to find the evidence. You'll have gone to Willesden, you'll have found my blood on the phone, you'll have talked to the foxes, talked to the pigeons, done all the things you should have done at the beginning if you hadn't been so stupid! Stupid blundering stupid bastards who took one look at the dead Mayor and thought, 'Ah-ha, let's go beat up a sorcerer. Hey, the apprentice of Bakker is still alive, and he should be dead, because he was last time; let's go shoot him just to be on the safe side!' Well up yours with a pineapple, lights out, good night, good luck, good evening, goodbye, good—"

Earle hit me. It was pure anger, pure anger and redness and scalded fire, a backhand swipe like a girl, wearing as many rings as a girl, with the strength of a man. We fell away, pain and fury and indignation burning every part of us, tasted blood in our mouth, wanted to set it on fire, just a little fire, a little blue electric fire and then they'd burn...and...

Oda said, "As I understand it, you're hitting your new master. Don't let me stop you. Tear each other apart."

I dragged my head up, fighting fire and blue sapphire fury. Something was wrong with my left arm, I could feel hot blood rolling over the pain. "She gets it," I whispered. "She understands. You kill me, then one of you will have to deal with all this shit. One of you will have to get flayed alive. There's a lot of you, so it's fairly good odds, but carry on like this and there'll be less and less and less of you. The thing that killed the ravens destroyed the Stone and killed the Mayor and it makes sense, if you're going about killing a city's defences, it makes sense to take out the Aldermen next. So shoot away—get on killing. It'll only speed things up. Fire, flood, crumbled, crushed, cracked, splintered, shattered, torn, tumbled—pick one. The city is going to be ripped apart because no one stops it. End of the line."

Earle's puffed angry face, Kemsley's not much better, Anissina behind them, doubt working its way down the arch of her eyebrows. I could feel blood seeping through my shirt. I looked down, saw redness crawling downwards and upwards and all around. I stammered, "You...you tore a..."

Never finished the rest.

*   *   *

She said, "Drink."

I said, "Uh?"

She repeated, firmer, "Drink."

I opened my eyes and was dazzled. I closed them again. I put one hand over one eye and risked opening the other a fraction, waited for that to get comfortable, then opened it the rest of the way. The dazzle was just a glow, a bedside lamp by a bed, bulb turned away to the wall. I risked opening my other eye, peering out between my fingers. Dazzle faded to glow. Somewhere distant and close all at once, a train rattled by. Oda sat on the end of the bed. There was a gun in her lap, and a humourless thing that looked stolen from the samurai section of the Victoria and Albert Museum perched by her right knee. She was holding a plastic cup towards me. It had a straw, and was full of a sharpness that could well have been orange juice.

She said, "Drink."

I took the cup in one hand. The arm that held the hand that held the cup was bare. The arm was joined to my shoulder. The shoulder was tied onto the rest of me by an igloo of fresh bandaging. I stared at it, stared at the orange juice, stared at her. I said, "I tore a stitch."

"Yeah," she sighed. "I noticed."

"You put a gun against my head!"

"You sound surprised," she said. She did not.

"No, not really. Just a little..."

"Disappointed?" She also had a cup of orange juice. She slurped from it through a stripy pink and white straw. "You know, sorcerer," she said, "I was always planning on killing you one day."

I did not credit Oda with a sense of humour. "Why haven't you?" I asked.

"The usual."

"Which usual?"

"Greater pictures, lesser evils."

"Oh. That usual."

"Make no mistake," she added. "You are the spawn of the Devil and will burn in all eternity for your sins, for your godless, soulless existence as arrogant minion of Beelzebub upon this earth. The fact that you may be useful to the greater good is neither here nor there as regards the inevitable destruction of your warped spirit."

"Thank you, Oda," I said, letting my head fall back against the pillows of the bed. "I'm pleased to see you too."

I drank orange juice, and looked round the room. It was a studio of some sort, bed and sofa and kitchen all sprawled across the same floor, counters keeping them apart. The floor was covered with great white rugs, far too clean to be lived on; a black grand piano was in one corner, a small cluster of chairs round a TV, a low dining room table and of course, the bed, pressed up into a corner by a window with the blinds drawn, into which I had been unceremoniously dumped. A clock on the wall said 16.33. I looked up at Oda and said, "Is the clock right?"

"Yes."

"Where'd the day go?"

She shrugged. "There was a lot of shouting. A lot of arguing. You will be unsurprised to learn that much of it happened while you were bleeding to death on the grass in Regent's Park."

"I was in Regent's Park?"

"Yes."

"Oh. I was bleeding to death?"

"Someone," she said, lips pursing round the straw, "someone might just have happened to have torn a stitch."

"But I'm not bleeding to death now."

"No. That was one of the conclusions of all the shouting. I had always imagined Aldermen would be good at holding committee meetings. They're not."

Thoughts returned slowly to us. I said, "Thank you."

"For what?"

"For not thinking I killed Nair."

She shrugged. "It's all the same to me. Kill him, don't kill him — one less freak on the streets."

"But . . ."

"You're useful, sorcerer," she said. "That's what it boils down to. You killed Bakker and that was a useful thing; you destroyed the Tower, and that was an extremely useful thing. Now you're on your own. And that" — she let out a long sigh — "is also, potentially, useful. The Aldermen are cowards."

We nearly laughed. "I guessed."

"They're terrified of whatever killed Nair."

"So am I."

"They think they're next."

"So do I."

"Do you believe this myth? That the ravens protect the city? That there are . . . *things*, whatever that means, waiting to come gobble up the innocent?"

"I believe in the Thames Barrier," I answered carefully.

"What does that mean?" she snapped.

"It means that I believe if the Thames Barrier failed, a great tide of floodwater would sweep over the city and sink most of its more fashionable areas beneath many metres of salt, sewage and slime. I have never in my life seen this, nor ever seen the Thames Barrier at work, but I believe it from the bottom of my heart. So, yes. I'm willing to run with the idea that we might all be well and truly buggered."

Oda slurped the last of her orange juice and put the cup to one side. She leant forward, looking us straight in the eye. "You want to know what was decided?"

"I've got a nasty feeling . . ."

"It's the stitches."

"That wasn't the feeling I meant . . . Why should we care what the Aldermen decided?"

"Because they were only two votes short of shooting you."

"When you put it like that . . ."

"It's your problem."

"What is?"

"All this. This imminent destruction thing. You're the Midnight Mayor. They agreed on that. You're going to have to sort it out. Your problem."

"They're saving on bullets," I sighed.

"That's the elegant thing about the Midnight Mayor. Even if you die, there'll be another sucker along soon."

"You really don't care, do you?" I asked. "Why are you here?"

"The Order may not care about your life. But we are naturally concerned when the actions of your clan of freaks may destroy the city that we live in. The innocent must be protected, even if it means cooperation with the guilty."

"Carry on thinking like that," I muttered, "and you'll be heading for sensible, fluffy normality before you know it."

"Not so fluffy. I'm here to keep an eye on things."

"What does that mean?"

"It means," she sighed, "that if at any moment it looks like you're not going to sort this out, that you're going to run, or betray, or double-cross, or generally walk away from this situation, then I'm the one who gets to shoot you." She added with a crocodile smile, "It'll be just like old times."

"Why aren't the Aldermen doing this?"

"They considered . . ." — she sucked in, choosing her words carefully — "that you might be more amenable to a conversation with an old acquaintance. It was suggested that I handle matters initially, lay out the position, tell it like it is. You're used to that, aren't you?"

"Tact and humour are not ideas I associate with you, no."

"Good. See — their reasoning had something going for it, despite their thrice-damned souls. You're going to have to work with them. Talk with them, let them help you do the thing you do until it no longer needs to be done."

"We're really not," we replied.

"Oh, I think you are. You see, you may be the Midnight Mayor—which is just another proof of how twisted is this life you lead—but you don't know what to do about it, do you? You don't know what it means. They do. They spend their lives learning the answer."

I said, suddenly suspicious, "Where are they?"

"There's five of them waiting downstairs in the car."

"Tell them to stick it up—"

"There's five of them, all very heavily armed, all annoyed, all trying their very best to be polite despite themselves. I never thought the day would come, sorcerer, when I would be *saving* you from your own withered walnut of a brain, but I have my instructions. They're going to have a word with you. You're going to play nice. If you don't, I will personally unpick those stitches from your skin with a blowtorch. Do we understand each other? I am that good."

Meekly, to our infuriation, I said, "Yes."

I got dressed. You can't be Midnight Mayor in your underpants.

Trains rumbled by. Somewhere in South London, I decided. Old brick arches filled in with other buildings under the railway lines; maybe somewhere near Waterloo, where the chaotic street plan had fallen like custard from a trembling spoon.

Someone had given us new stitches. They hurt, a dull throb that came and went with each pulse of our heart. Our face in the bathroom mirror could have frightened a dead horse that had already seen the innards of the glue factory. Our clothes were another bloodstained write-off. Again. Oda gave me new ones. The T-shirt read, "What Would Jesus Do?" and featured a big white cross on front and back, wrapped in thorns.

We said, "We can't wear this."

She said, "Will it burn your flesh?"

I put it on. It was that, or shiver and be undignified. More undignified.

Oda made supper. It was grey splodge served with undercooked pasta. Fanatical psycho-bitches clearly had different priorities from the rest of us. We ate it anyway, and tried not to look as grateful as we felt. We let the Aldermen wait. We could do that, at least.

It was 6 p.m. when Oda let the Aldermen in. I sat on the sofa; they stood in a row in front of me. Earle wasn't there. I wondered which way he'd voted in the should-we-shoot-him ballot. I wondered who'd voted for life.

Unfortunately, Earle's absence was not a total blessing. Kemsley stepped forwards.

"Mr Swift," he said through the corner of his slit-mouth.

"Mr Kemsley," I said.

"I am here as a representative of the Aldermen."

"I guessed."

"There are certain things that must be rectified between us. May I say firstly, on behalf of the Aldermen, that we offer an unconditional apology for the treatment you have received. We were acting on the best of intelligence, and I am sure, in time, you will come to see the reason of our ways."

"That's not unconditional, but let's stick with it for the moment."

His fingers twitched, but he managed to keep his face austere. "We have chosen to accept your appointment as Midnight Mayor."

"Big of you."

"It is unconventional." The word came out between his lips like thin bile when there's nothing left to vomit.

I folded my arms and waited.

"Mr Swift, I am sure you understand that the situation is complicated."

"It seems very simple. Someone is trying to destroy the city's defences, and you're too scared to stop it by yourselves. You want us to go and fight for you, find out why Nair was interested in the shoes, find out what's behind 'give me back my hat'. In short, you want me to be the one to find the guy who can flay people alive without laying a finger on them, and deal with the problem. Have I missed anything?"

A moment's hesitation. Kemsley drew in his lips, then smiled. "No," he said. "You seem to understand the situation. Issues arising?"

"A few."

"Deal with them."

"So much for the contrite apology."

"You know what's at stake."

"You killed my friend."

For a moment, his eyebrows drew together. "Did...oh...the White. Vera whatever-her-name-was. I might say that she turned into a puddle of paint, rather than the usual corpse."

"Yes, I noticed that. Curious, isn't it?"

"She was a White. They have different expectations of life than the rest of us. I'm sure you understand."

"If I'm Midnight Mayor, do I get to sack you?"

"What do you think?"

"Kemsley," we said calmly, "if you so much as breathe out of tune, we will kill you as casually as Vera died."

"I had no doubt. And for my part, may I say I find the idea of you as Midnight Mayor an abomination, a sickness, a degradation of the post and all the duties, age and time that it entails. But that doesn't change the fact that for you to be Mayor, Nair must have wanted it. He must have known what would happen when he dialled his phone, he must have known that the blue electric angels would be waiting. For his sake, I will respect the choices that have been made, and hope that they have not damned us."

There was almost a flicker of humanity in the man. The kind of human who pulled wings off flies as a kid, but still human. I smiled. "Well, it's nice to have that cleared up. Anything else I can do for you, gentlemen?"

"You have a badge. A cross within a cross. It belongs to my colleague, Mr Earle. He'd like it back."

"It's in my bag. Is it significant?"

"Sentimental value."

A lie. He knew that I knew, and brazened it out with a willpower that declared, yes, it's a lie, and no, I'm not going to say more.

I waited for them to fetch it, remembered Earle's face back in the flat in Bayswater, metalled over, and the shock when I'd pulled it from his chest.

Kemsley said: "We need to discuss strategy."

I shrugged. "Sure. What the hell."

"We need to find out who killed Nair. It makes sense that whoever — whatever — it was is connected to the other attacks in the city. We have links that could be of use. CCTV, police records, databases, forensic techniques..."

"What do you plan on doing with them?"

"We may be able to track the killer's movements."

"With CCTV? Good luck."

"You don't think we can do it?"

"I think that there's nine million people in this city, and of them probably two million wear bad suits and have slicked-back hair. And they're just the humans."

"There are other ways to track...creatures."

"And what do you intend to do, having found this creature?"

"Kill it."

"Any idea how?"

Kemsley smiled again. It felt like fingers being dragged down the back of our eyeballs. "That, we thought we might leave to you, sorcerer. *Mister* Mayor. In the meantime we're arranging for nine replacement ravens to be flown to the Tower."

"You just think that's going to fix the problem?"

"No. But I do think it might *help* with whatever the problem is. Even if it doesn't, it's better than sitting around radiating negative attitude."

"Did you just say 'negative attitude'?" we asked incredulously.

"I suspect you're not a team player," he added, all sucrose and teeth. "And what," he added, "do you propose to do?"

I looked round the room. "Where are my shoes?"

"If you mean the boy's shoes, Mo's, they're at the lab along with every other pair of shoes we could find in his bedroom. Also every pair of shoes we think you have ever worn."

"That seems like an overreaction."

"Nair thought the shoes were important—he didn't say how. Your wandering expedition might have been for nothing."

"You have a lab?"

"We consider all possibilities."

"I want the shoes back."

"Why?"

"To finish what I started before all this happened."

"Do you think that will—"

"*We want them back.*"

He bit his lip. "You can have them in an hour."

"Thank you." A thought struck us, slowly catching up with the rest. We said, "What do you mean, 'every pair of shoes in his bedroom'?"

"We acquired them."

"From Loren's flat."

"Yes."

"You talked to her?"

"Yes."

"What did you say?"

"Not much. It's better if civilians don't know."

"'Civilians'? Where is she?"

"We have her in a safe house."

We stood up slowly, pain dancing down our arm. "You took her away?"

"To keep her safe; to learn more."

"You took her away and didn't tell her why?"

"It is for the greater good."

"If we hear those words one more time, we will set the sky on fire," we snarled.

Kemsley seemed almost pleased. "Do you really care?" he asked.

"She is our...we said we would help her. She is lonely, afraid. We are...we will protect her. One hair of hers goes missing down the bathroom plughole, and we will tear you apart."

He smiled. Stood and stared at us and smiled.

I said, "You total bastard."

"Just covering base," he replied.

"She's not part of this."

"I am impressed that you care—really, I am."

"We will..."

"What? What will you do? What would you do if you weren't as mortal and scared as the rest of us? *Mister* Mayor. Mister Midnight Electric Mayor. What would you do?"

We slumped back into the sofa. I stared at my hands. A mess. "What happens now?" I asked.

"There's an inauguration."

I laughed.

"I mean it."

"I know you do. That's part of the joke. Will there be cocktail sausages, and bits of pineapple on sticks?"

"No."

"Sad."

"The Mayor must be inaugurated."

"What's the point of a party without the punch?"

"You want to live? Take it seriously."

"I am." I rubbed the palms of my hands over my eyes. "We do. What should I expect?"

"Ghosts," he said with a shrug.

"Thanks a bundle."

"See me smiling?"

"Ghosts," I repeated. "Terrific. When is this punchless, pineapple-less inauguration thing?"

"Tomorrow, midnight."

"Naturally."

"You need to do it if you're going to be Midnight Mayor, if you're..." He trailed away.

"Going to live?" I suggested.

"Yes."

"Didn't save Nair, did it?"

"Nair was a man."

"I thought he was Mayor."

"He was a man who happened to be the Mayor. You're something else."

"Sure. Blame the resurrection business. Go on. Why not? If in doubt reminding a guy that he got killed, got torn to pieces by black claws on a black night, saw the white light and the long corridor and all the things you see before you die, breathed a last breath—sure. Go ahead. Because that's really going to make me more inclined to help."

"This is about need, Swift. You need us, and we need you, and while we can both hate it, the sensible strategy would be to deal with the issues and move on. Keep your phone switched on, Mister Mayor. Remember to answer it when we call."

And that seemed all he had to say on the subject.

The Aldermen left.

All except Anissina.

She said, "I'm the shadow."

"Beg pardon?"

"I'm the shadow. The one that's going to keep your back."

I jerked my chin at Oda. "She'll do that just fine and she brings her own knives."

"So do I," she replied with a twitch of her lips that might have been a smile. "And mine need not end up *in* you."

"Does the little sorcerer need protecting?" crooned Oda.

Anissina didn't bother to reply. I sunk deeper into the sofa.

"Tea," I said. "Tea will make it all better."

I drank tea with a painkiller chaser.

It made things a little better.

Not hugely — but enough.

A knock at the door. Oda answered it, gun tucked away out of sight. A motorbike courier, all black helmet and padded jacket, presented a box. The box had a pair of shoes in it. We felt almost pleased to see Mo's shoes unharmed.

"What use are these?" demanded Oda.

"They're very good for walking in," I replied, and put them on.

Anissina had a car. It had a driver. He wore a peaked hat. I took one look at it and said, "Let's walk."

"To Willesden?"

"To the Underground."

Her nose wrinkled in distaste. Oda rolled her eyes. "Perks, sorcerer," she snapped. "I am sure you understand perks."

"I understand free lifts," I replied. "I also understand that driving around in a black car with windows shaded black and a driver in a black silk suit who opens a door with a black handle and black leather upholstery inside is not as discreet as you might want."

Oda grinned. "Not so easy to kill," she said. "Still dead, though."

"Remind me why you're here?"

"Sooner or later, someone's going to end up shot."

"Any idea who?"

"I'll write you a list."

We took the Jubilee Line. The station was new — glass doors and glass panels in front of the platform, just in case someone wanted to jump. The train driver missed on his first attempt, didn't slow down fast enough, didn't quite manage to align the doors of his bright new train with the shining glass panels. He had to reverse a few clunking inches, while the platform's scant inhabitants sighed and waited. Hard to tell which annoyed them more—delays caused by overshooting trains, or bodies on the line. It was going to be one or the other.

The Jubilee Line took us back north. Back to Dollis Hill. Darkness, cold, a slow sideways rain that came in across the streetlamps and stained the pavements, glaring reflective orange. I knew the route now, knew which way the shoes wanted to go, knew the swagger they wanted to walk with. Easier now, despite the drugs addling my brain and the ache in my bones. Despite being scared, despite the company. Easier to find a rhythm and strut like a seventeen-year-old jackass who should not, could not, must not be, and very clearly was, involved in this mess.

Back walking the streets with the swagger. Easier—much easier now I knew at least the beginnings of where we had to go. The empty skater park beneath the railway line, still empty, still dark, dry paint fading on old wood slopes. The pub showing the football, Arsenal up at half-time, an empty wall where the kids should have sat drinking booze, a pavement stained with the leftovers of some long-ago binge, the off-licence, shutters drawn down over the windows, no lights on inside, and on the shutters a scrawled warning:

ŞAPKAMI GERI VER

Along with the usual mess of scratched letters and names.
Anissina said nothing. Oda said, "If you're wasting our time..."
I ignored her. The swagger ignored her. It knew when it was dealing with the ignorant, not worthy of respect.

A patch of concrete that might possibly, sometimes, be a garage. A length of chain drawn low across the fence. Inside, a public phone, the receiver hung neatly on the hook, under a single fizzing neon bulb. We wanted to stop and stare, to look at it for hours and will the night to be another night, some time before; but the shoes wanted to keep on walking, and I didn't have the time or energy to care. It was how it was. The rain had washed off our blood.

I kept on walking. Unfamiliar territory from here on, never got past the phone in the garage last time. I turned my head down towards the pavement and watched the stones pass underfoot, trusting—despite our better judgement—in Oda and Anissina to warn us of impending cement lorries—and let the shoes do the walking.

I don't know exactly where we ended up. Somewhere to the south, doubling back on our previous route. It was a shopping street doing its very best to be trendy, and not quite making it. Pubs were pretending to be wine bars, condensation on the windows and punters pouring out into the streets, despite the rain; restaurants had hiked their prices up by two quid and added aubergine, even the curry houses, and the newsagents advertised local "cultural events" by amateur theatre groups or community choirs. We walked past it all, feeling water seeping through our shoes and itch inside our socks, shimmering bright blackness sparkling down the streets into the spitting drains. The rain drained away the usual smells of the streets—kebabs and bus exhaust—and left cold numbness in their place, invigorating until it started to stick.

Nor do I know how long we walked. Time was measured in strides, not seconds; distance in the warmth of our legs, rather than metres or miles. It seemed nothing at all. Oda said it was a long way.

And without warning, we stopped and turned, toes pointing in at a street wall. I looked up. The wall was an ordinary terraced house which had had extraordinary things done to it. Its entire surface was covered over with bright aluminium, into which a thousand glittering would-be diamonds had been implanted around a core of plastic purple jewels, the bulbs just visible within them, pulsing out in a hypnotic rhythm the blazing word "**VOLTAGE**".

Beneath the sign, a pair of aluminium doors, reinforced on the inside and padded with purple silk, had been swung back. They led into darkness; a red cord strung from a brass stand marked the beginnings of a queue line into this place. A man in black with a radio stuck in his left ear was standing on the door, gloved hands folded across his belly, one on top of the other. He stank of treacle, of deep dark maple syrup without the sugar, all thickness and no charm, a stench of magic that reminded me of Charlie, Sinclair's loyal assistant.

He was good at not meeting anyone's gaze, but scanned the street constantly as if we weren't looking at him, his ridiculous dark glasses pushed up on a great fat nose. Oda, seeing us stare, said, "*There?* You want to go in there?"

"Yes."

"*Why?*" she sighed. "When I last checked, you were a sorcerer, not a Jedi."

"You've seen *Star Wars?*"

"Seen it and denounced it."

"You've *denounced Star Wars?*"

She looked me straight in the eye and said, "Hollywood should not glorify witches."

"I think you've missed the point . . ."

"I also denounce Harry Potter."

"Really?"

"Yes."

"Because . . ."

" . . . because literature, especially children's literature, should not glorify witches."

"Oda, what do you do for fun?"

She thought about it, then said, without a jot of humour, "I denounce things."

"Let's forget I asked."

Anissina, as always, said nothing. I nodded towards the door. "I want to go in there."

"Do you really think this is the most productive way you can go about..." — Oda grimaced, then spat the words, "...saving this damned city?"

"You used 'damned' in a..."

"Purely literal sense. I do not blaspheme *nor* have a sense of humour."

"Mo's shoes want to go into Voltage."

"You speak as if they have a life of their own."

"You speak as if you can't imagine they could. I had a pair of shoes, a few years back, that had been rained on by the Singapore monsoon, got sand in them by the Indian Ocean, run the best part of the Bronx and been scoffed at by waiters in Istanbul. And that was after it was sewn together by a child in rural China, carted on the back of a truck across the country, boxed and flown around the world for me to buy. Find me a pair of shoes that hasn't got a life of its own, and I'll find you a blister plaster that actually works. Deal?"

Oda scowled, and looked towards the dark door of the gaudy club. "Voltage?" she asked.

"Voltage," I said.

The bouncer took one look at us, and said, "Wrong shoes."

You can't intimidate bouncers. It's not just that they're paid to be tough — it's that they're paid *and* bored. It's a bad combination.

I said, "Really? You sure?"

"Sorry, mate. You can't come in with those shoes."

As he spoke, a gaggle of kids, not out of their teens, were waved through without a glance, bundling down the dark passage of the stairs into the pumping gloom inside. I asked carefully, "Am I too old?"

"You know, mate, I've got my instructions..."

A CCTV camera was hanging over the door. I considered it, I considered him. CCTV cameras are easy to confuse, if you know how. I didn't even have to wave at it, and it was willing to turn the other screen. I said, "Shapeshifter."

He had shoulder muscles the size of an ox. They tensed. His coat nearly rode up a foot from his ankles. I waited. He said, "OK. Wizard."

"Not quite."

"It's not your kinda place."

We laughed. "I know that. What'll it take to get inside?"

"I'd like to help you mate, seriously, I'd ..."

We reached forward suddenly, not blinking in warning, and snatched the glasses from his eyes. Beneath, his irises were solid spheres of bright orange, tinted yellow at the edges and filling the expanse of his eyes. A pair of pigeon's eyes in a human's head. He reached for me instinctively, one hand pushing back my chin, the other going for my right arm, all martial arts glitter. A sharp and purposeful click stopped him. Oda's sleeve was pressed to the back of his neck. There was something in it more than a hand. She said, "If this wasn't an area of public view, it'd be *your* spinal cord on the pavement. Let go of him."

His fingers eased back; I staggered away. Oda looked at me nicely and smiled. "Are there any alleys round here?"

"Don't kill him."

"Imagine the trouble if I *don't* kill him. This is for your good as well as the city's."

"You're smart. Use your imagination. Don't kill him."

"He'll only ..."

"Cause trouble, yes, I know. We just don't care. Deal with it."

Her face flickered in annoyance. "You know, I could just ..."

"If you kill him, we'll know," we snapped. We weren't sure how we'd know, but she didn't need to know that. We looked her straight in the eye and added, "We'll know. Deal with it *nicely*."

"I'll go." Anissina. When she did speak, she was to the point. "Give me the gun."

Oda scowled, but carefully shifted places with Anissina, whose fingers slithered over the black metal pressed into the bouncer's neck. Oda pulled the Alderman's sleeve sharply down over Anissina's hand, to hide the worst of the barrel. "Don't think about it, sister," she hissed, wrapping Anissina's fingers tighter round the trigger. "When he tries something, don't think. It'll be easier that way."

Anissina said nothing. We had no idea if she was going to kill the bouncer either. But I figured he stood a better chance with anyone who wasn't Oda.

"Walk," said Anissina, and slowly, obediently, the bouncer began to shuffle from the door. I watched them walk down the street. It looked like trouble, all awkward movements and turns; but if an Alderman couldn't look after things, then who could? They vanished round the corner into a side street, and like the wise woman said, we chose not to think about it.

"Shall we?" asked Oda, looking into the dark mouth of the club.

"Dance?" I asked.

"What?"

"Shall we dance, it's a . . . forget it. Come on."

We went inside.

If the outside had been all glitzy gaudy glam, the interior of Voltage did its best to live up to the name. I could smell the electricity, sizzling the air, making every breath buzz. I could feel it, hear it like the hum of a computer battery kept overcharged; it made the hairs on the back of my hands stand on end, and it was all we could do to walk without sparking.

Flat plasma screens had been embedded in one wall, round circles of not-quite-glass within which wriggles of blue, green, purple and white mini-lightning danced and twisted. When we pressed our fingers against them, all the current danced towards our finger ends, turning them the colour of their own fire. The ceiling was set with twisting lights that gave off every colour except ordinary white, while above the bar in the corner deep UV blue mingled with a flickering strobe to set off the painted faces of the bartenders in psychedelic strangeness. And all the time, there was the music.

It went:

Dum dum dum dum dum dum dum dum dum dum dum

—too loud to hear anything else, though we knew from the open mouths of the dancers pressed close on the floor that they were shouting, screaming, talking, flirting, with all these inaudible things lost behind the relentless heartbeat of the bass. Lost too, any lyrics or other rhythms and beats; there was just *dum dum dum dum*, to which heads bopped, hips thrust, elbows flapped, knees jerked, feet turned, sentences tumbled, blood pumped. The air tasted of salty tea-spoons, smelt of thin slices of cucumber peeled away with a razored steel blade, and sweat, and static, and of course, there it was slicing through it all, a flash with every beat, the scarlet stench of magic. You don't have a shapeshifter guard the door unless there's something worth guarding.

There weren't any stools at the bar. Comfort wasn't part of the atmosphere. I leant on the counter and rubbed my temples, tried to drive the ache from the strobe out of my skull. Oda leant next to me, smiled at the barman and said, "You got anything that isn't alcoholic?"

The barman looked at her like she was a mammoth.

She shrugged. "My hopes were few."

There was a list of cocktails laminated to the surface of the bar. For each cherry-topped drink, I could have had three home-microwaved suppers. I pointed at one and said, "That."

"A Hot Red Sex?"

We weren't sure how to answer. "Sure," we mumbled. We'll try anything, once.

The barman turned; the barman worked. The thing he ended up putting in front of me was, in the UV light, the colour and consis-tency of lumpy custard. We sniffed it carefully and smelt booze and peach juice. We dipped a finger in it, licked it dry, couldn't really taste anything. We held it up to the light. Oda said, "Are you going to drink it or not?"

We took a careful sip. It was like swallowing a fermented mango soaked in a vat of acid. We wheezed. Oda turned away, and smiled. Teetotal. It made a sort of inevitable, self-righteous sense. I pushed the glass across the counter to a safe distance, just in case it started to melt, and turned my head towards the dance.

Dum dum dum dum dum dum dum dum dum

"See anything that sets your Satanic senses buzzing?" asked Oda nicely.

"Yes."

"Going to do anything about it?"

"Don't know. Don't know what it is yet."

"That's the problem with mystic forces," murmured Oda. "They tell you that you're going to die, but they never specify how. It's so you can feel the fear before the end, as some small redress for the life of arrogance you have led."

"You know, you could learn something from Anissina."

"I don't think so."

"No, seriously. You could learn how to be quiet."

"Information," she replied primly, "is not truth."

Mo's shoes didn't seem much help any more. Now that we had arrived, they didn't even seen inclined to dance. I looked at the people on the dance floor, faces coming and going like a jerking film in the glare of the strobe. All young: kids, teenagers, dressed in the kind of scruff that needs a rich man's budget, jeans slashed the right way, skin pierced with the right studs, hair done at a hundred quid for each gelled-up spike, brands artfully aged on cotton deliberately stained. The bouncer had been right—we didn't fit in. Too old, too mundane. Only our shoes were in the right area, all style and huff.

Their dance had a strange uniformity. It wasn't what we'd imagined dance should be; our thoughts filled with ideas of roses, moonlight, a boy, a girl, or at the very least two individuals with a thing for each other, an expression of something for when the crude mundanities of speech failed, a way to mention sex—a concept we found absurd, if fascinating—without having to go into biology. This was about sex; there was no denying it. But it had no sexiness, no intimacy nor sensuality, but was merely about fondling as many bottoms as you could in a single night, or peering down as many tops as your height would permit, all the time wiggling and shaking with strange expressions on your face as though to say, "you think I can do this with my hips *now*, wait till you see me naked". Some did it better than others, and danced in a way that spoke of sex but promised you this was the nearest you'd get, distance making it more alluring. Others just fumbled and writhed, but always, *always* the floor twisted and rose and fell and turned and moved to the relentless bass coming out of . . . where? I couldn't see speakers, couldn't see any source for the sound, it just seemed to shimmer into being behind the eardrums, not bothering to soften down its punches on the way in.

Oda said, "You're ogling."

"What?"

"You are staring lewdly at the dancers."

"I am not!"

"You are. It is highly distasteful."

We bit our lip. "Listen," I said, nearly shouting over the din, "there's something . . . off."

"You use 'off' like I use 'rotting', yes?"

"Where's the music coming from?"

She opened her mouth to say something smart, looked round, and closed it again just in time. There was a long pause as she scanned the room, peering into every corner, over the ceiling and through the faces bobbing on the floor. Finally she said, "All right. So there's no speakers. So?"

"So that doesn't surprise you?"

"I am never surprised."

"That doesn't interest you?"

"As a means to an end, perhaps it is of some curiosity."

"Where's the sound coming from?"

She shrugged. "You're our *saviour*." The word dribbled out like bile from an empty stomach. "You figure it out."

"Aren't you supposed to be helping me?"

"I'm supposed to be keeping an eye on you. The rest was left unspecified."

"Fat lot of use you are."

"I got you in."

"You were going to shoot —"

"I got you in."

I scowled and turned away. The music made my head hurt, the beat thrummed up from my toes and used the insides of my stomach as a trampoline. I edged along the counter, trailing my fingers along the smooth metal, almost frictionless, sterile and clean, drifted to the nearest wall, where the plasma screens wriggled and writhed, pressed my fingers against it, then my ear, listened.

Dum dum dum dum dum dum . . .

I could feel it *in* the walls, it made my ear ache. I squatted down and ran my fingers over the floor, and it was there too, setting the ground beneath my feet tingling like it was crawling with ants. A kid nearly trod on me, shouted some kind of abuse I couldn't hear, and went on dancing. Pressing my back to the wall and facing the dancers, I edged round the length of the room, trailing my fingers over every surface I could find, tasting the air, smelling the sounds, looking for a way down deeper.

I found it: a locked door, unmarked, the same colour as the rest of the room. I felt around in my bag until I found a key of the right make, slid it in, coaxed it to an appropriate shape, turned it, opened the door. A wall of sound hit me, louder even than on the dance floor, *deDUM deDUM deDUM deDUM deDUM deDUM*

UV light in the ceiling, nothing else; that uncomfortable blue that hurt your eyes, the brain aware that more was hitting the retina than it could understand. I walked down the corridor, found the manager's office; it was empty, papers and cash, mostly cash, strewn over the desk. I kept walking, found a flight of stairs, the sound crashing on my ears, deDUM deDUM deDUM ...

A door at the bottom of the flight of stairs. Above it a sign read, "Boom Boom — Executive Officer. By appointment only."

It was not our place to question a name like "Boom Boom". After all, you can't run a nightclub and be called Leslie.

I looked over my shoulder; no one behind, no one in front. I knocked, but my knuckles were a nothing in the din, so, I opened the door.

The room inside was UV blue. The great semicircular arc of the sofa bed was blue, the floor was blue, the walls were blue, blue lights were hung from a blue ceiling and the two goons standing inside the door with blood trickling down from their shattered eardrums were lit up blue by the reflection of all that blueness. They caught me as I came in, grabbed my arms, pushed me back against the door as it slammed behind me. I looked into a pair of young faces, boys, spotty and greasy and pale, dressed in hoodies and fashionable trainers. Their blood looked purple in the light where it had pooled in their eardrums and dribbled down the sides of their necks, the capillaries stood out gleaming from the wide sockets of their eyes, their faces were empty of all feeling. Our instinct to hurt them faded at the sight of those faces; two walking hunks of deafened meat guarding the door, two kids who'd never hear again; it seemed pointless to set their blood on fire now.

We let them pull and shove and generally manhandle us into the middle of the room, pleased at not killing them for their indifference. If we had, it might have demonstrated our nature to the thing we could only guess at being the Executive Officer. As we were dragged before him, he looked at us and said, "Are you lost?"

His voice was a roar, but even then it was barely audible over the thundering beat that filled the room. It came from jaws whose opening was the size of my head, a great, gin-smelling depth lined with tiny white teeth set in a base of a rolling length of opening bone. His eyes were two piggy grey marbles, his skin was flushed the colour of a grilled tomato, with a surface layer of darker capillaries threaded across his flesh like a road map of the Alps. His hair, if you could call it that, was three black strands slicked over a hillside scalp. He wore a suit the size of a wedding marquee. His belly sprawled out the length of my outstretched, tugged-on arms, his feet were two stubbly protrusions wearing — how we were thrilled by this sight! — black and white spats, poking out over the edge of the sofa. He could have crushed a buffalo just by sitting on it, he could have suffocated an elk between his thumb and forefinger, and it was from his chest that the great pounding roar of noise was coming.

A hand the size of my chest reached out to a control panel designed for fat fingertips, and pressed a button. A light went on beneath a bank of speakers behind his head, and at once the great roaring deDUM deDUM **deDUM** grew less, covered instead by an irritating hiss. It was still there though; I felt it rising through my stomach, aching in my gut.

He repeated, smiling, from his predator's mouth, "Are you lost?"

I tugged with deliberate weakness at the arms that held my own, testing their strength and doing my best to imply my own feebleness. I felt the stitches strain across my flesh, and grimaced in pain. "I guess so."

"You don't have an appointment." It wasn't a question.

We looked up and met his tiny eyes, almost lost in the folds of his face, then looked down. He followed our gaze and smiled. "Ah, yes," he said. "I often get that reaction."

Beneath the tent of his shirt, big enough to fill with hot air and fly in, something was moving *inside* his chest. I could see the shirt rise and warp, sink and flatten, then rise and warp again, as if a great big boil was being pumped in and out, or tectonic plate movement had decided to do its thing with his bone and skin. Its great rapid motion was in time to the beat, and it was moving above his heart.

I said, "*Oh*. I see."

"Do you?" he asked. "That's interesting. Most people go out of their way not to look."

"Couldn't you have gone to the NHS, like any ordinary Joe?" I asked.

"I'm not an ordinary Joe," he replied, "and neither, I think, are you."

He nodded at his two hooded guards. They pushed me forward; I stumbled, tripped, fell at his spat-wearing feet. The white and black leather filled our vision and we bit back on a hysterical laugh. A smile must have shown because he said, "Is something funny?"

"You're wearing spats!"

"And?"

"We just... it's so nice to... we've *always* wanted to see *someone* wearing spats. We thought it only happened in films. Sorry. It must seem irrelevant."

"You don't need to apologise," he grumbled, and now we realised what the hissing was, that irritating, needle-in-the-ear sound. The speakers were replicating the sound of his beating heart, the great swelling massive thing the size of a swallowed dog pounding inside his chest, but they were doing it a few instants out of phase. One sound met the other, and both were beaten down. That at least was the theory of it.

He leant forward. That is, his head bent down towards me half an inch. He didn't seem capable of doing any more. He said, "Is there something I can do for you, little man?"

"I've got to ask—sorry about this—but I've got to ask—why spats?"

"Style," he replied primly, "is more stylish if it's done to a personal agenda."

"And why is your heart pumping out enough decibels to shatter an eardrum?"

He smiled. This was a question he was clearly used to being asked, and enjoyed answering. "I," he declared proudly, "am the lord of the dance."

"You do realise that has slightly camp Irish connotations?"

His face darkened. "I," he repeated firmly, "am the master of the heartbeat, the music maker, the drummer of fate, the..."

"You're a cardiac patient with complications," I snapped. "Don't give me this destiny stuff."

I could see the flesh of his chest warp a little faster, hear the rhythm of his beat, faint behind the hissing of the speakers, slightly out, picking up speed. And if we looked closer still, we thought we could see his ribs rising and falling against his shirt, broken, out of joint, forced to snap up away from the breastbone to make space for that massive engine pounding away within him, and we could see the capillaries across his face flush and fade, flush and fade with each pounding of his heart. "What do you know of it?" he asked.

"Well"—I ticked the points off on my fingertips—"I know that one: cardiac problems account for a high percentage of premature deaths in the UK. Two: there's a very long waiting list for a very small number of hearts available on the NHS. Three: even if you get bumped to the top of the waiting list, sometimes it's hard to find a heart that will match you, owing to medicine, antigens, blood groups and all that medical stuff. Four—are we on to four? Yes, four: there are some backstreet clinics not registered on the NHS, or even popping up on the regular black market, where you can get a heart transplant if you're in a bad enough way and have a bit of ready cash, but you can bet your buttocks that the individual performing the operation believes in the power of incense and bad spirits in their work. Five: it's not just humans who can donate working hearts. With the right attitude, the correct approach and a hefty dose of obscure occultism... what did you get given? Sperm whale?"

He looked surprised. Then he smiled, a long, deliberate smile that clearly took a lot of effort. "You know more than I had expected," he said.

"That's me. Full of useful information, not that it's the same as truth."

"You are not just some lost buffoon."

"Well, that depends on your point of view..."

"What do you want, little man?"

"We'll get to that. First, I've gotta tell you—I don't like the fact that you've turned the brains of these kids here"—I jerked my chin to the empty-eyed hoodies—"to jelly. I mean, it's none of my business, but we do not like life when it is but a mimicry. Life should be lived. And they are not living it."

He shrugged. The ripples of the movement passed all the way down his arms to his fingertips, made his belly shake and shimmer. "I'm not here to manage your problems," he said. "I'm not here to have anything to do with you."

"Then I guess we'll come back to this one in a minute. Right now, what I'd really like to know, is whether you've seen a kid called Mo."

He hesitated. Not for very long. Then he laughed. We watched the great rising and falling of that blister in his chest, saw the pressing of his ribs against his shirt as they were pushed out with a creak, sharp broken edges scratching against the cotton. His heart was going faster now; the speakers couldn't keep down the sound: **dumdumdumdumdumdumdumdumdum**

"How should I know?" he chuckled. "I see very few people, in my condition, but some random kid? How should I know? Why should I care?"

"I've got a photo," I said, fumbling in my bag.

"Is this really what you came down here for? To ask me, *me*, if I'd seen a boy?"

"Didn't say he was a boy, and 'Mo' could be anything," I replied. "But yes, you have the gist of it." I found the picture Loren had given me, held it up for him to see.

"Recognise him?"

He studied it, too long, too deep, too carefully, a badly played act by a man who didn't get out much. "Nope," he said finally, chest heaving beneath his shirt, heart twisting and boiling within his shattered ribs. "Is that everything, little man? Would you like a back massage on your way out?"

"Look again."

"I've seen..."

"And you're fibbing. We are not in the mood for lies."

"Arrogance!" he laughed.

"Impatience," we snapped. "You have a great bursting blister contracting and constricting within your chest. A better liar might be able to stop it from accelerating. But like you said—you don't get out much. Should have waited for the NHS."

"Waiting was death."

"*This*," we retorted, "isn't living. But since you seem to value it so highly, let us make ourself clear. Tell us the truth, or we will kill you."

He just laughed, arrogance and error. We picked ourself up carefully, half-turning our head to eye up his deafened drones.

"Death couldn't kill me!" he said. "They thought it would, but I stopped it. I locked death out and now my heart is life, my heart is..."

"'Give me back my hat'."

His face froze. We smiled. "You recognise it," we said. "That's good. That means we're right. Tell us about it. Tell us about the boy called Mo."

"Who are you?" he asked.

"My name is Matthew Swift."

"So *who* are you?"

"I was the apprentice of Robert James Bakker. I'm sure you've heard of him." He had; his accelerating heart was a great thumping blister, an alien out of a monster movie trying to break free of his bones. "I am a sorcerer. I was there when Bakker died. We...made it happen. I too have met death, and did not have to peel the bones away from my chest to survive the encounter. I am also, and incidentally, the Midnight Mayor, the blue electric angels, the fire in the wire, the song in the telephones, and we are having a bad week. Be smart; fear us."

He licked his lips. His tongue was the colour of rotting strawberries. He nodded carefully and said, "OK. I get it. I see what you're saying. And sure, yeah, I'm smart enough to be scared of sorcerers, they always end in a bang. But the thing is, while it's sharp to fear you, I just fear *him* a whole lot more."

Like a schmuck, I turned my head looking for the *him*. I guess I wasn't at my best. There was no one there, just the two guys with the bloody ears. I looked back. He had one hand over the controls that turned on the speaker. His other was pulling at the buttons of his shirt.

He turned off the speakers; he pulled back his shirt. His ribcage was a mess of broken bones, sticking up from his skin, creating great dark voids between his flesh into which muscle had long since sunk and withered, ragged torn bone shattered away from the twisted breastbone protruding upwards like ruined towers in an ancient desert. We could *see* his heart beating beneath it, four great, coated valves smeared in clinging white flesh pumping one to the other, could see it shrink down to the size of a pear and then burst upwards again, pressing the ribs out so far that they creaked and cracked, little fracture lines running down the stuck-up grey bones where they had ruptured from his chest.

And his heart went: **deDUM!**

The shock of the sound had nothing to do with ears; it was long past the point where audible frequencies played a major part. His ribs twisted outwards with the blast, his whole chest rising up; then the force of the sound knocked into me and threw me back shaking, slamming into me so hard that all I could hear was a rumble like the sea.

We landed face-down on the floor and crawled away from him. It went again, **deDUM!** We covered our ears with our hands, with our elbows, buried our face in the floor and our knees in our face and again it went **deDUM!** The plaster cracked on the wall, and spilt trickles of dust; the lights hissed and swayed, flickered, began to shatter and go out. The two kids with the bloody ears were on the floor, blood running from their ears, their noses, their eyes, with ugly bruises where the blood from a thousand broken capillaries was spilling out beneath their skin. I tried to get up and another heart-beat knocked me down. We might have called out, we couldn't tell, couldn't hear anything but our own dying cells singing in our ears. His heart was going too fast, beating too fast for us to move, to stand a chance against the roar, everything we did took a heartbeat and one beat was one too many.

So we lay still. We pressed ourself into the ground, dug our fingers into the thick blue carpet, and let it buffer us, let the sound push us across the floor, **deDUM!** until we were up against the door, all twisted limp limb, and our head was screaming, bursting; our eyes ached in their sockets, such a frail little body to hold *us* and die and...

deDUM!

...think *sound*...

deDUM!

My fingers were knocked against the wall. Through a static haze, I looked at it. I pushed my fingers closer into the wall, sensed its warm dry touch. Then I pushed a bit deeper. I curled my fingers into it, felt the concrete slide around them, dug in up to my fingertips, up to my wrist, closed my fingers around the sense of it, and pulled.

deDUM!

I saw the wall warp and twist, seem to shrivel into itself as its middle was dragged out along the pipe of my arms, saw grey dryness wriggle over our skin, settle between the gaps in our fingers, stiff and locked in place, run up our arm, crawl into our armpit, slide over our chest, press against our neck, a thick, suffocating solid scarf that dug into our throat, made it hard to breathe, tiny twitches of the lung within its fixed frame. I pressed my lips tight shut and closed my eyes, but still tasted the dust on my lips, dry sickly nothing sucking out everything good from sense, felt it dribble into my ears, snatched one last frantic breath before it bunged up my nose, a bad cold backwards, felt it dribble over my eyelids, slide into the hairs of my eyebrows and close over the top of my head. As the concrete drained down my legs, the wall began to buckle and bend in on itself, its substance sucked away; and before it could set around my knees, I stood up, and turned to face what seemed to be the source of the sound.

deDum!

deDum!

deDum!

Concrete locked my feet in place. My fingers were turned towards the heartbeat, I could feel it shake my solid shell, see nothing but darkness, breathe nothing, smell nothing, every sense blocked, except that distant

deDum!

deDum!

deDum!

My head was burning up, air that was no longer air unable to get out of my lungs, blocking my throat, a stone sinking deeper and deeper down into my chest, every part withering inside, every blood vessel in my body stalling, warping, fracturing. We were going to die, us alone in a concrete shell, die from a heartbeat in a basement in . . .

. . . in *Willesden.*

We didn't want to die please no not the end not the end not back there not again not the end not us not no-sense not no-sight not no-colour please not prison again please not

Shut up!

please please please please

SHUT UP!

I listened for it, found the rhythm again, pounding against my shell, and as it came

deDum!

deDum!

I forced my legs to move. Strained against the concrete around my knees, forced my whole weight forwards, like a tree about to topple, felt it fracture, crack and as the *deDum!* split the world, I pushed into it. Against it. Turned myself against the sound, and sent it back.

The shock sent fault lines rippling up my shell, but that just made it easier to move, I listened again,

deDum!

moved again, pressing myself into it, pushing back on the sound with every gram of will and strength I had, saw light ripple across my vision as a fracture line ran across the concrete over my face, tasted dust worming between my lips, stepped again, each step a giddy flight up to boiling clouds and back down again, heart bursting inside, ready to pop, hammering *dedumdedumdedumdedumdedum* in tiny terror in our ears oh God not like this please please please

deDum!

Pushed against it, threw it back again, felt a shock run down the length of my spine as the backlash from the sound cracked my armour shell, felt concrete jar against my ribs as it began to tear and break, but I was moving now, dust falling from my legs, I had momentum and with each step I took, I sent as much sound bouncing back as I received. I could feel broken glass from shattered lights fall across the solid frame around my head, see the lights go out through the little spreading cracks across my vision, kept moving, pushing back against the sound like it was an avalanche and I a very angry rock.

deDum!

The concrete shattered around my right hand, I felt it fall away and my fingers come free, pale and dusted, felt the sound twist at my palm, try to crash down against the little bones in there, clenched my fist against it and kept moving.

deDum!

The lower concrete covering of my left leg fell away. I nearly fell with it; kept going, bowing head first into the force of the roar, and

deDum!

the concrete skull cracked; I could feel it rippling down my neck, playing pins-and-needles across my shoulders *deDum!*

began to shatter; not around my ears, I prayed, sound and pain, no
more pain, not there, not...

deDum!

and our right hand was on fire, blood seeping down our wrist and
we were nearly there, so close, red blood catching with blue fire, blue
electric flames that spat and hissed and threw angry sparks across the
floor as it writhed over our skin, electric oil burning electric flesh and
we let it burn, let the fire spread throughout our body, set the cracks
running through this concrete coffin ablaze, let the neon flame spread
throughout and carry us that last pace as our lungs prepared to give
up the ghost, fed them on fire and fury and

deDum!

and it was right there, right in front of us, we could feel it, hear it,
knew it. We reached out with a hand on fire and felt our fingertips
brush spiked bone as

deDum!

the shock blasted away the concrete across our chest, ripped it
from our neck, sent dust spilling out from around our ears and...

One more beat of the heart, that's all it needed, one more beat and
goodnight and goodbye and...

Our fingers closed around his heart. His contracted heart, waiting
to pump. We could feel bright hotness, stiff, solid flesh, like a lump
of uncooked steak, feel his ribs scratching at our dust-covered sleeve,
feel the valves trying to move and expand in the claw of our grip. We
held on tighter, fighting that strength back within his chest, pushing
his heart shut within him, and it was strong but so were we, and we
were on fire.

He screamed.

Big men shouldn't scream. It's the yowling of a baby with a soiled
nappy, the wail of the kid on the landing plane whose ears have just
started to pop. It's pure and animal and ugly.

I shook the last of the concrete shield from me, tumbling it to dust all around. Glancing over my shoulder I could see the whole near wall was largely down, just a few foundation spikes and a lot of shattered slabs, and in my wake a floor of dust and broken dirt, running from the wall to where I now stood, fingers buried in the Executive Officer's chest.

By the burning of our skin, by the bright electric fire running over our flesh, I could see his face, almost black now with the effort of death, and we hissed, "Tell us!"

His lips were the blue-black of an evening storm, his eyes were nearly all out of their sockets, the equators of the spheres starting from between his rolled-back eyelids. I relaxed the pressure on his heart a moment, let it beat a frail, constricted beat within my fingertips, then tightened my fist again. Someone, with a scalpel dipped in acid, had scrawled blessings, incantations, inscriptions and wards all over the inside of his ribs, carved them into the muscular wall of his heart. They were the only reason he wasn't dead. They were the things that kept him almost alive.

"'Give me back my hat'," we said. "Tell us what it means."

"Don't know!" he wheezed, tongue waggling like a sick pup between his lips. "Don't know!"

We tightened our fingers on a valve in his chest and he couldn't even scream, there wasn't enough blood and air. But his mouth opened, his head rolled back and every part of him spoke of agony until I relaxed our grip again. "What about the kid? Where's Mo?"

"Took him...hid him..."

"Why?"

"Paid. Told...paid. He came here...he said to take him, hide him. The kid used to come here with his mates, he said to take the kid, kill the rest, I didn't argue..."

"Why?"

"Didn't say. Just said he wanted kid hidden, just said...he said..."

I let his heart beat a shallow beat; then we dug our fingers in deep again. "Tell us!"

"Had to keep the kid hidden. Very special kid, he said, very special, gotta have a special end, needed someone who could get him snatched, keep him hid, kept him moved..."

"You provided the logistics to a kidnapping?"

"Didn't argue with him!"

"Where's Mo?"

"Took him...hid him..."

"Where?!"

"Kilburn," he hissed. "Raleigh Court. Gone, 53 Raleigh Court, took him, hid him, I was told, kill the rest, but Mo, keep Mo alive."

We almost forgot to let his heart pump. The breath slithered from his lungs, his head began to sink. We tightened our fingers and relaxed, tightened and relaxed, forced the blood to flow. "Where in Raleigh Court?"

"Top floor, fifty-three, safe house."

"Why?!"

"Didn't ask. Paid. Scared. Didn't ask. Just did."

"Who? Who told you to do this? What did he look like?"

"He wore a suit. A pinstripe suit."

"What did his face look like?"

"Pale. Slicked-back dark hair. Grey eyes. Pinstripe suit. Handkerchief in his pocket."

"Who is he?"

"He said...he said he..."

We jabbed at the arch of his aorta with a fingertip and he screamed, screamed and screamed, shrieked at last, "His name is Mr Pinner! You can't stop him! He's not human!"

"Boring name for someone who isn't human," we snapped. "What is he?"

"He said...he was...he said...he'll kill me..."

"Probably, sorry, sad loss. What did he say?"

His little eyes fixed on me from a face about to burst. He choked, "He is the death of cities. He's here for yours. End of the line."

His head started to roll back. We dug our fingers into his heart, but his mouth was a dribbling slackness, his great jaw hanging down almost as low as my fist buried in his chest. I let go of his heart slowly, saw it flicker feebly, and not move any more. We backed away a few paces, skin still burning by the fire of our blood running down our wrist. The furious blue glow of our anger began to recede into a paler neon-white shimmer. His blood, ordinary, boring, red, dribbled between our fingers. We backed away towards the place where there should have been a wall holding a door, saw the lights in the corridor burning towards the stairs. We walked away. His heart was dead behind me, a dead thing in ripped-apart flesh and we kept walking, but I wanted...

Walk away

I wasn't

walk away

we are

but that's not what I

we do

Not human.

I turned and looked back at him. A great dead whale beached on a fluffy blue sofa. I raised my hands up to the ceiling, spun my fingers for the bright burning electricity in the air, dragged it down, let it ooze out of the lights, out of the walls, the floors, the roof, let it drag in from the mains and spun it like a cat's cradle in the air in front of me, wove it between my bloody and dusty fingers, concrete mortar and human ooze fusing into ugly lumps on our flesh, twisted it into new and exciting shapes and, as we reached the bottom of the stairs, I threw it. It danced through the air, spitting our anger and frustration, and slammed into the Executive Officer's heart.

Which went *deDum*.

We started to climb the stairs, as the lights behind us died and went out.

Behind us came the rhythm.

deDum deDum deDum deDum deDum deDum deDum deDum deDum

I fumbled for the door, opened it in the dark, and slipped out into the chaos of the club.

The dancers were in uproar. The bass to which they'd been dancing had failed, the lights had died, the electricity had been sucked out of the circuits and all this after paying an £8 admission fee and ridiculous prices for cocktails! If they weren't so young and cool they'd write to the council and complain; as it was, being young and cool, they'd rather have free drinks or smash things, thanking you kindly.

Oda was leant against the wall inside the exit. The door was standing open, thin neon overspill from the streets pouring in. She saw me and said, "I'm guessing you didn't have a toilet break. You know, if you'd told me where you were going..."

We glowered at her and staggered out into the half-light of the street, trailing dust and blood in our wake. Anissina was leaning on the wall outside. I guess the two ladies felt they had nothing to talk about together. She looked me over and said, "Hurt?"

"My ears."

"We can get you to a doctor."

"No. No. Thanks. I'll be fine."

"He'll be fine," added Oda quickly. "They're good at blood and dust."

I ignored her, turned into the street. "I want..." I hissed, and then didn't know what to say. So I started walking instead, fumbling in my bag for a fistful of painkillers, my bloody fingers slipping off the cap. "There's a..."

"Where are you going, sorcerer?" demanded Oda, scampering to keep level with me.

"You"—I jabbed a finger at Anissina. "Tell the Aldermen, there's a guy in there who does things. Wrong things. Tell them to sort it out."

"Sorcerer!"

"Stop calling me that!" I had shouted. I hadn't meant to shout. "Sorry," I muttered. "Sorry. I'll ... I just need ..."

I kept walking, nearly running now. A few hundred yards ahead was a pub, still open, lights still on, a place for men with puffy noses and not much conversation. I pushed through the door, past the flashing bingo machine and tables an inch thick with old dried spillage, looked around, saw the sign, followed it, marched into the toilets. They were dirty, everything chipped, toilet paper across the floor. Who these people were who came into public toilets and threw paper around, I did not know. A guy with a faintly ginger beard and a ruffled blue shirt was already in there. We said, "Out."

He left without a word. Oda marched through the door behind me, while Anissina, more discreet, loitered in the opening. It took three taps before I found the one hot tap that was working. I stuck my hands under it and scrubbed, felt thick dust and clogged blood break free from my skin, saw it swish down the sink in red dribbles and little black lumps where the two had combined. My hands were shaking, we were shaking, as strange a physical reaction as we had ever experienced. I stuck my head down as far into the low sink as I could get it, threw water over my face, buried my face in it, closed my eyes and let the warmth seep into them, leach dust from my eyelashes, let it run over my lips and into the mortar-filled cracks of my skin. My sleeves were stained with blood, not mine, and I scrubbed uselessly at them with toilet paper and cold water until Oda said, "You know, that's not the way to do it. You need to get it in a soak."

"No time."

"OK. Why not?"

"I know where the kid is."

She gave a little laugh. "So all that walking was for something. Did this guy at the club do it?"

"No. He's just logistical support. A guy who knows a guy who knows a guy who has a van and a few friends who don't mind lifting a kid quietly off the street and carting him away with a gag in his mouth. He's just a bit of executive muscle, nothing more. Mo's in Raleigh Court."

Anissina looked up sharply. Oda shrugged. "And . . . is this is an ancient Indian burial site?"

"It's where Nair died," said Anissina quickly. "It's where the Midnight Mayor died."

"Does that make it mystically significant?"

"Not of itself," I said. "But I got a hint as to who killed him."

"You're full of it today, sorc . . . you're full of it today," she said. "Go on, then. Who did it and will they die quiet?"

I wiped my soaking hands on my coat, felt water drip off the end of my nose and trickle under my chin. "His name is Mr Pinner. That's who killed the Midnight Mayor."

"A name is a start. Anything else?"

"Yeah. He said he was the death of cities."

"How typically pretentious of the man," muttered Oda.

Anissina said nothing, but her eyes were locked onto mine. She knew, she said nothing, but she knew; she was that smart. "Oda," we sighed, "has it ever occurred to you that, if there's mystic protectors out there protecting us, there might be mystic nasties out there we need protecting from?"

"Sure it has," she said evenly. "That's the problem with all things mystic."

"That's the problem with life," I snapped. "By your logic, the communists would have nuked the capitalists and the capitalists the communists and never a bomb would have been irrational."

"Is this the time to talk philosophy?"

"No. Please shut up and go away."

She shut up. She seemed surprised. She didn't go away.

Finally, Anissina, seeing that Oda wasn't going to, said, "Raleigh Court?"

"Yeah. I guess so."

"I'll call back-up."

"You have 'back-up'?"

"Of course."

"Like guys in bulletproof vests?"

"Something like. Even sorcerers can't stop bullets."

"I don't think I like you either."

"I'll make the call," she replied, and reached into the depths of her black coat for a phone.

Back to Raleigh Court.

The bus was full of late-night revellers going home. At the bus stop, a guy with curly hair was bent over the nearest bin, bile dribbling down from the corner of his mouth. On the bottom deck, a young woman's mascara had run from crying and now she sat stoically next to a middle-aged stranger who looked older than he was, and who politely ignored the tears in her eyes. Three separate pairs of lovers were holding hands. Two of them were doing a bit more than that. On the top deck, a group of six revellers with big boots and matching black hair were jovially exclaiming on the woes of the world in loud, cackling voices, punctuated every now and then by a cheerful "Oops! Had a bit too much!" followed by more hysterical laughter.

The revellers thinned as the bus journeyed on, staggering away in small groups into the drizzle at the bus stops. A thick, rattling wind was picking up, a proper north-west stonker that came in sideways round every street corner and whistled across the chimney tops. We didn't want to go back to Raleigh Court. We didn't want to meet Mr Pinner, more than anything else, we did not want to meet him. There was more than just mindless pretension to the name of the death of cities.

Lights going out in the houses, streets reaching that moment when passers-by stopped being safety in a company and became lonely dangers walking through the night. Urban foxes poking their noses out, lured by darkness and the smell of wasting food, trotting down the pavement closer and closer to the wanderers every year, less fearful of humanity, stretching their thin bodies through the railings of public parks, the masters of daylight invisibility, and night-time rulers of the streets.

The driver of the bus, as his vehicle became emptier, began to drive like a proper night racer, the empty streets tempting his feet towards the accelerator and fingers over to the higher gears. We were at Raleigh Court quickly—too quickly for my taste, and the three of us got off, as unlikely a collection of mystic storm troopers as had ever assembled.

Anissina said, "Kemsley is bringing support."

"Support and back-up—you do take your work seriously."

"Yes," she replied flatly. "I do."

I looked at Oda, half-expecting her to want to charge straight in. She saw my look, and said simply, "It's only in computer games that you get to reload after the zombie kills you. I can wait for support. I am good at waiting."

"We're not."

"Deal with it."

I waited.

Every second we spent standing by the bus stop, looking up at the square slab wings of Raleigh Court infuriated us, made our skin itch, hair stand on end. But I'd seen the films, and I knew—the guy who went in first was either the first one dead, or a tortured hero going solo because no one else could do it. I wasn't prepared to be either. So I waited, fingers turning blue, hair slowly soaking through with drizzle, laced with a slight sting of acid.

I knew it was Kemsley the second I saw the big blue truck turn round the corner at the end of the street; I just couldn't bring myself to believe it. When it lumbered to a halt in front of us, the back doors opened and five men with body armour and rifles got out. I laughed. We couldn't help ourself; I put my head back and laughed.

Kemsley climbed out of the front seat and glared at me. "Funnies?" he asked.

"Sorry. Serious face."

"You wanted back-up?"

I jerked a thumb at Anissina. "She wanted back-up."

"Any good reason why?"

"You don't seem pleased to be here."

"And you don't seem to consider the cost to the local councils this little operation will incur," he replied. "Overtime fees, vehicle rental, health and safety, logistic support, equipment and maintenance, property damage, personal and third-party insurance, property insurance. Management and finance aren't your specialities, are they, sorcerer?"

Our jaw tightened. "We're looking for a...thing calling itself—himself—whichever—Mr Pinner. I imagine he'll introduce himself something like this. 'Hello. My name is Mr Pinner. I am the death of cities. Do you think bullets can really stop me?' I mean, I'm just speculating, but that's all I've got at the moment. Thanks for coming."

"What do you mean 'the death of cities'?"

"I don't know. It's a bit vague. I mean, on the one hand, it might be a pretentious title adopted by a man who spends too much time playing online fantasy games or an attempt to confuse and befuddle his opponents—in which case congratulations to him for a successful scheme! On the other hand, it might be exactly what it says on the cover. A walking talking thing in a pinstripe suit who is, quite literally, the death of cities. The embodiment of the end made flesh upon this earth, one of the riders of the urban apocalypse and so on and so forth. It's just not clear yet." We put our head on one side, stared straight into his eyes. "Are you going to stick around to help us find out?"

Now it was Kemsley's turn to tense. "Tell us where and when, and we'll handle the rest—if you're not up to it."

I pointed into Raleigh Court. "In there. Where Nair died. We're looking for a safe house run by an individual called Boom Boom. The Executive Officer of a nightclub called Voltage who got a little bit scared of a guy in a pinstripe suit and agreed to help him kidnap a kid who liked to visit his club. That's where the shoes went, by the way. They like clubbing. Pity the owner lacked moral fibre. And a heart. But anyway—somewhere in here, we hope, is the kid Mo. And that would all be fine and grand of itself, except, you may have noticed, this is where Nair got the skin peeled from his flesh. It's number 53, top floor. Shall we meet you up there?"

"You know," murmured Oda, "testosterone is one of the many ways in which God tests our natures—women, as well as men."

"Sorcerer..." began Kemsley.

"I swear, I *swear*, the next person to call me 'sorcerer', as if I *didn't* have a name and a small intestine, will get a sharpened pencil shoved firmly up their flared nostril."

There was a slightly taken-aback silence. Then Kemsley said, "Mr Swift."

"Yes?"

"Are you ready?"

"Sure."

"Good. As Midnight Mayor..."

"You want me to go first?"

"No. I want you to stay as far back as you can."

"With pleasure."

They did the assault/SWAT thing. Rifles, corners, kneeling, standing, running, climbing, gestures—fist, two fingers, flap, twiddle—the whole lot.

We tried not to laugh as we trailed along behind. Even Anissina was playing along, pistol in hand. You have to have a lot of training to be a storm trooper, we concluded. It wasn't just about learning when to duck and when to fire; it was about learning to take yourself seriously as you did it. I looked at Oda in the hope she was appreciating the humour. It was a naive look.

As council estates went, the interior wasn't so bad. Someone had recently painted the stairs an unoffensive pale blue, and there was a general soft smell that I associated with my gran's cooking and fat cushions on padded chairs, and the regular shifting of dirt by plastic brooms and warm soapy water. The troopers stormed the stairs; I shuffled along behind. Number 53 was, as promised, on the top floor, a long balcony punctuated by the occasional bike, kitchen windows and wilting geraniums. The Aldermen and co. clattered along to the green door, spread themselves out around it, and at a cry of "go!", kicked it open with a heavy studded boot, and threw something in there that went *snap!* There was a burst of bright light and a high buzzing noise. I leant against the edge of the balcony and looked down into the courtyard below, wondering where Mr Fox had gone and if my furry friend was eating enough kebabs. The armoured men counted to three, then burst inside the flat, shouting impressive things like "clear!" or "go go go!" as they did. Oda said, "Gum?"

"You chew gum?"

"No. But I always carry it, to use as barter when visiting prisons."

"Do you see how I'm not asking?"

"Smart. So, how scared are you?"

Inside I could hear the thumping of many heavy boots, the slamming of many light doors, the rattling of many, probably futile, loaded weapons.

"On a scale of one to ten?"

"If you insist."

"Where one is 'so doo-lally-happy I could jump off a cliff and whistle numbers from *The Sound of Music* on the way down' and ten is 'can't open the window in case the air eats me' scared?"

"If you feel obliged to use these assessments—then yes."

"Pretty much up there."

"Why?"

"Why do you care?"

"Because," she said carefully, as in the flat lights began to be turned on and orders barked in brisk military voices, "being, as you are, an arrogant spawn of the nether reaches of creation, for something to have frightened a creature so relentlessly self-certain as you, it must be significant. It is in my interest to know about it."

I smiled sideways at her. We respect honesty, even if we can't stand its owner. "You've never heard of the death of cities."

"As a concept?"

"As a man."

"Then no. I never have."

"It's a myth."

"Like the Midnight Mayor?"

"In that sort of region, yes. Just a rumour, a legend. You hear stories. Stuff like...when the atom bomb was dropped on Hiroshima, there was a house right in the middle of the blast, at its very heart, untouched while the rest of the city was levelled. They say that there was a man in the house, who had his face turned towards the sky as the bomb fell and who just smiled, smiled and smiled and didn't even close his eyes. But then again, you've got to ask yourself..."

"...who survived that close to the bomb to tell?"

"Right. It's always the problem with these sorts of stories. Or they say that when Hurricane Katrina struck New Orleans, there was a man who walked through the flooded streets and laughed and the water could not buffet him, or when they firebombed Dresden there was a guy untouched by the flames, or when the child tripped running into Bethnal Green station during the Blitz, that there was someone who knocked her down and climbed over the bodies piled up in the stairway. Myths. That's all. Rumours and myths. And just in case these things aren't scary enough on their lonesome, they just had to go and give this smiling, laughing, burning man a name, and call him the death of cities. Naturally, I don't believe a word of it. And yes, of course I'm scared. Just in case."

She looked, for a moment, like she was going to say something else. Then Kemsley was there, and his face did not glow with happiness.

"There's nothing in the flat."

I shrugged. "Makes a kind of sense."

"If you thought..."

"I thought. I thought that Boom Boom probably wasn't going to lie to me, what with me having my hand in his chest cavity at the time. Then I thought Nair came here; Nair was killed. It makes sense that whoever—whatever—killed him would only do so if Nair was getting close to something important. It makes even more sense to have moved that something to somewhere less likely to be found. Sorry. I just can't pretend I'm surprised."

"Then why are we here?" he growled.

"Think how stupid you'd feel if we'd known about this place and just ignored it," I said, beaming as sweetly as we could in the face of his dentistry. "Let's have a gander, yes?"

Kemsley was right.

The place was empty.

Surgically empty. You could have removed cataracts in the kitchen; you could have skated across the bathroom floor. It smelt of bleach, a stomach-clenching, eye-watering smell. No furniture, no curtains, no pictures, no nothing to indicate any sort of life. Even the carpets had been bleached a faded grey-white, even the pipes. An estate agent would have called it "full of promise", and that's all it was, four rooms of great potential and not much else, being walked over by size-twelve assault boots.

Kemsley said, "Nothing. See? This hasn't helped at all."

"Mo was here," I replied firmly.

"How'd you know that?"

"The Executive Officer didn't lie to us."

"Sure. Because no one would."

"Because we had our fingers closed around his heart," we replied. I felt cold, hearing us speak so flatly of these things. "Because when a place is cleaned this thoroughly, it's because there is something to hide."

"Great. Good job the hiders, I think it's pretty well hid, don't you?" I looked around.

He was right. It made our chest ache to think of it. Kemsley was right. There was nothing here.

Then Oda said: "There's a CCTV camera in the entrance hall. So much for mystical stuff."

I could have kissed her.

"A CCTV camera," I repeated firmly, trying to hide our sudden thrill. "And only one way in and out, yes?"

"I think so."

I beamed at Kemsley. All praise the poor fire regulations of North Kilburn. "We can use CCTV," I said. "There's...what? At least a dozen cameras around this estate alone, probably more in all the high streets. You lot seem like escapees from an American spy thriller, right? If they moved him, we can track it."

"Assumptions..." began Kemsley.

"Not really," retorted Anissina. "Not at all. We know Nair came here, and Nair was killed. We know that the shoes of this boy were regarded by Nair as important; we know they led us to Voltage, we know that Voltage led us here. We know that this room was sometime full and is now recently empty. We know that these things are connected. You're wrong, Kemsley. If the boy was here, we must find him, and we can."

We fought down the desire to say something triumphant, to stick our tongue out at Kemsley and hug Anissina round the middle, to hop on the spot and gloat that despite everything, despite our fear of *oh God* of too many things, we were *right*. This was *right*.

Then a voice from the door said, "There's a guy in the courtyard."

Kemsley ignored it, turning to Anissina, face red, clearly trying to find something to say that wasn't the grown-up equivalent of a farting sound, trying to be rational in the face of his own crippling irrationalities. We turned to the man who'd spoken. A trooper, an escapee from another world, all gun and big boot and only the slightest whiff, the merest tracery suggestion that on the inside of his bulletproof vest, someone had stamped a set of defensive wards. We walked slowly towards him, his face turned down across the balcony edge into the courtyard below. I could feel Oda watching me; the Aldermen busy in their bickering. The man on the door had a face like a swollen mushroom, from which peered a pair of sharp, smart eyes. I said, "What guy?"

He nodded down at the courtyard. "That guy."

I shuffled to the balcony and looked down.

He stood in the middle of the courtyard, black shoes planted firmly on the cracked paving stones. His hair was dark brown, not quite black but doing its best, sliced back thin over his almost perfectly spherical skull. His suit was black, his hands were buried in his trouser pockets, buttoned jacket swept back behind his wrists, as casual as a primrose in spring. His skin was that special kind of pale that has been tanned by neon strip lighting. His smile was polite, expectant. His eyes were fixed on us.

We jerked back instinctively. Our heart, without asking permission, started doing the conga down our intestines, our intestines tried to throttle our stomach, our stomach tried to crawl up our throat. I looked at the guy with the gun; he looked at me and said, "Sir?"

"We have to get out," we whispered. "We have to get out *now*."

"Sir," he muttered, and he was too well trained to pronounce fear, but it was there, we could smell it, "there's more."

We crawled like a child to the edge of the balcony, peeked over the edge. There was more. A kid in a hoodie had joined the man in the pinstripe suit, standing behind, bobbing to an unheard beat. I couldn't see his face. I didn't think there was going to be a face to see.

"We have to get out," we whimpered. "We have to go!"

Oda had noticed. "Sorcerer?"

"He's here. He's here, he's here, he's here, he's..."

She leant over the balcony. "Who, him?"

"Him!" She was reaching for her gun. "Don't shoot!"

"Why not? He's just a guy, and even sorcerers can't stop..."

"Bullets don't stop spectres."

"The kids in the hoods?"

"Spectres, yes! You'll just make holes in them."

"All right. So how do I kill them?"

"Beer and cigarettes."

"If this is one..."

"Beer and cigarettes! Get down!"

We dragged her down from where she was leaning over the balcony behind the protection of the yellow brick wall. She looked at us in surprise. "Are you really that scared?"

"Really, honestly and entirely. From the bottom of our being, yes."

"But he's just..."

"No just."

By now, everyone was paying attention. Kemsley strode forwards, looked at us in contempt, peered over the balcony, turned to the man with the mushroom face and said, "What is this now?"

"Possible hostile down below, sir," replied the soldier briskly.

"It's just a man in a suit, and a couple of kids."

"See the kids' faces?" we snarled.

"Well, no..."

"Spectres!"

"And you propose what? Cowering behind a brick wall until he goes away?"

"It's a sensible start."

"Is this... did this man below kill Nair?"

"He peeled the skin from his flesh."

"Then that is Mr Pinner?"

"I'd guess so."

"Then this is it! This is our chance to end it, right here!"

"Didn't you pay attention to the part where he peeled skin?"

"Someone has to do something."

"Someone doesn't know what that something is!"

"And you do?"

"No!"

"I don't have the patience for this game..."

"Kemsley, if he could kill Nair without touching him, think what he'll do to you."

"Sir?"

It was the note of urgency, that ever so slightly unprofessional rise at the end of the trooper's words, that brought all attention to him. He nodded down at the courtyard and said, "He's gone, sir."

We all peered over the edge of the balcony.

There was no one there.

"Well," exclaimed Kemsley brightly. "Not so much trouble."

"So much worse," we whimpered. "So much worse."

"Pull yourself together! My God, you're supposed to lead us! Sorcerer, angel, Mayor, get your arse in gear, Swift!"

I climbed to my feet, leant against the balcony wall, looked, looked again, saw nothing, staggered back, pressed our back into the wall behind us, safe and solid and reassuring. I turned to Anissina and said, "Call 999."

"You want me to bring the emergency services?"

"Yes, fire, ambulance, police and the Good Samaritans too, please. Do it! You—" I turned to Kemsley. "Find out if this place has a big and loud fire alarm. Then start it. You—" I looked at the trooper with the mushroom face. "I don't suppose you know anything about magic?"

The end of his nose twitched as he thought about it. "*Yes*, sir," he conceded. "But to tell the truth, there's nothing a magician can do that a shotgun won't do better."

"Don't hold on to that thought," I sighed. "Get back inside the flat.

Watch windows and doors. And walls, for that matter—you never know where they'll decide to come in. You—" I stared at Oda. "You know, I have no idea what it is you do to stay alive, but I guess you must do it well, so do that."

"Leadership skills," she retorted. "You can look them up another time."

We were going to say something rude, but nothing seemed to come to mind. We hustled back into the flat, a tumble of black coat, armoured soldier, armed fanatic and sorcerer in "What Would Jesus Do?" T-shirt. What *would* Jesus do, we wondered? He seemed to have an occasional temper.

The last man in was Kemsley. He closed the door behind us, pulled the chain across, as if that would make a great deal of difference, and hustled us all into the largest room of the flat, at the end of the hall. The troopers took up various armed-to-the-teeth positions, and I found myself shuffled to the back wall. The street was behind us, neon yellow light sifting through the curtainless glass, the occasional distant swish of traffic. I could hear Anissina on the phone, whispering quietly and urgently.

"Yes...they're armed...armed men...shotguns...and burning bottles. Raleigh Court, they're at...yes...yes...no, Raleigh Court..."

I thought of the phone in my bag. Where was the Midnight Mayor to rescue us? I'd died once before and the bastard hadn't shown up then on a chariot of winged steel, and now that we had the job, who was going to get us out of trouble? I opened my satchel, looked inside at the spray paint and old socks. Nair's phone sat sullen and silent in one pouch. I pulled it out. There was a number there, it occurred to me, just one number in that great list that might actually be some use. Not yet, though—not quite yet. I slipped his phone into my pocket and looked up at the door. Kemsley half-turned and whispered, since this seemed to be what the moment called for, "What now?"

"Oh, you just had to..." I began.

The lights went out. They went out on the balcony outside, and in the stairwell. They went out in the streets behind us, in the street-lamps and the little "ready" LEDs on the TV sets in the houses opposite, they went out in every room of every flat in the court, they went out in number 53, they went out in the waiting warning lights of the sleepy cars below.

Londoners almost never see proper darkness, not true, black-as-black, turn-from-the-sun, smother-the-moon darkness. Even when the curtains are drawn in their darkened rooms, there will be the shimmer of street light through the tiny gaps at the edges of the window frame, or the ready waiting light of a radio, or the glow of their mobile phone left on in the dark. There is no darkness darker than the darkness of the city, when all the lights go out. The stars and the moon are lost behind the bricks of the buildings. I snatched a sliver of neon as the last lamp went out outside, cradled it to my chest, let it warm the skin of my face and my curled fingertips, a tiny yellow shimmer in perfect black suffocation.

Then a trooper said, "Lights."

I heard the racketing of equipment, the tearing of Velcro, and as the first torch went on, it nearly blinded us; we flinched away from its white glare. Oda had a torch too—where she had concealed it I didn't want to speculate—and for Anissina and Kemsley...we had to look twice, but yes, for certain, as I looked at the Aldermen, their eyes glowed. The mad, wild, spinning marble glow of the dragon that guards the gates of London. The sinking red vortex of an angry tiger burning bright, the kind of stare that looked at you and saw just an inanimate object standing between it—for those eyes weren't human—and some more worthwhile meal. There's reasons people fear the Aldermen.

We waited.

Silence. Nothing. On the whole surface of the planet, there is nowhere that silence is perfect—an engine will rumble in the distance, a bird will sing, an insect will scuttle, a leaf will sway in the wind, a footstep will fall, a brick will crumble. This was not a perfect silence either: the wind was humming outside, a low mournful tune from some forgotten folklore that had accepted death and now found the subject mundane; the drizzle was turning into rain that rattled like a thousand tiny ball bearings against the glass. But nothing in it that was human. I felt for Nair's phone in my pocket, felt the burning brand on my right hand, aching.

Then Oda said, "I smell fumes."

At once I looked up, and it seemed that the whole room in unison drew a long, deep breath through the nose, and all at once we all smelt what she, sharper, had detected — the unmistakable warm dry whiff of car fumes drifting across the floor. I risked a little more brightness to the neon glow in my hands, pushing the orange-pink bubble of illumination towards the door, and saw it, thin greyish-brown trickling smoke crawling in through the gaps, spilling over the floor.

I drew my light back, half-crawled to the window, and looked out. In the street below, a thing that might have been fog but for the sickly brownish thickness of it was rising, tumbling out of the exhaust pipes of the cars parked below without a sound, filling the streets like some swaying alien sea and still rising, crawling up the sides of the buildings and slithering through the gaps at the sides of the doors.

The troopers were already reaching for gas masks — say what you would, they were prepared. Kemsley and Anissina didn't seem to care, their skin taking on a strange silverish tone, their nails already two inches too long, but in Oda's eyes, even as she tied a scarf across her nose and mouth, I could see the fear. I drew my own scarf across my nose and mouth, but that still left eyes, already starting to sting and itch with the dirt crawling up in gaseous form from the door and floor.

And we heard, somewhere not so far off:

Dedededededededededededededede . . .

And perhaps a hint of:

Duhdeduhduh duhdeduhduh duhdeduhduh . . .

I looked back out of the window. It was a long way down, deeper since we now couldn't see the bottom. By the faint neon clutched between my fingers, I could see the sickly fumes twist and spin around Anissina's breath, as it seeped slowly from her peeled-back lips. She still superficially resembled a human — two arms, two legs and all the bits in between — but her skin had a metal shimmer to it, her hair a wire quality, her tongue a twisted red forked sliver on the air. The fumes didn't seem to be bothering her. They were bothering us.

Then the door opened. I said, "No, wait, don't..."

Kemsley said, "Shoot it!"

Gunshots in a confined space are like having popcorn explode inside your eardrum; automatic gunfire was the popcorn, the bag, the oil and the whole microwave. I half-saw in the flashes from the barrels a figure, all hood and faceless shadow, staggering back as his clothes were ripped to shreds, as fabric popped and burst backwards and outwards and severed and snapped and spat and the men emptied out every bullet they had in the barrel, I could hear the clitter-clatter of falling casings, smell over the stench of the exhaust fumes the sweeter stench of burning powder and overheated metal and, when it stopped, I could hear nothing but banging in our head and taste nothing but dirt and smoke and see nothing but afterburn star flashes on the inside of our eyes. "Stop!" we screamed, "Stop!"

And they stopped. Eventually.

I crawled to my feet, pressed my neon bubble into my chest for childish safety. In the torchlight, I could see the thing standing in the door. Its clothes were nothing but a scalded, smoking spiderweb, blasted threads clinging to each other by the thinnest strain of grey fabric, hood shot straight through so I could see the smog rising *behind* it, look straight through that non-face, through the nothingness, empty air, that supported the almost nothing of its clothes. The spectre seemed more surprised than hurt, its hood turning downwards as it examined the shrivelled remnants of its garb, no flesh beneath, nothing to suggest that anything worse had happened to it than a saunter through a very thick shrubbery. Then its head—the emptiness that was its head—turned upwards and seemed to fix its attention on the nearest soldier, who, without a finger falling upon him, started to scream.

It was an animal noise, pure and without thought. It wasn't just that his vocal cords were tightened by agony or terror, it was his whole throat, his lungs, every part of him that had anything to do with air, seemed to clench. His feet left the floor, his fingers spasmed wide, the gun falling down at his feet, his face went back and his throat seemed to buckle. He screamed and screamed so loud and so high and I could see the bottom of his ribcage seem to twist into it, heard it buckle, snap and crack like dry cereal hitting hot milk, pushing more air up through his mouth.

Then we saw it. A thin line of redness drew itself across an eyelid, tiny and vivid in the torchlight, then another across his cheek, then another down his chin, then another over the twisted, warped pro-trusion of his tortured windpipe, then another, and another, slashing through his nostrils, inside his nostrils, across his lips, over his gums, over the white of his eyes that began to fill with scarlet blood as, faster than the mind could register them, his skin began to break and crack, tear and slice and slide with a thousand little dribbling cuts, never longer than an inch, never wider than the thickness of a sheet of paper, and now there was no air left in his lungs to scream by nor nothing in his body that seemed to let him inhale but he hung sus-pended there as his skin cracked and parted and sliced and his eyes went red and filled with blood and his teeth stained with blood and there was just blood and the rattle of his bones and breaking cartilage of his windpipe and Kemsley was screaming, "Do something, do something!" in a voice that rolled unnaturally deep and full of bubbles from inside his throat and we realised he meant us, do something, and there was still the spectre in the door just watching and Oda stepped past us, levelled her gun at the soldier's head and fired. Just fired, just...did it. But his head rocked back and his body jerked by the cuts still kept cutting, slicing under his nails, tearing apart his flesh, wiping away all trace of skin except a few loose white shreds like the thin roughness of dry skin exposed to too much sun, drooping off bright red flesh.

We looked at the spectre. We opened our hands and snarled, let the neon bloom around us and bending our head like an angry bull, charged for it, past the dead body being turned into dead meat in an assault jacket, through the door and slammed the top of our head crown-first into the spectre's chest. We felt something resist, the strength and softness of a pillow, and kept on pushing, driving the spectre back to the edge of the balcony and there, on the very edge, bent down all the way and tipped it, grabbed it by its trendy trainers and hurled them up with all our strength, vision a blazing blue, and threw it hood-first into the smog below.

It fell without a sound. No voice, to make no noise.

We straightened slowly as it vanished into darkness, turned and by our neon glow stared into the face of the man known as Mr Pinner, the death of cities. We were sure of it. He stood at the end of the balcony walk, head on one side, smiling at us. Just smiling, hands in pockets. He looked...ordinary. An ordinary man in a silly suit, no taller, possibly a few inches less, than we stood, in his thirties and trying not to think about middle age, smiling, an expression of almost fond amusement, like a teacher watching the smug pupil in the class struggling with an idea that the other kids have already grasped.

He didn't seem to have anything to say, just stood and smiled.

Then we said, "Mr Pinner?"

And his smile flickered. Just for a moment, it flickered. Recognition—surprise.

Then Kemsley had pushed past me, he was shouting, roaring, an animal snarl from animal lips, he'd forgotten which fire was anger and which was fear, which was cause or effect, and just shoved straight past me, gun in one hand, flames, bright, gas-stink flames shedding carbon crispiness, in the other. He fired, emptied the entire magazine at Mr Pinner and threw the fire, a billowing burst of cooking stench and searing heat. We covered our eyes, heard it hit, heard the soft *whumph* of it slamming over a solid mass, smelt burning, just charred and crispy burning, heard tortured warped glass crinkle and crack.

I opened my eyes. Mr Pinner was standing in a shroud of smoke and fumes. His pinstripe suit was untouched, not even scorched; but the bullets had entered his flesh. I could see a mass of them, five, bunched in the middle of his chest. He looked at them with mild dis- interest. Then he reached carefully with thumb and forefinger, and stuck them into the nearest bullet hole. His lips and eyes narrowed in concentration as he twisted and turned his fingers inside the gap in his flesh. They tightened; he pulled them out. There was a small, snub bullet in his hand.

I looked for blood. There wasn't any. The hole in his chest was white, an off-white beneath the padding of his suit, and the only thing that seemed to come from it was a tiny slip of paper. It slipped from his flesh, dropped onto the floor, tumbled over the balcony towards us. I bent down to pick it up, even as Kemsley screamed and threw more flames, belched electric sparks from his sharpened teeth, fum- bling in his pocket for more ammo as he did.

I scooped up the piece of paper. There was lettering on it, faint, in dull ink. It said:

Thank you for shopping at Tesco.

Mr Pinner was still standing, still unscathed, Kemsley pushing another magazine into his pistol. I grabbed him by the shoulder, was shrugged off, grabbed him again and hissed, "You can't kill him like this!" and dragged him back into the flat.

I kicked the door shut behind us and Kemsley collapsed against the wall. His eyes were streaming, clear lines streaking down the dirt clinging to his face, to all our faces, from the ceiling-high smog now filling the room. Oda was coughing, even Anissina looked unhappy, and our lungs burnt, ached, our eyes stung, every part of us calling for water and none to hand. Our head wanted to fly away from our stomach, our stomach wanted to see what it was like where the feet were at. We pressed our hands against the door, whispering, *"Domine dirige nos, domine dirige"* — the old blessing of the city, "Lord, lead us" — telling the lock, dear lock, be our friend, just for a minute, be our friend.

"My bag!" I wheezed. "Paint!"

Oda staggered forwards, half-tripping over the skinless, faceless, humanless flesh that had a few moments before been a guy with a gun, opened the satchel hanging off my back and handed me a can of paint. I drew quickly, the first ward that came to mind — a cross within a cross, in bright blue paint. Someone was trying to force the door, slamming it back on the hinges, but as the last dribble of paint went on, the thundering stopped.

A voice from outside said, "Are there Aldermen in there, by any chance?"

It was a polite, well-educated voice. It knew the answer to its own questions. The paint on the door began to burn, to bubble and peel. I turned to the window and said, "Only way out."

No one, not even sobbing Kemsley, seemed inclined to argue. Not any more.

"No way down," pointed out Oda.

We strode to the window, slammed our palms towards the glass. Not touching, we didn't need to get that close, the movement and the magic were enough. The glass burst out, not a shard left in the frame, and tinkled merrily away down into the swirling smog below. Oda leant out, tears — not of sorrow, but of pain and chemical suffocation — running down her dirty face, and said, "We don't know what's down there."

"Gotta be better than in here."

"We've no way down."

"Don't troopers carry rope?" We turned to look at them. They shrugged, and didn't offer rope. "Terrific," I sighed. I looked up to the ceiling, smelt paint simmering, roasting, heard Anissina say, "He's coming through the door!"

I reached up to the ceiling. I could taste electricity, still feel it lending me a little more strength, a little more speed. Electricity that happy meant something friendly to carry it in. I heaved with all my strength, closed my eyes and told it to come to me, to bring its friends with it, strained and dragged until my head spun and my knees bent, felt dust falling in my hair and down my face, mixing with dirt, smog and tears, and here it came, the great coils of wire, twisting out of the ceiling, the floor, the walls, spinning and spitting like angry snakes on a hot plate, rising at my command. I waved furiously at the cables, commanding them towards the window, imploring, *please, please, please be my friends . . .*

Bricks tumbled from the walls, the whole building seemed to creak as length after length tore from the crackling gaps in the floor: a tarantula's web, an earthquake's playground of cracks rippling and writhing as the cables crawled at my command down the side of the building. I gestured furiously at the nearest trooper, "Get your arse down it!"

He looked with doubt for a moment at this snapping, angry coil vanishing into smoggy darkness, but good training and a better brain were his saviour, and he threw his leg over the window ledge and wriggled down into darkness without a word. Coughing and hacking, I gestured more troopers towards the cable, caught Oda as she staggered, legs wobbling in the fumes, and felt her immediately pull away from my touch, as if I was somehow dirtier than her. Even with death knocking, I had time to feel a soft warmth in my throat that might have on a better day been sorrow.

Then Anissina said, "The door!"

I turned, saw a flash of light around the hinges, heard the bolts snap, then bury themselves in the ceiling, saw Anissina stumble across the twisting floor as more cables crawled from beneath us and lashed out of the walls in a zigzag of twisted wire. I saw Kemsley raise a child's face, too much going on for that mind of his to comprehend, look up towards the door, and see for a moment in it a man in a pin-striped suit, from whose chest thin wafts of paper tumbled where there should have been blood.

Then Kemsley started to scream, and it was the same pressed-down scream of Nair, of the soldier who had died, of lungs that couldn't stop, of a throat drawn too tight for anything other than sound to escape, and I grabbed Anissina and half threw her out of the window, one wrist tangling in cables as she dropped, heard her shoulder crack and a cry burst from her lips, saw those mad red eyes that weren't her own.

"Oda, get..." I began, but my words were lost in the sound of Kemsley's scream, and there was Mr Pinner in the door, smiling, just smiling like always, and the spectres behind him, filling the balcony, faceless non-eyes staring straight at us. I felt a tear down my arm, felt a stabbing across my hand, a burning below my eye, tiny, micro-scopic, agony. We looked at our fingertips and saw the ringed pattern of our flesh part in a tiny, crawling line of blood, too shallow even to ooze, and knew in an instant we would scream like Kemsley and die like Kemsley and that would be the end, *it*, unnameable *it*, whatever that was, goodbye to sense, goodbye light, dark, fear, sorrow, pain, blood, flesh, humanity, mortality, Midnight Mayor...

So I said, "No!" because that was all I knew.

And we saw a tiny droplet of blood rise from our breaking flesh, and that was enough, just enough. We looked into Mr Pinner's smil-ing grey eyes, and raised our right hand, skin breaking inside the fin-gerless mitten, and screamed with the beginning of our final breath, *"Domine dirige nos!"*

The world went blue.

Beautiful, electric blue. Blue blood dribbling down our fingers, blueness blazing across our eyes, blue fire spilling from our hands, blue fury in our veins, blood blue inside and out, soul blue electric rage, we are the angels, we be light, fire, life, freedom, fury . . .

and all I knew was

set our blood on fire!

he wasn't scared

not even of us

but then, that hadn't been the point.

We turned our hands down towards the floor of writhing wires and spitting cables, burst up from the carpet and the concrete, and turned the fury of our fire downwards, shook our fingertips until that single drop of blood that had wormed out of the paper-thin cut on our flesh shook itself free and fell.

When it hit the floor, it went *boom*.

And for a moment, even Mr Pinner looked surprised.

The floor buckled. It creaked, it twisted, it bent, it sagged. The cracks ran across it, up the walls, and crawled into the edges of the ceiling.

Then the floor collapsed.

It went out beneath me, beneath Oda, and beneath Kemsley. We tumbled in dust and shattered cable that flopped like dead creepers from the hole of our passage, spilt like so much old flour in a torn sack down into the floor below. I bounced, head hitting the lower end of a sofa, feet knocking over a coffee table—we had fallen into someone's living room. Oda landed on her feet, like a cat, rolled and rose in a movement, twisting away from the radiator against the wall and coming up by a small shelf of cheesy books. Kemsley fell where he had fallen above, a limp bloody sack in the hall towards the door. I rolled to my front, then crawled to my feet. Nothing felt broken but that meant nothing, we were on fire, blazing inside with fury and terror and stolen electricity snatched from the wire, pain wasn't going to get a look-in until it was too late to care, so we didn't care, staggered forwards, tried to pick Kemsley up and found his sleeve saturated with blood that slipped from our fingers. "Oda!" we screamed. "Help us!"

She was forward in an instant, ducking her head under one arm and lifting him bodily, crouching and rising like a weight-lifter at the gym to get the man to his feet. His face was a nothing, an acid burn from which strips of loose whiteness dangled, but his breath still came, even as the hair fell from his head, the roots torn loose by the laceration his skull had received. I heaved open the front door, ran onto the balcony—no spectres, not yet—ran to the end, snatching electricity from the walls around me until our skin was bright white lightning and our hair stood on end, saw the stairwell by the faint neon glow clutched to my hand, heard above,

De de de de de de de de

And maybe:

Kaboom kaboom kakakaboom kaboom kaboom . . .

Even Oda, superhuman, subhuman, inhuman, utterly human—didn't know, didn't care—even Oda was struggling with the dead weight of Kemsley. I took his other arm, slipped it over the back of my neck, dragged him into the stairwell and downstairs, staggering and stumbling in the faint glow of neon by which we ran. Ground floor; courtyard, the courtyard where Nair had died, smog, so thick that two steps were two too many and now behind was nothing more than a vague recollection lost of all geographical meaning, and "out" was a naive illusion from brighter times. I felt in my pocket, found Nair's phone, shrieked at Oda, "Road! Get to a road!" and she chose a direction; faith, random, someone had to choose.

So we staggered/ran/fell in our bubble of stolen pinkish-orange light, could have been at sea, could have been alone in the world, no way to tell, just silence and perhaps:

Chachachachabang chachachachabang . . .

De de de de de de . . .

Kakakaboom kaboom kaboom kakaka . . .

Nair's phone took all of time and much of space to warm up; then did; I found the phone book, I flicked through; a number, a long shot, but still a number. It was labelled Black Cab and nothing more, no company, no nothing, and that was why it was a shot fired in the dark. I called it, our staggering in the smog had found a wall, not an exit, Oda pressed us to it as she directed our course and used it as a guide, coughing and choking as we staggered through the dark.

A voice on the other end of the phone said, "Black Cab, how may I help you?"

"I need a ride!" I whispered it, but the words came out an old man's wheeze through the scarf across my nose and mouth.

"From where to where?"

"Raleigh Court, Kilburn, to anywhere safe!"

"What time do you require collecting?"

"As soon as possible!"

"Very well, sir, please make your way to Raleigh Road and a cab will be there to collect you in the next few minutes..."

I hung up, Oda had found dustbins, dustbins rang a bell, it was near where I'd found my Mr Fox. I hissed, "This way!" and dragged her by the weighty bridge of Kemsley in the way I thought I remembered the road. A few steps on, and Oda trod on something and hissed. I looked at it. A trooper, one of the Aldermen's, lay on the pavement in front of us, a penknife stuck calmly through the wrinkled pipe of his throat.

"Quiet!" I whispered. "Quiet!"

We stopped, and listened.

De de de de de de de de . . .

"Where is he?" hissed Oda.

"Don't know. Shush!"

Kakakaboom kakakaboom kakakaboom . . .

"Sorcerer..."

Fear, not question, reassurance, not answers. She could probably have done with answers, but knew better than to think I'd have any going spare.

I curled my fingers tighter around our neon bubble, let it become nothing more than a tiny flame between my clutching fingertips. "This way," I whispered. We staggered forwards at an old man's totter, each step the one before the last that ruptures that ageing artery, this one, maybe this one, maybe now...so we kept moving, counting maybes, no sound except the tiny whisper of a bass beat in a pair of headphones and our own gigantic shuffling steps.

When we reached the pavement of the road, I nearly tripped on it, feet staggering into a gutter full of foul, blocked and rotting leaf-mould-rain. I hissed, "Here!" and Oda stopped too.

"What now?" she asked.

"Shush! Listen!"

We listened. There was a faint wind now, blowing in from the edges of the smog, promising, somewhere, a slightly fresher air. It blew something else. I looked down at my feet. A small piece of paper had blown up from the gutter and tangled round my ankle. I half-bent down to pick it up. It was a piece of newspaper, torn at the corner. It said:

SHOCKER IN
CHERYL SAYS

**utrageous party pranks have led
commented to said that she wo
me back my
of the
en**

I looked up.

The only light was coming from my fingertips. It seeped upwards over a foot, no more, from where I stood, before becoming lost in the smog. I should have been able to feel his breath, had he lungs to breathe. I felt his toes brush mine; hard leather toes pressing down on the soft space of my too-big shoes, where my toes should have been. Mr Pinner smiled. We screamed, "Oda, ru—"

His hand came up. It was holding something bright and shiny, which stabbed down towards our eye. We caught his hand, wrapped our fingers around his sleeve and let the neon blaze, let it burn from inside us and screamed again, "Oda, run, get to the end of the—"

His other hand came up and pushed into our throat, pressing our chin back and taking the rest of us with it, and now we could see what was in his raised hand. It was a fountain pen, titanium-gold, hinting at all the shiniest colours of the silvery rainbow as he brought it down towards us, the end stained slightly with black ink. Even ignoring what he was, what he might be, the threat of that stuck through our eye filled us with enough terror to lend us strength, and we let the electricity blaze across us. It should have killed him, would have killed a man, set his hair on fire, but it just flickered harmlessly over his flesh and down to earth, didn't even singe his suit, and we could hear Oda staggering down the street and see the nib growing bigger and bigger, filling the left-hand side of our world.

The phone in my pocket started to ring. I screamed, "Oda, get to the cab, get to the..."

An engine started at the end of the road, I saw a light, a bright orange-yellow light, letters lost somewhere in the smog. "Oda! Oda, get to the—"

Mr Pinner's fingers tightened around our windpipe, pushing down on the thick muscles, and his eyes were our universe and he murmured, "What are you, blue-blood?"

The orange light grew closer. I could hear the rattle of a great, old engine, that would one day shake itself apart in a shower of bolts and blackened iron, and run without a hitch until that happened. We looked him in the eye and replied, "We are Swift, and I am the angels!"

I let go of his wrist. I let his fingers push back on my throat, I tumbled head-over-heels, flopped back like someone had replaced my bones with jelly and caught him off-balance, threw his entire weight forwards as I went back and kicked and jammed my elbows together as we fell, tried to push my bottom into the pavement as being my least delicate part, landed badly, felt my leg twist beneath me and rolled, heaving him to one side and pushing him away. His fingers fell from my neck and I crawled up, my fingers tangling in his suit, which didn't tear. It didn't come away from his flesh, didn't reveal the shirt beneath, but stayed fused to him, as if a very part of his body and skin. No time, not now, not now...

We staggered back onto our feet and ran, waiting for the pain of a thousand paper cuts, ran towards the yellow light, saw Oda already by its source, pushing the bloody Kemsley into the back of the cab, and there it was, TAXI in large letters against the light and it was big and black and curved and belched black smoke from its rear and shuddered on its rickety suspension and it was a black cab, no, not enough: it was *the* Black Cab, its skin so black it stood out deeper against the darkness; its windows so fouled over with dirt and unwashed filthy rain that you couldn't see inside, its wheels spitting smoke, its engine roaring like a caged animal. Oda was already half-way inside. I tumbled in after her and shouted at the driver, "Out of here! Go!"

He put his foot to the accelerator.

We went.

There are stories. Some of them, unlike most, are true.

Stories of...

A train that goes round and round forever on the Circle Line, will go for ever, will never stop, never rest, never take on a new passenger except for those who know the secrets of the Last Train and when it runs.

The Night Bus, which collects the spirits of the dead who died sleeping and alone in the dark.

Lady Neon, whose eyes are too bright for any mortal to look on without being driven mad.

The Black Cab, which can go anywhere, whose driver has heard of Isaac Newton and thinks he missed a few points, and which will always charge a fare. Usually, a very high fare.

Something to worry about at a later point, we decided.

One problem at a time.

Oda said, "He's not dead."

Kemsley lay on the floor of the cab. The driver's voice drifted in from the intercom, his face lost somewhere in the murky darkness behind the glass shutter. *"If he bleeds on my floor, you've got to pay for cleaning."*

I said, "Strap him to something."

She scowled but, grunting and groaning, heaved him into one of the fold-down seats on the backwards-facing side of the cab, and strapped him in. I buckled myself into the seat behind the driver, and added, "Now strap yourself in." The belt felt hard across my chest, stiff, and a little bit too slippery.

"Why?"

I pointed at a sign. It said, "Passengers Must Wear Seat Belts At All Times".

"Is this . . ."

"Do it."

She looked at us, saw through the dirt and grime and knew better than to argue. She strapped herself in. Kemsley was something from the butcher's yard that had been left out in the rain and the sun for too many weeks, and by this process acquired a twisted mimicry of life. The driver said, *"So where can I take you?"*

His voice was a muffled crackle over the intercom, the red LED on the door a little bit too bright, the windows between us and him a little too dark. All I could see was smog in the bright headlights of the cab. I leant forward and said, "The City. Corporation of London. The Thames."

"That's three places."

"Are we caring if the Alderman dies?" asked Oda carefully.

I looked at her, saw a face hacked by stone out of an iceberg, looked at Kemsley. It occurred to us, for a moment, that we didn't care. Not our problem. I said, "Damn. Damn damn damn. Elizabeth Garrett Anderson Hospital for Women, Euston Road."

"*Righto.*"

I could see the red lights of the tariff metre in the front of the cab. They were clocking up numbers and letters as we drove, but not by any mathematics I knew.

"You want to go to an abandoned hospital?" asked Oda. She was getting her breath back, wiping dirt from her eyes with hands dirtier than her face: instinct, not practicality.

We turned sharply to her. "If the Order raids it, when this is done, if they attack the hospital, if they dare go after the healers, we swear, we *swear* we will bring you and them down."

She just smiled. "Right," she said. "More magic."

"Sure, because black cabs just happen to drive into magical war zones on a regular basis," I snapped.

"I *am* serene, am I not?"

"Getting used to it?"

Her face darkened, but she said nothing. The head of our driver was just a black outline peeking out from behind the slab of his head-rest, lit up only by the reflected glow of his headlights and the dull red illumination from the tariff metre. I looked across at Oda and said, "You carry much cash?"

"No. Why?"

"Cab rides are always expensive."

Especially this one.

"You're worried about the fare?"

"I thought you'd be pleased with me. A good, noble, avoiding-whichever-sin-it-is sentiment."

"He sees your heart, not your smile," she intoned.

"What does that mean?"

"It means that twenty quid slipped to a cabby can't redeem your soul."

"That's a 'no' on the fare, then?"

"Yes, that's a no."

"Fine." I turned away, and our eyes passed over Kemsley. He was leaning forward against his seat belt and wheezing. I could see the veins pumping through the remnants of the skin on his neck, jerking in and out like some obscene production line in a food factory, filling with thick blue blood and then deflating to a bruised tube among the ruined mess of his skin. We looked away. Outside, the smog seemed to be lifting, streetlights flashing between the sickly mist, reflected orange stains moving from back to front across the ceiling of the cab, too fast and too erratic to pick out any shapes or shadows. I thought about Anissina. I slipped my hand into my jacket pocket for Nair's phone, thumbed through the address file, found her right near the top, dialled.

"Who are you—" began Oda.

"Anissina."

"Why?"

"She might still be lost."

"We can't do anything for her, even if it should be done," replied Oda primly. "She falls or she fights. That's how it is."

A phone rang on the other end of the line, and kept on ringing. There was no reply. It went to answerphone. We hung up. We knew better than to leave our voice floating as electricity in the wire. Outside the window, the smog was almost entirely gone, just a few loose traceries being washed away by falling rain, that slipped sideways like tiny transparent snakes across the taxi's window. I could see flashes of houses, but that's all they were—shadows that came and went in some impossible, too-far-off distance, perspective playing tricks, architecture playing tricks as terraced house melted into flashy apartment melted into rickety shed melted into bungalow. It gave us

a headache to look at it, would have set an epileptic screaming. Oda
had noticed too, a warning was in her voice: "Sorcerer?"

"Don't look too hard."

"What is this?"

"It's the Black Cab. It goes anywhere."

"Does it take the North Circular?"

"Oda! That almost sounded like desert-dry humour."

"It wasn't."

"It doesn't take the North Circular. If Einstein had seen how the
Black Cab moved, he'd have given up physics and gone back to playing the trombone."

"Einstein played the trombone?"

"I don't know. But it would fit the hairstyle."

I had the sense we were picking up speed. I risked glancing out
of the window. Signs drifted by, seemed to hang in gloomy nothing,
pointing at nothing, suspended in nothing, just floating by in the
darkness outside, lit up by no source I could see. The road was nothing but a black shimmer beneath us, defined only by the painted-on
markings that lit up blinding yellow and white as we skimmed over
them. In the distance, I could see neon signs drifting by like a lit-up
ship far out to sea, promising plays, shopping, films, long hours and
cheap prices. A billboard drifted by too slow for the speed our wheels
were spinning at, the long eyelashes of a perfume-soaked model
blinking at us from the pale paper; a single pedestrian, hat drawn
down across his eyes, every inch of him as dark as shadow, without
variety in texture or tone, vanished round an unseen corner, not once
looking up. We felt suddenly tired, sad and alone. A blazing billboard
advertised a car whose engine revved inside the hoarding's plywood
frame; it floated up overhead, drifted above the roof of the taxi and
set down on the other side. A great fat rat, larger than any urban fox,
looked up from where it was chewing a grey-green soaking ham-
burger, and blinked a pair of bright red eyes at us as we drove by. A
short road of bright pink streetlamps flashed, came, went; a lorry, as

tall as a house, driver lost in the soot-black, burnt-black darkness of his roaring vehicle, streaked by outside, horn blazing: a sheet of spray containing more than its fair share of goldfish and flapping river eels slapped over the cab. A pair of headlights flashed for a second, then vanished; a pair of pulsing yellow bulbs declared a zebra crossing, on which a zebra grazed, its skin carved from curved aluminium, its legs glued together out of old toilet rolls. It chewed on spilt chicken tikka with a patient gnaw and watched us as we sped on.

Oda whispered, "Obscene. Damnation. *Obscene*."

We replied, "Beautiful. Just beautiful."

She stared at us in horror. "How can you pretend to be human, and not be afraid?"

"It is beautiful," we replied. "You've just got to look at it right. Of all the things, the frightening and inexplicable things, the terrifying and the chaotic and the uncontrolled, you just had to pick on magic to fear and hate, in that order and in equal measure."

"Don't think you know me, sorcerer."

"Is there anything more to know?"

That seemed to silence her. We were almost surprised, and felt again a thing, strange and hollow, that might have been sadness. The beat of Kemsley's blood, pushing and falling against the protruding pipe of his veins, was slowing. There was no point pretending it was our imagination; that just made it worse. No point asking the driver to go faster. If Einstein couldn't work out how the Black Cab moved, we certainly couldn't; and besides, back-seat drivers just made the fare steeper when the cab stopped.

One problem at a time.

"Oda," I said carefully, "when we get to where we're going, we'll have to pay a fare. It'll be...more than money. It may be...almost anything. Don't argue. Don't shout, don't haggle. And, for the sake of all that's merciful, don't try and shoot anything."

"Why more than money?"

"The Black Cab can go anywhere. I mean...*anywhere*. Get your mind outside the boring three-dimensional trivialities of geography and you still haven't come to terms with it. We're not going there. Humans can't abide 'anywhere'; they . . . we are built for very specific environments. It is only natural that the fares are steep."

"Sorcerer?"

I sighed. "Yes?"

"The man in the suit. He's not human."

"No."

"He bleeds paper."

"Yes."

"Why?"

"I don't know. There are constructs that can bleed things other than blood, but I've never seen one looking so ordinary as him. And he's clearly not ordinary. Not human, not ordinary, mortal. His suit was part of his flesh; he bleeds receipts, old bits of newspaper. A summoning of some sort? But then he shows so much independence: he speaks, he enquires, he demonstrates amusement. Most things summoned from the nether reaches are incapable of much more than slobber and slash."

"You don't know how to kill it?"

"No."

"That seems like quite a major problem."

"Yes."

"You're bleeding."

"What?"

She tilted her chin up to my face. I felt under my eye, found a tiny, almost imperceptible brownish stain of blood running down from my eyelid, where a paper cut no longer than a child's toenail had been drawn across my skin. "We be blue-blood burning," we sighed, wiping it away.

"What does that mean?"

"Mean? It is what we are." I glanced out of the window, saw the distant windows of a lit-up Underground train fading into the night, the flicker of a traffic light going red, amber, green, green, amber, red, too fast and rhythmic to be real. "He didn't seem to realise that I'm..." I rubbed my right hand. "He doesn't seem to know I'm the Midnight..."

"Didn't do you much good, did it?"

"Kemsley"—drooping flesh with a pair of shaven lips sitting opposite us, couldn't look—"said something about inauguration. Ghosts and streets and midnight mystic doings."

"Didn't do Nair much good, did it?"

"No." We were silent a while. A thought was pushing at the edge of speech, trying to get out. It was strong, angry, with claws for fingers. We let it out. "But that may have been the reason Nair made us Midnight Mayor." Oda raised an eyebrow, a perfect half-moon. "The Midnight Mayor is just a human with complications. And we..."

"Aren't," she concluded. I said nothing. Thinking too much was always trouble. "What happens now?"

"There was a CCTV camera. In the hallway below, a CCTV camera, and only one really viable way out. CCTV everywhere."

"So?"

"So even if Mr Pinner—the man in the suit, the death of...even if whatever he is destroys the camera, there'll be an archive somewhere, records. Better than sharing the memories of pigeons, they couldn't muster more than a day of recollections. There'll be something, somewhere. The Aldermen can trace it, they have...they take their work very seriously. We can still find the boy."

"You think it's that important?"

"I think that if Kemsley dies, then it's because Mr Pinner thinks it's that important. I think that Mr Pinner had Boom Boom abduct the boy from his club; I think that's interesting. Why keep him alive? He said alive. So yes. Find the boy, find some answers. 'Give me back my hat'. He might know...he *has* to know something."

"What if he doesn't?"

"Well, I would hope that if I get flayed alive and the city burns, you'll have the good manners to die an excruciating death with the rest of us."

"Sorcerer, have you ever wondered why you have never been appointed to a managerial position before?"

"My honest honest face?"

"Don't flatter yourself." She paused, sharp eyes fixed steadily on Kemsley. "You really think finding the boy will make this better? Stop what happened to Nair happening to you?"

"Yes."

"You sure?"

"Yes."

"I'm not."

"Why?"

"I think you're doing it for this woman—Loren. I don't think there's enough proof for any of it. Mo, Mr Pinner, the club, the shoes, the ravens, the Mayor. A lot of circumstance, but nothing else. I think you want the boy to be involved. Then you can help *her* while helping yourself."

I thought about this a while.

Lights turned and drifted outside, a thousand miles away, as tall as a skyscraper pressed up to the eye of the window.

"OK," I said. "All right. Yes. She's lonely. She's scared. And we are ... we have never had a friend. Just strangers out to get something done. Acquaintances with an agenda. Never this thing, 'friend'. I want something ordinary. It was *nice*. It was unremarkable. Just a friend. That's what they say, isn't it? We're 'just' friends."

"Matthew?"

"Yes?"

Silence. Just the rumbling of the taxi's engine.

A moment that might have been something different.

"We're slowing down."

Just a moment.

I looked out of the window. I could see the reflective black slab of Euston station, the slow flickering lights of Euston Road, crawling into existence in the darkness. "Yeah," I said. "We are."

My satchel was on the floor. I picked it up, rummaged through for my wallet. I had £40 left. It wouldn't be enough, but it'd be a start.

The streets were becoming more solid, pavements growing out of the gloom, shopfronts edging closer and closer towards us, growing bricks and settling their way into solid reality. The driver's voice came in over the intercom.

"Anywhere round here in particular?"

"If you could just drop us off outside the main entrance..."

"No problem."

We turned, actually turned, something I couldn't remember the cab doing in our whole journey, down a side street off from Euston, round the back of a grey office block and a Gothic fire station, towards a red, turreted building with broken windows and bright blue hoarding all around its walls, stuck with signs saying, "DANGER KEEP OUT" and posters for dubious gigs and, of course, scrawled in white paint over the blue hoarding by the door:

GIVE ME BACK MY HAT

The Elizabeth Garrett Anderson Hospital for Women. Abandoned by almost everyone and left to rot. Almost being the important part.

The taxi slid to a stop outside the padlocked dark entrance, covered over with plywood. There wasn't any traffic on the street, not at this hour, not even night buses turning onto Euston Road towards King's Cross. Even the lights in the hotels ahead were out, even the receptions just distant dim puddles. I had to remember to breathe, watching the dark shadow of the driver's hands reach up to check the tariff, to stop the clock, watching a hand push back the Plexiglas between him and us, waiting for the damage.

"It's thirty quid," he said, just a voice drifting in from the driver's compartment.

"What?"

"Thirty quid," he repeated.

"OK. Great. Thanks."

I fumbled in my wallet for the money.

"And her gun."

I glanced at Oda, whose lips pursed. I mouthed, *please*, and she reluctantly pulled a gun from a pocket, all black metal and power, and pushed it through the gap between passenger and driver compartments. As her fingers slid in, a hand moved in the front, locked down on her wrist and dragged her forward so sharp and hard I heard the seat belt lock around her chest and saw her face wrinkle in pain.

"Her hand," said the driver. "You seen her hand?"

I realised he was talking to me. "Um... yes?" I hazarded.

"You seen the blood?"

I glanced instinctively at her fingers, grasped in his, stretched across the panel separating front from back. I couldn't see any blood, not a shimmer of darkness on that deep chocolate skin, dry and thick.

"No?" I mumbled.

"Hey, now, I just drive cabs you know, but I gotta tell you, I've noticed, and it wasn't like that a few years ago. Fucking government!"

"Um..."

"Immigrants! I mean, I'm no racist, some of my best friends are foreign, but no one can deny it's a problem and now look at this." He dragged her hand forward and Oda cried out as her chest strained against the seat belt, which seemed to refuse to budge. "Look at this! A disgrace!"

I couldn't see his face, couldn't see if he was smiling, joking. There was just a dark oval where features should have been. "Here's your thirty quid," I mumbled, leaning forwards against the line of my seat belt, forty pounds in hand. "Keep the change."

"£30, her gun, her hands."

"What?"

"*What?!*" Oda didn't do shrill, but she was close.

"You see the blood?" asked the driver. "Look at it! Dead wizards, dead magicians, dead witches, dead warlocks, dead, dead,
dead—and you know, none of my business, but the *smell*! It's just
been rotting down under the skin for like, you know, like years. Little
brother and little sister and little sister and all dead and rotting and
you know, sure, you know she buried them back home but they're
still rotting, can't stop the air, you know? It's like the fucking taxman,
gets everywhere and you'd be surprised how long it takes the eyes to
decay until they're no longer staring, it's the casing, you see, once the
outer muscle's gone then the jelly just sorta evaporates. Nah, trust
me. Better this way."

He pulled at her hand, so hard that Oda now cried out, face
bunching in pain, dragging her forward against the tightness of her
belt. "Wait!"

He meant it, he actually meant it, the silhouetted black oval shape
of the driver: he was going to pull the hand from her arm, pop it out
of the bones and just pull until the muscle tore and it was snapped
away from her flesh, just like that.

"Wait!"

I tried to lean forward, but the belt held me back. I fumbled at the
catch, but it wouldn't open, wouldn't unlock. I tried to duck my head
beneath the diagonal strap, and it just tightened, so sudden and so
hard I was pressed back against the seat barely able to breathe, choking and wheezing. Oda wasn't a screamer, wasn't a moaner, but every
part of her shook with pain; I could see the skin around her wrist
turning strange beige-white, hear every terrified breath.

"Wait!" I shouted. "For God's sake, wait! Look at my hand before
you take hers!"

The dragging stopped. The pressure on Oda's arm seemed to
relax for a second. The strain of the seat belt against my chest relaxed
a little; in the tiny extra space it allowed, I gasped for breath.

"Let's take a gander," said the driver.

The belt let me lean forward just far enough. I got the glove off my right hand, slipped it through the narrow gap in the dividing glass, unfolded my fingers. The twin red crosses were still burnt on my skin, glaring in the gloom. I felt a pair of hands, metal-cold, steel-hard, take my palm and turn it this way and that, dragging me further towards the driver's compartment. The belt was cutting into my throat, a dull knife against my windpipe.

This close, I could see more of the driver's face.

Nothing to see.

The black, face-shaped, featureless thing that I had glimpsed from the back of the cab was, close to, the same. Empty, a pair of carved eyes around a carved nose and a pair of carved, slightly parted lips, drawn out of ebony darkness. Taxi drivers are among that great mass of people in the city who you go out of your way not to notice — just extensions of the machine. This one had taken it literally. His back melted into the chair he sat in, his feet were the pedals. His fingers clackered like the click on the fare indicator when he moved them over the palm of my hand, tracing with one metal fingertip the twin crosses.

"So," he said finally, "you're like, you know, Midnight Mayor, yeah?"

"I guess so."

"What happened to the last guy?"

"Killed."

"Shit. See? Didn't I tell you? I mean the radio talks about it plenty but no one listens — times are getting hard. Fucking politicians. Corrupt, the whole lot. Need a clean sweep, if you ask me."

The pressure around my hand released. I drew it back, rubbing at the fingermarks in my skin. Then Oda's hand was released as well, and her gun handed back.

"Keep the thirty quid."

"What?"

"Yeah. Midnight Mayor's got an account. Direct debit. I'll send the bill to the Aldermen. Receipt?"

"The Midnight Mayor has an *account*?"

"Yeah. Jeez, didn't they fucking tell you?"

"I'm new."

"You should get your act sorted, I mean, seriously! The perks, man, the perks of a cushy job like that — if I had the damn perks you think I'd ever walk anywhere? Hell no. Bureaucrat fat cats — hey, but all respect, like."

Oda had undone her seat belt, so I undid mine. It snapped free in a perfectly ordinary, respectable way. A piece of paper was handed back to me. I took it carefully. It was a receipt. It said:

Thank you for using Black Cab Ltd. Your account will be billed at a later date. Have a pleasant onward journey.

And a serial number.

One problem at a time.

Keep moving. Don't stop to think. Thinking only led to trouble. Keep moving. Your body is smarter than your mind. It gets hurt easier.

Oda and I unloaded Kemsley from the cab. There was no gentleness in what we did; there didn't seem any point. Nothing we could do could possibly make it worse than it was. The taxi rumbled away behind us; Oda dragged Kemsley by the armpit. I hammered on the plywood door of the hospital, slashed at the padlock, which was smart enough to know when not to argue, unlocked the door, barrelled Oda and Kemsley inside.

"Hello?! We need help!"

Dead, dark corridors. Buddleia was growing out of the walls, water dripping down into stagnant, green-drifting pools, walls of faded drained colour, floors of broken forgotten trolleys and shattered old glass. I dragged neon out of my skin, tired, we were so tired now, wanted to sleep, hadn't slept for too long; too many days, too many nights, it seemed longer than it was, too long; by the pinkish glow I managed to drag into my hands I spread light across the corridor, called out again, my voice inhumanly loud, "Help! We need help!"

A voice from the darkness said, "Well, don't stand there fussing, come on!"

I dragged the light across the shadows cast from the shattered, badly boarded-up windows, to where a nurse stood, wearing an old-fashioned blue and white uniform, complete with peaked hat, hands folded neatly in front of her apron, watch hanging off its silver chain by her breast, a pair of sensible shoes turned slightly outwards, toes towards the distant walls. Her steel-grey eyes fell on Kemsley. She tutted. "Well," she said, "hardly nothing, is it?"

Oda looked at me in surprise and unspoken question. We didn't answer, but helped her drag Kemsley down the rotting hall, following the nurse to where a chipboard blue door had been pushed back into a room full of yellow foam. It had been dribbled along the cracks of the walls and floor, along even the ceiling, in an attempt to stop the cracks spreading, and keep out the wind; but it had expanded too much, and now the room looked like a great yellow fungus had come up from the bowels of the earth to colonise with sticky alien threads this friendly, dripping, rotting warm planet for itself.

There was a trolley in the middle of the room, all metal slat and thin white covering, and a single lamp. The lamp wasn't connected to any power source, but hummed and glowed with white electricity despite itself. The nurse clapped importantly, and we lowered Kemsley onto the trolley. She waved us back, barking, "Are you friends or family?"

"Neither."

"Then you cannot remain for the procedure!"

"But we..."

"How was this done?" she asked, examining the shattered skin.

"By a creature who bleeds paper and calls himself the death of cities," I replied with a sigh.

"Have you given him anything?"

"No."

"Not for the pain?"

"We didn't have anything."

"Does he have any allergies?"

"I don't know."

"Disabilities, is he diabetic, asthmatic, cursed, bane-spawn, epileptic, any long-term medical conditions?"

"None that I know of."

"He's an Alderman, isn't he?"

"Yes."

"Very well. Kindly call the office of the Aldermen and request full medical information is sent here as soon as possible."

"Can you do anything for him?"

"I can always do something, but that may simply be the relieving of pain. This is not a place for miracles! This is merely an A and E ward that happens to have a subspeciality in magical injuries! That does not mean we can perform magic beyond the laws of nature!"

"Is he going to die?"

"Everyone is going to die," she replied. "And when, is a question no one, not even the NHS, can predict with any accuracy. Now if you will excuse me, I have work to do and you are not going to be able to assist me. Shoo!"

In the corridor, Oda turned her gaze upwards and murmured, "What kind of place is this?"

"It's what it says on the cover," I said. "An A and E ward that happens to have an unusual speciality."

"And is there a fee here?"

"It's NHS."

She shrugged, waiting for my meaning.

"Free."

"The NHS runs a unit specialising in magical injuries?" It was a question that maybe wanted desperately to be a shout.

"Yes."

"Taxpayers' money is going to..."

"Magicians pay tax."

"You don't."

"I did. I know the thrill of a rebate and all. And look on the bright side—the Order kills so many magicians so efficiently so much of the time that we are rarely a burden on the NHS in our old age. That, or we feast on newborn babe's blood by moonlight and thus spare ourselves the indignity of the nursing home."

Her face darkened. "In the taxi..."

"Let's not talk about it."

"What he said..."

"Is true. We'll only fight if we have this conversation. You want to keep me useful, I want to keep you useful. We don't want to get hung up on the details. Let's not talk about it."

She shrugged. "OK."

We were silent a while. Then, "What now?"

"I guess we should do what the nice lady said."

"The nice..."

"The nurse. Let's talk to the Aldermen."

Just a thought.

Anissina?

Dead meat in assault gear.

Smog and biting cables dragged from the floor.

Anissina?

Just a thought.

Too much thinking is trouble.

Someone had to call Earle.

It was always going to be me.

"H-H-Harlun and Phelps."

The boy with the stutter was on duty on Earle's number, even in the little hours of the morning.

"It's Matthew Swift. You might remember me. I want to talk to Earle."

"M-M-Mister Earle is a-asleep."

"Does he sleep in the office?"

"I'm his p-personal assistant."

"You should get another job."

"C-can I..."

"Tell Mr Earle that Kemsley is in hospital, probably going to die; that Anissina might be dead already, along with a number of your pet mercenaries; and that the death of cities is in London and wearing a pinstripe suit, please. He'll know how to contact me."

He did.

He contacted me in under two minutes, and didn't sound like a man who'd been asleep.

"Swift? What in God's name is going on?"

"Nothing in God's name, unless you want to discuss theology with Oda. But enough to go around for the rest of us."

"What is this about Kemsley? And Anissina?"

"He's dying, Mr Earle. His skin has been peeled from his flesh — most of it, from what I can see. Anissina is...I don't know where. She isn't answering her phone. She vanished into smog and that's the last I saw of her. We were attacked by a Mr Pinner. He bleeds paper, bullets won't stop him, magic won't stop him, his suit is sewn into his flesh. And...no, no I think that's about it. I don't want to rush to conclusion, but I think we're buggered. Oh, and the nurse wants to know Kemsley's medical history."

"What nurse?"

"We're at Elizabeth Anderson Hospital."

"Have you been followed? Is this Mr Pinner there?"

"We took the Black Cab."

"I wish you hadn't. The bill will be..."

"We were being flayed alive by a man with a smug smile, Mr Earle. I'm sure you don't want to go through the trouble of having to find another Midnight Mayor so soon after the previous incumbent died that particular death."

"Christ. Jesus fucking Christ," muttered Earle. "Don't move. I'll be there in twenty minutes."

*   *   *

He was there in fifteen.

What kind of man wore a suit to bed?

He brought minions. Aldermen: nameless, stone-faced men and women. How we loathed Aldermen.

"Where's Kemsley?"

I jerked my head at the door. I'd had to let the light go out in my fingers, too tired to hold it. I'd found a bit of wall that didn't look like it was going to collapse immediately, and made it my friend. The Aldermen had torches. They hurt our eyes.

"In there. There's a nurse looking after him. You'd better not be too rude. The NHS has a policy on rude visitors."

Earle gestured at the chipboard door, and one of the black-coated silent Aldermen detached himself and drifted through it, pulling it shut behind him.

"What about Anissina?"

"I told you. I don't know."

"What about my—"

"I don't know. One is dead, at least. We got separated. Mr Pinner was waiting. I guess he must have known we'd go looking again after Nair died there. I guess he didn't mind, until we got too close to the flat where the kid stayed. Then he did his thing."

"What about this kid?"

"Not there."

"So at least one of my men is dead for nothing?"

"No. At least one of your men is dead for confirmation that Mr Pinner is a mean son of a bitch who would probably have a bit of a giggle at a strategic nuclear strike. Also for confirmation that Nair was killed by this...thing. And to prove that the kid is connected; to conclude that this whole bloody thing has been tied up in a way that gives me a migraine just to think of; and to find that there was a CCTV camera in the stairwell. I know it's not like dying to save puppies and children, but I'd go to the funeral and we'd honour their memory with true gratitude."

"You're gabbling, Swift," snapped Earle.

"I'm a little fried."

"How did you survive?"

"It was all a bit of a blur."

Earle glanced quickly at Oda, who turned her head away. It meant something, that movement—I just didn't know what. Add it to the list.

"This CCTV camera"—the guy could prioritise—"It was working?"

"When I last checked. You people have a thing for this, right? I mean you've done the assault rifles and stuff"—we wanted to laugh, or possibly cry, or some hysterical thing in between, a madness on the edge of my voice—"so you've gotta be up there with the whole spy surveillance shit, right?"

"We can probably manage something."

"Good. You should probably do it soon. I'm guessing Mr Pinner is kinda pissed that anyone survived. He'll probably come looking. And we're not in any condition to fight, not against a guy who can't die."

"There are scratches on your face."

"Paper cuts."

"He..."

"Yes."

"What is he?"

"You're asking me?"

"Yes. You were Bakker's apprentice, and whatever he was in life, there is no denying that he was an expert in these matters. Do you have any idea what this Mr Pinner is?"

I thought about it long and hard. "No."

"No?"

"Not a clue. Not a finch's fart. He's going to kill us, isn't he?"

"From the sounds of it, yes," murmured Earle thoughtfully.

So we laughed. And realising that what we really wanted to do was cry, we laughed just that bit harder, so no one would see the truth.

Safe places.

Strange how these things get redefined. A guy walks behind you in an empty street and safety is the home. A couple of kids burgle your house and safety is with Mum and Dad's home. A bomb goes off at the end of the street and safety is in the countryside. A guy comes looking for you who bleeds paper and shredded the last bloke with your job title like an unwanted telephone bill, and safety is...

Thinking is trouble.

The Aldermen found me a place to stay. They didn't want me in the office, and I didn't want to be there. I had no home of my own, hadn't had one since my death certificate had been put on file. So, grumbling all the way, they found me a hotel to spend the night.

I wanted to sleep.

I wanted to feel safe.

And as safe goes, it wasn't bad. It ticked the mundane choices — twenty-four-hour security staff, police station practically across the road, busy streets outside, CCTV surveillance up the kazoo and Aldermen stationed on the corridors and doors at all times. It also met some mystical choices — the River Thames only a few yards away in one direction, the lights of the West End only a few yards the other way; and, just down the road, Charing Cross station, generally accepted as the heart of the city. There was power in that, even if it wasn't true. Ideas are power, and the constant burning of the lights gave the place a magic that we could practically float on, an electric-orange lick in the air. Look out of any window, and whether you saw reflected lights on the water or the flashing signs of the Strand, it was beautiful. Even we could sleep, safe in so much busy, beautiful life around us, trusting to strangers and their ways to keep us from danger.

And whaddayaknow?

It even had room service.

As a rule, I dislike hotels. Too much money, too little soul. Plus the bed had ten layers of sheet and blanket that needed a hydraulic pump to pry them away from the mattress, and the radiators were turned up too high. But it was peaceful, and it was safe.

So we curled up beneath the sheets, and we slept.

Sorcerers are supposed to have prophetically insightful dreams.

I guess I wasn't in the zone.

My dreams were drenched in terror. They woke me every half-hour, gasping for breath, face burning and arms goosebumped, without being able to name the dread that hunted me across the synaptic snooze of my mind. When I went back to sleep, turning in the wrecked mess of blanket, it would come back, beating against the edge of my skull the chant:

GIVE ME BACK MY HAT
GIVE ME BACK MY HAT
GIVE ME BACK MY HAT!
GIVE ME BACK MY HAT!!
GIVE ME BACK MY HAT!!!!

Another thing to add to the list of things that needed to be thought about, and about which I did not want to think.

We slept.

Morning began at three in the afternoon.

Still here.

Still not dead.

Surprise!

Our heart missed a beat as we opened the bathroom door, but no, no flayed victims or vengeful pinstriped … things waiting for us.

Surprise!!

I didn't get up in a hurry, reasoning that if Earle had anything heartbreakingly important to tell me, he would. It occurred to me that, it now being three in the afternoon, Earle might already be dead along with the rest of the Aldermen and for all I knew the remainder of the city, and we were all alone in the ruined remains of London—but the water ran hot from the shower and the slippers were too fluffy for this to be Armageddon quite yet.

Besides, there was a phone call I had to make before the end of everything, the death of the city. I made no conscious decision to do it. But I knew, with the certainty that comes over you in a hot shower after a long day, that it had to be done.

While I slept, someone had cleaned my clothes, even my coat. Polishing my shoes had been out of the question, but the worst of the dirt seemed to have been scraped off with a hard brush, my trousers folded and my "What Would Jesus Do?" T-shirt, for which we were starting to develop a strange and uncomfortable fondness, smelt of fabric softener. They'd even managed to shift the worst of the blood from the cuffs of my coat. I was impressed. Suspicious, but impressed.

There was an Alderman on the door, when I opened it. He had a face that had been polished in olive oil. He glanced at me, I stared at him. He didn't smile. I guessed he was one of the ones who'd voted to have me shot. I guessed he wasn't currently a fan of the democratic process. I said, "Have we met?"

"No."

"I'm Matthew."

"I know who you are."

Five words were four too many to prove that this line of enquiry would get nowhere. I gave up on good manners and snapped, "Where's Earle?"

"Mr Earle is working."

"At what?"

"At the current situation."

"Where can I find him?"

"His office is Harlun and Phelps. Overlooking Aldermanbury Square. We're under orders to keep you safe."

"Whose orders?"

"The majority's orders."

"What's Harlun and Phelps?"

"Trust fund managers."

"The Aldermen are trust fund managers?"

"It pays to be paid."

Couldn't argue with his reasoning. "Has he found the boy, Mo?"

"I would inform you if he had."

"Has he found Anissina?"

"No. But then, he hasn't found her body. Unlike those of four others of our employees."

I thought of the mercenaries skidding down the cable into the smog of Kilburn. "I'm sorry."

"They were just employees."

The Alderman intoned it like a bored priest too indifferent to care that he'd lost his faith. He didn't look at me, but focused his attention on a part of the wall just above my left ear. He had a ring on his left hand; it carried the twin crosses.

"Where's Oda?"

"She had to consult with her employers."

"Why?"

"We need a coordinated strategy if we are to tackle the current situation."

"Who's 'we'?"

"Everyone."

"You don't like me, do you?"

"I would not presume to question your judgement," he replied.

I took a deep breath. "Fine. I want to talk to Loren."

*　*　*

Loren wasn't in her flat.

The Aldermen had moved her.

Sure, they'd moved her to a reasonably comfortable B & B just north of Mornington Crescent and made sure her boss didn't mind; but they'd still plucked her out of her home and dragged her, strangers, to a strange place, and not bothered to explain themselves.

Which explained why, when I rang the number that the Aldermen had given me, she said: "WHO THE FUCK IS THIS?!! I SWEAR I WILL GODDAMN KILL YOU, I'LL KILL YOU I'LL..."

"Loren?"

The shouting stopped. There was a long pause, full of a rapid and distant drawing of breath. Then, "Who's this?"

"It's Matthew."

"Jesus, *shit.*"

"Are you all right?"

"No. I am very much not all right. I am the least all right I think I have ever been in my whole life, and it's been pretty shit so far anyway. Where's Mo? Have you found him? I'm in this place in Camden, these men turned up and they... they said they were the police then I asked for ID and they said they weren't but that I'd have to come and... have you found Mo?"

"Not yet. No. I'm sorry."

"God. But you haven't... I mean, you haven't not found him because he's... I mean, you haven't not found him and you're just not telling me because you think I can't... look, I want to know, OK, I need to know whatever way it is if you've..."

"I haven't found him. In any sense, I swear. I'm trying. I'm... getting there."

"But if you can't, then why..."

"Loren, I need to know some more things about him."

"Matthew, what's going on? Anything, but..."

"The guys who took you to Camden did it, for all their screwed-up reasoning, to keep you safe. You'll be safe."

"What's not to be safe from?"

"There are things happening. Different things; I mean, different. But I'm looking, they're looking all the time. I promise."

"This is... there's mystic stuff, right? Bad?"

"Maybe."

"Involving Mo?"

"Perhaps. Yes. Probably."

"Tell me."

"It's..."

"You told me the truth, Matthew. When that thing came up from under the street you turned and said, sorcerer, magic, monster, just straight out. And I thought 'hell, this guy is either so whacked off his own head that he just can't tell the difference any more so might as well run with it or, shit, this stuff is real, deal with the madness'. That's the only way, do you see? I thought about it. If I don't know then I'll just imagine, all the things I might not know, all the terrible things that are out there, without limits, without reason, I need to know that it makes some sort of sense!"

There was no reason not to tell her.

No sensible reason.

We couldn't.

Good sense had nothing to do with it.

We couldn't, and didn't know why.

"I don't know what's happening," I said. "Not yet. Not all of it. I promise, when I know, when it's finished, I'll tell you it all. But anything I tell you now would just be a white lie or a bad lie or a half-truth with nothing to sit on and that might be OK for a time, but when it's done, if I got it wrong... I'm sorry. I am looking. Please. I just need to know a few more things about Mo."

"Is that it?"

"Yes. For the moment."

"I see." Her voice was the flat distant fall of the criminal who's been caught, who knows it's the chair, who knows the lawyer is just making noise, who knows there's no way out, no point left in crying. "What do you want to know?"

"Everything."

And, as much as she could, she told me.

Mums and sons.

We struggled to understand. It was something people seemed to think would be instinctive. Flesh of my flesh. We found the idea distasteful.

There was more. Of course there was. Problem about asking questions is that most of the time, you only know what the question is once you have the answer.

He'd met some friends.

At the city farm, of all places. It was part of being young in the city; you got shipped off to do healthy, hearty things in order to make you a better person, until that day comes around the age of thirteen when you suddenly realise that goats *are* horrid, and the city is clean.

She didn't really know them. They were from the Wembley area. Sometimes he'd come back late at night with them, but they never came in. Always polite—sort of—but never came inside, as if they were embarrassed or afraid of her. And in time, that's how he seemed to be. Embarrassed.

And then he kept on not coming home.

And the school complained.

And she'd send him to school but what could she do? Her job didn't let her stand at the school gate all day to watch him, a job meant no time; no job, no money. She knew the others weren't going either, just knew, without having to be told—what's there for a kid on his own to do, when the rest are in the classroom? He'd disappear and not say where he'd been. He'd come back stinking of beer and sweat—when he came back. He'd talk about being "down the club". She didn't know what club, or where.

Then the police had called.

He'd stolen a bike.

The whole gang had been involved, and he was the youngest, so he got a caution, because they couldn't really nail anything bigger onto him.

Then they called again.

ASBO, they said. She'd thought it was just a phrase journalists used on the TV. Riotous behaviour, drinking, shouting, threatening behaviour. They'd grabbed an old guy's shopping and thrown it into the street—not because they wanted anything in it, but just because they could. Just for something to do. You should keep an eye on Mo, they said, this is the start of a downhill path that ends in a very thorny thicket.

Not that the police were big on metaphor.

And then one day, a few weeks ago, he'd come home, and he was hiding something. Something in his bag, something he didn't want her to see, and he banned her from his room and didn't talk to her and just spoke to his friends and there was something...shameful. Something shameful had happened, had been done, he had done it, something shameful. And then he went away and didn't come back, his friends didn't come back, and she'd spoken to the police and it wasn't just Mo. The patrols up in Willesden, where they used to hang, had noticed it, an absence. The whole gang, however many there were, had just stopped. No more hanging outside the pub, no more skating beneath the overpass, no more spitting in the off-licence, no more stealing old guys' shopping, no more doing, just because it could be done. All at once, they had just vanished.

They'd done something shameful.

A gang of kids, bored, arrogant, cocksure, cock-up kids, who liked to go to a club in Willesden, just vanished.

I could have told her I thought they were still alive.

It would have been a lie, and one that she would probably have come to hate.

So I just told her nothing, just the same tune as before.

I'll look, I promise. I'll find Mo.

We went to see Earle.

Harlun and Phelps were trust fund managers.

I wasn't entirely sure what this meant. I associated it with suits, shiny shoes, gleaming teeth, polished hair, questionable moralities and big glass foyers. I wasn't disappointed.

The sunlight falling on Aldermanbury Square was promising a glorious spring and a scorching golden summer, just as soon as this part of the planet could get on and lean closer to the sun. The sky was the glorious blue, with clouds of fluffy whiteness, that you find in a child's drawing. Trees, spindly half-grown afterthoughts, lined the space between the buildings of the square; and the old guildhouses nearby competed with the giant glass growths of modern offices. Overhead, concrete walkways from the heady 1960s, when everyone believed the Future To Be Today, jutted across the slim gaps between constructions.

The foyer of Harlun and Phelps was three storeys high of itself, a great swimming-pool expanse of slippery white marble in which a small forest of potted plants and trees had been installed. Water ran down one wall behind reception, into a small pond of zen pebbles designed to create an impression of serene, expensive tranquillity; and even the receptionists, sitting behind desks adorned with artfully twisted metals including labels (to assure you that they really were art), had the most expensive, modern headsets plugged into their ears. The future is here, and it wears pinstripe.

"The majority of employees here are civilians," explained my Alderman guide/protector/companion/would-be-executioner as we strode without a word to the security guards through the foyer towards the lifts. "They conduct themselves within perfectly standard financial services and regulations. There is one specialist sub-operational department catering to the financing of more . . . unusual extra-capital ventures, and the executive assets who operate it have to undergo a rigorous level of training, psyche evaluation, personality assessment and team operational analyses."

We stared at him, and said, "We barely understood the little words."

"No," he replied. "I didn't think you would."

The lift was all in green glass, even the floor. It crawled up the side of the building, faced outwards to the falling city below. Alderman-bury Square became just a blob within a maze of streets, alleys, bus-clogged roads, cranes, building works, Victorian offices and gleaming new towers, and then lost amid the snake of the river and the sprawl of the city, the familiar floodlit landmarks of London, the sun fading into evening towards Richmond, the early winter gloom spreading in from the estuary.

Earle's office was on the very top floor. From there, presumably, he could stare down and survey all his little people toiling below, from his nest of triumphant endeavour.

The office itself was in the same stylised, soulless vein as the rest of the building. It took ten seconds to walk from his door to his desk. Ten seconds is an eternity, when it's just you and another guy in a room that could have hosted the Olympic curling championship.

He wasn't dressed like an Alderman. His black coat was hung on a deliberately old-fashioned coat stand behind his black marble desk. He wore a suit, dark, dark blue with a matching navy-blue tie, and cufflinks on which were engraved a pair of ebony keys on a back-ground of pearl. As I approached across the endless floor, he smiled. It was done for good manners' sake, not that that was a cause for which he had much time.

"Mr Mayor." He waved me at a chair designed to give you good posture and a bad temper.

"Mr Earle."

"Have you slept well?"

"I slept. What news?"

"We have been working on finding the boy, Mo."

"And?"

"There is some progress. CCTV cameras in the Kilburn area saw the boy being removed two nights ago from Raleigh Court and loaded into a van. He appeared to be unconscious but alive. We are attempting to trace the men who moved him, but most likely they were just hired help."

"Was Mr Pinner there?"

"No. We do, however, have his face on CCTV from your encounter, and are circulating it to all relevant areas. We were unable to find further information on Anissina. The smog obscured all imaging."

"I'm sorry."

"It isn't immediately relevant," he replied with a shrug. "The focus of our investigation must be on the boy, as he appears to be the strongest link we have to this Mr Pinner, this death of cities. So far we have tracked the vehicle entering and leaving the congestion charge zone on the same night. It appeared to be heading in a southwards direction, leaving the congestion charge zone after crossing Waterloo Bridge."

"You can access the congestion charge database?"

"Of course."

"And where is the vehicle now?"

"There are teams working on it."

"Teams?"

"Human Resources allocated us some appropriate assistance."

"When will you have an answer?"

"Mr Swift," he said, fingers whitening on the edge of the table, "do you know *why* Big Brother isn't watching you?"

"Because he has my death certificate on file and a literal mind?"

"Because, Mr Swift, *because*, in this city there are anywhere between eight and nine million other people to watch. In a single day, tens of thousands of people will pass through one Underground station alone; in a single week, hundreds of thousands, all moving, all turning. Millions of vehicles every month will pass in and out of the congestion charge zone, *millions*, and at any given moment you can be certain a train is breaking down or a pipe is bursting under the strain or a police car has been called to clean up the blood or a window has been smashed or a bomb threat has been issued or a fire alarm has been sounded or an ambulance has been caught up in traffic behind a stalled pair of traffic lights and a confused learner driver. Big Brother isn't watching you, Mr Swift, because there's just too much for Big Brother to keep an eye on. You are . . . not important."

"You're breaking my heart."

"Do you understand what I mean?"

"Yes. I understand. You mean that I should be patient a little while longer and let you people find Mo in your own time, right?"

"Essentially. Yes."

"You want us to wait."

"Yes. Besides, there are other matters."

"What other matters?"

"Inauguration."

I sighed. "Oh, yes. This pineappleless, cocktail sausageless party of an inauguration."

"There's more to it than you think."

"There usually is."

"All the Midnight Mayors have to do it."

"Of course."

"It can be dangerous."

"I was waiting with baited breath for you to say that."

"You were?"

"It seemed like you were building up to something — 'dangerous' made a certain inevitable sense. What do I need to know to live — you do want me to live, don't you?"

He took just a moment, just a *moment*, too long to answer. "Of course. We've made the investment in you now. We need to see it come to maturity."

"Then tell me."

He sighed, swivelled slightly in his chair. "Do you know," he said at last, "how the Aldermen are chosen?"

"Nepotism. And the old boys' club."

"You might be thinking of our more mundane counterparts..."

"Perhaps. I don't know much about them."

"It is not nepotism," he said. "It is about dedication. To an idea; to a cause bigger than any individual. To become an Alderman requires a lifetime of study, work and commitment, and most of all, it requires an understanding of the smallness of man within this great machine of the city. London is an antheap, Mr Swift. It is a great, sprawling, beautiful nest, built by two thousand years of man, so deep and so dark that its people can never see or know it all, but live their lives rather in this or that complex of the city, burrowing deeper and deeper into their little caves, because to know the full extent of the nest is to realise that you are nothing. An insect crawling down tunnels which only exist because two thousand years ago, a thousand, thousand other insects also crawled this way, each one as unimportant as you, each one a stranger. There is nothing that binds these ants together, that stops them from ripping each other apart, save that they share the same structure, the same city, the same physical structure that only exists because, for two thousand years, the ants have carved. We are tiny, Mr Swift. We are insignificant, living in a world of life and wonder and miraculous existence and excitement, not because of who we are, or whom we know, but because the construction around us, the bricks and stones of London, shapes and guides us, and gives unity to the millions of strangers who inhabit its caves, so we can all say, 'I live in the city'. Do you understand?"

"Yes."

"Then this is what the Aldermen are. We are the ants who climbed to the top of their hill, who looked down from the highest tower of the maze and saw the darkness and the time and the caverns, and realised the smallness of man within this heaving world. We are the ones who saw this, and were not afraid. Do you understand?"

"Yes."

"I have been told that for sorcerers, magic is life, that to live is to be magical. The same is true for Aldermen. We find our magic in being nothing. Ants on top of a heap. Do you understand?"

I smiled. I tangled my fingers together between my knees. "Yes," I said. "I understand what the Aldermen are."

"Then you understand why the Midnight Mayor has always—usually—come from the Aldermen's ranks."

"Maybe."

"It is the city, Swift. The city is so old, now. So many millions of dead men and dead women buried beneath it. They all scuttled through the streets and made the city what it is, and now they are forgotten. Millions of wandering forgotten ghosts; but the city! It is so alive. The Midnight Mayor must protect the city. Do you understand what this means?"

"I understand what you think it means."

"Swift..."

"I have a theory as to why Nair made us Midnight Mayor."

"Well?"

"I think he knew the Midnight Mayor couldn't fight Mr Pinner. Of course he knew it, he was dying as he made the phone call. But I think it was something more, something earlier."

"Go on."

"I think Nair understood that cities change."

Earle was silent as he contemplated this. Then he shook his head, almost sadly. "Would you like to hear my theory?" he asked. "I've been thinking about it too, of course. We all have, all the Aldermen, all the ones who seemed more qualified."

I shrugged.

"I think..." He took a deep breath, as if perhaps this was too important to bungle. "I think that Nair made you Midnight Mayor in order to eliminate a threat."

"Mr Pinner?"

"No. Well—Mr Pinner too. But another threat, possibly one even worse."

"Which is?"

"You."

"I'm confused."

"*You.* I think Nair made you Midnight Mayor in order to force you to take responsibility, to *make* you become involved, to drive you to take a side and fight for it. I think he did it to control you, to bind you, to curse you with this office. I think he did it to eliminate the threat of the blue electric angels."

We stared at him long and hard, too surprised to say anything. He let us stare, then smiled a real smile, cruel and dry. "If you can't beat them..."

"We don't believe that."

"That doesn't matter, does it? What matters, is whether Nair believed it. And there, I fear, is something we'll never know."

We didn't speak. He let out a great, tummy-clenching sigh, and stood up sharply, his leather shoes snapping against the polished floor. "Still, none of this is really to the point, is it? You want to know about the inauguration, how to survive? The answer is I can't really tell you. It's always different for each new Mayor. Being, as they are, just a man with a brand on the hand. I know it has to be done, in order for the transfer of office to be complete. And if you are going to survive any more encounters with Mr Pinner, I suggest you take every advantage presented to you."

"What do I need to do?" A voice that might have been ours, somewhere a long way off.

"You have to walk the old city walls, seal the gates against evil."

"That's not just unhelpful, it's pretentiously vague."

"It's what it says on the cards."

"And how do I do that?"

"I don't entirely know. Not being, myself, Midnight Mayor."

"I'm a sorcerer, not a Jedi."

"Is that something you tell yourself in times of doubt?"

"It's something a religious nutcase pointed out to me in a moment of prophetic insight."

He shrugged. "I can only hold your hand so far. You'll work it out."

"You're really not much use, are you?"

He treated me to the crocodile smile. "May the Force be with you," he said, and gave me a Vulcan V for good luck. And then his smile almost became a chuckle. "No one else is."

Afternoon melted into evening.

Evening asked night if it was free for a coffee.

Night sheepishly went in search of its dancing shoes, having left them somewhere behind the spotlights.

The orange glow of urban darkness slithered over the sky.

We ate Thai fish cakes with sweet and sour sauce.

We felt a bit better.

We ordered more food.

Pad Thai noodles with chicken, lemon and crushed peanuts.

We felt a lot better.

The smiling waitress at the restaurant, a small place shimmering in soft candlelit cleanliness on Exmouth Market, asked us if we wanted anything more.

We thought about it, and said yes. Anything with a theme of coconut.

The evening passed on by nicely.

We almost managed to forget.

That special, subtle "almost", that drives the fear out of the stomach, leaves only a few claws scratching away at the junction of small and large intestine.

We went to the toilet more often than was our inclination.

We had no reason to believe that there was a God, but if he/she/it existed, it had a sick sense of the silly.

Time passed.

Can time take its time?

It did tonight.

Then, just when I was getting used to its saunter, it started to jog, and my Alderman watcher/carer/guardian/assassin said, "We have to go."

They took me by car to the base of London Bridge. They unloaded me in the bus lane on the south side, and sped off, citing traffic regulations. The tin shed of London Bridge station squatted behind, the yellow towers of Southwark Cathedral across the other side of the street. It was midnight in London, and the city was taking its time, or maybe time was taking it. The wind carried the sound of the bells of St Paul's as they banged out the hour. Behind HMS *Belfast*, Tower Bridge was lit up in dangling red and green lights. The Tower of London sat squat and orange, like an angry garden gnome in the family too long to care that it was now cracked and ugly. The black lampposts along the river, stretching out past Butler's Wharf, were hung with shining white bulbs; the grey concrete of London Bridge was lit up with shimmering pinks and purples the entire span of its length.

I took a deep breath of clear Thames air.

It made me feel cooler inside, sharper on the edges, drove the weariness out of my eyes and the lead from my brain. They say yogis can live a whole day on just one breath. If it was the breath of the river of the city they loved, then I can see how it might work.

Earle had said: magic is life.

He'd got it only slightly wrong.

The rest of what he'd said seemed, to our mind, utter bollocks.

I started walking.

Or maybe, we should call it processing.

Whatever that walk was that the Midnight Mayor did, I did it that night.

*   *   *

Second Interlude: The Inauguration of Matthew Swift

In which various dead things make their point, the ethics of urban planning come under scrutiny, and a new Midnight Mayor learns some important lessons about some old ideas.

The Lord Mayor, when he gets inaugurated on that cold, drizzling November evening, doesn't just get cocktail sausages — he gets champagne, pineapple, cheese on sticks and someone to hold the umbrella.

So much for perks of office.

I wondered, as I walked across London Bridge, trailing my fingers along the railing and watching the water gush and slide beneath me, if Earle was just holding out on the cocktail sausages as a matter of principle. The life of Midnight Mayor seemed a precarious one, obtained for the most part after years of questionable service. And to be Midnight Mayor and face various unnatural and, in my case, unkillable dangers, all of which seemed out to get you, thank you kindly, without even a piece of pineapple on a stick as a reward, seemed...

...unnatural.

Which was probably the point.

So much for the ruthless application of reason.

I walked.

Earle had said I had to follow the old route of the city wall. All but a few pieces had been demolished years ago, and those I'd seen were nestled away.

GIVE ME BACK MY HAT

Lock the gates against evil, whatever that meant. If I took "evil" in the traditional Christian meaning, 90 per cent of the city's inhabitants wouldn't be able to get to work in the morning, ourself included. Even limiting the definition to things actively out to kill and maim, it still presented semantic as well as practical problems.

You'll work it out, he'd said.

Assuming he even wanted us to live.

Still, any advantage, anything against Mr Pinner, seemed worth getting, and it couldn't take more than an hour, maybe an hour and a half, to walk the course of the old wall. Even if it achieved nothing material, it would calm us down, let us soak up some of the older, quieter magics that slithered across the pavement like low mist, as we fed off the rhythm of the wander.

Magic is life, my old teacher had said.

Turn it round, and you begin to get something.

We walked.

Shops, shut; camera shop, TV in the window showing our face in a dozen screens from a single camera as we passed by; shop selling suits and ties; Monument station, shut; the Monument itself, its golden ball of fire peeking over the top of the surrounding buildings; cobbled streets leading to ancient, low, forgotten churches, smothered in the gross concrete buildings bursting up around. A giant chemist, where you could purchase things to make your skin brighter, darker, tighter, softer, gentler, warmer, hairier, smoother—and who knew, even find some medicines too. Spitalfields off to my right, the streets empty, the city workers long since gone home, the traffic nothing more than a lost 15 bus on its way to Blackwall, before the night buses took over. A wide street, concrete buildings edging against black reflecting windows that stared angrily down on the grand decadence of the older Victorian offices squatting in tight streets with names like Cornhill, Leadenhall, Fenchurch Street, St Helen's Place, Clark's

Place, Camomile Street, Houndsditch, Liverpool Street, Wormwood Street, and all their little friends and relations scrabbling away into the crowded gloom of the night-time emptied city. A few miles to the north and a few streets to the south, the night would be loud and lively, full of partying, drinking and general wassail. Here, where the offices were, no one lived, and little stirred except myself and the occasional passing dustbin man.

I headed for Aldgate, that strange junction where the run-down old window frames of the East End met the pampered corniced doors of the City, no apology, no excuse; just bang and there it was: humming, buying, selling, smelling, bustling squalor and the death of brand names. A subway beneath a broad roundabout where the narrow city roads began to spread out into the urban-planned highways towards the estuary, the east, and the Blackwall Tunnel; newspaper drifted beneath the dull lamps; shops, built underground as part of a cunning scheme that had never worked, lurked behind abandoned blankets too tatty even for the beggars to take. The writing was on the wall, declaring such mystic statements as:

BHN CCI ABP RULZ!

Or:

I LOVE CALIPER BOY

Or in sad scratched letters:

make me a shadow on the wall

I kept on walking, ignoring the signs that lied about which exit led where with ancient yellow arrows half torn from the walls. The feeling that I was not alone crept up on me with the gentle padding walk of the polite assassin. I let it get close, until I could feel it tickling the back of my neck, then stopped, hands buried in my trouser pockets, and turned.

There was no one there.

I felt like the justifiable fool I was.

I turned back, kept on walking.

I was still not alone.

I reached the ramp up from the subway, and stopped again. This was, I figured, the last chance to check for followers and get it wrong, without making a fool of myself in public.

Still no one there.

There was, however, something on the wall.

I looked at it carefully.

Someone had spray-painted on the image of a woman. She wore blue jeans and a white T-shirt and appeared to be drinking some sort of yoghurt drink from a plastic cup. Her top lip had folded over the pink straw from it to her mouth and the movement had tilted her head down, but her eyes were up, and fixed on me. They were laughing.

They were also blinking. A rhythmic, silent, steady on-off, one-two count, long eyelashes moving over the soft reflected pink of her eyes.

I recognised the painted woman's face.

I said, "Vera."

The painted face stopped drinking the painted yoghurt through the painted straw and looked up. Then the two-dimensional flatness said, "Ah, shit."

Her lips moved; a pink thing wiggled inside the redness of her mouth. No depths to it, just a change in colour to imply an alteration of perspective. A cartoon on the wall, and the wall was speaking. Her voice echoed the length of the subway. I repeated numbly, "Vera?"

She gestured with the plastic cup, which slid silently over the chipped concrete as if paint was nothing more than a sheet of silk to be moved and slid back at will. "You gotta keep walking," she said. "You don't walk, and it won't work."

I turned, and kept on walking. Never argue with the surreal; there's no winning against irrationality. The image of Vera slid off the wall behind me and onto the wall by my side. She was walking with me.

I could only see her profile, like an ancient Egyptian painting turned sideways in a Pharaoh's tomb, and her outline was wobbling, uneven, as if the invisible cartoonist sketching her onto the concrete couldn't keep up with the speed of her swagger. I said, "This is peculiar."

"You think?!" she chuckled. "*Jesus.*"

As we neared the top of the ramp, her whole form was gently eaten away by the lack of concrete on which to project itself, until there was nothing more than a pair of knees, a pair of ankles, a pair of feet walking beside me, before even that was erased by the lack of wall onto which to walk. Then there were just a pair of painted footprints walking next to mine, that landed with an audible *splat splat splat* as they stepped along beside me, drawn in white paint. As we passed by a lamppost she was briefly back again, her image keeping track of her footsteps, painting itself onto the nearest handy surface: postbox, telephone box, as we walked on.

Not having a mouth didn't stop her talking. Her voice drifted out of the air, somewhere above those painted steps on the floor.

"So, how's it going, Swift?"

"Not too well," I answered, watching the street around me for someone with a straitjacket and a literal mind. "I've wound up Midnight Mayor, been chased, pursued and misunderstood, and now I'm talking to, with all respect, a dead pair of painted footsteps."

"Yeah. That must be a bit freaky."

"It could be worse."

"Seriously?"

"Someone says 'inauguration' in my line of work, and you can just bet there'll be freaky shit. It's like quests. You get told 'go forth and seek the travelcard of destiny' and you know, I mean, you seriously know that it won't have just been left down the back of the sofa. You read—seen—*Lord of the Rings*?"

"Yessss..."

"Ever wondered why they didn't just get the damn eagles to go drop the One Ring into the volcano, since they seemed so damn nifty at getting into Mordor anyway?"

"Nooo..."

"See? Fucking quests! So talking to a dead pair of footprints. Fine."

We passed a parked white van, and for a moment Vera was back, her painted form shimmering across its glass and metal sides. She looked worried.

"Something bad is going down, isn't it?" she said.

"Yup."

"Seriously bad?"

"Pretty much."

"I know. I guess what you said about the whole quest thing — it makes sense that I should know, yeah?"

"I guess so. Any useful tips?"

She'd vanished off the side of the van. For a while there was nothing but the *splat splat splat* of her footsteps, as the only sign she still walked by me. Then, "End of the line."

"Thanks."

"Swift?"

"Yeah?"

"You heard of the death of cities?"

"Yeah."

"You know he's real? That he's been real ever since Remus turned to Romulus and said, 'hey, cool digs, bro'?"

"Yeah."

"You know he can be summoned? Sometimes he's called by the volcano, or the thunder, or the war, but always, something summons him."

"Yeah. I'd heard."

"Swift?"

Her voice was fading, the painted footsteps on the ground growing fainter.

"Yeah?"

"Am I really dead?"

"You got shot and turned into a puddle of paint."

"That's not normal corpselike behaviour."

"No. It did occur to me that it was a little unusual. You are — were — leader of the Whites, a clan with a big thing for life, paint, graffiti and all the magics in between. But then again, if you're not dead, what are you doing here?"

"Good bloody point."

Her footsteps faded to a thin splatter, then a little smear, then died altogether. We didn't look back. It wouldn't have been appropriate to the vibe.

Just above Aldgate, I turned west, heading towards Old Street and Clerkenwell Road, watching offices dissolve slowly into a mixture of shops and flats, piled up on top of each other, joining briefly the ring road that was at all hours laden with traffic, and then heading further along, skimming the northern edge of the Barbican to where those painted statues of those mad-eyed dragons holding the shield with the twin crosses stood guard over the city. The white towers of the churches built after the Great Fire were mainly behind me, twenty-six in all, most of their bodies gutted in the Blitz.

A voice said, "Spare some change?"

A beggar with a big beard sat in the doorway of a recruitment firm, dark eyes staring up at us. I fumbled in my pocket, found nothing, dug into my satchel, felt the desire to keep on walking, the rhythm briefly broken, found my wallet, found the £30 I carried inside, handed it over.

"Cheers," said the beggar.

"Any time," I replied, and kept on walking.

A few doorways later and a voice said, "So you like to walk?"

It was the same voice.

It was the same beggar.

"Sure," I replied, and kept on walking.

By the bolted metal door round the back of a photocopy shop, he was still here, knees huddled up to his chin, blanket pulled over his shoulders. "It's the new thing, you know. Walking," he said.

"No it's not. In the old days people used to walk all the time."

"Yeah . . . but that was because it was walk or sit behind a shitting horse in a flea-infested coffin smelling of sawdust and widdle."

"You may have a point, although I imagine that most of the early modern period smelt of sawdust and widdle regardless of your means of transport."

There was a long brick warehouse ahead, its back turned to the street, no doorways for the beggar to sit in. That bought me a few more moments to gather my thoughts, and sure enough, sat in the next doorway past that, there he was again, lighting a fag.

"You know," he said, "it's amazing it took until 1865 for some bright spark to build a proper sewerage system."

"Antheaps," I replied. "Or wasps' nests. With a small nest, you don't have to worry. It's got to be big before you wonder if it'll fall off the tree."

"Someone's been using metaphor on you, right?"

I had to wait two more doorways to reply.

"Yup."

"Sounds to me like a paddle full of shite."

"You've got to admit it has a certain chaotic something. London burnt down in 1666 and everyone went, whoopee, let's rebuild! A golden city! But look what happened. Chaos and fluster. Everyone was so eager to live in this golden city that they didn't even have time to build it."

Goswell Road. Nowhere for a beggar to sit on the junction of the Goswell Road and Clerkenwell Road, just two staring dragons in a traffic island. I waited, leaning against the traffic lights. They changed. I crossed, still heading west. There were very few doorways on this side; a pub ahead, but it was occupied by a group of scruffy trendies in carefully slashed jeans sharing a bottle of wine. I kept walking. An art studio of some kind presented a low, grubby doorway.

The beggar said, "Can I make a suggestion?"

"You've got an agenda, right?"

"Sure."

"OK. Suggest away."

"Don't do the walk. Don't get inaugurated."

"Why not?"

Art studio to chippy; he was in the door between that and the strip club pretending to be a pub.

"You want to be Midnight Mayor?"

"No."

"There you go!"

"It's not that easy."

"Sure it is. You be free."

I kept on walking.

He wasn't in the next doorway.

Or the one after that.

He'd had his say.

We kept on walking.

Keep moving. If you keep moving you might just manage to leave thoughts behind, you might get it done before they catch you.

Keep on walking.

Come be me . . .

Aching right hand.

We be light, we be life, we be fire!

What would Jesus do?

We sing electric flame, we rumble underground wind, we dance heaven!

I like walking. Each step is a thought without words, a thought without words is a thought without blame, without retribution, without consequence.

Come be we and be free . . .

I think he did it to control you, to bind you, to curse you with his office.

...we be blue electric angels!

Mr Mayor.

"Mr Fucking Mayor."

I looked up.

Kemsley's face was a badly peeled tomato, grilled at a high heat and left to sag. You couldn't look like that and be alive, and there was no way the Kemsley I had seen a few hours—maybe a day?—ago was up and walking. No way he'd be here, just to talk to me. I skirted south towards Holborn Viaduct, and he fell into step beside me. Boarded-up butchers' shops, renovated Victorian ironwork painted green, red, gold, with the little dragons guarding the city wall, the shields, twin red crosses on a white background, one cross smaller than the other, one cross a sword; *Domine dirige nos,* the motto of the city, everywhere, once you looked, if you stopped to look.

"You want to know what I really think?" he said.

"Not really, but I guess you didn't go to all this trouble not to tell me."

"*You* are a fucking disgrace to the office of Midnight Mayor."

"Thanks. I really needed a skinned mystical projection to tell me that."

"You want my advice?"

"No."

"Lie down and die. Let Mr Pinner do his thing. Let someone better take over the office. That's the best thing you could do as Mayor, for the Mayor. Just lie down and die."

"You know, people pay therapists to get this kind of abuse."

He just grunted, turned his back on me, started walking briskly the other way. We called out after, "Where are you going?"

He looked back.

Just a guy. Just some guy in a black jacket, frightened at a stranger's voice shouting after him in the night.

I raised my hands in apology, smiled, shook my head, turned and kept on walking the way I'd gone.

With my incisive detective skills, I was beginning to notice a pattern at work.

I could see the golden cross of St Paul's Cathedral peeping above the nearby offices. As I walked, the streetlamps flickered, flashed unevenly when I passed beneath them, splitting my shadow into a dozen different mes that spread out like a sundial around my feet.

I heard a squeaking.

At first I thought it was some sort of cartoon rat.

It would have made a strange kind of sense.

Then the squeaking grew nearer, and now it was more a sound of metal sliding off metal. I kept on walking, figuring that if it was something important, it would catch up with me.

It did. But it gave us a strange pleasure to make it work for the privilege.

For a moment I thought I smelt curry powder and plastic bags, heard the distant muttering of the mad old lady with her trolley of bags, *buggery, buggery, youth today, buggery...*

But it wasn't her. Not tonight.

"Hello, Matthew."

I looked to the voice, and didn't stop walking. Our fists curled in anger.

The squeaking came from a pair of big wheels behind two smaller ones. Above the wheels was a black leather chair. Attached to it was a man. Attached to him were two stands on more wheels, trailing along behind. One stand held a bag of some clear liquid, drugs or fluids or whatever; the other held a bag of blood, and I could just guess whose it was.

Pushing the wheelchair was a man dressed all in shadows and my old coat.

Angry.

Don't look.

Angry.

"Matthew," said the man in the wheelchair, "how exactly do think this business is going to end?"

"Terminally," I replied. "But at least it *will* end. Dead is dead is dead. Especially for you."

We walked/wheeled on a little further. "Matthew," said the man in the wheelchair, with a slightly reproving tone in his voice, "do you really understand what it is to be Midnight Mayor?"

"Nope. Totally winging it."

"You have to serve the city."

"Sussed that."

"Not the people, Matthew. The city."

"I wasn't signed up to be Robin Hood, if that's what you mean."

"Let's please not be coy about this."

"This isn't me being coy, this is me being angry."

"Why are you angry?"

"Because I didn't ask for this gig. Because some *bastard* chose me for it without so much as a cocktail sausage and pineapple on a stick, because Vera was shot and Anissina fell into smog, because Mo is gone and Loren cried, because the spectres stabbed me and Earle sat in his office drinking coffee, because I saw a guy flayed alive and another bastard lumbered in hospital with no skin, and because *you*" — I stabbed an angry finger at the man in the wheelchair — "*you*, Mr Bakker, *you* are dead. We killed you. We killed you and we did it because you... because... We killed you and you should stay dead and so should your bloody fucking shadow!"

I was shouting. My voice echoed off the buildings on the empty street, hummed in the cold water pipes. I turned away, looked down at the paving stones, counting my own steps, how many stones they covered with each stride, how many they'd cover in ten, in twenty, how many strides to a mile.

The wheelchair rattled on peacefully beside me. Mr Bakker sat, his pale, spotted hands folded across his belly, his head tilted up and to one side, being pushed by his shadow. His blood-soaked shadow in the bloodstained remnant of my old coat, the one I'd died in. The one I'd been killed in. That coat.

"What's the point of all this?" I asked at last, as we swung into the mess of up-down streets between Farringdon Road and Fleet Street. "I get that there's mystical shit going on and all that, but what exactly is the point? Am I supposed to derive some great moral message from all this, become a better person, a nicer Midnight Mayor? From what I can tell, 'nice' isn't the qualifying term."

"I think," said Bakker, drawing in that long, slow, thoughtful breath he'd always used as a teacher, just before the answer "maybe", "I *think* that you're supposed to find out what kind of Mayor you're meant to be. I don't know. It's not really my field of expertise."

"Great. You know, that implies all sorts of unpleasant things about higher powers."

"Or a lot about your current state of mind. How is your current state of mind?"

"I see no reason to tell you about it."

"But isn't that the point?"

"I don't know. No one has told me the point. And until someone does, I'm just going to assume there isn't one and keep on walking for the hell of it."

I kept on walking.

"Matthew?"

"Still here."

"On the subject of higher powers . . ."

"Yup."

"I'd like to posit one to you, purely, you understand, hypothetically."

"I'm paying attention only because there's nothing else to occupy me at the moment."

He took a deep breath and went, "The city."

"Yup."

"As higher power."

"I'm still only here out of shitty luck."

"Well, *no*. If you see what I mean."

"I don't."

"Let me try and explain it."

"Happy day."

"A woman gets up for work. Her alarm is powered from the mains, and doesn't go off this morning because on the other side of the city another woman whose clock was powered by battery missed the wake-up call and didn't press the right button at the transformer station. She's running late. She doesn't have time to make breakfast so she runs to the supermarket where at three a.m. the previous night three students and a disgraced manager loaded freshish sandwiches onto refrigerated shelves so that this woman could run in all a fluster, buy one and get out. She's still running late. She runs for a bus that doesn't come. The driver has been caught in traffic because pipes have burst further up the street, and it's going to take him twenty minutes to get moving past the junction and then five minutes to do double that distance. The bus comes. She gets on. The bus takes her to work. At work, she toils for eight hours without much of a break then has to go and see friends in the evening. They're going to have a Chinese takeaway. The food is being prepared by a chef, whose cousin runs a Chinese goods import-export on the edge of Enfield. Every day he receives and delivers a whole city's orders for mandarin duck, chilli sauce and yaki noodles, a fleet of two dozen vans at his command, fifty workers on staff at any time, collecting orders from airports, delivering them to cities within a two-hundred-mile radius. The woman gets her food because the van turned up on time, the driver paid his congestion charge zone fee, the MOT was clean, the engine was full of petrol. She eats her Chinese meal. As she goes home, the streetlamps come on, the rubbish is removed, the buses drive along lines that have been painted, roads that have been laid, the water mains are repaired and it is an easy run back to watch the telly, and so goes her day."

I waited a moment after he'd finished talking, to see if there was something else.

"Yessss?"

"Matthew—does it not occur to you that even to live in the city as we do, to go day by day and do what is done, see what there is, live surrounded by eight million strangers, dependent on strangers to drive the bus, prepare the food, clean up the rubbish, pipe the water, supply the electrics, answer the—"

"I get the idea."

"Then you see my point?"

"Not quite..."

"Matthew! I taught you better than this!"

"You killed me better than this too, remember?"

"'You killed me too'—must we be playground infants? Dead is dead is dead."

"OK. Your point?"

"My point is this: that the city even exists, even lives, so alive! So gloriously, wonderfully, amazingly alive! That for all this to be so, day by day, is a miracle. And since miracles are by definition rare, is it not possible, even *reasonable* to turn what seems a constancy of miracles into the idea of a higher power, and call it simply, the city?"

"Oh. I get it now. Philosophy 101 for Midnight Mayors."

"Life *is* magic, Matthew. You said it yourself. Even the boring, mundane acts, even breathing, seeing, perceiving, being perceived. Life is magic. That is all a sorcerer is."

"I know," I sighed. "I remember."

We were nearing Ludgate. A great joining of places, confused, wriggling in from all sides, monuments to the war dead, supermarkets for the living, and coffee shops for all. The squeaking of Bakker's wheelchair was growing less. I glanced down at him. His face was sunk, dark, grey, fading into shadow. His chair was fading into shadow, stretching thin and flat across the floor.

I looked away.

We had no need to see such things again.

There was something wrong. It wasn't that Bakker faded into shadow; it was that he faded into his own shadow, and that shadow faded into my shadow, and my shadow was doing the pencil-thin thing behind me as I walked towards the light, and in front of me, and around me, and it wasn't so thin as it ought to be and wasn't so flat on the pavement as the normal laws of optics demanded. If water was nothing more than moonlight on the earth, this is how it would behave.

My hand hurt.

It more than hurt.

I cradled it to my chest. The stitches in my skin hurt. My head hurt. The paper cuts stung across every part of me. We could feel warm blood rolling down from the tiny slice below our eye, feel itching in the palm of our hand. The travelcard of destiny is never behind the sofa, these things are never as easy as a party with pineapples. I opened my hand. The twin crosses were burning, the blood in them turned to warm red flame. I didn't know if this was a good sign or a bad one. We turned our face away. I walked the southern edge of Gray's Inn, past shuttered shops and gloomy, lights-out banks, past bus stops declaring on their orange boards:

1. *341 — North'land Pk — 14 mins.*
2. *11 — Liverpool St — 15 mins.*
3. *17 — runrunrunrunrunrunENDOFTHELINErunrunrunrun run — Due*
4. *11 — Liverpool Street — 18 mins*

Want flexible hours and excellent pay? Be a bus driver! Then you too can become a shadow on the wall! Phone Arriva on 0800 924 7100.

A splat of a pub was turning out for the night, customers, mostly drunken students, spilling onto the streets, arms full of stolen ketchup sachets and packets of brown sauce, cackling merrily under the streetlights. A couple of taxis went by. A woman was leaning against the window of an electronics store, arms folded, head turned towards me. I recognised her as I approached, but turned my eyes away from her face. She fell into step with me as I passed, saying nothing. It's hard to say anything when your throat is half missing. In films it's always neat, a single cut, one slice and that's it, just another scarlet smile a bit lower than your first. This wasn't a neat missing throat. This was a five-fingered yawn torn from muscle and flesh, that gaped and laughed obscenely with each rattle of her jaw.

In life, the woman whom this obscenity mimicked had been called Dana Mikeda. My former apprentice. The half-Russian daughter of a sandwich shop owner in Smithfields. She'd been taken in by Mr Bakker, when I'd died. She'd been the one who cast the spell that brought us back.

She hadn't died a tidy death.

When she talked, her voice bubbled through crimson blood popping out of the gaps in her neck. She said, "You can still run away."

"Yeah," I said. "Sure."

"Seriously. Find another city, find somewhere else. The world is big enough, even for you. What loyalty do you have to this city?"

"I was born here."

"And what loyalty do *you* have to this city?"

"We were born here too."

She smiled, and so did her throat. "Haha. Deep. You should write Christmas crackers. Still, plenty of people stuff their domestic loyalties."

"Nah. You get born in London, you get raised in London, sooner or later you'll put 'Londoner' on your passport. Hey — I can even give you a bit of Midnight Mayor pep talk, while you're here, Dana, not being dead. How's this for Alderman crap: the city defines you. Or even better — I am born in this city and it makes me who I am. The streets, the stones, the strangers, everything, whether I meant it or not, made me me. Ergo, we will not abandon it. You like?"

"Christmas cracker."

"Yeah. Flawed logic, in my opinion."

"Then why'd you say it?"

"I think it's the point. Of the walk, I mean. To get that whole sense of perspective. Get whacked up on the conviction that I'm fighting for something and, most likely, being flayed alive for something."

"You feeling convinced?"

I looked at her face. We felt...almost pleased...to see it again, talking, moving, even above that shattered throat. A mimicry of life, an abomination, but perhaps, a recollection of something living, whose memory had threatened to die. I remembered, so she lived, just like the poets went and said. Easy to forget, when you want to.

"Sorry," I said.

"What?"

"For what happened to you."

"Me? You really think I walk around with this shit in my throat?"

"No, that's not the point. I fully comprehend that you're just another metamagical manifestation of whatever crackpot Mayorish madness this particular acid trip is. But you have her face, and I never got to say sorry to the real one. So...sorry. I'm sorry. We're sorry. I'm so sorry."

"Aw," she said. "Nice of you to say, bit late."

Slipping down past Lincoln's Inn, alone again on the empty streets, following the route of the old wall as best I could, shadows thick at my back. Look out of the corner of our eye and we could see them, bubbling, twisting, rising up the walls, crawling out of the streets, dark faceless masses trying to be heard. Earle had said: so many millions of dead men and dead women buried beneath the city.

Dead is dead is dead.

Dead memories, dead names, dead things.

Dead is dead is dead until someone happens to remember.

And life was, after all, magic.

So here we are, heading towards Fleet Street, and the lights are being smothered in the shadows that follow us. Here we are, wandering past old-fashioned terraced houses of black brick and white facings, of thick wooden doors and cross-sashed windows, of pointed roofs and old, disused chimney stacks, past old forgotten greenery tucked into car-filled streets. And here's the shadows, the memories that no one bothers to remember: who put down the stones and laid the streets and painted the lines and powered the wires and pumped the water and stacked the sandwiches onto the shelves; and who died and were buried and covered over by the spread of the city, and the bones of the more recently dead, whose families could pay for their lot in a currency that buys more interesting things to smother over the smell of sawdust and widdle. And our hand is bleeding and our head is aching and the dead should just stay dead is dead is dead, just like me.

Now we knew what Vera—the painted cartoon of Vera—had meant. If we stopped walking now, the tidal wave of darkness writhing at our back would fall, tumbling under its own weight, spiral tip-down on top of us and suffocate the life from our chest, press until we couldn't breathe and that would be it: so long, goodbye, goodnight, farewell. Keep walking and you didn't have to look, didn't have to stop and notice the bricks laid by dead hands on a plan drawn by a dead stranger who was commissioned by another stranger who earned his money off the thoughts of strangers who ate the food of strangers who sat huddled kissing-close every day to strangers on a train, armpit-close because that was what you did, that was how you got around, as intimate as a lover and probably more honest too, blood in our hand, shadows at our feet. And here it is, Fleet Street, the mad-eyed dragon guarding its shield with the twin crosses that burnt brighter than the red glow of the traffic lights, watching us with a spinning chaos in its eyes as if it too had seen the endless hole into which the forgotten dead of the city had plummeted and knew how deep the bones went below.

And there was someone leaning against the base of the dragon. I couldn't stop walking, not now, and he didn't seem inclined to follow; just watched me calmly from where he stood, drinking a cup of coffee. I walked straight by, heading back towards the river, dragging the darkness and the shadows and the memories and painted footsteps and whispered voices along behind me and he, at last, drained the remainder of his cup, threw the thing into a bin, and followed, hands buried in his pockets. He was wearing a coat I'd seen already in the night. He came level with me as I headed down the side of a newsagent's towards the river, a tight little street of too few lights held too high up above too little pavement.

I said through gritted teeth, almost too breathless to talk, too busy to slow, "What the hell do you want? This is a walk for the dead."

Blood dribbled from my closed palm, splattered onto the street at my feet, slipped into the mad gaps in the tarmac.

"Oh — I'm totally dead," he replied. "I mean, *totally*."

"You're not. Unless we're talking prophetically."

"Noooo," he said carefully. "No, I think we're dealing with the past here. See, I got gutted by the shadow of my former teacher. He let me die by a phone box near the river. The last breath left my lungs, my heart beat its last, my internal organs decided to give the open air a try and my brain stopped crackling. Medically, dead. You seen *Star Trek*?"

"Of course I've seen *Star Trek* — do you mind, I'm busy here?"

"You thought about the teleportation stuff?"

"No."

"You should think about it. A beam comes out of an empty vacuum and dissolves your entire body. I mean literally, *everything* stops. Your brain stops, your thoughts stop. You are nothing more than a 01010101001 in a computer! Jesus Christ, if that isn't the definition of so dead you could drop it down a pyramid for a party then I don't know what is! Sure, you get assembled at the other end, but it's by a machine that could assemble spare ribs just as easy — it's piling you back together bit by bit, like some ready-made sausage squeezed from a tube. That's not life! That's...cloning, at the very best.

A reconstruction, probably a flawed one, of an entity that naturally died when you went and bloody dissolved its entire nature! So you see, and this is really the point, I'm dead. I mean, seriously, totally whacked."

I could see the river ahead, blue lights on the other side, shimmering reflection of a thousand shattered colours on the black racing water.

"But," I croaked, as the lights went out behind me and the mad eyes of the dragon spun and sunk down for ever in the streets, "if you're dead, then what the hell am I?"

The man in my old coat shrugged. "Dunno. If I were you I wouldn't worry about it too much."

"Why not? Dead is dead is . . ."

"Is dead, yeah. But, you feel like Matthew Swift, don't you?"

"Yes."

"And remember like Matthew Swift?"

"Yes."

"And hate like him, and fear like him, and want like him, and live like him, and marvel like him, and bleed like him?"

"Ticking all these boxes."

"So I figure, fuck it! Sure, I might be dead," he said. "But you're an excellent copy of me."

I looked at him out of the corner of my eye.

They, whoever They are, say you'd go mad if you ever saw the back of your own head. Or the universe would explode or something; paradox and physics and something along these lines. I didn't see the back of the man's head. But he had my face, he *was* Matthew Swift, right down to the blood soaked through his clothes and the tears across his throat and chest which had killed him. But his eyes were brown, not blue, and there was no scar upon his right hand.

I said, "This is turning from the surreal to the downright sick. I want my money back. I want to reload, reboot, try again without the psycho shit!"

"You think?" he chuckled. "You should see what's behind you!"

I wouldn't have looked.

I really wouldn't.

But if you can't trust yourself, even when you're dead, then who are you going to put your faith in?

I looked.

"Ta-da!" said Matthew, the other Matthew, the one who died and didn't come back, because you couldn't, dead is dead is . . .

It was . . .

. . . *dragon* didn't quite cover it.

Dragon implies something made out of scales, with a nod in the direction of reptilian ancestry: dinosaur meets flamethrower with wings. Sure, it includes anything from fluffy through to ferocious; and we could see a case for this thing fitting into both categories. But it felt impolite to try and tie it to any particular biology. Impolite to impose anything as mundane and boring as up, down, sideways, forwards, back, in, out, here, then, there, now. It would have cocked one black eyebrow bigger than the sky above an eye madder than the tiger, tiger that once upon a time burnt bright in some acid-drenched brain; and looked at you as though to say, "Oh. So you're *that* small."

To say it was made of shadows would be to imply that light or darkness even got a look-in. Sure, it had crawled out of them, in the way that the diplodocus had once crawled out of the amoebae of the sea. And if a comet came from the heavens to smash it, it wouldn't be squished, just spread so wide and thin across the earth that it would look like night had fallen down, dragging all the stars with it — before, with a good thorough shake to push the stardust off its skin, the creature slid back to its brilliant, angry, maddened shape.

If its wings bothered to do something so mundane as beat, they took a hundred years to do it; if its tongue found anything in the air worth tasting, the lashing spike as it sampled the drizzle would knock down every chimney from Fleet Street to Piccadilly; if it deigned to press a claw into the earth, the Underground trains rumbling beneath would screech to a stop as the clatter of their engines became lost in the roaring of the tunnels that cowered from its touch.

And if it found any reason, and it would have to be one hell of a reason, to bother to look at you, in its gaze were a million ghosts who pressed up against the cornea of its eye and stretched their fingers through the blackness of its pupil to try and suck you down.

And it was looking at us.

We, who were born from the chatter of mankind, from the things that got left behind in the wires, who were bigger than any city or mortal, were nothing: tiny, insignificant, footsteps walking on stones where a thousand million feet a year would walk, nothing more than ants in a heap. A blink, and our lives were over. Our voices and our footsteps and all that we were would sink into its great black belly. And, while not lost, we would be too small to merit interest from anyone other than the insignificantly small librarian interested in the history of the insignificant: little stories to comfort little people who liked to believe that the heroes mattered, because otherwise, they would be nothing but forgotten ghosts before the city could even deign to shake itself free from yesterday.

It looked at us; we looked at it.

I didn't want to know.

I closed my eyes.

And, without us wanting to attribute a digestive system to the beast, it gobbled us up.

Part 3: The Death of Cities

In which a wife is lost, an enemy is found, and a sorcerer expostulates on the cruelty of strangers.

He said, "Fag?"

I said, "What?"

"You wanna fag?"

I considered this. We were almost tempted. It seemed to calm people down. He held out a packet in a hand that had passed the point of being dirty, into the pure cleanliness of compressed earth so ground into the skin that it's hard to imagine it could ever rub off.

The packet said, "SMOKING GIVES YOU CANCER".

I said, "Nah. Thanks."

He shrugged, stuck a cigarette in his mouth, and struck a flame from a bright orange plastic lighter. He sucked long and deep, coughed, and exhaled. "Jesus," he croaked. "Fucking fags."

I tried to work out what was happening.

I was in a gutter.

Fair enough.

The gutter was on a bridge.

To the left was Tower Bridge, to the right was Southwark.

The guy sitting next to me had my satchel open at his feet. He'd gone through the contents. My wallet lay beside it. He'd gone through that as well, and been disappointed. Now he was offering me a fag. His face was too bloodless for a beard ever to find enough strength to grow. His eyes were lost in the soft tissue round the front brain; his neck was two long tendons on a stick. At some point, and not too far away, he'd messed around with drugs, and they'd messed back. I sat up slowly. I didn't hurt as much as I'd expected—even my hand, burnt with the twin red crosses, didn't pain me as it should. I looked up at a sky in which a few shy stars peeped between black cloud and orange wash, and watched the flickering twin lights of aeroplanes passing overhead.

Not dead.

Still not dead.

Again.

Something had changed.

Couldn't put our finger on what it was...

...but even we knew that being consumed by a metaphysical, metamagical, meta-most-things dragon while on a semi-philosophical LSD trip for Midnight Mayors changed something.

I said, "I need to find the boy."

The guy smoking the cigarette chuckled. "Whatever gets you off."

"I'm serious."

"Sure. Serious guy like you."

On the other side of the bridge, a taxi swished by. At the end of the bridge, a bendy bus scooted past a stop. I crawled onto the pavement, as it rushed by with the racing glee of night buses everywhere.

We looked at the messed-up man and said, "Where did you find us?"

"Here," he replied. "Lying in the gutter, looking at the stars."

"How did I get there?"

"Dunno. Not my business."

"You didn't see...anything peculiar?"

"Fuck shit hell."

"No, then."

"Hey—you got cash?"

"No. Sorry."

"Watch, credit cards, you know?"

"Nothing."

"Come on! You gotta have something. I just need a quickie, you know? Just a little."

I staggered up onto my feet, looked east towards where, in a few hours — quite a few hours, judging by the thickness of the sky — the sun would come up between the yellow-blue pinnacles of Tower Bridge, crawling over the Thames Barrier and sliding across the white bulb of the Millennium Dome, to where I stood.

"I could do you," said the man with the fag. "I could do you and take your shoes when you're stiff."

He didn't say it aggressively. He wasn't laughing either.

We half-turned. "No, you couldn't," we sighed.

"You ain't tough."

"Sure."

"I got friends who've done it, you know? They know places; you send the bodies down and they don't ever come up, not as anything thicker than soup. A fiver? A quid?"

"Bigger picture," I said, stooping to pick up my satchel, piling its contents inside, sticking the wallet back in my pocket without bothering to look if he'd taken anything, knowing there wasn't anything to take.

"I'll fucking do you!" he called after me, not moving from his perch on the edge of the gutter.

We walked away.

Sunrise in winter, in the centre of town. A quiet greyness rising between the streets; lamps on the edge of extinction, hovering with just that tiny sense of unease, not entirely sure if this is dawn, or dusk, or if the sun really will make it. The light brought a slow hum with it, subtle and growing, one bus on an empty street becoming one bus and a cab, two buses, a cab and a bike, three buses, a cab, two bikes and a delivery van, the streets thickening like porridge as the hot milk of the city was poured back into its veins.

It excited us, that slow wakening, like the dawn chorus thrills the druids skulking in the countryside. This was a choir playing the carburettor and the travelcard beep, tinkling on the brakes of the postman's van and playing a chorus of ATM dispensers and Underground rattles. It made us feel awake, alive, our heartbeat in time to the turning over of the double-decker's engine, our breath coming in the slow pumps of the blasts of wind up from the Tube tunnels, our feet moving in that sharper banker's step that went *click, click, click* at the busy brisk leather walk of the City worker. It would be so easy, so *simple*, to turn our fingers towards the oncoming one-way streets and catch the life building in them, tangle it like water against the dam of our hands, and fly on nothing more than the pressure differential created before the sunrise, and after.

I kept walking.

London Bridge, Monument, Bank, King William Street, Cheapside, Guildhall, Aldermanbury Square.

Harlun and Phelps.

Still open, a rising buzz within its halls.

The security guard just waved me through.

Lift to the top floor, city falling away below you, only gods and great men could feel this big over something so endlessly small. Down the corridor, an office designed to make you work for the privilege of talking in it; and knock me down if Earle wasn't there, *still* there, sat behind a desk on which a wicker tray of yoghurt, jam, croissants, toast, Danish whirls and boiling coffee had been laid, sipping from a stainless steel cup, eyes turned towards a newspaper open on his lap.

He glanced up as I entered, and for a moment, looked almost surprised.

"Mr Swift!"

"Ta-da!" I exclaimed weakly.

"You're still..."

"Still not dead. That's me. It's my big party trick, still not being dead, gets them every time."

"You..."

"Did the walk, talked the talk. Went down memory lane, Tarantino-style. Where's the boy?"

"The..."

"Boy. The boy. I've been out all night and I'm a firm believer in what they say about Big Brother never sleeping. Have you found the boy?"

"As a matter of fact..."

"Yes?"

"We just might have."

I beamed. "Mr Earle," I said, "I got a good feeling about all this."

CCTV.

Someone, probably a journalist, claims that there's one CCTV camera for every twelve people in the UK.

Or in other words, Big Brother could so very, very easily be watching you, if he had a reason. That's the whole point, really. He, or it, or them, or best of all, *They*, can track you by ATM, by Oyster card, by mobile phone, by CCTV, by loyalty card, by licence plate, by items bought and items sold, by programmes watched and calls made, and while the Good People need not fear—for what reason should their lives be seen and judged by strangers?—the problem arises when no one knows what that reason is. No one even knows who's going to make that choice.

There are advantages to being legally dead.

So here's how it goes:

About a day after Nair died and a telephone rang, a blue van, registration LS06 BDL, pulled up outside Raleigh Court. Three hired men with unsympathetic faces and unstable morphic structures, friends of a friend who knew a guy called Boom Boom, got out of the back, walked up to number 53 and pulled a kid out from inside the flat. He wasn't looking great in the few grainy seconds of footage that the Aldermen had recovered. He wasn't looking alive. But then if he wasn't alive, what was the point?

They stuck him in the back of the van.

The van drove south.

The congestion charge cameras caught it entering the zone around 4 a.m. They didn't care a damn, because at 4 a.m. no one pays £8 to drive, but they were still watching, and even if they weren't, the Aldermen had *means*. I didn't want to know, found that I didn't really care.

Roughly half an hour after entering the zone, the van left it, heading south from Waterloo, and was glimpsed briefly at Elephant and Castle, then caught for a moment heading round Clapham Common. No wonder it had taken a day and a half to find — too many cameras, too much watching, too many things to watch, too much to see; no one mind could take it in. A heap built on a million dead heaps built by a hundred million dead ants on the crunched-down skeletons of their predecessors; who'd track one little van?

"This is all very interesting," I said, "but where did it end up?"

"You won't like it," said Earle.

"Hit me."

"Morden."

"Morden."

"Yes. Morden."

End of the line. We did not like Morden.

"Where in Morden?"

"You won't like it."

"Worked that out already. Where?"

He told me.

And no, I didn't like it.

Morden.

Sometimes there are places so far, so obscure, so unlikely, so implausible and so utterly . . .

. . . well . . .

. . . *Morden* . . .

. . . that there's no point driving there.

A friend once put it like this: One guy gets on a train to Isleworth,

another guy gets on a train to Cardiff, and you can bet the guy going
to Wales gets there sooner.

The same rule applies to Morden. A mainline train to Ipswich will
get there faster than a driver departing at the same time from Liverpool Street will make it to deepest, darkest Morden.

To even the odds a little, I took the Northern Line from Bank,
right down through the strange wildernesses of Monument, Borough,
Elephant and Castle, Kennington, Oval, Tooting Bec, Colliers Wood,
South Wimbledon and, right at the bottom of the map, Morden.

End of the line.

The driver even announced it as we arrived.

"End of the line," he said. "All change, all change, end of the line."

Oda was waiting at the top of the stairs. She had a big sports bag over
one shoulder. As I came out through the barrier, she said, "You feeling
inaugurated?"

"Sort of. Does that make me a higher priority for the hit list?"

"There's an argument there. On the one hand, the Midnight
Mayor is a magical entity whose very existence is an insult to the
works of Heaven. On the other hand, we don't yet know how to kill *it*,
the title, even though the men die easy. So there's a school of thought
that says we should keep you alive, just so we know who you are, and
how to hurt you."

"Goodie."

"Pleased to see me?"

"Thrilled."

"Where are we going?"

"The Aldermen have traced our blue van to a place not far from
here."

"Why Morden?"

"It's the end of the line."

"Does that mean anything?"

"Maybe. Come on."

*   *   *

Suburbia. Squalid suburbia, to be exact. Close enough to the inner city for rich retirees seeking a rural dream in proximity to a convenient supermarket to find it unpleasant; far enough away for rich workers in the centre of town to find it unsatisfactory. Morden was a left-over borough for the ones left behind. Streets of white concrete bungalows, and half-timbered semi-detached villas with lattice windows, and panes of fake antique glass in each front door, bulbous and distorted. And, every few hundred yards, a run-down shopping parade boasting the chippy, the betting shop, the newsagent and the launderette. A few unlikely hangovers survived: here the frontage of the little shop where they fixed watches, there the open garage door of the bicycle-repair shop, across the road, the post office selling beach balls, plastic toys, birthday cards with kittens on and, if you were lucky, a first-class stamp as well.

It could have been anywhere, any town in any place; and only the intrusion of the Underground and an old music hall converted for bingo let it still claim to be London.

We walked through the streets of Morden, following the instructions Earle had given me. I counted CCTV cameras, imagined a blue van driven all the way from Kilburn sliding through these sleeping streets. The sky was grey and overcast, the wind smelling of rain yet to come, the lunchtime bakeries selling suspicious sausage rolls: quiet, business not really interested today. Oda said, "No back-up?"

"They'll meet us there."

"And where's there?"

"Not far now."

"No patience for cryptic, sorcerer. 'Cryptic' is something people use in order to feel smug about their knowing and someone else not."

I sighed, but she had a point. "Earle's people traced the van to a site near here. We think it's where the boy, Mo, is."

"And the boy is still important?"

"Yeah."

"To whom?"

"To me."

"That's what I thought."

We kept on walking.

"What did you see, last night?"

"What?"

"The Midnight Mayor is supposed to see things. It would be useful information for us to know what you saw."

"The Order are the last people I would possibly ever tell."

"But you did see something, didn't you?"

"Yes."

"Will you tell me?"

"Is there a difference?"

"What do you mean?"

"If I tell you, aren't I just telling the Order?"

She thought about this half the length of the street. Wheelie-bins, parked cars, delivery vans, mothers with buggies, bright red postbox, pigeons scuttling out of the middle of the street as a learner driver pootled uneasily past. Then, "One day, I'll kill you."

"Yup. I know."

"Because you're a sorcerer."

"Yup."

"And one day you might have to kill me."

"The thought had crossed my mind."

"Because I'm part of the Order."

"Pretty much. I think you'll probably shoot first. But what if you miss?"

"It has nothing to do with my being Oda or your being Matthew. It's just how it is."

"Yeah. I know." We kept on walking. I said, "I saw a dragon."

"Cheesy."

"It wasn't *Jurassic Park*. I mean, I saw a thing that looked like a dragon simply because if it had looked like itself my brain wouldn't have been able to comprehend it. Things we do not understand . . . the brain does its best to fit them into some sort of vehicle that allows us comprehension, to simplify it down so that the part of us that thinks with words, not instincts, has even a vague chance of understanding. It wasn't a dragon."

"OK."

"It was everything else. Up, down, in, out, forward, back, time, width, length, depth, stone, brick, leaf, pipe, iron, steel, gas, breath, dirt, dust, fear, anger, madness, fury, hurt, life . . ."

"You're rambling."

"It was the city. Too big and wild to ever understand, except to call it a dragon and hope your brain doesn't dribble at the thought."

"Uh-huh."

"Oda?"

"Yes?"

"There's a reason I don't tell *you* things either."

And then, she smiled. It was such a strange and alien expression on her lips that at first, we couldn't comprehend it. But it was in her voice as well, a moment, an actual moment, when psycho-bitch wasn't anywhere to be seen, and there was just a woman with a gun in her pocket. "Matthew," she said, "if you weren't already thrice damned and stuck on a spit, it would almost be human that you tried."

We didn't know what to say, couldn't think of anything except a sudden awareness of all the air inside our chest, that slipped over our tongue without being able to take anything but the feeblest of shapes.

Too much thinking, too much trouble.

Our solution for everything.

We kept walking, and said not a word.

And there it was.

It crept out of a corner and announced with a blaring self-confidence, "*Voilà!* Here I am and buggered if you'll find a way round me!" It lay between two red-brick railway lines racing south towards more exciting, less smelly destinations, and on the chain-link fence someone had stuck up a sign in crude paint saying:

!!!SEAL'S SCRAP, WASTE & REFUSE SERVICE!!!
!!WASTE NOT WANT NOT!!
VAT NOT INCLUDED

Oda looked at the metal fence and said, "If this is a symptom of your sense of humour..."

"You make it sound like a disease. And no, it's not. This is where the blue van went. It's somewhere in there."

I nodded through an iron gate.

Beyond it, a long way beyond it, and in it, and over it, and just generally doing its impression of the endless horizon, was rubbish. Every possible kind of decay had been placed within the boundaries of SEAL'S SCRAP, as if iron and steel might, after ten thousand years' compression, have mulched down into rich black oil to be tapped. Dead cars, shattered and crushed in the vices of lingering, sleepy cranes; dead washing machines, dead fridges, pipes broken and the chemicals spilt onto earth and air, broken baths, old shattered trolleys, torn-up pipes, ruined engines with the plugs pulled out, tumbled old tiles shattered and cracked, skips of twisted plywood blackened in some flame, bricks turned to dust and piled upon bin bags split into shreds, shattered glass and cracked plastic, white polystyrene spilt across the tarmac, cardboard boxes in which the weeds had begun to grow. It seemed to stretch for miles, oozing into every corner between the railway lines, locked away behind its see-through fence and a small cabin for the delivery men to sit in and have their tea.

Oda said, "Where's back-up?"

I looked for the Aldermen, and saw none.

"Don't know."

"We could..."

"I've seen enough American TV to know what happens to people who go in without back-up."

"Jack Bauer manages."

"You've watched 24? Did you denounce that too?"

She pursed her lips. "There's a forum on the subject, but so far, no."

"Is this why you're a psycho-bitch with a gun?" I asked carefully. "You saw too many thrillers?"

"I think we both know that isn't true, and I think we both want to avoid discussion on the matter."

No smiles now. Perhaps we'd imagined it after all.

We waited. It started to rain. This is what usually happens when you're outside and not too busy to notice.

Oda had an umbrella in her sports pack, along with a rifle and a sword. She didn't offer to share.

I rang Earle.

"H-H-Harlun and—"

"Ask Earle where this fabled back-up of his is."

The stuttering boy asked Earle.

Earle said, "Swift? What do you mean? They should have been there an hour ago."

His voice was big enough that Oda could hear it over the phone. She looked at me, I looked at her.

We both looked at the scrapyard.

"Earle," I said, "if I should die, I want you to know that the phones will scream their vengeance at you when you sleep."

I hung up. I figured he'd work out the problem all by himself.

Oda said, "What do we do now?"

"Did you denounce *Alien*?"

"No."

"Why not?"

"It's just a film."

I wagged a finger at the scrapyard, half lost now in the falling rain.

I felt dirty just looking at it, and the seeping through my clothes of heavy London drizzle didn't help. "Let's say, hypothetically, that back-up has been and gone and it ended badly. The biggest mistake made in *Alien . . .*"

"Was going in after the monster?"

"Yes."

"Then we should walk away."

"But that's the point, isn't it? A blue van drove into the scrapyard with a kid inside who should hold the key to this entire farcical cock-up of a disaster. It didn't come out. Now, if we go in there . . ."

"The kid is probably dead."

"Then why not kill him at Raleigh Court?"

"You want him to be alive."

"Yes! Of course I do! For so many, many reasons, and only one of them is mine! And if he is, and we just walk away then how stupid will we feel when everything goes splat?"

"You want to go looking for him. Now?"

"Yes."

"In there?"

"Yes."

"You know, I never had you for a fool."

"Thanks, I think."

"A coward, yes, but not a fool."

"Wait here, then. You can save your bullets." She sighed, reached into her bag, pulled out a gun, ugly, big and black. "Thank you," I said.

"I know where my soul is going," she replied sharply. "I don't think this enterprise is helping the cause of yours."

I was almost touched my soul had a cause to fail.

We went into the scrapyard, as the rain grew heavier.

There was no one inside the gate cabin. I found a kettle, as cold as dead men's flesh. Our terror had subsided to a calm and level fury, as if every receptor for sense was so bombarded that the whole system had shut down for a diagnostic reboot, unable to believe this was the information it was meant to process. It gave the movement of our hands in front of us, the tread of our feet, a detached quality. We were observers, observing someone else, no more.

Rain pooled grey-black on the uneven tarmac floor of the yard. A few twists, a few turns, and all was lost behind the great piles of stuff, the endless cairns of dead equipment rising up taller than three basketball players with an acrobatic fondness for each other's shoulders. The railway lines were quickly gone behind the tottering pyramids of broken metal, twisted plastic, rusted iron, pocked steel, rotten stuffing and slashed foam, just dead bits of comfortable lives, left over to no purpose that I could see. The rain helped keep it a bit real, tickled down the back of my neck and bit ice into my spine, oozed through my shoes — still not my shoes, still too big — and started wrinkling itchy around my toes. I buried my hands in my pocket, stuck my chin inside my collar and kept walking, scanning each great mound of abandoned nothing stuff from top to bottom in search of something softer than metal.

There wasn't a smell, not with the rain and the heavy, sinking cold. There was a taste, salt and dry spilt chemicals, old bleach and broken bottles of things that shouldn't have had the safety cap removed. Two turns in the maze and the sounds of the road were already a long way off; a train rumbled by distantly, wheels screeching like a maddened witch. I slipped on a torn pile of builder's bags, sand still clinging to their inner edges; ambled past a wall of shattered safety glass, so safe that the million greenish pieces hadn't had the heart to fall away from their friends. A fat black-brown rat scuttled away towards the gutted and half-burnt remnants of a sofa, the cushions long since vanished. I scuttled after it, bending down towards the ground and holding out my hands, cooing gentle noises.

"Come on, come on . . ."

The rat looked back at me uncertainly, hesitated on the edge of a hole chewed through the stuffing of a mattress, which thin orange fungus had long since made its own, then started to edge back towards me, its oval body shimmering and bright in the soaking rain, its pink claws sliding through the rising puddles on the floor. Oda looked at us with distaste, but said not a word as bending down, we picked it up in our hands, smelt slime and old rotting things from its coat, saw tiny sharp teeth in a tiny pointed mouth, felt little sharp claws tap dance on the surface of our palm. Pigeons and rats; no one knows more in a big city.

We stroked its back, our fingers sliding slime-covered off the greasy surface of its coat, whispered gentle implorings and polite commands, and bent down, let it scuttle free, followed it as it passed along small trails through the rising water. It scrambled over old black Victorian pipes dragged up from some forsaken corner of the sewers, past broken pots and vases smashed into a dozen white shards on the earth, over a hundred cracks where the grass had somehow managed to peep its way up from the grey concrete soil, round a rotting slab of sandy clay where the buddleia was trying to take root, little purple flowers crawling out of tough brown roots. I almost had to run to keep up with it; staggering past the broken hull of a yacht, a great fat tear through its belly; the twisted remains of a car, bonnet pressed up almost into its boot; wrought-iron back of an old bedstead; a lonely rocking chair, the screws just about to fall free.

"Sorcerer…" whispered Oda, a note of urgency in her voice. I glanced back at her, then back again and could see nothing but the towers of broken things all around, like metal hills blocking out the sky.

"Not far," I muttered, as much for my sake as hers. "Not far…"

I could smell the bright warm stench of a sandwich rotting in the rain, see the yellow blur of the rat's eyes in my own, sense the twitching of its whiskers as if they grew from my face, and there it was as well, another thing rotting, a different kind of rot, the kind that didn't taste of bright orange rust and broken metal. I remembered the fox in Kilburn. I remembered the way Mr Pinner didn't smell.

Old kettles turned calcium-white on the inside; half a chimney pot, through which the buddleia was beginning to peek, a shattered TV aerial still carrying traces of pigeon poop on its strands, a satellite dish, face turned upwards to receive a signal, in which now nothing but stagnant water pooled. There would be ice in the night, thick frost in the shadows; our breath was white smoke.

And then the rat stopped.

It looked at something, then looked at me, then scuttled away into a tunnel an inch wider than itself, dug out of a tower of tumbled detritus. At first we couldn't see what it had seen, but stared at more of the same: rust and black burnt nothings. Then Oda's hand brushed ours, just for a second, and we, startled by the touch, looked to her, then followed her gaze.

There was something in the rubbish.

It was a shoe. At some point, it had been a trendy shoe, big, white and gold and blue, all the right marks to declare that here was someone who knew who they were and it was all about the feet. That had been then. Now it, like everything else in this place, was rotting, dirt and rain and ragged tears pulling out the soft stuffing of the inner sole, limp sodden brown laces dribbled, undone. It stuck out of the pile of dead machines at a strange angle, like someone had stuck it there on a pole like a defiant flag. I looked closer. There was something in the shoe. It might have been a sock.

Oda whispered, "Oh, God."

There was something in the sock.

It might have been an ankle.

I snapped, "Help me!"

We scrambled up the sides of the heap and started pulling. Old rusted bike frames, crinkled-up drink cans, broken bottles, a thing, all withered bone and hair, that might once have been a dead cat stuffed inside a cardboard box, a shattered lamp, a gutted radio, the panels for a speaker trailing wires, the drawers of some old filing cabinet, snapped along the lines on which they should have slid. The ankle became a leg, blue slashed jean stained the colour of black rust; the leg joined onto a hip, at the wrong angle, sticking out too far to one side; the hip was half-covered by a T-shirt, soaked through and torn; the T-shirt covered a chest, into which half a broom had at some point buried itself just hard enough to pin the body it impaled to the ground. We threw broken things aside, feeling the great mound of decayed waste shift beneath us, creaking and clanking as old lynchpins of its structure were tossed away; and there were fingers, hands, arms. And they were wrong: black — not the deep rich brown of Oda's skin that foolish mortals called black, but the black of an ocean night when the stars are lost, coal-black, dead-black, ink-black. I could see black blood pumping through the veins beneath his skin, still moving, still, just alive, and we knew without a doubt, that it was ink-black, black as ink, black, because it was ink.

Some sort of whisk had fallen over his face, its broken wires clinging to his throat and jaw. We untangled them, metal hooks twanging merrily as they came free, and ink flowed from the pinprick wounds. The whites of his eyes were stained with the same ink that ran through his blood, his lips were the colour of festering bruises, his hair was falling from his skull in fistfuls, barely a few handfuls left on the grey dome of his head. Alive. Still alive, bleeding, wheezing, freezing, shivering, dying, pick one, they were all leading in the same direction, racing each other for the prize.

"Is that..." whispered Oda.

"What do you think?"

I dragged him up by an arm and he came, a puppet without the stuffing. Oda took the other arm, slung it across her shoulder and between the two of us, we pulled him free. A rusty screwdriver was embedded in his back, just offset from his spine, sticking out like some obscene fashion accessory. Oda pulled it free with a thick pop of dead muscle, and black ink began to flow from the hole down to the seat of his fouled pants. He stank of urine and shit, dragged uneven and lumpy in our arms as we pulled him along. His legs didn't move, his head didn't rise; there was nothing in him to suggest life except the slow beating of black blood in his veins. I turned my head, looking for the way out, trying to judge by the distant rattle of trains the way to the exit. Picked a direction; staggered, walked, ran, dragged, tripped, stumbled, all at once, towards the way out.

"Ambulance?" whispered Oda.

"Can't save him now."

"The . . . hospital place?"

"Maybe. They have means at Elizabeth Anderson . . . can you reach the phone in my bag?"

My satchel was swinging uncomfortably from my shoulder; to grab it was to drop the ink-stained boy. As Oda snatched for it, I glanced at his face and saw, through the black stain under his skin, that his cheeks were still slightly puffed with puppy-dog youth; just a kid, and he was going to die. Oda grabbed my satchel, reached inside, pulled out the mobile phone.

"Black Cab," I said. "He's the only one who can get us there in time."

She thumbed it on. Continents drifted in the time it took the phone to power up. "Sorcerer . . ." Fear, unashamed, numb-the-senses fear. ". . . there's no signal."

We never call bad things "coincidence".

"Help me," I grunted, and she took more of the kid's weight again. "We need to run."

We ran, tripping and staggering through the thick rain, the sky a sullen gloom overhead making no concession to the time of day, determined to keep things uniform and dead. My hand burnt, my head burnt, my *eyes* burnt inside their sockets, I could feel them aching and stinging.

"He's here, he's here, he's here, he's here," we whimpered.

"Shut up!"

"He's here."

"Shut *up!*"

I remembered the mad eyes of the dragon. Too big, too...too much of anything, too *too*, an endless fall into a thing too big for the mind to grasp.

So we ran, dragging the kid who I guess once upon a time had answered to the name of Mo, son of Loren, blood turned to ink, eyes turned black, dribbling black ink tears down his stained face, draining black blood from a screwdriver hole in his back, from wire tears in his neck, clothes the colour of rust, trousers the smell of shit, shoes the brown stain of rot and decay. We rounded a corner and pulled immediately back, pressing ourself into the pyramid of fallen debris.

"He's here," we breathed.

Oda peered past us, towards the exit from the junkyard, and immediately drew back, shoulders heaving with the effort of breath. She had seen what I had seen. Just a guy in a suit, standing in the exit. I wondered if Earle's back-up had seen him too, and if they had lived long enough to see anything more.

"What do we do?" she hissed.

I glanced forward again, and there he was: pinstripe suit, one hand buried casually in his trouser pocket, the other holding a huge blue umbrella over his head, the water tumbling down from the edges. Smiling—just smiling. Mr Pinner, patient as the dustbin man, just smiling in the way out.

Mo, as if sensing the terror that we could see, groaned.

I turned, twisting my head towards the junk above us. "Get him to the station," I said. "Buy him a ticket. We can hide behind the barriers."

"What are you going to do?"

We reached up and brushed the tip of an old, cracked fishing rod, sticking out from the black stinking piles of junk. "Litterbug," we whispered, closing our fingers round the stubbly end of the rod and snapping it like a dry summer twig, "we're going to have a conversation."

We wrapped the end of the rod in the palm of our hand, took a deep breath, and stepped out to meet Mr Pinner.

*   *   *

He was smiling.

Had he ever not smiled?

He stood under the umbrella in the chain gateway to the junkyard, and smiled.

Mr Pinner, the death of cities.

After all, if the ravens and the river and the Stone and, God help us all, the Midnight Mayor protect the city, then that should suggest there's something you need to protect it *from*.

We stopped ten paces from where he stood, and hoped our jelly-trembles would be mistaken for the cold of the pouring rain. Our hair itched where the water had dragged it down towards our eyes, our stomach felt like it had been sucked clean by a hoover that someone had forgotten to switch off after. We wanted to speak, and found we couldn't.

Then he said, "Hello. My name is Mr Pinner. I am the death of cities. Did you want to talk about something?"

I nodded numbly.

"I'm all ears."

His voice was polite, level, well educated, with just a hint of something more aggressive, something that deep down loathed the good grammar he used, loathed the sharp suit and the expensive watch, and dreamed of Friday night down at the pub, and the old farting motorbikes the kids used to use.

"Well?" he prompted, as we stood and stared for too long.

I licked my lips, tasted the falling rain, clutched our piece of fishing rod so tight it burnt in my hand. "Why are you here?"

"To kill you and your lady friend," he replied easily. "Somewhere in here there are some men who had no luck. Or some of their bits. I don't concern myself with the details."

"Why?"

He looked slightly confused. "Because I am the death of cities," he repeated. "I'm sorry; didn't I make my position clear?"

"Just...just to clarify..." I stammered, "you are using it in the literal sense, right? I mean, you're not just some twat who spent too much time playing Dungeons & Dragons as a kid, you're the actual, I mean...the literal..."

He beamed. "When the bomb fell on Hiroshima, I saw the sky blossom above me like a flower, saw the beauty of the flames, the majesty of it. When Dresden burnt, I breathed the smoke — the night has never been so bright! When the levees broke during the storm, I let the water run through my fingers, washing away corruption and a surplus of time; when the plague came to this city, I stroked the backs of the black rats as they ran off the ship. When the baker in Pudding Lane left his oven open, I was the customer who took the last loaf before the ashes scattered onto the straw and ignited. The bread was the sweetest food I have ever tasted. When Rome burnt, I stood on the tallest hill to watch the temples tumble; when Babylon fell, I licked the dust off my lips to taste on my tongue. I stood on the walls of Jericho, danced on the lip of the earthquake when it shook down the Bosphorus, bathed in the burning rivers at Pompeii, drank vodka on the rooftops of Stalingrad, and when the order was given, spare not man, woman, or child, I raised the standard high and gave the battle cry that mortal men were too afraid to utter. I am as old as the first stone laid beside its neighbour. I feast on the fall of walls, on the shattering of roofs, on the breaking of the street, the bursting of the pipes, the snapping of the wires, the bursting of the mains, the running of the people. I have come to this city half a dozen times before, to watch the cathedrals burn and taste the terror on the bridges just before they sink beneath the weight of runners. And now I've come again, to finish what was started when the first stone was laid." He smiled. "Does that answer your question?"

"Yup," I squeaked. "Pretty much." He reached up to close the umbrella. *"Although,"* I said quickly, "it seems to me, in an academic way of things, that you didn't actually *cause* all those things. You encouraged them, maybe, you rejoiced in them, you found...*beauty* in them, sure. No one would deny that a mushroom cloud is magical, outrageous, obscene, beautiful. Whatever. But unless you're telling me you stood next to Truman's shoulder and whispered, 'press the red button' or told Bomber Harris that it would just be a little, little fire, you seem to be more of a consequence, not a cause. A feeding parasite who finds magic in life, life in death. So I gotta ask you: what brought you to London this time?"

He seemed almost to hesitate. Then he smiled. "You must be Bakker's apprentice," he said. "The sorcerers are dead, which saved me killing them. The Tower has fallen, which saved me destroying it. When you killed Bakker, you made my life so much easier. I would not have come here had he still been alive. I should thank you for that, sorcerer."

The vacuum cleaner in my stomach turned from suck to pump, filled it with ice and vomit and dust.

So I said, just to see, because if I didn't ask, I'd never know, *"'Give me back my hat'."*

His face darkened, his fingers tightened in his trouser pocket. We grinned. "Come on," I said. "Like it was never *not* going to be important."

And for a moment, just a little, little moment, Mr Pinner, the death of cities, was afraid.

Then I felt the first slither of blood run down my face, felt the first sting of the paper cut. We drew back our right hand, behind our shoulder, and then flung it forward, throwing the snapped end of fishing rod like a dart, like a spear. It slammed dead-centre into his chest, point-first through the place where there should have been a breastbone. He looked at it, a little surprised, then back up at us. "Nothing can stop me," he murmured. "You cannot begin to comprehend."

I shrugged. We opened our palms out to our sides, felt the

electricity crackle through our blood. "Waste not, want not," we said. He reached to pull the fishing rod from his chest, utterly unconcerned to have it sticking from his paper flesh; and as he did so, we *pushed*.

Not at him; we pushed sideways, backwards, down, closed our eyes and twisted our fingers towards the great piles of discarded junk, remembering the smell of it, the rusted touch, the slime, the rot, the stink, the decay, the dead cat in its cardboard box, the fungus oozing over rotted things, the torn stuffing, the biting wire, the razored shattered edges, the tumbled glass, the melted plastic, the burnt steel, the broken pipes, the shattered cans, the twisted hinges, the abandoned everything. Everything we didn't want to see and didn't want to know, thrown aside; didn't care, didn't think, didn't need, didn't use, didn't work, tossed and discarded and abandoned and forgotten and alone.

Life is magic, magic is life. It's a conundrum sorcerers have always worried at. So much that had once been alive, so many abandoned forgotten things that had been a part of life. It was only logical, only natural, only the most sensible conclusion in the world that with so much association and neglect piled up in one place, there would still be a shard of forgotten life, waiting to burn. And it, being lonely and abandoned and left to die, was *angry*.

Mr Pinner pulled the piece of fishing rod from his chest, and looked at it with an expression of surprise. Small scraps of paper drifted down from the wound, caught in the wind and billowed upward for a moment, before the falling rain cast them down into the puddle at his feet.

Then, quietly and off to our left, something went *thunk*.

He looked up sharply and, just a bit too late, realised. Something else went *eeeeeeeeeeeeeeeiiiiiiiicccccccccckkkkkk* . . .

A plastic bottle tumbled from a pile and bounced away. A piece of rotting brown string snapped free from a Gordian knot. A sprout of purple buddleia twisted and shrivelled, its roots dislodged. Then came the scuttling. It started as a distant tap dance performed by a flea circus, rose into a tumbling of meltwater, the ice still in it, became a high chattering noise, and only at the last moment did we understand. The rats were coming out of the junk: hundreds of fat brown rats. They slithered from inside the humming piles of twisted debris, plopped down onto the earth, onto each other and scuttled for the exit, worming past my ankles, brushing against my legs, flowing over my feet and past me without even bothering to slow down, streaming around Mr Pinner and away, tumbling into the street and gutters, searching for a way out.

Then I felt something move past my head. I ducked instinctively, shielding my face with my hands. Through my parted fingers I could see what it was. A fishing rod, the end snapped off. It spun past my ear and struck Mr Pinner across the side of the head, too fast for him to dodge. A broken umbrella flew point-first from a pile of rubble and embedded itself in his shoulder; a deflated plastic football spun from the ground and tangled around his feet, a blackened barbecue spun past me and knocked into him; and now it wasn't just one thing, it was a dozen, a hundred, the whole yard spinning and screaming and rattling and twisting and rising and turning and falling, all falling in, tumbling down from the great pyramids like iron filings drawn to a magnet, like a rocket into the sun.

We threw ourself on the ground as the tarmac cracked and splintered beneath us, covering our head, tucking our arms into our ears and our hands over our eyes and willing fury and life still into the old dead things left to rot around us, pushing every drop of fear and anger and strength we possessed into the rust and mould and telling it, *him, get him*. Somewhere nearby I was vaguely aware of running; I half thought I heard Oda call my name; kept my head down and started to crawl on my belly, the last rats running over my spine and the back of my neck in their desperation to escape, as I headed for where I thought the exit might be.

I couldn't see; the air was too full of spinning broken objects that, even as they travelled, shed spare parts, clattering to the earth around them. A thick orange dust of metal shavings, sawdust, sand, rust, old spilt chemicals, shattered moulds, ripped-up mosses and bits of thick purple fungus and thin green slime filled the air, turning clear lines of perspective into a maddened oil canvas painted by a drugged-up loon. I breathed through the sleeve of my coat, and even that hurt, my nose burning with the rust that tried to slash and tear the soft tissues, my eyes running and every sense overwhelmed with so much information all at once that I could barely register any thought at all. Just crawl, keep it simple, too much thinking, too much trouble, too much of too much, just keep crawling . . .

I bumped into the chain fence, bent back like a clifftop tree in a storm, and crawled along it, feeling my way to the edge. I half thought I heard Oda again, but it was hard to tell, beneath the tumbling of a thousand dead bits of steel, iron, plastic, brick, concrete, rubber, glass, Plexiglas, clay, tin, plywood, chipboard . . . a hand closed over our ankle and we whimpered, glancing back into the storm and half-blinded by the blast of everything that hit our eyes, so weak, small, frail, mortal,

Mr Pinner

his hand was paper

for a moment we blinked and pushed back against the storm and saw

the skin torn away. It was just white paper, covered in tiny illegible writing and the suit, his suit tearing in the wind, was sewn into the paper; I could see the tiny stitches as the cuff was pulled back by the whirlwind. His eyes were full of blue ink; his hair was unravelling, each strand unfolding into a tube, a receipt or a bus ticket or some small marker, that flew away and unfurled behind him. His teeth were rubbers, tiny white rubbers set into a broader rubber gum; his tongue was some sort of thick moleskin or leather, dry, like the kind used to bind an executive diary. It occurred to us quite how much he looked like a thing summoned, a creation of someone's fury: consequence, not cause . . .

His other hand came up, holding a not-quite-gold-nibbed pen, the end dripping black ink drops that were snatched away into the whirlwind. He was on his belly, an arm, part of a head sticking out from beneath a falling tonnage of rubbish and scrap, which writhed and twisted above him like a great angry worm, bits of old fridge and shattered chair rising to the surface and falling into the depths, like a liquid creature, not a thing of solid mass at all. I kicked at the hand that seized my ankle, grabbed the strength in my chest, the heat and the fear and sent it blasting down my leg, smoking and spitting electric anger off his fingertips. His grip relaxed for just a moment and I crawled free, staggering onto my hands and knees even as Mr Pinner shrieked in frustration and a wardrobe, the doors gaping like jaws, tumbled down on him from out of the whirlwind.

I turned away from the storm and ran, sparks flashing off the surface of my skin as I struggled to control it, too much, too much magic, too much electricity, too much of anything that was too too much...

And there was the street, the road, the cars, alarms wailing in furious distress, the windows opening in streets around, the telephone lines swaying and jangling uneasily, and Oda, already halfway up the street and headed for the station, Mo slung across her shoulders, not looking back, never looking back. I staggered after her as behind me the great mound of scrap that had upended itself on Mr Pinner heaved and warped, buckled and screamed and

it was going to go.

I ran down the street, staggering and bumping against the sides of the cars, heard the little jangling sound of the iron fence giving out behind me, heard the whooshing of the telephone lines as they tore free from their moorings, heard the distant screech of some passing train slamming on the brakes and an almost sad, gentle, *whumph*.

I threw myself down into the gutter, crawled underneath the bumper of the nearest car and put my hands over my head as behind me, the scrapyard blossomed like a mushroom cloud. It went up into the air, spread out in blissful photographic slow motion, and fell. It rained stuffing, wire, broken pipe, rusted metal, old fridge and split tyre. Half a dresser smashed through the bedroom window of a nearby house; a truck found its roof caved in by an upside-down van, the engine, tyres and windows gone, that fell from the heavens like a burning bush. An armchair managed to catch itself on the sharpened antennae of a rooftop TV aerial; a chimney pot smashed down on a garden gnome. Everywhere there was dust, and dirt, and rust, shimmering like orange snow down onto the ground. It seemed to take a lifetime to settle; it probably took less than five seconds.

I looked around me. A grandfather clock had landed half a foot from my hiding place, top-down, and spilt its ancient blackened gears across the pavement. An old crowbar was buried like King Arthur's sword in the bonnet of the car in front of me; a sheet of thin insulating foam drifted from the sky to land at my feet. Wherever there was an alarm, it was wailing, on every house, and in every car. I crawled to my feet and looked back at the scrapyard. Black smoke obscured everything, but it seemed like most of the contents of the yard were now spilt across an area roughly five times wider and five times shallower than before. A piece of paper drifted past my feet, turning rapidly grey in the rain. It said:

Gas bill in the period 06-07 to 12-07 — £257.13

I looked up.

There was a man standing in the smoke.

Smoothing down his suit.

We ran.

Oda had been knocked flat by the blast. As I caught up with her, she was trying to pick Mo up with one arm while pulling the remnants of yellow sealing foam out of her hair. "Help me!" she snapped, and I guessed she meant with the kid.

I dragged him up and together we staggered towards the end of the road.

"Did you kill him?" she asked.

"Ha ha," I replied.

"Terrific. Where is he?"

"Smoothing down his suit. If we're lucky I've rattled him and we'll have a few minutes. If not..."

"Where are we going?"

"The station."

She glanced sharply at me. "You're going to..."

"Power of the travelcard," I replied. "You know how this song goes."

If anyone paid us attention on the streets of Morden, they paid just enough to get out of our way.

They'd heard something explode and were thinking of terrorist bombs and the ten o'clock news. And we were moving too fast now, as we dragged Mo down the rain-drenched street, for anything to make us stop. I could hear sirens, getting closer, every pitch and tone of distressed vehicle, see people running in equal measure towards and away from the blast. We got Mo across the street towards the station, saw the bright sign of the Underground, that most holy of symbols, protection and safety and movement and freedom, and tumbled into the station even as the guard started to close the gates. "Hey, there's been a—" he began.

"He's got a gun, fucker!" Oda screamed at him.

The station manager looked from me, to Oda, to Mo. Oda, to prove her point, pulled out her own gun, fired two shots in the air and shouted, "Run for your lives!"

They ran, guard, manager, passengers and all. I loaded the full weight of Mo into Oda's arms and staggered towards the ticket machines, fumbled for ever in my bag, looking for coins, anything, found some, bought a ticket for him, pulled out my own, handed Mo's to Oda and snapped, "Get him through!"

We passed through the barrier and nearly fell into the hall inside,

Oda crudely dragging Mo as she held their two tickets in her teeth. "Down, down!" I snapped, waving at the stairs. I felt movement behind me, turned back towards the half-open grille on the entrance; and there he was, Mr Pinner, walking in calmly out of the rain, shaking the droplets off his umbrella, which wasn't even scratched, *he* wasn't even scratched, the illusion of skin back on his face, all hint of paper gone, nothing torn, not even a thrown stitch in all his suit. He smiled at me and started to walk towards the barrier. I raised my travelcard, bracing myself for the spell, and began the incantation.

"These are the terms and conditions of carriage: 'If you do not have an Oyster card with a valid season ticket and/or balance to pay as you go on it, you must have with you a valid printed ticket(s)...'"

He hesitated, seeing what I was doing, seeing the air thicken between us as I threw myself into the protective spell, invoking all that was sacred about the Underground.

"'...available for the whole of the journey you are making. You may use your printed ticket in accordance with these conditions.

All printed tickets remain our property and we may withdraw or cancel...'"

Then, he turned his head towards the nearest ticket machine, and walked towards it. The spirit went out of me; I nearly fell under the weight of my own travelcard. He pressed a button, chose a ticket, started to dig into his pocket for change, couldn't find any, looked up at the empty glass where the station manager should have been selling, then smashed it with the end of his umbrella in a single swipe and reached through for the cash till.

I screamed at Oda, "It's not going to work! Move!"

She'd already dragged Mo down to the bottom of the stairs. We took the steps two a time after her, skidded on the dirt-engrained tiles at the bottom, grabbed her by the sleeve and pulled her towards the platform.

"What do you mean it's not going to work?" she shrieked. "I thought that spell of yours stopped everything!"

"It stops everything that doesn't have a *right* to be on the Underground," I replied, looking up for the indicator board, "and he's buying a fucking ticket as we speak!"

And there was the indicator—

1. High Barnet via Bank—3 mins
2. Edgware via Bank—9 mins
3. Edgware via CharingX—15 mins

GIVE ME BACK MY HAT GIVE ME BACK MY HAT GIVE ME BACK MY HAT GIVE ME

"Can we use the train?"

"Depends how much change he can find for the ticket," I snapped, shoving her towards the further end of the platform. We dumped Mo on the concrete floor, and I turned to look back, searching for inspiration, protection, anything. I felt in my satchel, found a can of blue spray paint, started to draw the symbol of the Underground; then I thought better, switched to a can of red and drew the twin crosses, one inside the other, muttering, "*Domine dirige nos*, please, please, *domine* bloody *dirige nos . . .*"

The paint began to burn on the concrete in front of me.

"Sorcerer!" shrilled Oda.

"Not right now!"

"*Matthew!*"

I glanced back.

Mo was lying on the floor, and he was blinking.

"He's awake!"

GIVE ME BACK MY HAT GIVE ME BACK MY HAT GIVE ME BACK MY HAT GIVE ME BACK

"I'm glad for him!" I snapped. "Seriously!"

"*Matthew!!*"

I glanced back and Mo was pointing; he had raised one hand the colour of a spilt biro and was pointing at the indicator. "'Give me back...'" he whispered, and his voice was full of popping bubbles, little spurts of black ink ruptured from his lips as he spoke. "'Give me back...'"

"'Give me back my hat'," whispered Oda, and for a moment there was almost a kind woman there, leaning over a dying kid. "What does it mean?"

"'Give me back...'"

"What does it mean?" she hissed, shaking him gently by the shoulders. "What does it mean?!"

"I took it," he whispered. "I took her hat. I'm sorry, I'm sorry I'm sorry I'm sorry I'm so sorry Mum? I'm sorry I'm sorry Mum! Fuck shit please God fuck!"

"Whose hat? Whose hat did you take? His? Mr Pinner's? Did you take his hat, is that why this has happened? Whose hat did you take, Mo?!"

"Mum! I'm sorry I'm sorry I'll never again honest please you fucking help me fucking shit please help bitch help me sorry so sorry please...!"

I looked up sharply, there was something happening at the far end of the platform, a shadow in the corridor.

"Whose hat did you take?!" screamed Oda, shaking him now, not gentle at all. "Tell me!"

A light went out at the end of the platform, then another, and another, the long neon strips dying around us. And there was someone moving in the darkness, a man moving in it, the twin red crosses painted on the floor burning now with thick angry smoke, popping and spitting in rage. I dropped the spray can, backing away from the smell of it. One minute, said the indicator, just one little minute and then it'd all be OK, the train would come and we would go and Mo would live and Loren wouldn't cry and we'd live ohgodohgodoh-godohgod just let us live please just live a little longer just a little live and see and smell and

"Whose hat?!" shrieked Oda's voice as the darkness spread.

"Hers," whispered Mo. "*Hers*. The traffic warden's hat."

"Oda," I whispered, as the light went out from the twin red crosses and the last neon tube died. "Oda, get away..."

"Which traffic warden, what traffic warden..."

"Dollis Hill," he whispered, "the traffic warden's hat."

"Oda! Get away from him!"

She staggered back just as he started to scream. I grabbed her, turned her head away, turned my face away, heard him scream and scream, heard his skin tear and part, saw in the dying neon glow the blood tumble black across his flesh, spill black into the platform, roll black down into the trench for the trains to run in, spitting and sparking when it struck the tracks, and he just screamed and screamed and screamed until there was no breath left to scream with, no mouth left to scream with, no human left to scream, just a piece of dead, flayed meat lying on the platform and Oda was holding us, she was holding *us* as if we were going to be any use in the buried darkness of that place.

And that was it.

Polite silent death.

A drip, drip, drip of black, ink-stained blood rolling down off the platform's edge. The rapid breathing of Oda, her face pressed against my shoulder, my head turned into her hair. The only light came from the indicator board, orange letters scrawling across the thin rectangular screen.

1. High Barnet via Bank — 1 mins
2. Edgware via Bank — 7 mins
3. Edgware via CharingX — 13 mins
GIVE ME BACK MY HAT GIVE ME BACK MY HAT GIVE ME BACK MY HAT GIVE ME

A pair of footsteps, leather soles, walking down the platform, a smiling face half-lit up in reflected orange glow. Mr Pinner, not a mark on him, examining the burnt-out twin crosses I had painted onto the concrete.

"*Domine dirige nos,*" he said at last. "The blessing of the city."

I couldn't speak, we couldn't breathe.

He looked up slowly, considered first me, then Oda, then me again. Then he started to smile. "Oh," he breathed. "How unlikely! Not *just* a sorcerer and some Aldermen. The Midnight Mayor made a phone call before he died."

I held up my right hand, trembling with fear, and cold from the rain. The twin crosses ached across my skin. "*Domine dirige nos,*" I whispered. "Keep back."

"*You!*" breathed Mr Pinner. "Well...I have to admit I'm surprised! Considering that it was you who killed Bakker, *you* who brought down the Tower, *you* who destroyed the only institution that might have kept your city safe from my revenge...and Nair made you Midnight Mayor?"

"Believe me, it's as inexplicable to me as it is to you."

1. High Barnet via Bank
GIVE ME BACK MY HAT GIVE ME BACK MY HAT GIVE ME BACK MY HAT GIVE ME

It didn't say the train was due—these things were never clear. Did the lack of a "1 min" statement mean it was due right *now*, or in fifty-nine seconds? I doubted if we'd survive fifty-nine seconds of this conversation.

"So...this makes you what? Sorcerer and Midnight Mayor? A heady combination! How do you sleep at night, how do you not get lost in it, all the power you could have, heart beating in time to the rumbling of the engines waiting at the lights, breath gusting like the vents up from the kitchens, eyes moving with the twitching of the pigeons and the sweep of the cameras? So much *life*, so big and so mad and so wild and so bright—I'm impressed you're not drooling! Seriously. Man to man—well, as the phrase goes, respect. Still not enough to keep you alive."

The last ashes of my twin crosses, burnt onto the platform floor, shimmered out. I wrapped my arms around Oda, felt her tense against the touch, looked into her eyes and smiled, hoped she would see my apology for what we had to do.

"OK," we murmured. "OK. You've got us. A sorcerer can't stop you, the Midnight Mayor can't stop you."

A distant rumbling, a distant breath of cold air in the tunnel, a distant grumbling of wheels, a distant white light in the darkness...

Too distant.

"You missed something," I said. "About me."

"What was that?" he asked, sounding genuinely interested.

A cold push of air from the tunnel, a pair of white lights grinding down towards us, an asterisk running across the indicator board, wiping out all previous statements, clean slate, end of the line, goodnight, good luck, reload, reboot...

"Us."

And holding Oda by the waist, we pulled both her and us head-first onto the tracks.

There is an idea: the live rail.

We have always liked it.

Electricity, alive.

They say: don't step on the live rail.

We tumbled over tracks rumbling with the approach of black razored metal wheels, slipped into the mouse-infested, litter-filled dip in the middle, and I heard Oda gasp as her nose came within an inch from the live rail, raised on its insulating white supports just above the height of the tracks. She tensed, pushing back against my weight, and above us I heard Mr Pinner start to laugh, start to clap.

She looked at us, saw the blue of our eyes, whispered, "No."

We grinned, raised our hand burnt with the sign of the Midnight Mayor, and as the approaching train saw us in the blackness of the station and slammed on its brakes, too late, much too late, we pulled Oda closer to our chest, and wrapped our fingers around the raised bar of the live rail.

It takes a lot of electricity to move a train.

The shock of it blasted us up and sideways, pitched us into the air, fingers fused to the metal by a screaming, writhing tangle of white lightning snakes that bit and snapped with poisoned teeth, scorched the air black and sent furious screaming sparks spurting out of every join of the tracks. We let it burn through us, set our blood on fire, our skin on fire, our eyes on fire, let it blaze and scream and burn and dance and flash and flare and fury and

I screamed God just screamed and

we sucked it in through our burning hand

my skin on fire

caught it up beneath our feet, let it fill us, sucked in every drop from the live rail and then a little more, fed on the left-over neon clinging in the snuffed-out tubes, ate up the orange glow from the indicator board, sucked in the taste of black blood running down the rails, feasted on the screaming of the train's brakes, and more still

I could taste more as my tongue ignited with blue burning

going from here to there faster than the electricity in the wire

just a little mortal going to burn going to catch fire going to

here it is...

...blue blood burning...

...blue electric angels...

We spread our wings.

We dragged in the fire from the live rail, the rushing of the train, the pumping of the cold air in the tunnels, the light, the darkness, the blood, the heat in my stomach that I couldn't give, the strength in my blood that I didn't have left, the warmth in Oda's body clutched to our chest; we dragged in a million million million ghosts who had died to dig the tunnels, who had lived their lives on the train going from here to there and back again, touch in, touch out, ticket, escalator, platform, chair, a million, million, million dead and living things who every day prayed for their train to come for the seat to be free for the paper to be left for the strangers to be kind for the journey to be swift for the ticket to be cheap for the stairs to be empty for the tunnels to be cool for the announcers to be gentle. And with all this life poured into the tunnels beneath the streets, was it any surprise that here, of all places, *here*, we could grow a pair of blue electric wings?

Was it any surprise that here, where the business was movement, with our hand burnt to the live rail, we could fly?

The electricity blasted us into the tunnel ahead of the incoming train and we let it. We lifted our feet from the earth and let the fire burn across our flesh and outside our flesh and with a single beat of the burning blue electric wings, beautiful and immortal as the darkness in the tunnels, we flew into the waiting depth of the Underground.

When the first train was built, back in Victoria's time, the passengers who rode it were terrified that having got to about 40 m.p.h., they would die, the human frame unable to support such strains.

NASA probably had a similar worry the first time they blasted a man at 11 kilometres per second into outer space. But that worked out OK.

This wasn't escape velocity. The London Underground was not designed for rocket testing. On the other hand, the electricity that fuelled our flight, gave us blue electric wings whose brightness split the darkness into a sapphire blur as we passed by, was intended to power a train at reasonable speeds, and we were a lot lighter than a train.

Ergo, a lot faster.

The tunnel turned and bent, the darkness ahead parting to the blue fire spilling off every inch of our flesh, the live rail lit up as far as I could see with writhing white lightning. Behind us we shed dollops of blue sparks that hissed and crackled on the black floor of the tunnel;

turns and twists took care of themselves, we were anchored now to the live rail, feeding off every volt it had to spare to propel ourself along. A flash of light to our right might have been South Wimbledon station passing us by, but it was gone in the speed of a blink, the cries of the passengers ducking down from the spinning blaze of flame that was what we were

lost in an instant, snatched away by the scramble of the parting air to get out of our way or be lost to the flame. Another flicker of light ahead, seen and gone

Colliers Wood

and we were laughing now, spinning and turning in the air, beating electric wings and listening to the roar of the flame and so much more the beat of the tracks the rumble of a thousand parted trains the breath of the Underground air the special dry stench of the black dirt that stained your spit the swoosh of the door the endless echoed voices of a million million million announcements please mind the gap please mind the gap please mind the gap please mind the

Tooting Broadway

going to burn going to burn going to burn oh god please

we laughed and laughed and laughed, thrilled and danced in it, revelled in the burning flames and

too much of too much this is why sorcerers forget their names

I am

Blazing blue electric glory as

Tooting Bec

Listen to me!! Listen!!

We blazed blue fire light life fury freedom

Listen to me!! We are going to burn!!

Light up ahead blink and it'll be gone, we will be in the heart of the city before you can whisper our name blink and it'll be gone we'll be gone too fast to stop and catch and

Train up ahead.

And we'll be

Train up ahead!!

for ever free and fast and just like we were before this human flesh and

There's a fucking train!

A train up ahead, sitting squarely in the platform of Balham station, rear lights showing red, doors just closing, just starting to pull into the tunnel ahead, engine whining slowly as it tried to eat the electricity we were feasting on. And even though we were greater and mightier than ever any mortal machine, it was sucking down the power, eating up our speed as we competed for the live rail and besides, there wasn't enough room for it and us in the tunnel, one would have to go and we weren't going to stop never stop never give up the fire or the blaze or the

I pulled our hand free from the live rail.

The burning blue fires went out.

The great angel wings, blue electric angel wings that had carried us from the end of the line to here, spat and fizzed, began to melt and dissolve into a thousand wriggling blue sparks, that flashed and popped like exploding blue maggots on the line for a moment behind us, before dissolving into nothing. I twisted in the air as the last furious blast of electricity faded from across our skin, pulling Oda tighter into me and turning my body towards the platform as with a sad *snap* of electricity the lightning on the live rail went out and we tumbled, hissing and smoking with speed and fire, onto the platform of Balham station.

Oda came free from my arms as we fell, sliding across the concrete and tiles, people scattering to get out of our way. I felt dull pain, followed by the hot burning of blood starting to seep through my skin, almost a friend now, an agony I knew how to deal with; and I rolled across the platform, didn't try to fight it, just rolled until I bumped up against a wall covered in posters and bits of old chewing gum, and stopped.

Above me, an Indian-looking man pulling a heroic face so manly it

was surprising his jaw didn't pop straight from his skull, stared sombrely down at me from beneath a sign proclaiming "*THE MIGHTY
ALI SINGS BOLLYWOOD'S GREATEST HITS*". I looked to my
left. A collection of B- and C-list celebrities stared back at me in various character-filled poses, from a poster declaring, "**NOW IS THE
AGE OF HEROES!!!**" I groaned and rolled onto my side. I could
feel blood running down from my left shoulder, blood pooling in
the palm of my right hand. Our eyes drifted past the platform edge,
fell on the live rail. We whimpered, tried to crawl towards it, digging
our fingers into the dull, dry tiles. I tried to get up, we staggered and
fell back down, still moving towards the rail. I tried to turn my head
away, but we couldn't, could still taste the electricity on our tongue,
beautiful burning brightness.

"Please," we whimpered, "please please please."

I closed our eyes.

"Please, please, please," we whimpered.

I hid my head in my hands, brought my knees up to my chest, felt
the blood seeping through the twin crosses carved in my skin, staining my hair where my fingers had curled around my skull.

"So beautiful," we whispered.

So beautiful.

This is why sorcerers go mad.

I crawled onto my hands and knees, head turned away from the
live rail. We wanted to look please one last look one last breath
one last

I dragged myself up onto my feet, turned away, leant against the
nearest wall, gasping for breath, dirty, wonderful, spit-staining tunnel
air. We were going to scream, just like a child, like an injured animal
with no words to express the idea that it was going to die, we were
going to scream.

Then someone said, "Uh . . . mate?"

I opened my eyes, stared into a stranger's face. He was wearing the
slightly undignified bright blue and white uniform of an Underground

worker, holding a radio in one hand, a white signal paddle in another. He was about twenty years old. He looked terrified: his hands shook, his voice stumbled over the simplest sounds.

"Uh..." he began.

I started walking, pushed past him, keeping our eyes turned firmly away from the rails. Oda had fallen some few yards behind me, and was struggling to pick herself up. We helped her, dragging her up by an arm; she looked at us and said not a word, but turned and started to stagger towards the escalator up from the platform, and I followed.

"Hey, mate?" The platform manager's voice again, weak and uncertain.

I didn't look back, couldn't look back. We stumbled to the bottom of the escalator and started climbing it, leaning on the black rubber handrail that dragged a little faster than the stairs could rise.

At the top of the stairs stood the station manager, flanked by one of his assistants, radio in hand. He raised his hand as we approached, and said, "May I have a word?"

Oda waved her ticket at him. I waved mine.

We pushed past, tapped out through the barrier, and walked away before he could recover from his surprise.

A witty man once announced in that very special 1950s English accent that today can only be used in parody:

"Balham: Gateway to the South!"

Balham—last chance to turn back, last chance to escape and get back into the city. Last place where the Underground meets the overland, last chance at least to pretend you live in the centre of town.

Balham. A place where all good Woolworths go to die; suburbia that just wishes it was something more.

I was bleeding.

As we staggered out of Balham station I turned to Oda and said, "My stitches have torn."

She looked at me, and for a moment, I was scared again. Then she took me firmly by the wrist and dragged me like a child across the street to the nearest chemist. She bought a thick pile of bandaging and a first-aid kit, and hurried me into the nearest passport photo booth.

It wasn't a unit designed for two, but I wasn't about to complain. She said, "Coat!"

I pulled off my coat.

"T-shirt!"

I pulled off my shirt. "What a mess," she tutted, and started mopping.

After a few minutes, a security guard pulled back the curtain to enquire what we were doing. Oda told him to call the police, or an ambulance, or both, and to get stuffed. Paralysed by the wide range of choices available, he just hovered, and when the bandages had been applied and my Jesus T-shirt pulled back on, he hustled us out as quickly as possible and snuck away to call the police.

Oda propped me against the glass window of a supermarket and ran across the road to a charity shop. A minute later she came back with a black T-shirt in a paper bag. It said, "**GARAMOND IS THE WORLD'S GREATEST FONT**".

I said, "Please. No."

She said, "Shut up and put it on."

This time we used a coffee shop. She bought two strong coffees that turned out to be brown hot water in a cardboard cup; but I appreciated the gesture. It was something to wash the painkillers down. I changed in the toilets. By the time we emerged, cups in hand, the sirens were starting nearby. She said: "Can he follow us?"

"Who?"

"Mr Pinner."

"I don't know. Let's keep moving."

We took a mainline train to Clapham Junction, sitting in silence by the window. I couldn't face the Tube; just couldn't face it.

From Clapham, we took the mainline train to Waterloo.

She didn't look me in the eye, just stared out of the window in silence and dug at the dirt under her nails. It was black and red from dry blood. She still didn't look at me.

At Waterloo she said, "Do we need to find you a doctor?"

"Eventually," I said. "I want to see the river."

Down into the subways that ran beneath the roundabout before Waterloo Bridge; a loop past the Imax and then north. I could smell the river, taste its old magics on the air, they cooled down the burning in my skin, eased some of the weight from my legs. The rain had stopped, the pavement gleaming with clean washed darkness, the tide low, with soft, perfectly smooth sand peeping out from beneath the high walls of the embankment. I slid gratefully down on a bench in front of the National Theatre, beneath the leafless branches of the fairy-light-hung trees. The wooden bench was still damp from the rain, the city a faded grey behind a monotone haze. It was quiet and beautiful. Somewhere behind all the walls a million people were doing whatever it was people did after their lunch break in offices like these. And I didn't need to know about a single one of them, but could sit at the centre of the universe and listen to the river, flowing just for me, just mine.

Oda stood behind me.

Bang, I thought.

Bang, three to the chest, two to the head.

Bang; bang bang.

Public place—cameras, CCTV, always CCTV, eyes in the windows of the cafés of the theatre, buying tickets, reading books, walking by the river, tourists with little kiddies holding balloons.

I slipped my fingers beneath my "**GARAMOND IS THE WORLD'S GREATEST FONT**" T-shirt and felt the sticky seeping of blood through the bandage Oda had wrapped round my shoulder. The blood that came away on my fingertips was thin and red. I wiped it unconsciously on my trousers and breathed a little deeper the smell of the river.

Then, because Oda didn't seem to want to talk to me, I stood up, walked to the edge of the embankment and climbed over the railing. A stair, practically frictionless with thin green slime clinging to it, led down to the soft almost-entirely-sand of the river's edge. I climbed down, walked to where the Thames water slid over the bank, washed my hands in it, then walked back to the sand. Oda had come to the top of the stair. She looked... nothing. Folded arms and nothing in her face. Not speaking, not doing, just watching.

I prodded the sand with my toe, saw thin clear water ooze out from the surface, and very carefully with the end of my shoe wrote,

GIVE ME BACK MY HAT

"Is that smart?" asked Oda from the top of the stairs.

I looked up at her. "Oda?"

"Yes."

"I think I know what's going on."

"Do you." Not a question, not wanting an answer. But I had one to give, and the novelty kept me talking.

"Oda?"

"Yes?"

"I think I know how to kill Mr Pinner."

Now, and for the first time, Oda started to look interested.

Legwork.

I loathe the Aldermen, but it is nice having someone else's legs to do the working.

We went to Aldermanbury Square.

Earle said, "You're still...!"

"Not dead, no. I noticed."

Still behind that desk. Still in an immaculate suit, still unfluffed, still not rattled. Still drinking coffee. No wonder the man never seemed to sleep.

"Forgive me, I did not mean to sound so..."

"The good thing about my party trick, is that it is *always* surprising," I replied, slumping down into the chair in front of his big desk. "Your 'back-up' is dead."

His face darkened. "You found..."

"Dead. They're dead. And the kid... and Mo... dead."

Loren.

I hadn't thought but

what would we say?

"But you appear to be..."

"Still not dead, yes, I know. Funny, isn't it? I have a theory, Mr Earle. Actually, I have a whole fat bundle of plausible hypotheses which, taken together, may make one great whompha of a theory. Wanna hear it?"

He shrugged. "If it's relevant to our current dilemma."

"Mr Earle, does it worry you that, if I *am* the irreparable prat you seem to think I am, I'm still alive?"

"It is conceivable that you are a villain rather than a prat, Mr Swift."

"You want to hear this theory or not?"

"Will it offer possible solutions to the deaths that seem to be occurring in ever-increasing quantity?"

"Quite possibly. And I'm just half an hour of medical attention away from divulging it."

They had a small medical room in the offices of Harlun and Phelps.

Of course they did.

They also had a gym, two canteens, an ATM and a psychotherapist. Everything to make the running of orderly business more orderly.

They gave us painkillers.

We were beginning to understand why, in pre-anaesthetic days, the Bible had stipulated that suicide was a sin. Anything other than the prospect of eternal damnation, and the human race would probably have done away with itself at the first sign of the dentist.

Oda stood by the door, arms folded, eyebrows low over her brown eyes. Earle sat with his legs folded on the small chair of the medical room, looking displeased to be holding a meeting in a place without a PowerPoint projector. I sat on the paper-covered bed and ate. We hadn't realised how hungry we were, until someone had offered us food. Now we scraped gravy off the plate with our fingers, and licked our fingertips, and wished I was not too inhibited to just run our tongue round the edge of the dish.

I said, "'Give me back my hat'."

Earle said, "This had better be good, Swift."

"Didn't it strike you that it was a strange thing to appear with the arrival of the death of cities? The ravens are killed and there it is; the Wall is defaced and the writing says 'give me back my hat'. The London Stone is smashed and there it is, always, 'give me back my hat'. I mean, I know that mystics tend to be obscure; it's the only way they can stay in business in this litigious age. But surely this phrase, occurring endlessly across the city streets, is about as unlikely a harbinger of the end as Abba at Armageddon? It has to have a meaning, it has to have . . . something more than just random words to it, otherwise why would it appear? That's the first thing.

"Second! The death of cities. Why is he in London, here, now? Look at the patterns of his appearances . . . Hiroshima when the bomb fell, Rome when the Vandals came, Babylon when the walls fell, London when the fire burnt, Pompeii when the volcano blew, New Orleans when the levees broke. Are we to assume that he *created* all these events? If so, then why hasn't he just obliterated London already? The death of cities is not the creator of these disasters—he's *summoned* by them. Sure, his presence might exacerbate them, might make them worse; he might fan the flames or shine a light in the dark to guide the bombers to their targets. But always he's there because something is going to happen. He's *feeding* off the death of cities, he is not the cause.

"So what has brought him to London? Why now? What could be so catastrophic that he has come to our city and interests himself in the activities of a kid who likes to hang around in Willesden, and goes out of his way to kill the Midnight Mayor, to poison the ravens in the Tower? What summons him to our city, when there is no war and the Thames Barrier still rises and falls? I think we can safely assume that his presence bodes a disaster of a mystical nature—if we're talking a bomb in Westminster then I suspect Mr Pinner would be far too busy killing MI5 officers to bother with us. This is about magic, straight and thorough.

"In other words: something magical has summoned him to London.

"Are we happy with this so far?"

I looked at the faces in the room.

They looked unhappy, but no one wanted to say anything, so I ploughed right on.

"Mo said before he died, before Mr Pinner went out of his way to make sure that Mo died, having hurt him, punished him, inflicted on him...terrible things...Mo said, 'the traffic warden's hat'. He took a traffic warden's hat, and for this he has been punished. The death of cities—and I think we can be fairly sure that's what he is—doesn't bother with individuals. He's about bricks and stones and streets, about ideas bigger than you or me. So why bother with Mo? He was punishing him, very deliberately, very cruelly. He got Boom Boom to lift him, and him alone from the club floor, specified the kid must be alive. Alive, in order to hurt him, throw him out with the garbage, turn his blood to ink. Mo took a hat, a traffic warden's hat, and on the walls the writing now says, 'give me back my hat'.

"And Mr Pinner said—I made his life easier. By destroying Bakker. That...that by bringing Bakker down, I gave him a way into the city.

Now, the Tower was powerful, but I don't think even Mr Bakker was up to keeping out Mr Pinner if he wanted to come. But what Mr Bakker did do, did so brilliantly and without even a thought that he was doing it, was kill sorcerers.

"When Nair died, you assumed I killed him, because I am the last trained sorcerer left in the city. You dislike sorcerers, Mr Earle. You regard us as dangerous, unstable, running the constant risk of madness. You think that most of all about *us*. You are wrong; but just this once, that's not the question. When I killed Mr Bakker, I stopped the systematic murdering of sorcerers, but not before we had nearly all been wiped out. There is no one left to train new apprentices. And if anyone would go mad, an untrained sorcerer is a loony job waiting to happen.

"So here's how I think it goes.

"I think that 'give me back my hat' is a warning. Not from Mr Pinner, but from the city. The London Stone, the Midnight Mayor, the ravens; these are all part of the city's defences, and while even one of them is alive, the magical defences still stand. I think it's a warning, trying to tell us what's happened.

"I think when Mo stole the traffic warden's hat, he stole something from someone who has enough anger, enough vengeance, enough fury and enough power in them to summon the death of cities. Mr Pinner was summoned here by the traffic warden. I stole her hat, Mo said. That's why Mo was left to die in the scrapyard; it was a punishment, vengeance on a kid who was scornful and contemptuous enough of strangers to steal from them, just for a laugh. So, for revenge, a stranger poisoned him and left him to die as agonising a death as they could manage. 'Give me back my hat'; that's what it says on the walls. Think about the geography — Mo hangs around in Willesden, Mo is kept in Kilburn, Nair dies in Kilburn, the hat is stolen in Dollis Hill, in all these places just a few miles apart. Think about the writing on the wall, think about the timing of when Mr Pinner came, about what happened to the kid, about why Nair died, about the nature of all that has happened so far. There is no profession in the city more hated than traffic warden — not even the police get as much abuse or assault or common cruelty. Think about what that would do to an untrained sorcerer, who knows that the city is screaming to them, who can taste the life and the magic on the air, and finds in it nothing but hostility. Think about why you suspected me. A sorcerer could do it, a sorcerer is perhaps the only person in the city who could do it, who could summon something as powerful and vengeful as the death of cities. The traffic warden is the mystical disaster that is going to happen. She is going to destroy us, the death of cities is *her* vengeance on the contempt of a stranger.

"Of course, all of this is 99 per cent hypothesis.

"But unless you've got anything better to go on, I think we should find this traffic warden whose hat was stolen.

"Stop her, stop the death of cities.

"I think we should kill her, before it's too late."

Part 4: GIVE ME BACK MY HAT

In which a damnation is discussed, a hat is found, and the nature of strangers gets a thorough going-over on London Bridge.

Legwork.

Someone else's leg, someone else's work.

There's pros to being management.

I sprawled across an ornate curly sofa at the back of an office just below Mr Earle's and waited.

Occasionally people came in. The office doctor who came to check on my stitches, take my blood pressure; the office caterer who came in with cups of coffee and biscuits of such quality and expense that our taste buds, accustomed to custard creams and jammy dodgers, found them slightly unease-making. Once or twice Oda. She seemed to have something to say, and then not, and would just look at us, nod as if to say, "still here, good, don't try leaving" and walk out again.

Once—just once—Earle.

He came in with a big white box, put it down on the table in front of me.

"Open it," he said.

I did carefully, expecting snakes.

It was a big black coat.

I said, "Umm...?"

"It's for you."

"Uh..."

"An Alderman's coat. The symbol of our office."

"But I'm not an Alderman."

"No. But you are Midnight Mayor, and the relationship between our two offices has always been close. And your current coat is in sad need of replacement. There's a card in there for a tailor, to make you a suit. You don't own a suit, do you?"

I felt the comfort of my bleached and bleached again old coat, felt the little sticky enchantments stitched into the lining and did my best to smile. "No—but thanks," I said. "I appreciate the coat. If it's OK, I'll keep this one on a little longer, just because . . . you know . . . there's spells and stuff that'll take time to sew. I'm sure you understand."

He smiled a smile the width of a tapeworm's eye, and walked out, leaving the damn white box with its damn black coat sitting in front of me.

Legs worked.

Afternoon drifted towards evening.

Evening turned the lights on in the great glass faces of the offices, sketching out mad mathematical patterns of light and dark across the towers of the city.

Somewhere in an office on another floor, someone who didn't know why they had been given this task and didn't understand what it was meant to achieve got their slightly grubby hands on a police report from Dollis Hill.

Somewhere else, another person who didn't know why they were doing what they did but understood promotion lay in combining plenty of dutiful obedience with just enough initiative to be noticed found a piece of CCTV footage from a camera in north-west London.

A few minutes later, the same person would call someone in Brent Council, name a few names, offer a few figures and make a polite enquiry about traffic regulations in Kilburn.

Their promotion was looking up.

I stared at the ceiling.

It was one of those panelled things, white boards laid on a metal frame, with a strip light embedded in the middle. It looked like the sort of thing Bruce Willis would crawl through in a sweaty vest.

Rush hour.

Didn't need to look at the clock to feel it; just close my eyes and it was there on the edge of perception: a rising heat in my skin, a brushing prickly feeling in my stomach, an itching at the end of my toes. A city that big: even to begin to comprehend the scale of it was to risk madness; and here it was, rush hour, elbow pressed into elbow on the Underground, head bumping against head with each swaying of the train, thigh rubbing thigh, close as lovers on a cold night, bags bumping and newspapers being tossed aside, rubbish bouncing in the streets, buses crawling under the weight of bottoms sitting and legs shuffling towards the exit, *beepbeepbeep* for the doors to open, not enough room to breathe, windows misted up with bright steam, a thousand strangers' faces on the platforms, pushing towards that deadly yellow line; the live rail. Engines whining into life, cafés steaming, coffee and frothy milk, lights coming on in the streets, feet clacking on wet pavements, umbrellas turning inside out in the rushing wind funnelled down the streets. The live rail.

So easy to go mad, if you just let it. That's why there were sorcerers, and sorcerers' apprentices, and kindly old men who found you in your teenage years and took you to one side and said, "Now, Matthew, let me explain about the health and safety procedures you must follow in your use of magic." Because if you looked close enough and began to understand the size and the beauty of it, you'd forget that somewhere there was a you at all.

And when he should have been going home, somewhere in the offices of Harlun and Phelps a young employee with a bright career ahead of him, so long as he didn't ask too many questions, was reading a complaint filed by a traffic warden assaulted on her duties in Dollis Hill, some few weeks before, and slowly coming to realise that this was *exactly* what Mr Earle had asked for.

It even had a name and address on it.

Oda opened the door, stuck her head round, said, "They've found her."

I blinked my eyes open blearily and said, "Uh?"

"The traffic warden. The Aldermen have found her."

Not so hard, if you know how.

All praise be unto the Metropolitan Police and their effective data entry systems.

We met in a conference room—Earle, me, Oda, those Aldermen who hadn't already fallen at the mark. Even Sinclair, who sat some seats away from me and didn't meet my eye.

Afraid of us.

Judging by the number of Aldermen who were no longer meeting our eye, not even to glare, they were afraid too.

Still not dead.

Surprise!

Earle had a neat file on his desk. Someone had taken the time to print out multiple copies and staple the sheets together.

He said, "I shall be brief, as I cannot abide long meetings. Ms McGuiness is taking the minutes, and I would like to welcome Mr Sinclair, a...concerned citizen...whom I'm sure we all recall from previous dealings. Ms..." He hesitated.

"Oda will do fine," said Oda calmly.

"Ms Oda, representing the Order, and of course, Mr Swift, our new Midnight Mayor. The agenda is brief and to the purpose; you should all have copies."

We did, on a neat, "Harlun and Phelps"-headed piece of white paper.

The items were:

1. Outstanding Matters, and Apologies.
2. The Death of Cities.

I wondered which secretary had typed it up.

"Mr Kemsley is, as I am sure you are aware, currently undergoing medical treatment. His condition remains stable but critical. Flowers have been sent, and a card is being circulated round the office; I would appreciate it if you could all sign.

"The second matter arising is the issue we have come to label 'the death of cities'. I appreciate that this is a rather more grandiose and melodramatic term than we usually like to use at such meetings, but I fear it may fit the occasion perfectly. For those who require clarification on the matter, I refer you to the minutes of our last meeting. In the meantime, Mr Swift has come up with a rather unusual suggestion."

He turned to me. So did everyone else. I shrugged and said, "Yeah, right. I think the traffic warden did it. I think she summoned him, the death of cities. He's her tool for vengeance, destruction, retribution, whatever. She's going to be the thing that pops. Anything else?"

Mr Earle gave me the kind of smile I imagined he reserved for that special category of employee who came to his office at 1 p.m. on a Friday afternoon to announce there was nothing else to do so could they, like, go home, yeah? It was the kind of smile that guaranteed you a plywood coffin.

He said, eyes on me and voice for the rest of the room, "If I may refer you to the files on your table. Three weeks ago, a traffic warden on duty in Dollis Hill walked into her local police station to report that a gang of youths on bikes had stolen her hat and cycled off, in her words, 'laughing and calling me racist names'. The police report says she was extremely distressed, which may be understandable in light of the fact that this was her third visit to the police station in three months. Two weeks before she had been spat at in the street. A month before that, and the driver of a Corsa parked illegally on a double yellow line had beaten her so badly she had required stitches, and treatment for two days in the local hospital. It was the opinion of the writer of the police report that having her hat stolen by a boy who laughed at her as he cycled away was the last straw. An act of random, careless cruelty by a stranger to a stranger; the kind of thing that, to the right mind, in the right place, with the right... disposition... could push you to do unwise deeds.

"The day after her hat was stolen, she quit her job as a traffic warden.

"I should also add further that our credit-check service reported a bad rating on her financial situation. Her family were immigrants; she was granted leave to stay by grace of being born in the UK, but her parents quickly abandoned her and ran back off to wherever it was they came from, leaving the state to handle matters in their usual way.

"Gentlemen, may I be bold to say that this is the kind of extremely flawed and volatile individual who could well, if circumstances were right, be so reckless—perhaps without even knowing what she did—as to cause extreme harm to our city. If we were the Samaritans then I would suggest a nice cup of hot soup and a gentle talk with the counsellor; but this situation is far beyond that. The facts are in front of you to see. If this woman is indeed the reason why Mr Pinner has come to our city—as circumstance suggests she is—then I move immediately to vote on the course of action suggested by our Midnight Mayor. That this woman—this traffic warden whose hat was so unfortunately stolen—be considered a threat intolerable to the safety of the city, and be eliminated before the death that Mr Pinner is clearly seeking comes to London. If there is no objection, let us take this vote now."

There was no objection.

They took the vote.

Not a hand went against it.

Mr Earle said, "Mr Swift? You haven't voted for the motion."

"I didn't realise I was meant to."

"You are a member of this board."

"I am?"

"Yes. This was your idea, your deduction, your motion."

"Oh. I see."

"Well? How do you vote?"
"I...we...I mean, I..."
I lowered my head.
"What's her name?" I said.
"Is it relevant?"
"Just curiosity."
"Her name is Penny Ngwenya. How do you vote, Mr Swift?"
We studied our feet.
What would the Midnight Mayor do?
I raised my hand.

Penny Ngwenya.
   Spat at, assaulted, her hat stolen.
   Give me back my hat.
   Dollis Hill.
   Too much coincidence.
   Mo had stolen a traffic warden's hat in Dollis Hill and was punished for the crime.

GIVE ME BACK MY HAT

And Penny Ngwenya, refugee stuck in the system, no money, spat at, assaulted, robbed, had filed a report, on which no action had been taken.
   And Mr Pinner had come to the city.
   Penny Ngwenya.
   Poor little Penny Ngwenya; she probably didn't even know what she had done, or what had to be done in reply. I hoped she did. Then it would be easier. Then I could tell Loren.
   We drove.

Not that far, as it turned out.
   St Pancras International. Some wisecracker had announced in the 1830s that, what with the Houses of Parliament having burnt down,

there should be a competition to build the replacement. St Pancras was one of the entries. If British MPs wore sweeping cloaks and cackled at the moon, it would have been the perfect place for government. Red towers with spikes on; a clock that could never quite agree with its neighbour on the tower of King's Cross; a long, pale blue-grey arch that you could see from on top of Pentonville Hill, or from the tower blocks of Camden. Tiled steps, marbled pillars, red bricks hiding a decayed interior of exposed cables and pipes just locked out of the public's sight. It was not a delicate building. Nor was there anywhere to park. There are downsides to putting international terminals on main roads.

I said, "You sure . . . ?"

"She works here."

"Doing . . . ?"

"Cleaner."

I looked up at the bright clock on the tallest tower, at the heaving traffic stop-starting down the numberless traffic lights of theEuston Road, at the people waiting for taxis under the metal overhang of King's Cross. "Let me out here," I said. "You find a place to park."

"Where are you going?"

"If this Penny Ngwenya is the cause of all this, I'll know. Seriously. You find someone better qualified to look, and I'll give back the coat."

Oda came with me. No point in saying no. They let us out just past the British Library, pulling, illegally, into the bus lane so I could duck into the shelter of the great beige stone buildings that kept their backs turned to the traffic, their faces towards the quieter streets of Bloomsbury. The wind was nose-bite icy, ear-dropping cold. I pulled my coat up tighter around my neck and hurried towards the traffic lights, while the Aldermen in their big cars that deserved every penny of congestion charge they had to pay went in search of a place to park.

"We're not doing anything without the Aldermen," said Oda.

"Sure. Just looking."

"Sorcerer..." Warning in her voice.

"Just making sure. You wouldn't want an innocent to get blasted, would you?"

"You misunderstand my cause. Bigger pictures."

"Of course. Silly me."

The station was divided into three parts: Underground, international and overland. It seemed easier to find our way in through the low sculptured doorways to the Underground at pavement level, than through the high arches above street level leading to the mainline station. Glass and bright lights; beeping gates, whirring ticket machines, men and women in blue uniform: police. Of course—police. An international terminal, where else?

"You know," I murmured, "if this Ngwenya is the one responsible, St Pancras may not be the best place to..."

"There are ways."

"Really? You mean you can..."

"If I told you my methods," she said calmly, "then I might not be able to use them again."

We looked away.

The mainline station combined trains to Glasgow with services to Paris, Brussels, Lille and, for the truly masochistic, Disneyland. It was built to impress. The roof was higher than the average winter cloud on the city, the platform longer than the distance between most bus stops. Everywhere was the same pale, cold blue light, shining down on glass and steel, built one into the other like they were elements of the same nature, modern simplicity melted into Gothic grandeur. The effect should have been an uncomfortable clash of old and new, but both periods were united by the drive to achieve splendour and space, to make it clear to anyone who hadn't guessed as they stepped off the train, that this was London, capital city, and you'd better hold on to your wallets.

The sound was the constant rumbling of the Eurostar engines, which sat right next to the main foyer, separated only by a thin glass sheet, some unsympathetic coppers and international law. Tourists about to travel could buy champagne at £70 a throw from the leather-sofa champagne bar that sat by the nearest long platform. Shoppers with space left in their bags could nip downstairs to where passport control kept its booths and, from the shops huddled around the X-ray machines and metal detectors, purchase anything from a trashy novel to an exploding bubble bath. Cafés offered travellers from Paris croissants and thick dark coffee, to cushion them against the baked-beans-based culture shock they were about to receive; off-licences offered cut-price booze to bring your family, whose present you'd failed to buy on holiday; luggage shops offered businessmen the best leatherware, and everything shone with commerce.

And everything shone, because someone was there to clean it.

Oda and I stood above the escalator leading down to the main shopping hall, and watched. The station was buzzing with people, arriving, or heading for the last train to the Continent; bags and coppers and immigration control, shoppers and sellers elbowed each other for room.

Oda said, "Do we know what this woman looks like?"

"We'll know."

"Because of your Jedi nature?" she snapped.

"Because you can't just summon the death of cities and not have something peculiar going on. Doesn't your bigger picture involve using me for my essential and potent grasp of these things?"

"You haven't been very potent so far," she grumbled.

"We saved your life."

Silence.

"I didn't expect it to . . ." I stopped. "Sorry," I said finally.

"Sorry? You're saying this as though there's some meaning. As in, repentant, remorseful, regretful?"

"Don't know. Just seemed like the thing you wanted to hear."

"I should hit you."

"There's a queue. You still need me."

"Even less than you could possibly comprehend. We do have your theories."

I shrugged. "Just theories. And if I'm wrong, you still need the Midnight Mayor. Why do you think Nair lumbered me with this?" I asked, genuinely interested.

She shrugged. "What does it matter?"

"Plenty. He seemed like a sharp guy. Smart enough to find Raleigh Court; smart enough to have a good address book in his mobile phone. Earle thinks he did it in order to tame us. To *make* us get involved."

"There is a logic to it."

"It could have just been a good combination. A complete and utter accident. A stranger dials a random number on the phone, and you can guarantee that sooner or later, they'll call us. Your fingers must twitch at the thought. You hate the idea of sorcerers per se; you despise the blue electric angels, you fear the Midnight Mayor. Wrap them up in one bundle...I'm impressed you aren't even hitting."

"Utility."

"That's what they said about the nuclear bomb. It'll come in handy one day—sure, let's keep it around."

"Matthew," she said sharply, and then seemed to catch her own breath, draw it in, as if she could suck the word back down. "Sorcerer," she added, firmer, "unless you have something useful to say, shut up and work."

I shut up.

We worked.

It didn't take long. People go out of their way not to see the cleaners. There's a shame involved—we let the crap fall from our nerveless fingers, and someone else picks up after.

Look; and ye shall find.

When she shuffled into view, dragging the trolley with its twin bins and collection of brushes and mops hooked onto the side, we knew before I had time even to reason it through. We snapped at Oda, "Wait here a moment," and tripped briskly downstairs to the lower concourse, elbowed through a gaggle of schoolkids just off the train, ducked the swinging banjo of a musician dressed as Mickey Mouse headed for Disneyland and walked straight up to where she was carefully laying down a yellow sign proclaiming "Caution! Slippery Floor!" She had her back to me.

Sorcerers are good at killing people. It's not in the job description, it just...comes naturally.

We stopped in front of the sign. She looked up. We opened our mouth, and she said, "Can I help you?"

A hundred ways to kill.

Stop it right here, right now. That's the plan.

Burn out her heart, set her brain on fire, boil her blood, break her bones. A hundred ways to die, a thousand things we could do. Just human.

"Hey — can I help?"

There was a badge pinned to her blue overall. It said "P. Ngwenya — Hygiene Care Assistant".

I looked into a pair of perfect brown ovals set in a face that was itself almost a perfect oval, except for the wide protrusion of her slightly squashed nose. Her black hair was done in plaits wound so tightly to the curve of her skull that the fuzzy hair in between each row looked like thin grey paint rising to a carved ridge.

Looking at her, there was something I recognised.

I said, "Uh..."

The empty sounds you make to buy time.

She waited patiently, not smiling, not moving, just waiting to see what I'd do next, almost as if she knew what had to come.

"Um..." I stumbled.

I was aware of Oda coming down the stair behind me. I heard a voice say, "Do you ever clean round the University of London?" The voice was mine.

"Yes," she said, as if I was a child asking whether falling was always down. "Do I know you?"

"Um, no. I just..."

What would the Midnight Mayor do?

Save the city.

Save the stones, the streets, the roads, the stories, the treasures.

Dead is dead is dead.

(Ta-da! Still not dead.)

"Do you have the time?" I asked.

She looked at me sideways for a moment, trying to hide the scepticism in her face, then carefully raised a latex-gloved hand and pointed upwards. A clock the size of a park playground was projected onto the main wall overlooking the terminal. It said 9.23 p.m. I smiled at her, and said, "Thank you."

And then, because Oda was at the bottom of the escalator, I turned my back to her and walked away.

"Well?" demanded Oda.

"Well?"

"Is it her?"

"What?"

"Is she the sorceress? Did you see? Is it Penny Ngwenya?"

"She's Penny Ngwenya," I sighed.

"Then we have to find a way to get her away from these people — the cleaners must have a supply cupboard, a place behind the..."

"She's not a sorceress."

Still me talking?

Surprise.

"What?"

"I looked at her. We read her like a book. Just an ordinary mortal, just a cleaner, nothing more. She's not the cause of all this."

"But you said..."

"I had a good hypothesis and she happened to fit it. But it's not her. Either the theory is wrong or the Aldermen screwed up. Ngwenya isn't our woman."

I started climbing the stairs upwards. We wanted to breathe, proper, cold, rain-drenched London air, get a smell of bus and car, get something pure into our lungs, walk and think, get to the river, give me back my hat, just think.

"Where are you going?"

"For a walk."

"Where are you walking?"

"Don't know. Doesn't matter. Don't know."

"Sorcerer!"

I turned back so fast she nearly walked into me, tripped at the top of the stair. "You keep shouting that in public and I won't need to worry about the gun in the dark, the stranger, silence, knife, wire, drug, needle, bomb—the NHS will get there first with a fucking straitjacket!"

Turned again, wanted out, reload, reboot, try again without the psycho shit!

(You should see what's behind you!)

Oda scuttled after me. I felt the aching in every part of me. Strangers who'd just taken it on themselves to come and cause me pain for no damn good reason, just because I happened to be there, happened to be me, us, sorcerer, us, whatever, pick one.

Out in the cold, good wind, proper wind, a proper coat-flapper of a blast, straight up the nose and down into the lungs, a decent whallumph of a city storm, just what we needed. We ran across Euston Road in front of the angry traffic, picked a street heading away at random, started walking, past suspicious hotels with drooping neon signs, gloomy old B & Bs, Bloomsbury terraces, that could be fit for millionaires, inhabited by students behind plywood and broken glass. We let the shadows drag behind us, could taste them on the air again, just like the night we'd walked and the dead had come for a chat, clutching at our coat-tails, trying to pull us back.

The paving stones bounced loosely beneath our feet; second-hand bookshops, cafés selling suspicious sandwiches, schools of English and plumbers' supply shops, all poking uneasily round corners where bombs had fallen on the older houses; gated crescents of withered green and leafless trees, neon lights illuminating the black fall of drizzle so thin that if I hadn't seen it, I wouldn't have known it was falling.

"Sorcerer!"

Oda still behind us.

"Sorcerer!"

Walking and thinking, they went naturally together. Thinking without words. "Sorcerer, stop!"

She grabbed our arm. We grabbed hers, shook her where she stood, pushed her back into the street. "Get away from us!" we snarled. *"Get away!"*

She fell back, stumbling into the gutter and then to the middle of the narrow street, staring at us in... something that on an innocent face might have been surprise and horror, and on hers was nearer contempt.

"I won't kill her," I said.

Revelation in Oda's eyes. "She is —"

"No."

"She *is* a sorcere —"

"No."

"Why won't you kill her?"

"Damnation."

"What?"

"Damnation. Burn in hell, Oda. Damnation. You kill an innocent, you go to hell, isn't that how it is? Do you think that your God is up there keeping score—hey, sure, she gunned down an innocent in cold blood, stood and took away a human life; for that, technically, she should spend all eternity suffocating in a vat of elephant dung, sure, but hey! Look! She killed guilty people too! Gunned them down just like the innocents, bang, bang, two to the head, three to the chest, isn't that how it goes? A simple bit of mathematics, the bigger picture, let the evil live so that the good need not suffer extraordinarily—and look, she sacrificed her principles to let the blue electric angels live, because that way the innocent could be saved by the guilty, and the innocent mustn't die, mustn't be gunned down bang!

"Equations—let's say one innocent soul is worth a hundred guilty ones—have you killed a hundred and one guilty people? Will their deaths buy you the way into heaven, or do you suppose at the pearly gates blood is blood is blood regardless of whose heart it was squeezed from? Greater evil, lesser evil, let's do a risk-assessment analysis, weigh up the pros and cons, award percentage points based on who is more likely to slaughter the newborn babe, and who'll settle for a three-week-old with hearing problems? Burn in hell, Oda! Go burn with the rest of the damned! *I will not kill her!*"

She looked at us like . . . we don't know. We couldn't see.

"I'm going to end this," I said.

"How? If you won't . . ."

"She's not a sorceress."

"You just . . ."

"She's not. Tell the Aldermen. Scream it until the straitjacket comes. I'm going to end this."

"How?"

"I'm going to find the damn hat. Keep away from us."

"Sorcerer . . ."

"Burn, Oda. Let's vote and kill a stranger. Do the maths. Then burn. Get out of the city. Run. It's what we would do, if we had the chance."

This time, she didn't follow.

* * *

We walked.

Didn't matter where.

Thinking and walking.

Brunswick Square; restaurants, supermarket, cinema—this week's speciality: Romanian arthouse. Russell Square. Hotels and ATMs. The British Museum—great Doric columns, windows too big for a single floor to contain, posters. Those special shops that cater only for tourists: a hundred little waving Paddington Bears; shortbread at two quid a slice; tartan kilts, and "art" made almost entirely out of masking tape. New Oxford Street; Gower Street; Tottenham Court Road; Oxford Street. The shops still open, even the ones selling "I LOVE LONDON" T-shirts and big leather boots, the cafés buzzing, customers of the pubs in every by-street and up every alley spilt out into the street regardless of the cold and the drizzle. Women with piercings, wearing more metal rings than cotton clothes, men with shaven heads and white T-shirts that warp under the weight of over-eating trying to explode from their innards. A thousand bright lights as far as the eye could see: the hot, tight magics of Soho to the south, the easy illusions and enchantments of Great Portland Street to the north; I could taste them, dribble my fingers in them. The shadows dragged behind me, snagged and snared on my fingertips, slipped across the palm of my hand like water blown sideways in a gale. So much magic, so much life; and it was all going to burn.

Penny Ngwenya.

Give me back my hat.

I *am* the death of cities.

What would the Midnight Mayor do?

Our fault—no, not quite right. Our *responsibility*. Our problem. Reload, reboot, without the psycho-shit.

We were going to find the hat.

Her hat.

And it occurred to me as I passed Bond Street station, I had an idea where to look.

The Jubilee Line runs through Bond Street. It's sometimes a detail hard to remember; people think Bond Street and automatically start counting stations the long length of Oxford Street—Marble Arch, Oxford Circus, Tottenham Court Road, pleased that in this one case, the map of the Underground and the map of the city actually have some sort of geographical symmetry going for them.

Bond Street is therefore easy to take for granted—an in-between stop for people who don't quite know where they're going, unless they're shopping for something extremely rare and expensive. Jewellers make the streets around the station their own, but the station itself is still on Oxford Street, still just a doorway on the way to somewhere more conclusive.

We caught the train. Jubilee Line, again, swishing new doors, clean blue and red chequered seats, not too much yet scratched into the glass, just the usual statements of:

KEN WAS ERE

Or:

MEGA!!

Or (and of course):

GIVE ME BACK MY HAT

Headed north. Baker Street, St John's Wood, Swiss Cottage, Finchley Road—overtaken by the mainline train to Coventry, *whomph* and the Underground carriages gently swayed at the pressure of its passing—West Hampstead, Kilburn, Willesden Green, Dollis Hill.

Back to Dollis Hill again.

The indicator board read:

1. Stanmore — 5 mins
2. Damnation — 9 mins
3. ENDOFTHELINEENDOFTHELINEENDOFTHELINE
   ENDOFTHELINEENDOFTHEL

But by now, I'd got the message.

Out into a dark and sleepy street, the rain falling harder now, the chill retreating on the air, aware that the water was the main business tonight and it wasn't quite cold enough to make it into ice.

Into the deep dark wilds of windy Willesden, where no traveller dare venture without a copy of the London A–Z, a bus map, a travelcard and ideally, a compass and all-purpose urban survival kit, through streets that changed their nature every five minutes, as if the whole area had lost faith in itself and now needed to ask its neighbour if *this* style was all right after all, or whether they should have stuck with terraced grot.

Back to the wide high road, with big red buses irregularly lumbering down the middle of the carriageway. Back to the purple sign above the gleaming door — **VOLTAGE**; and now it was locked shut, no bouncer on the door, no kids going in. A council notice had been stuck up on the front of the door, informing any would-be visitors that this place had had its licence to serve alcohol withdrawn, and if anyone wanted further information they should consult their local borough offices. I hammered on the door, shouted various obscenities until someone paid me attention, a window sliding open upstairs, a head sticking out and a man's voice saying, "Oi, fuck off out of it!"

I stepped back into the rain, looking up at the face, and said, "I'm looking for the guy who ran this place — the Executive Officer. A prat with a cardiac condition who called himself Boom Boom! You know where he is?"

"Got his arse shifted out of here, didn't he?" came the reply. "Try doctor."

The window slammed shut.

I cursed quietly to myself, marched back up to the door of VOLT-AGE, pressed my fingers into the padlock and chain and whispered loving placations to it until with a well-mannered click the thing came open and free in my hands. I pulled the doors open, saw nothing but darkness inside, snatched a bubble of neon from the streetlamp above, which hissed and dimmed in complaint, and lobbed it down the stairwell ahead of me.

Few things are as unsettling as a place which should have been roaring with noise, turned quiet. No windows, no lights, no sounds, except the tread of our footsteps. We pushed heat from our fingers into our floating bubble of neon, forced it to expand and blaze to drive away the clinging darkness that slipped in like loose silk from every corner. An empty bar, an empty floor, sticky with old spilt beer. Empty stools and silent speakers, unlocked doors, and switches that when flicked didn't bother to turn anything on. I could taste the thick, lingering afterburn of that place's magic, felt the shadows, silent and sad, faces that should have been dancing now fallen into nothing more than a sullen, bored and resentful sleep.

Downstairs. No lights, no sound, just us.

I found an office, which I had ignored last time, following the *deDum* of the beat. Now the door was open. I went in. Papers on a desk, a computer, an executive toy made out of ball bearings and wire. We picked it up by one bearing, let it drop, watched the whole thing swing. It was hypnotic. How could anyone work, with such distraction? The walls were covered by posters of various DJs, and bands with names like "Thunderchazz!", "DJ Grindhop", "The Bassline Slutz" and other excitingly ungrammatical things. I sat down in a chair too big for me, too small for the Executive Officer, twirled a few times, watching my shadow shrink and grow on the walls around me as I moved and my bubble of stolen neon stayed stationary overhead, humming faintly with trapped electric glow. I went through a couple of desks. Strange bits of wire, electronics, jacks and plugs designed to operate on systems that were never, ever as easy as it claimed in the manual. Old batteries rolling around on the bottom of a drawer, dead biros, scrap paper, a half-used box of tissues, an unopened box of "Her Pleasure" condoms, a pack of Blu-Tack, a broken keyboard, the front panel ripped off and the number keys mostly gone. Not what I needed. I kept on looking.

The solution was inside a black organiser bound with a thing that wasn't quite leather, but dreamed of one day making the leap. I flicked through it, tried "D" for doctor, "G" for "GP" and eventually found what I was after under "Q" for "quack". The entry in the address book said:

Howard Umbars,
158 Fryer Walk,
London W11 58P
(Emergencies call: 0208 719 9272)

I took the contact book, just in case I was wrong. The shadows dragged behind me, empty nothingness turning to watch as we walked out. In a few years, there would be ghosts in that basement, if nothing was done soon, and they'd dance to an invisible beat for the rest of time. It didn't take much to make these things real.

To double-check my guess, I walked through the rainy streets of Willesden until I found a bus shelter. I climbed up on a ticket machine until I could lean over the top, stretched across the gap and pulled down from the stagnant pool of dirty water on the roof a sodden and sticky copy of the Yellow Pages. Quite how the Yellow Pages found its way on top of most bus shelters in London was a mystery beyond our knowing, and we put the whole thing down to higher powers and tried not to think about it. I sat in the bus shelter, shook the worst of the water out of the soggy book, and peeled my way through the glued-together pages.

What the Yellow Pages was doing on top of the bus shelters was one mystery we didn't explore; why the Yellow Pages that we found up there happened to contain a directory for "wizards" was a mystery we actively walked the other way from. I was in there, somewhere. Matthew Swift (sorcerer), just waiting for some clumsy oaf to grab a copy of the book from on top of the shelter and read our name.

We tried "H" for healers, "M" for mystics and, with growing frustration, went back to "Q" for "quacks".

Howard Umbars was there, in the Yellow Pages on top of the bus stop.

Higher powers had a sense of humour after all.

I tossed the book back into the puddle on top of the shelter, and went to see him.

Acton.

Acton is a borough that prides itself on not being Acton. Wherever you live in Acton, it is your noble and firm intention to make it clear that you don't really live in Acton. You live in Ealing, or maybe, if you're low on luck, in Ealing Borders. Or you live in Park Royal, or maybe you're Almost Chiswick, or borderline Harlesden — wherever you are, however deep you may be inside the boundaries of the borough, if you live in Acton, then you don't.

Howard Umbars lived in Acton. He wouldn't admit it, but anyone who is five minutes' walk from North Acton station lives in Acton.

Low, semi-detached houses. Fake timbering in their perfect triangular sloped roofs, set in white, gravelly stuff too smug to admit to being painted concrete. Driveways containing a mixture of slightly foxed and extremely battered cars, pubs with big gardens and expensive beer, local twenty-four-hour stores selling suspicious cakes, French cigarettes and chocolate fingers.

158 Fryer Walk could have been anywhere, and was most certainly Acton.

There was a six-pointed star on the roof above the front door. Once upon a time, this was where the Polish emigrants had come to stay, back in the days when Acton was considered practically countryside. The door itself was painted blue. There were chain curtains drawn across the windows and no doorbell, no lights on upstairs, a dim yellow glow from downstairs. I knocked on the door.

No one answered.

I knocked harder and waited.

After a while, the door was drawn back on its chain. A voice from inside said, "Yes?"

"I'm looking for Mr Howard Umbars. Actually — that's a total lie. I'm looking for the turd with the heart condition who uses Mr Umbars as his mystical quack. He here?"

There was a moment's pause. Then the voice said, "Please wait a moment."

I waited.

The door stayed on the chain. There was movement in the gloom behind it. A watery blue eye appeared in the crack, looked me up and down. An indignant male voice said, "Who are you?"

"Me? I'm Matthew Swift, the last sorcerer left in this damn town, the blue electric angels made flesh, the Midnight fucking Mayor. Are you going to make me stand in the rain until I blast your bloody door down or what?"

There was a moment's silence from behind the door. Then it closed, the chain was pulled off from the inside, and it was opened up. A dark corridor, possessed of coat rack (empty), mirror (clean) and coffee table (bare). I stepped inside carefully, looking for the owner of the watery blue eye. He stood at the top of a steep, narrow flight of steps, hands folded around a detachable TV aerial, which he held like a shield. He was bald — not just with a shaven head, but every inch of his visible anatomy shining with taut, stretched pale skin, as if the distance between bone and air was so narrow that hair simply didn't have the chance to grow. He wore a white shirt and dark trousers; his little face, too small for the neck it sat on, wore an expression of serious mistrust.

"Who are you?" he demanded again. "What do you want here?"

"Strangely, I've been entirely honest with you. Are you going to try and use that"—I nodded at the TV aerial in his hand—"to hurt *us*?"

"If you're what you say you are, it wouldn't make much difference."

"Well, *quite*."

"If I believe you're what you say you are."

I shrugged. "Think of it as being like a nuclear bomb. You don't want to give the terrorist his million quid not to detonate on basic principle, but on the other hand, are you *really* going to take the chance that that little red button is fake?"

"What do you want here?"

I looked up the dark stairwell, then past Mr Umbars to the gloomy corridor into what I guessed was a kitchen. I said, "Look. You're a quack, right, in a business where quacks seriously do try to make gold from lead or whatever. I don't really care. You know a guy I'm looking for. He calls himself Boom Boom—the Executive Officer of a club called Voltage. I'm thinking you did some work for him, on a cardiac problem. I'm thinking he's had a relapse lately owing to some... *unforgivable* fool... grabbing his beating heart in an angry and electrified fist and squeezing it until it nearly popped. Where is he?"

"Why do you want him?"

"I'm going to save the fucking city," I replied with a chuckle.

"Are you for real?"

"You'll never know until you press that button. We aren't in the mood for pleasant games. Where is he?"

There was a basement.

There's always a basement in these circumstances. You got into it via a small triangular door cut into the side of the staircase going upstairs, down a flight of grey concrete steps, beneath a bright white bulb swinging from the ceiling. I said, "For a quack, you're not big on disabled access, are you?"

He looked at me with the expression of a man thinking about red buttons.

"Humour," I said cheerfully. "It's my only redeeming quality."

The basement had been turned into a . . .

Surgery did it too much credit. That implied bright lights, scrubbed floors, needles, plastic chairs and steel beds, people in overalls and machines that went "ping". This wasn't a surgery. It was a nightmare out of the mind of a surgery patient scheduled to have their heart bypassed in the morning, who knew, just knew, that they'd be one of the ones for whom the drugs didn't take. The longest wall was covered with all the alchemical ingredients an urban magician might ever require — feather of albino pigeon, leg of rat drowned in a burst of raw sewage, fat from the bottom of the basin in the chip shop, buddleia from the derelict mansion on the corner of the high street, burnt tyre carved carefully off the base of a burnt-out bus, tail of squirrel that found the winter too warm to sleep through, dribble of oil from the bicycle that skidded into the cement truck, black tar scraped up from the street that had started to melt in the summer's sun, ground ballast from the furthest platforms of Paddington station, kebab feasted on by King Fox, vodka bottle still bearing the red lipstick-kiss of Lady Neon, found left behind the bar at a club in Soho. No longer did young apprentices to the great alchemist seek silver buried at the bottom of enchanted mines. The time was of tar and plastics, of synthetic compounds and decaying reactive products in a jar.

In the middle of the room was a table the size of a double bed, made from titanium steel. On it, and that barely, was the great blubbering rolling twisted body of the Executive Officer. Over *him* were several layers of Plexiglas casing, with air in between each level, which between them managed to reduce the great rumble of the man's heart to nothing more than a faint *deDum*. Pipes and tubes had been threaded in between these layers to provide blood (mixed with a few parts petrol) for his veins, air (mixed with a tad of exhaust) for his lungs, and, sure, why bother to ask?, electricity for his heart. I could see the wires running into his chest, taste their sharp fizzle on the air. Boom Boom, the Executive Officer, was running on little more than enchantment and luck.

But he was awake.

We walked towards the great table with its layers of casing, and tapped on the glass. He half-opened his eyes, saw us, and turned the colour of old bedlinen left out to dry in the rain.

We smiled and waved. "Remember us?"

A fat pair of fingers scrambled across the table inside the transparent casing that contained him, found a switch and pressed it. His voice wheezed from a speaker overhead; "Fucking get him away from me!"

He remembered us.

We felt almost proud.

"Hey!" I replied. "If we were going to kill you, we wouldn't have hesitated for a moment. I need a bit more information—I was wondering if you might just be the guy to help."

"Umbars! Get him away from me!"

I glanced at the door. Mr Howard Umbars stood with his hands folded neatly in front of him, a zen-serene expression of blank nothing on his face, eyes looking at some point a few years behind the back of my head.

"Oi, fatso! Me here to save city; you possibly vessel for valuable information, so stuff it!"

It occurred to as, as we said this, that there had been a voice before Mr Umbars had come to the door, someone else in the house. I heard the click. Nasty little clicking sound. It reminded me of Oda. We said, "Of all the things in this mortal world that frighten us, guns are right down at the bottom of the list."

I half-turned to look at the source of the sound. Guns dropped another rank in the list of frightening things, displaced by . . .

. . . technically . . . a man. He wore a neat white shirt and black jeans, a pair of leather loafers and a loose fleecy jacket. He held a gun in one hand, and from the neck down looked in every way to be a boring member of the human race. Where the problem arose was from the neck up. The windpipe at the front of his throat had been carved out with a very sharp knife, the muscle removed and a bright blue plastic tube inserted as a replacement, emerging from just below the soft base of his jaw and disappearing into flesh again behind his sternum. Skin had been carefully grafted to the edges, some further into the middle, and a futile attempt made at some point to paint the thing pink, but neither attempt could disguise the truth of this disfigurement. One half of his jaw had been broken and plied away, replaced with a small metal frame through which I could see the teeth and hollow inside of his mouth. Into this frame had been slotted what looked like an old-fashioned cassette player, the top controls embedded in his gums. I could see the spools turning, hear the faint clacker of machinery from within his lips, and realised that, through some means we had no desire to comprehend, this was his tool for speech.

Yet if all this shocked us to our core, when we turned our eyes to his we had a worse horror to see, for his left eye had been entirely removed, along with the best part of that side of his face and all his left ear, and the long snout of a CCTV camera, glass window and all, had been stitched and fused and moulded into his skull. Its long metal nose stuck out three or four inches past the length of his nose, and I could hear it whirr faintly as it adjusted focus on me, and see my own faint reflection in the square glass. The wires seemed to have been plugged direct into his brain, and his nose pushed to one side to make space for it, so that the creature I saw was as much machine as mortal, and neither to completion. His other eye was bright green, and looked steadily at me, just like the gun he held.

I breathed, and found that was about all I could do, hypnotised by the sight of such extremity.

"Addison is my assistant," said Mr Umbars, moving down from the doorway. "You should be afraid of the gun, Mr Swift—not of him."

"Sure, bullets don't kill people, *people* kill people," I muttered. "Long live the National Rifle Association. What exactly..."

"Addison suffers from a rare condition. It's not infectious. His brain is randomly shutting down parts of his body. First it was his voice, then his left eye, then his left ear, then his lungs. The NHS can't help him. So I did. He is my assistant."

As he said this, Mr Umbars reached carefully past me and took hold of my right hand, with the same firm, unsympathetic grip that all doctors seem to possess. He peeled back the glove from my hand and held it up to the light. I watched the CCTV camera of Addison's eye, and it watched me.

"Fascinating," murmured Mr Umbars, running his fingers over the crosses carved into my hand. "The mark of the Midnight Mayor."

He let my hand fall and then without a word reached up to my head, dug his fingers in under my chin and pulled my head towards his, tilting it back and then down, staring at my eyes. "Bright blue," he murmured. "Not your natural colour, is it, Mr Swift?"

"I am so not in the mood for this," I snapped. "I've told you everything you need to know and like I said, guns are right down the list of things that frighten me."

"You know," sighed Mr Umbars, "if I didn't believe you, I would drain every drop of blood you have and make a fortune flogging it, I mean a *fortune*. It's not every day you get to drain the blood of the blue electric angels, after all."

"Tougher guys than you have tried and died," I replied. "And thankfully you *do* believe me, which will make all this a lot easier. I need to talk to the guy on the table."

For a moment, Mr Umbars hesitated. I could see him thinking about blood, and fire, and telephones, and electric gods and expensive golf courses. Then he smiled, and gestured at that. "It's all right," he said. "Put it away."

The gun was slowly lowered. Mr Umbars gestured at the plastic casing. "He's all yours. Try not to kill him again. Think of me, if the NHS should ever let you down."

"I'll think of you," I said coldly. "But I don't think I'll ever see you again, will I, Mr Umbars?"

He smiled. "Possibly not, Mr Swift, quite possibly not. Addison!"

His voice was a command; Addison obeyed, shuffling dutifully up the stairs with Mr Umbars, leaving me in the basement alone with Boom Boom, the Executive Officer of club Voltage.

I could hear his heartbeat, still faint through the casing: *deDumdeDumdeDum.*

"You should try and relax," I said, leaning my elbows on top of his transparent cover. "You'll do yourself a mischief."

"What do you want?" came the voice over the intercom.

"You just calm yourself down. If we were here to kill you, we would also have killed everyone else." I could see the great mass of his heart rising and twitching quickly below the protruding spikes of his ribcage, torn upwards from his flesh. "You're a mess, mate."

"What do you want?! I told you about the boy."

"Yeah, thanks for that. Found the kid, saw the kid flayed alive while I stood powerlessly by — you know, I see why Mr Pinner has you so freaked, why you played flunky for him. Now we're going to talk about the traffic warden's hat."

"I don't know what you mean."

"The hat. The traffic warden's hat that Mo — the kid — stole. He took her hat and she's a sorceress, although she probably doesn't know it; but she is. I took one look at her and knew it, and now I've gone and fibbed to the Aldermen; so let's assume I'm running on a bit of a clock here. Mo stole a traffic warden's hat, and she, God knows how, has summoned the death of cities. I don't think she meant to, not really; I'm still hazy on the details, but there it goes. And so it is. Where's the traffic warden's hat?"

"I don't know anything about a hat!"

"You wouldn't be lying to me, would you? Only it seems to me that you're a guy inside what could well be an airtight jar dependent on a whole host of fluids being fed in from the outside and that really the Gestapo couldn't have done better if they'd tried..."

"I don't know anything!" he wailed.

"Would you lie to *us*?"

"I swear, I swear, I *swear*..."

"Righto," I sighed. "Well, I'll admit it's a bit of a disappointment. City going to burn because of an untrained sorceress's rage and all that. Skin torn from flesh and so on, death by ten thousand paper cuts. You know. Good news is, state you're in, you'll probably be dead first. So is there *anything* you can tell me that might just stop London from being obliterated in a blast of untamed magical fury?"

"The...the woman," he stammered.

"Which woman? The traffic warden?"

"The contact. There was a woman, I dealt with a woman to arrange it. To get the boy. I dealt with a woman, working on his behalf. Someone else helping Mr Pinner."

I folded my arms on the top of the casing, pressed my nose against it, smiled. "Which woman?" I asked, softer than warm honey on a summer's day.

"I was told to contact a woman, by Mr Pinner, if anything happened, this woman..."

"A contact? An associate of Mr Pinner? She did notice that he's the living death of cities, the harbinger of destruction, the feast in the fire and so on and so forth?"

"I was just told to contact her."

"Did you?"

"No. There wasn't any need, he said. Emergencies only. He said I'd be spared, if I helped him, that I'd be spared and could live and rebuild and survive and have a new heart and..."

"He said everything you wanted to hear and you just thought the silver lining was a cliché," I sighed. "Great. Tell me how I can contact this woman."

"There's a number."

"Which number?"

"In my organiser."

"Seen it, stole it, got it. What name?"

"Smith — Ms Smith."

"How inspired. You're really not very good at this, are you? Just a fat guy with a cardiac problem. If you weren't such a pustulent testicle with it, I'd almost feel sorry for electrocuting you. But whaddaya know!" I was rummaging through his organiser, flicking through and there it was, under "S" for Smith, written in the same neat hand, just a name and a telephone number. "You know if this doesn't work, or if we die in the attempt, you'll die, right?"

"I'm telling you everything..."

"Not our meaning," we sighed. "But keep up the moral revival!"

And once again, we walked away.

The number was for a mobile. That was good; that could help us.

We went to North Acton station, sat down on the nearest platform bench, thumbed on our mobile phone, and started to compose a text. It's easier to lie briefly than to invent lies at great length.

We wrote:

IT'S BOOM BOOM, SERIOUS PROBLEM NEED HELP DANGER MEET?

Predictive texting might lend itself to good spelling, but it can't fill in the punctuation. I entered the mobile number for "Ms Smith" and sent the text.

The reply came back in less than five minutes.

WHAT PROBLEM, WHAT DANGER, HE WILL BE ANGRY.

I replied:

MIDNIGHT MAYOR ALDERMEN HELP ME MEET?

This time, the response took nearly ten minutes. I watched the trains go by, counting down towards midnight and the last train.

Then it came:

HACKNEY MARSHES; NAVY CADETS BUILDING, TWO HOURS.

This, we could do.

I caught the first train heading east.

We could taste the beginning of the end.

I just felt tired.

Disrupted sleep patterns?

Too much of too much.

Ta-da!

Still not dead.

Still *alive*.

Watch us burn.

Central Line, heading east. North Acton, East Acton, White City, the beginning of the descent into tunnels, Shepherd's Bush, Holland Park. The stretch that ran beneath Oxford Street and I could still feel it overhead, its vibrancy, brightness, tacky, gaudy glee making me feel more tired by comparison, a great fire raging just overhead and me down in the cold, empty carriages of the tunnels. Holborn, Chancery Lane, our hand ached, how it *ached* as we passed beneath the Square Mile, the Golden Mile, the City, the Corporation, call it what you wanted, the oldest part of the city, where the shadows were most thick, where the dragons with the mad eyes guarded long-forgotten gates. *Domine dirige nos*, Lord lead us, city protect us, a higher power, a miracle beyond comprehension.

St Paul's, Bank—a vortex in space and time that made the weird corridors of the Barbican seem straight as a Roman road—Liverpool

Street, Bethnal Green. We climbed off the train, the last train—well, maybe not quite the very last—up onto a crossroad junction, mainline track to one side, museum and park grounds to the other, traffic still waiting by the lights, passengers still milling around for the buses. A strange place, Bethnal Green. It sat at a junction of more than just geographical borders. Druids call it ley lines, paths of power, but the Glastonbury "away days with the faeries" had undermined some of the pride of those who believed in such things. Didn't mean such things weren't possible. At Bethnal Green, things met and melded into each other. Hackney borough met Tower Hamlets, and on each side of border streets hung banners proclaiming that *this* borough was the best in London, don't believe the lies of your neighbours! The rich towers of the city were but a few minutes away to the west, the low slabs of Mile End but a few minutes to the east; and in the middle, old Bethnal Green, just far enough from squalor to be respectable, far enough from wealth to be poor, winding enough to be old, open enough to be new, where all the buses met and divided, to take their passengers to a place more certain than the crossroads where all these things converged.

Sure, there are ley lines. Transport for London could probably draw a map.

It was an easy hop from Bethnal Green towards Hackney Marshes, made only less so by the cordon of signs warning "Olympic Site Development—Road Closed". I got off the bus at the edge of the marshes, and the shadows were thick, crawling up from the pavements, gnawing at our feet, aching in our fingers. The old was dying, they whispered, glaring at the Olympic signs, all going to be knocked down, washed away. East End, end of the east, place where things ended, rejects and slums, squalid history of neglect, all being washed away behind gleaming steel and glass. Wipe away the history; wipe away the shame; forget that the shadows were once alive.

Midnight Mayor, protector of the city.

Remember those memories?

"Busy now," I snapped at the darkness. "Next time."

Hackney Marshes—get them while you can. A few more years, and they might have been mown away to make place for a running track, a tennis field, a sports ground, a swimming pool, something, where the world can come and celebrate this strangeness that mortals seem to find so fascinating—Olympic games. We do not understand why mortals, trapped in a fleshy shell, must make their own flesh suffer.

The place had once been a swamp or marsh, and still looked it. The Lee Valley might have been tamed, the river diverted to a more useful course than through valuable real estate on its way down to the Thames, but the drooping, green-brown grass and thick, razor-stemmed reeds still told you, if the spongy ground didn't, that this was a place with a history humanity had not fully managed to tame. It was not by any means a public park—since that implied benches, bins, children's play areas, flower gardens, ordered hedges and tactfully planted trees. Hackney Marshes had none of these things, and was all the purer for it. It was a place for the dog walkers to ramble, for the kids to slouch, for the fishermen to wait hours on end to catch a trailing shopping bag; an open patch of sullen, sagging land just like it might once have been a thousand years ago, full of unreliable dips and delves, strange smells and unlikely strangers. We liked it, although as a meeting place, it had one serious disadvantage. It was a long way from the roads, the power lines, the gas mains, the water pipes; these things that were the most natural and useful tools of an urban sorcerer's trade. There was magic here, time and shadow and proud defiance of the "here we are, here we remain" category—but it was fainter, unfamiliar, harder to tangle our fingers in and command to our use. It was, in short, exactly the kind of place where you might stand a better than usual chance of killing a sorcerer.

We should have taken the gun from Mr Umbars's house.

As it was, I took a few precautions. I rummaged in my satchel for my penknife and, feeling halfway between extremely clever and utterly inane, stuck it in my right sock and pulled down my trouser over the bulge. I put a torch in my coat pocket, not wanting to risk a possibly futile effort in summoning a light so far from a reliable source of neon. I pulled my gloves off and stuck them in the bottom of my bag. We didn't know anything about fighting with fists, but if worst came to worst, ignorance was not going to stop us.

And then, because she had guns, and I didn't, I texted Oda.

HACKNEY MARSHES, NAVY CADETS. DANGER. SHARPEN YOUR KNIVES. SWIFT.

She didn't text back, so I went in search of Ms Smith.

The Navy Corps building was a corrugated-iron shed whose great-great-grandfather might once have held the *Titanic*. It was now little more than an iron curve over a bit of concrete floor, but it was still an interior, among the dank grasses of the marsh, and above the battered wooden door a battered old wooden sign declared:

R YAL NA Y CADET
O EN 14-21 YRS OL
BE T E BEST

I knocked at the door with the knuckles of my scarred hand.

The wind went through the reeds, the thin waters of the tamed river dribbled and stirred in their uncanny paths. A druid might have found it beautiful, magical, might have breathed deep of that cold, slightly muddy air and from it summoned the lightning. I could see how such things were possible. Life is magic. It just wasn't the kind I liked.

No one answered, so I kicked the door until it opened, half falling in when it swung back suddenly on its rusted old hinges. The inside of the iron building consisted of four rooms, each one as low, grey and unimaginative as its partner. One might have once been a kitchen, with great rusted pots in which litres of baked beans had been boiled at a go. One had been a dining room, the tables kicked aside; one a bathroom, the sink long since broken, the taps too depressed even to drip ominously in the dark. Broken bulb glass was on the floor, the mirror cracked from a single smashed point. The last room had, once upon a time, been a place for people to feel proud. Pictures still hung on random hooks across the wall, showing beaming boys (and some less so) and stretching back generations to the days when stripy knee-length socks and rounded caps were considered the height of fashion. Here they proudly waved from on top of a canoe; there they sat in sombre rows, their captain holding a battered football, their coach with whistle clasped firmly in hand. Wooden panels had been nailed into the walls on which were emblazoned the names of extra-special boys who had done such and such a deed while serving in the Navy Cadets, the little silver shields now tarnished faint green, the little flags, proclaiming victory at this game of rugby or honourable inspection by such and such a rear vice admiral, now drooping limp, threadbare. There would be rats living in a building like this, hiding away innocuous in the dark. Rats we could work with.

There was no one else in the building.

We were early.

A brown sofa in one corner had had its cushions stolen, revealing the thin veil of fabric beneath. We sat down in it, stretched out our legs, folded our fingers behind our head, feeling the thick scab of the cut down the back of our skull from that night—however many nights it had been—when the telephone had rung and it had all begun—and waited. We were usually very bad at waiting. Tonight it was the most thrilling boredom we could ever have conceived.

There was no risk of sleeping, regardless of how tired we felt.

Weight, not fatigue, was the symptom of our restlessness; a great shallow pressing down on our heart and chest.

Not sleeping, we heard them coming a quarter of a mile off, feet rustling through the reeds while the wind whispered its sad resentments over the marsh.

More than one set of footsteps; we half-turned our head to the window and saw torchlight, heard the faint snatch of voices lost in the twisting of the grass. The bouncing uneven strays of white light from the bulbs sent crazy shadows across the wall, that twisted and writhed and proclaimed *runrunrunrunrunrunRUNRUNRUN!*

I slunk back deeper into my gutted sofa and waited, tangling my fingers in my hair to keep them still, rubbing at old scabs and scars, keeping alert through the faint pressure-pain. A footstep outside dislodged something; I heard the scuttling of little ratty feet over concrete. Then the door opened. Two men with pistols and torches slunk in, doing the SWAT-team stuff. The way they moved seemed familiar, something straight off the TV, all signals and armour and guns. They saw me straight away; one gave a cry of "Hey-oi!" and the other turned to look.

I said, "Surprise!"

Two more men, slightly more heavily armed than their colleagues, also entered the room. The four of them took up positions in a semi-circle around my sofa. I sat up, pressing my feet down on the concrete floor, listening for the scuttle of ratty claws.

"Ta-da," I added weakly.

They just stared at me. None of them looked like they had a sense of humour.

"Ms Smith?" I asked nicely.

Another person at the door, another figure entered the room. This one was a woman. She wore a big black coat. She said, "Mr Swift."

You can get big black coats almost anywhere.

And hell, it wasn't like I was hard to crack.

But I knew her voice too.

I reached into my pocket for my torch, and at once the guns, which had been doing little more than pointing, came closer, making their point a little more pointed. I put my hands carefully by my side, smiled my nicest smile and said, "Just looking for my torch. Dark in here." And then, because the terror was starting to set in, we blurted, "Hello, Ms Smith. You couldn't have found a more inspiring name, could you?"

The shadow from the door became a darkness behind the four points of torchlight, moved between them, said, "He's coming, Swift. Coming to end it all. No phones, no redial, no ringing in the night. End of the line. He's coming, and then it will be done."

"I'm guessing by 'he' we're talking about Mr Pinner?"

She didn't answer.

I stood up, as slow as I dared, and the lights and the guns kept on following. "You know, I never trust people who don't have anything to say."

No answer.

"And you knew that it was *me* asking for the meeting...because you have my number already on your phone?" I added carefully, trying out the idea for size.

No answer.

"Silence is contempt."

And, because even people who don't have anything to say have nerves to touch, she stepped into the torchlight, and the big black coat was stained with dirt and smog, but her face was still clean, and still familiar, and she was still, when not the unimaginative Ms Smith, comrade of the death of cities, a woman I had called Anissina.

She said, "You can't begin to understand."

"Try me."

She said, "If you move, we'll shoot you."

"I guessed."

"I don't want to shoot you."

"Bless."

"If you die, the Midnight Mayor will still come back. Mr Pinner says he has ways. We are waiting for him."

"Mr Pinner...death of cities Mr Pinner? Mr 'I feast on the flame, stand beneath the bomb, drink the flood waters, rage with the burning and lick my lips on mortal terror' Mr Pinner? This is the ducky we're talking about? Don't get me wrong, but I think I'd rather get shot."

I took a step forward, and all the guns moved, and all the breaths were drawn. "Don't!" she snapped. "There's a reason I chose this place to meet. I know that you are weaker away from the streets and the lights and the electricity! Don't make this be worse."

"Nice to think you care."

"I don't."

"Ah. So much for that consolation. I know it's cliché, Anissina, but I gotta ask you: what exactly are you, an Alderman, and one who should theoretically be dead with the rest of her men, doing here, pointing guns at me?"

She thought about it, and then, because we had nothing to do but wait, she told me.

*   *   *

Third Interlude: Damnation, Contempt and Traffic Wardens
In which all is explained at the point of a gun.

"The city is going to burn," she said. "It has been damned, cursed, blighted. The death of cities has been summoned, the ravens killed, the Wall defaced, the Stone broken, the Midnight Mayor weakened. You cannot be weak in the city. He should defend the stones, the streets, the history, the ghosts. Two thousand years of ghosts are sitting on the banks of the Thames, on whose bodies the houses were raised and the stones settled, a history too big, a life too immense for any one mind to comprehend. That is why the dragons are mad, Swift, the ones who guard the gates of London. When you look into their eyes you see nothing but endless insanity. They comprehend how big the city is, how great and how deep and how beautiful and how dark, and it sends them mad.

"But you...Midnight Mayor...for you to be here, you must be seeking the traffic warden's hat. You must know about her. You must know that Penny Ngwenya *is* a sorceress, though she does not understand it. To know this and to not have killed her is unforgivable. For a one in eight million, for 0.0000000125 of a city, you will let London burn. Damnation waits for you, Midnight Mayor. It is the ultimate failure of your office.

"I am sure you have learnt much — much too much — of what you need to about Penny Ngwenya. I have no interest in what motivates you in your mistakes. At the end of the day, regardless of the brand on your hand, of your bright blue eyes, you are also 0.0000000125 of a city, and even fewer will notice your passing this time than they did the last.

"The death of cities is coming for you, Matthew Swift.

"A child stole her hat, a kid on a bike stole Penny Ngwenya's hat, and a stranger beat her for doing her job, and a stranger spat in her face, and strangers abused her, and strangers called her names. Little frightened sorceress, who saw life and beauty and magic in the city, who stood by the river's edge and felt the beating of its heart as if it were her own, who stared down on the lights of the city and saw the starlight of the world spread beneath her feet for her to tread lighter than the breeze. Do you remember how it was, sorcerer, when you first began to breathe the magic of the city, to taste its burning brightness, to dream in neon and rejoice to smell the streets in your sleeves? She could have been so bright, little Penny Ngwenya, but not any more. Strangers beat, robbed and spat at her, faces she will never see again, and who will never see her, too many million between her and them. They did it not for who she was, or why she was, or what she was — but because she was there and they did not have to care for her, a stranger. A cruelty without consequence, a deed without responsibility.

"The night that this boy, Mo, stole Ngwenya's hat, she walked to the river. You and she have that in common; you seek the river to calm you; you breathe deep of its magics and become lost in time and movement, for that is what the river is. She went to the river, as you would, and stood upon the bridge at the height of rush hour. She turned her head towards the sky and her arms towards the water. Tourists, commuters, workers, travellers, call them what you will—the bridge was full, London Bridge, the heart of the city, the oldest bridge, the last barrier to the city, the final part of the city wall, she stood there as the city moved around her and—for whatever reason it was, for whatever cruelty—she turned her hands towards the water and her head towards the sky and called out to these passing strangers, 'Give me back my hat.'

"And no one listened.

"Not a single man or woman turned their head.

"Crazy woman alone on a bridge.

"Crazy shouting woman alone.

"Leave her alone.

"Give me back my hat—sorcerer. This was her curse. Give me back my hat!

"And no one listened.

"Except Mr Pinner.

"Sorcerers love to burn.

"It is why the blue electric angels love the sorcerers—you are moulded of the same light and fury, the same madnesses.

"You see magic where there is life.

"So it was with Penny Ngwenya.

"She stood on the bridge and saw the magic of the city, a harsh, cruel, unloving thing, stood alone and cried as a hundred strangers ignored her, and came to realise that this city, this place she had thought so beautiful, was a diamond she could never possess. A gleaming ornament on someone else's glittering coat. A thing bought with money, carved out with blood, cold, beautiful, unyielding, cruel.

And not knowing what she did, she wove on London Bridge a spell, as cold and cruel as the city that despised her. Damnation upon the cruelty of strangers, she breathed, curses on the unkind unfamiliarity. Let all who are strange be afraid, let all who are alone be left alone to their furies. 'Give me back my hat,' she screamed. 'Damnation upon this city!'

"Hundreds of people must have heard.

"But as we avoid seeing the cleaners, the dustbin men, the drivers, the road painters and the sewage workers, no one heard.

"Only Mr Pinner.

"Her anger was as beautiful to him as the diamond to an avaricious eye. It summoned him, brought him up out of the streets, built him from the papers drifting in the wind, stitched the suit to his flesh and the fury to his soul, bound him to one purpose, and one purpose alone—damnation on this city! He is the tool of her vengeance, the vehicle for this city's demise. Her magic created him, fuels him, he cannot die while her fury still lives. You cannot kill him, Matthew Swift. I am sorry that two Midnight Mayors had to die to learn this truth.

"Mr Pinner—the death of cities—is Ngwenya's revenge made flesh. He has destroyed the protectors of the city, wiped them out, enacted vengeance on all who would hurt her. The man who spat drowned in his own spittle; the man who beat was flayed alive and his skin stitched to the ceiling of his bedroom while his eyes could still look to see. The boy who stole her hat, infected with lingering death and thrown aside like the ruined rubbish he was, condemned and tossed with the contempt he showed a stranger. But her damnation is much bigger than just her personal enemies. She said, a curse on the unkindness of strangers, and the city is nothing more than a commune of strangers, eight million of them, each of whom will never know more than a few hundred faces, a tiny sliver of a per cent of all that there is to know, who will never walk more than a few hundred streets, a fraction of the hive. She has damned the city. Her will be done. Mr Pinner is here to see to that.

"It will be soon.

"She will return to London Bridge.

"She will raise her face to the sky and her arms to the river.

"The city will burn, Mr Swift.

"Mr Pinner has seen that nothing will stop her vengeance. It is simply a matter of time; of bringing down the defences. It is strange that you should be one of these. Another sorcerer. Too late. End of the line.

"For me . . .

"I have little to say.

"I am a true Alderman.

"I look at the city and it is a miracle. That for two thousand years these streets can have stood and grown; that for two thousand years a ragged union of strangers pressed in tighter than blood to a boil can have lived together, fed together, worked together; that now eight million strangers can reside in one place, pressed in like lovers—that it works! That the water flows, the electricity burns, the gas rumbles, the streets hum, the wheels turn, that this works is a miracle! Wonder! Glory! Ours is a world full of strangers, that is what gives it such life. That in this place, at this time, we live; through the actions of strangers, faces we shall never know, miracles we shall never comprehend, history we can never understand. Madness in depth; we can only scratch a tiny percentage of the life, the power that is the city. To understand any more than our little part in it is to slip into spiralling madness. I think you've seen it, sorcerer. I think you know what I mean.

"And now it is taken for granted.

"*Obscenity.*

"Damnation.

"How *dare* anyone, anyone who lives in this city, how *dare* they ignore the miracle? How dare they shrug and say, 'whatever'; how *dare* they forget the size, the beauty, the wonder, the scale, the life, the vibrancy, the glory, the miracle! How *dare* a stranger spit in another's face, how dare a stranger strike a woman down, knowing it is cruelty without consequence, how dare you throw your litter into the street and wait for the cleaner to pick it up, how dare you park your car and shrug at the rules, how dare you scream at the policeman, how dare you curse the bus driver, how dare you steal a traffic warden's hat, how dare you show such *contempt?* Contempt! Take it for granted, damnation, contempt! Strength in the city, strength in survival, strength in being strong, in being hard, in caring for yourself and none other, a jungle in the city, preserve thyself and let the others burn, how dare you walk down the street and not notice its wonders, how dare you look just at your shoes, how dare you turn your face away, how dare you leave the man to die, how dare you, *how dare you?!*

"I am a true Alderman.

"Magic is in the strange.

"The cruelty of strangers.

"The kindness of strangers.

"The things that strangers have done, built, made, maintained.

"Beauty in the city.

"I am a true Alderman.

"This city is going to burn."

* * *

She finished speaking.

We considered.

"Well," I said finally, "you've clearly thought hard about this."

She said nothing.

"To tell the truth, I'd figured a good part by myself."

Still nothing.

"You couldn't have gone to a shrink instead?"

"Weakness," she replied. "Kemsley was right—you aren't fit to be Midnight Mayor."

"Yeah," I sighed. "I'd kinda sussed that too. But, see, if there's one thing we're going to agree on about the nature of the city, it's this: time has come for a bit of change. How long before Mr Pinner gets here, do you think?"

She shrugged. "He doesn't move like mortal creatures."

"Sure. Why not? Hey—if you shoot me, right, do I get any say in who becomes Midnight Mayor? Like—could I make *you* Midnight Mayor with my dying breath? That'd be a turn-up for the books, wouldn't it?"

"You wouldn't know how."

"I've been inaugurated."

She shrugged, but there was a hint of unease behind it. "So?"

"I saw the dragon."

"And?"

"I know quite how big the madness is, Anissina. Ms Smith. Whatever. Would you like to meet it? Would you like to look into its eyes until *your* brain dribbles out of *your* nose?"

Nothing.

"Scared?"

Nothing.

"Fire and fury," we sighed. "People say these things as if they were meant to make us feel ashamed. As if a bomb going off were not, secretly, obscenely, immorally, indefinably, beautiful. We are not permitted by the customs of this world to say such things. It is regarded as unhealthy. But it is so. Has been so ever since the first caveman became lost, staring into the firelight. Where is the traffic warden's hat? Did you destroy it? It would be the smart thing to do."

Nothing.

"I don't think you destroyed it. It's like the Midnight Mayor, yes? A symbol of everything you don't like about the city. The cruelty of strangers, a kid on a bike steals a stranger's hat. Not to speculate too deep about your sexual predilections, but I'm just betting you couldn't destroy it. Where's Ngwenya's hat, Anissina? Where did Mo hide her hat?"

"End of the line," she said.

"Been there, done that. Where's the hat?"

"It's nothing personal, sorcerer."

"I know, you said, you did maths at me you stupid, *stupid* woman! Where's Ngwenya's hat?!"

"You can't do anything here, not here, not..."

"We are the blue electric angels! We were born from the left-over breaths of humanity, by the fears and the thoughts and the ideas and the truths and the lies you poured into the telephone lines. We were created by *you*, bigger and brighter and more alive than any mortal could aspire to be! Do not think to tell us what we can or cannot do! *Where is her hat?!*"

The men with the guns wanted to shoot, we could feel them aching for it, see them watch the burning of our eyes, just a twitch away from firing.

"Do it," we snarled, "and you will have the brand on your hand, Midnight Mayor. Let the city watch, the shadows drag, dream the dreams of the sleeping stones, Midnight fucking Mayor! Protect the city, protect the streets, protect the stones—and nowhere did anyone bother to mention that this tiny little ant scuttling within the heap is a best buddy of this tiny little ant who knows this ant who knows this ant who knows that ant who lives on the other side of town whose family all know these ants who just happen to know another ant who knows our initial scuttler and it's not strangers, we are *not* strangers, Anissina! It wasn't a stranger who stole the traffic warden's hat; that would be fine, that would be nothing! It was a *Londoner*. It was one of the family, united because of the streets and the stones and the stories! That's why the city is going to burn, it was a *betrayal!* We will kill you before we die, Anissina. Burn and be damned—*GIVE ME BACK MY HAT!*"

We screamed it, the curse on the city, and as we screamed, we raised our right hand, felt the twin crosses blazing blue-blooded brightness, saw the men with the guns flinch away, and felt something more, felt a stiffness in our skin, glanced at our flesh and saw . . . a darkness settled over it that hadn't been there before, a clawing, growing darkness spreading out from the palm of our right hand but now wasn't the time, one by one, and there was something wrong with our eyes, something hot and prickling and

Here they were!

Come on, my little beauties, you know this song . . .

Up came the rats. They tumbled out of every hole in the wall, hair raised on their backs, teeth bared; they spilt from the pipes and the cracked vents in the ceiling, crawled over each other to come through the doors; and they were angry because we were, because their home had been invaded when they hadn't asked, no invite, no reboot. They spilt around our feet and crawled up the legs of the men with guns, who screamed and,

of course, as frightened men do,

fired.

Something went *boom*. I couldn't name where, the blast spread so fast through my skin, tore up the back of my throat and liquidised my knees, a great big rolling cloud of mushroom-shaped fire spreading through my nerves. I went down and backwards because that seemed to be the direction the pain was headed in, and I wasn't going to argue with the pain. The rats parted beneath me, ran across my arms, my face, my chest, scuttling still in their hundreds out of the walls, bearing down on each of the men, who didn't have lips left to scream, just fell, black bundles melting under black bodies, the torches going out, the lights going out, everything going out inside the room. I could hear shouting, screaming, gunfire as they shot at the rats, and I could feel the blasts, little fat bodies bursting on the earth as the bullets went in, little yellow eyes dying, little claws twitching, little whiskers flicking through the air, little teeth nibbling and biting into soft, warm, human flesh, sinking in like they were eating raw pink chicken. And there was blood on my hands burning bright blue wriggling bright blue blood our blood and I'd been shot bugger that *shot* after all the things that could have happened some *bastard* had

the rats were going

running into the night

too frightened to stay

couldn't stop them, my friends, come back and sing this song,

what *bastard* shoots strangers anyway?

A man was lying on the floor a few feet from me. He was still alive, wailing, just wailing like a hurt child, too low and pitiful to be a scream, too quiet to be a roar, just...crawling and wailing. Half his ear was hanging off. The rest was too bloody for me to see. We were grateful for that. His comrades lay behind him. One of them was going, "*huhn...huhn...huhn...*"

The blood in his breath caught the sound in his throat, made it crackle.

The others weren't moving at all.

I tried to raise my head.

A shadow was standing against the furthest wall.

I could see a pair of red eyes blinking in the darkness. They were perfect marble spheres in the black oval of the creature's head, deep and mad and endless. They moved towards me. A torch had fallen from the hand of one of the men; the light cut across the feet of the creature as it moved. Human legs, wearing a long black coat, but still attached to those mad red eyes. The creature knelt by me. Its skin was a silverish metal colour, its veins dark black beneath the surface. Its hair was fused black wire that trailed behind its head, its ears had stretched to spiked points, its fingers were black curved claws coming out of strangely jointed arms, and when it breathed, black smoke rolled from its nostrils and lips. If dragons were silver and human, then this was a dragon. Its eyes were the insane brightness of the creatures that guarded the city gates.

I whispered, "Anissina," and was pleased to feel the breath move, not lungs then, still had my lungs, for the moment.

The half-creature curled back its silvered lips to reveal sharpened teeth. The shadows moved behind her, the metal walls of the shed creaked. One shadow seemed to have my name on it. Time for that in a moment...

"Anissina," I breathed again. "True Alderman." Then I added, because I was feeling depressed, "You should see what's behind you."

She didn't get it. She closed her metal fingers around our throat.

And the shadow behind her said, "Now... that doesn't look like first aid to me."

Anissina turned, hissing, claws reaching up to tear at the shadow that had spoken, and I closed my eyes. Even then, the gun was near enough and the flash so bright that I could see it explode, star-pattern, on the back of my retinas, feel it jolt through my brain. I heard an animal scream, a piteous, wailing mewl, and opened my eyes again in time to be dazzled by another bang, another flash, and Anissina fell, rolled to one side screaming, the metal shimmer vanishing from her skin, her claws retreating back into nails, hair regrowing from the metal strands on her head, and she was screaming! There was blood flowing from the half-blasted remnants of her left leg, and worse, blood now in her belly, her hands clasped over the middle of her gut and she lay on the floor screaming until the shadow that had pulled the trigger knelt down next to her and very firmly put a hand over her mouth.

The torchlight fell on that hand, the colour of rich chocolate melted in a dark pan.

I wheezed, "Help me."

Oda said, "Of all the people to ask that of me, I would have thought you'd know better."

Oda's voice, Oda's hand, Oda's gun, Oda's general sense of humour.

"Shot," I breathed. "Shot."

"Yeah. I noticed. Entry and exit, Swift, left side of your upper abdomen, just below the ribs. Stop complaining. As bad news goes, it's one of the best of the bads. Care to tell me why this should-be-dead Alderman was throttling you, or was it just your nature again?"

"She's working with Mr Pinner," I groaned, trying to sit up and thinking better of it. "Jesus, he's coming here—we have to go!"

"An Alderman? *This* Alderman? With the death of cities? Why?"

"Screwed-up reasoning."

"She know anything?"

"The hat," I hissed. "The traffic warden's hat."

Oda's eyes widened in the torchlight. She carefully pried her hand back from Anissina's mouth, who started gasping and wheezing, on the edge of a scream but without the strength to make it, clawing at the blood flowing from out of her belly. Then she leant over to me, gun still in her hand, and carefully ran her fingers down my throat.

"*Liar,*" she whispered. "The sorceress...Ngwenya..."

"We can find her hat."

"We can kill her, end it, *should* have killed her, ended it!"

Her fingers rested on my windpipe, applying just the gentlest little pressure, just enough to let me know. "Innocent," I whispered. "She didn't know...she didn't know! Spat at, beaten, stolen, hurt! *Innocent!* Damnation, strangers, damned, hell, burn! For God's sake help me!"

"For *His* sake?"

"Help me," I whimpered. "Please. Anissina knows where her hat is. Give me back my hat! I can break the spell! Please! You still need us!"

"I can kill the sorceress."

"He's coming, Mr Pinner is coming, end of the line, damnation, give me back my hat, he's coming please..."

"You couldn't even be Midnight Mayor, could you?" breathed Oda.

"Please," I whispered. "I saved your life. I could have let you die. Please. Help me. I saved your life! Oda!"

She grunted in reply, lifted her fingers from my throat, turned to

Anissina, twitching on the floor. She leant over her, lowered her face in so close it was not an inch off Anissina's, breathed gentle, steady hot breath into her clammy face, and, as softly as a mother rubbing a child's tummy, pushed the barrel of the gun into Anissina's belly.

The woman screamed.

I turned my head away, tried to bury my cheek in the floor.

"Where is the hat?" asked Oda.

Screamed so loud the floor hummed with it.

We closed our eyes, counted, maths, if I am one eight millionth of a city what does this make me in percentage terms? Do the maths, divide and...

"Where is Ngwenya's hat?"

"He'll...he'll...he'll..."

"Mr Pinner will flay you alive, yes," breathed Oda softly. "Of course he will. But the thing is this. You've been shot in the stomach. Right now, the contents of your bowels are spilling into your bloodstream. Faeces, gastric juices, stomach acids, digestive enzymes. They're going to get into your veins, and start eating. The acid is going to burn you from the inside out, the enzymes are going to gobble away at your body until there's nothing left for them to chew on, *digest* you from the inside out, the faeces spilt from your stomach are going to turn your blood to sewage. If you're fortunate, septic shock will take you out before the worst of it. If not, then having the skin peeled from your bones will seem the balmy mercy of the Almighty compared to the death you will endure. And that's just the start. Damnation awaits you, Alderman. I cannot say what manner of suffering it will be. That is a secret that will be shared only by you and the Devil, and *he* does not care for reason. Where is the hat? Anissina? Where is the traffic warden's hat?"

"H-H-Harlun and Phelps," she whispered. "Boom Boom took it, didn't r-r-realise its power, what it m-meant. I hid it in Harlun and Phelps. I th-th-thought they would n-never..."

Oda stroked Anissina's chin with the end of the gun. "God loves you," she whispered. "Remember that, when the Devil comes. God is suffering as you suffer, crying out when you cry out. He loves you. He weeps for you. He sees that there is only one way for you to learn."

So saying, she leant down, and carefully planted a kiss on Anissina's forehead. She stood up briskly, looked down at me and said, "Are you still not dead?"

"Still *alive*," we replied. "Ta-da!"

"Do you want to end this?" she asked.

"Depends on what you mean."

And for a moment, Oda, psycho-bitch, almost smiled.

"Lucky man," she said, and bending down, helped to lift us up. "He must love you too, in His own special way."

She pulled me to my feet.

I felt things moving beneath my skin that shouldn't have been moving, and we bit so hard on the scream that we caught our tongue between our teeth and for a moment, the pain was almost a welcome relief.

Anissina whimpered, "Swift? Help me?"

We looked down at her.

"Remember Vera?" we asked.

She didn't answer.

Oda helped us limp away.

Hackney Marshes.

Running. There was blood running between my fingers, blood running down from my side, too fast, too hot. I hissed, "Shot..."

"I know. Come on."

Grass and bumps and sticky wet mud and little flowing streams that sunk up to our ankles and reeds that pulled at our legs and I couldn't see magic here, now, not tonight, but there it was, the bright neon glow of the city, so close, just a little more and there it would be, electric fire!

"Nearly...there..." we breathed.

"I know. Come on!"

She'd stolen a car, a Volkswagen Passat, the most boring car manufactured by man, parked it on the edge of the marshes. She opened the back door, threw me in, stepped into the driver's seat, turned on the ignition, handbrake down, clutch up, boy-racer to the full. I groaned and rolled onto my back in the passenger seats, fumbled for a torch in my pocket, found it, shone it down onto my own abdomen. Something small and angry had torn a jagged smile in the upper-left side of my flesh, just below the floating ribs, and blood was now merrily dribbling out from the grin. I cursed and swore and threw in a bit of blasphemy just in case, groped in my satchel, found the first-aid kit, unravelled pads and bandages and pressed them in, but no sooner was one white pad applied than it had turned scarlet with blood and had to be tossed aside.

"Oda," I croaked.

"I know," she snapped. "You're losing plenty of blood, which probably means it grazed your spleen. You'll get anxious, your heart rate will pick up, your breathing will accelerate. Then you'll lose more blood and get calmer, but that won't be a good thing. Your blood pressure will plummet, your head will spin, your peripheral nervous system will essentially shut down. Then you'll just collapse. You've got a few hours. Like I said: could be worse. Lucky man."

"Anissina..."

"We're going to Harlun and Phelps. If we don't find the hat, I'll kill her. Ngwenya. I'll kill her, Swift. And if you try and stop me, I'll kill you. I'll tell the Aldermen everything. I know...why...you protected Penny Ngwenya. It was...human weakness. The Midnight Mayor cannot be so...soft. If you cannot break the spell, I will gun her down. Do we have an understanding?"

"Yes."

"Good. Lie still, apply pressure, and consider whether you need a deity in your life."

"I thought it was too late to repent."

"Never too late to repent. Just too late to avoid your fate."

"Thank you."

"Any time."

"I mean, thank you."

"I know what you meant."

The lights of the sleeping city.

What time was it?

"Oda?"

"Yes?"

"For any hurt I did you. For any hurt you think I have done. For all that there needs to be something said, that I . . . that we did not know to say. I am sorry."

"It sounds like a death speech."

"I mean it."

"I know. Too late, sorcerer—it's too late. But thank you for trying, Matthew Swift. It means nothing to me, but I imagine for you, it is important."

Sleeping roads, sleeping streets. Even Bethnal Green was turning out the lights, the buses slinking away up Mare Street towards the mysteries of Dalston, Clapton, Stamford Hill and the north. I watched the lights go by the back window, pressed my fingers into the blood seeping from my skin. Anxiety, high breathing, high heart rate. What did a spleen do anyway? Little mortal little fleshly death by a dribble at a time.

Railway lines overhead, a face that might have been ours reflected in the black background behind the glass. Names with a hundred years of history slipping by on the street signs, the shadows watching as we swished through the soaking streets. Midnight Mayor, protector of the city, stay and fight for stones, shadows, memories, strangers, family, whatever, pick one, pick them all, all of them valid reasons to die, if that's what it came down to. Three Colts Lane, Dunbridge Street, Shoreditch, Grimsby Street, Oakly Yard, Great Eastern

Street, Holywell Lane, Curtain Road, Willow Street, Blackall Street, Old Street, City Road—and there it was! The silver-skinned dragon holding his shield, red crosses in red crosses, eyes too mad to comprehend, tongue rolled out in a hiss against the night-time air! We almost jerked with the touch of it, felt its magic hit us like electricity; closed our eyes and the shadows were still there, bleeding into the red lines of the city cross, *Domine dirige nos*, Lord lead us, trust in a higher power, a miracle day by day, *this* was what it meant to be the Midnight Mayor, mad eyes in a dragon, City Road, Finsbury Road, Moorgate, Swan Alley, White Horse Lane, Kings Yard, so close, Masons Alley, Basinghall Street, just there, Aldermanbury Square.

Empty, sleeping; but the lights still burnt in all the offices around, windows into an empty room, a thousand empty rooms, coats hung up on the backs of chairs, pictures of kids and wives, executive toys that distracted from any work and even more the personal touches of the little empty rooms. A model yacht on the lit-up sixth floor of a sleeping office tower, a conference room, table covered in old coffee cups, a meeting room with pads laid out in perfect geometric style, a floor entirely of computers in rows, an office with a tiny roll-out crazy golf course stuck into a corner. Close your eyes and you could imagine the windows of the lit-up office blocks watching you back, a thousand insectoid eyes peering out of the towers, just like the shadows.

"Oda!" we hissed. "Can you see?"

"See what?" she grunted, dragging us out of the back of the car.

"Look!" We waved at the lit-up towers.

"See *what*?"

"Magic!" we exclaimed. "Can't you see? The city is the magic, we made it, we made the magic out of the stones and the streets and the life! How can you not *see*?!"

"This had better be the pain talking," she growled, and half dragged, half carried us across the lit-up neon courtyard to Harlun and Phelps.

The doors were locked, but seeing us, the security guard lounging sleepy inside unlocked them, the great swish spinning door beginning to turn automatically as they sensed our approach. We staggered inside; Oda half-dropped me in the foyer, marched up to the security guard, grabbed him by the lapels and snapped, "Get Earle, get the Aldermen, get a doctor and then get out of here. Do you understand me?"

He nodded numbly.

"Good. Which floor was Anissina's office on?"

We took the lift to almost the top floor. I sagged against the glass walls as we rose, breathed the lights stretching beneath me. Our palm left a bloody print on the pristine glass. We could feel blood running down the outside of our leg, too much blood, couldn't sustain this for long.

The doors opened on a dimmed floor of white strip lights and silent computers. I staggered, fell onto my hands and knees as we clambered out of the lift. Oda dragged me up. "Come on!" she snarled. "Think of Ngwenya, think of her brains on the wall, her blood on the wall, little Penny Ngwenya dead, because if you die now and don't find this hat, don't undo her curse, then I swear to God I'll do it. You thinking of this, Matthew? You watching Ngwenya die, you hearing her skull burst, her blood splatter? Are you there yet?"

I nodded dumbly, she dragged me along the corridor. Pale beige doors on either side, white walls you could stick a pencil in, pictures of valued clients and random token works of could-be art, strange bits of sculpture next to the coffee machines and beside the water coolers, potted plants so bright and shiny they should have been made of rubber and saved everyone the effort. Names on the doors; I recognised Kemsley's as we went by, locked doors, venetian blinds lowered over the window panes.

(You are a fucking disgrace to the office of Midnight Mayor.

Thanks. I really needed a skinned mystical projection to tell me that.)

We passed a kitchen, Oda paused for a minute, propped me against the door frame, grabbed a green first-aid kit from above the sink, then dragged me on. "Come on!" she screamed, almost lifting me off my feet as we lurched down the corridor.

And there it was.

Ms Anissina, Senior Executive, engraved in boring white plastic on a boring beige door. The door was locked. Oda kicked it and got nowhere, Oda shot it and got in. The office inside was quiet, dull, uninspired. A harmless company picture, showing a couple of trees by a waterfall, hung on one wall; a grey filing cabinet had been wedged into a corner; a shelf above drooped under the weight of uninspiring cardboard folders. The desk had a laptop, not a computer, a thin white thing too trendy to be plugged into anything else, next to an immaculate white pad of paper and a line of perfectly ordered biros. Oda dumped me in the nearest chair, started sweeping folders off the shelves.

I opened a drawer, saw a stapler, a couple of highlighters, a notepad, a box of paperclips. I opened the one beneath it, found papers, full of numbers, including figures that were surely too big to have anything to do with money, except possibly in the City. I opened the one beneath that. There was nothing in it except a calendar. The calendar read, "*Take That 2001!*" It was worn, battered, fondled, and clearly much loved. I flicked through it. Various male faces plonked on various male bodies, vacuum-sucked into distressingly tight trousers. They pouted, smiled, frothed and flirted at me out of the semi-cardboard pages. I put it carefully on the desk by Anissina's computer and stared at it long and hard.

We wondered what it was like, being digested from the inside out.

I stuttered, "Oda?"

I heard a bang from behind me, flinched away instinctively from the noise, raising my hands to cover my face. When death did not ensue, I looked carefully back. Oda had dragged open the drawers of the filing cabinet, and was going through them, throwing paper and files onto the floor in great armfuls.

"Oda?" we stumbled again.

"There's stuff in the first-aid kit," she snapped back.

We picked up the kit in our bloody hands, tried to undo the zip; our hands were shaking. Anxiety first, then calmer and goodbye to the peripherals, that's what she'd said; and we'd been grateful to not fully understand her meaning. Bandages and padding, not enough; antiseptic, as if that wasn't the least of our concerns.

"Oda?"

Silence from behind me. I half-turned in the chair, kicking it round to see.

She stood in front of the wide glass window, eyes turned down towards her hands, hands turned up towards the ceiling. Something small, quaint and black was resting in her upturned palms. It was made out of the hybrid offspring of felt and plastic, its top dully reflecting the white light. A band of small white and yellow squares ran round its base, just above the shallow, upturned rim, and a small silverish shield had been stuck to the front, that a gleeful child might have mistaken for a sheriff's badge. It was, in short, a very boring, rather small, quite old-fashioned not-quite-bowler hat, a piece of headgear that in the 1950s would have been the embodiment of modern style and which now was just...a bit sad. A piece of uniform that time forgot.

Oda murmured, "Um..."

I took the hat carefully from her hands and turned it over.

Inside, a rim of elastic had been sewn in to make the hat sit easier on the head. On this rim, in faded yellow letters, someone had written in lopsided capitals:

PENNY

We put the hat down carefully on Anissina's desk.

We looked at it.

Silence.

"Well?" demanded Oda. "Is it . . ."

"Shush!"

She shushed, then in a lower whisper added, "What's the matter?"

"I'm having a moment of reverence. I would have thought you'd appreciate it."

"For heaven's sake, I don't have time for this. Is it . . ."

"Yes. It's the traffic warden's hat. It's *her* hat."

"And can . . ."

"Yes. I can break the curse."

A pause. Then, "Well? Do it! What are you waiting for? Full moon?"

We reached out tentatively, ran our hands over the black dome of the hat, picked it up by one side and turned it over in front of us. "He's coming," I muttered. "Mr Pinner is coming."

"*What?*"

"He's just passed across the boundary of the old London Wall. We can feel him. He hurts, right here, in the palm of our hand. He knows we've got the hat. The hat is the key to the spell that summoned him. Break that, undo the curse, and he'll die. He's coming."

"Then do it! *Do it!*"

"I need Ngwenya."

"If this is . . ."

A voice from the door said, "The traffic warden?"

I looked up slowly, ran my eyes up the immaculate length of Earle's suit, his black coat, his stern face. There were other Aldermen behind him. None looked happy. Earle carefully pulled off a pair of black leather gloves, passed them over to an Alderman in the corridor, slipped through the door, reached out for the traffic warden's hat. We snatched it back defensively, cradling it to our chest, and seeing this, he smiled.

"I thought Ngwenya *wasn't* a sorceress, Swift? After you ran off at St Pancras, Oda informed us she was...just an innocent. And yet you seem to be holding a traffic warden's hat, and seem to think that the death of cities is coming *here*, and seem, may I add, to have been shot and to be breaking into the property of one of our missing colleagues. You've clearly been busy these last few hours. Did you...*lie* to us about Ngwenya?"

We met his eyes. "Yes," we said. "Deal with it."

His fingers tightened on the edge of the desk. "You lied to us about the woman who has damned this city, cursed it, condemned it, whose anger summoned the death of cities, whose power is going to rain mystic vengeance down on our streets, and you...*you* dared to lie?"

We thought about it, then nodded. "Yes. And would do it again. Anissina, by the by, is a loony backstabbing bitch, and yeah, thanks for your concern, I've been fucking shot and yes, Mr Pinner is coming. Very very much is he coming: we can hear him on the stones, inside the city. He's coming for this." I twiddled the hat in the air. "So, since there's not much time left for you to get angry in, Mr Earle, why don't you ask me the incredibly important question—why, Mister Swift, *Mister* Mayor, why oh why oh why did you get shot trying to find this damn hat, and quite how are you going to save the city with it?"

"Doesn't really matter, now I know to kill Ngwenya after all..." he began, turning away.

We reached up, grabbed his arm, pulled him tighter towards the desk. "It matters to *us*. We can break the spell, and she doesn't have to die."

"Weakness! Stupid ineffectual blind stupid weakness! You are a..."

"Disgrace to the office of Midnight Mayor, yes, I know!" I snarled, climbing to my feet. "Every bloody stranger in the fucking city has been telling me this at every given moment and you know what, I have had it up to *here*! I am a disgrace to everything that the office used to be, to the bigger picture, to the sensible solution, to the pragmatic deeds, to the necessary sacrifice, to the stones and the streets! And good! Frankly, excellent! I am honoured to have got this brand on my hand and be able to say with it, up yours, this is the big city! We exist to change the rules, and here I am, changing one now! Ngwenya doesn't have to die! I have her hat! I can break the curse, I can destroy Mr Pinner, I can stop the death of cities. We can do it!"

"And how, exactly," growled Earle through gritted teeth, "do you plan to do this?"

"I'm going to give her back her hat."

There was silence while the collected Aldermen considered this. Finally Oda said, "What?"

"Thank you, Oda, for your essential ignorance of mystic procedure," I sighed, the energy suddenly gone back out of my bones, groping for my chair again. "I am going to give her back her hat."

"And that'll just do it? That'll break the curse?"

"Haven't you been paying attention? 'Give me back my hat'!"

"But that's . . . you said that was just . . ."

"A warning. A solution. You ever wonder how the ravens, the London Stone, the river, the Wall, the Midnight Mayor get any of their defending done? Bloody mystic forces and their uselessly obscure ways."

"We could have killed her, sorcerer," growled Earle.

"Yeah. The most efficient strategic solution in response to the on-site risk assessment analysis. The police would never have known, a crime without consequence. A stranger kills a stranger and that's it, goodbye, goodnight, end of the line. Cold, efficient—very *financial*. As cruel and distant as mankind can ever really get. We will not sink to your level. We are going to give her back her hat."

Silence.

I sighed, rubbed my eyes, and regretted it, felt sticky blood slither from my fingers to my face, heard it crackle like Velcro against my skin.

"All right," said Earle.

"You sure?" I asked, eyes closed and turned up to the too-bright afterburn of the neon light overhead.

"Yes."

"Good. So if you gentlemen will excuse me, I need to get this hat to Penny Ngwenya before I bleed to death."

I staggered back to my feet, pushed past Earle towards the door.

"Is that it?" asked Earle. "The end of it? The death of the death of cities?"

"Ha-ha," I said.

"Then . . ."

"Mr Pinner isn't just going to *let* us bring this hat to Ngwenya! The curse that she made is his life, it is what summoned him, what sustains him. He'll do everything he can to stop us. Which is, sadly, quite a lot."

"But if he . . ."

I waved at the window. "Have a look out there and tell me what you see."

Oda was nearest the window, so she was the first to look, and the first to see. She sighed a long, sad sigh. "Kids in tracksuits and hoods."

"So?" snapped Earle.

"How many?" I asked.

"Maybe . . . fifty. They're looking right up at us, if that's of any interest to anyone. Can't see any faces."

"Are they? Is it? What do you think, Mr Earle?"

His jaw was locked tight, his fists clenched at his side. "All right," he said. "Mister Mayor. What do you want done?"

"You expecting a big speech? Get off your lazy arses and fight, damnit! Oh—and *pop*."

"And po—?"

The lights went out with a faint pop.

They went out in the office, in the floor, in the building, in the buildings around, in the streets, on the wings of the planes overhead, in the tunnels underneath. We grinned. "Told you so," we said. "Where's the nearest way out?"

*   *   *

Spectres.

How we *loathed* spectres.

And turning the lights out was just cheesy, a distraction, an itch of an inconvenience, nothing compared to the big wallop. Mr Pinner, he's coming, always coming, can't hold back the death of cities for ever, sooner or later they'll die along with everything else and here he is right now, coming for *you*.

How we loathed mystic forces and their uselessly obscure ways. Why couldn't the travelcard of destiny ever be left behind the sofa, why couldn't the prophets of fate write up a spider diagram with useful footnotes and references?

So here we were, in the offices of Harlun and Phelps, surrounded by the Aldermen (how we loathed Aldermen!), who in turn were surrounded by empty hoods playing loud bass beats through their headphones, while somewhere down in the streets below a man in a pinstripe suit looked up at the black windows of the darkened office and just kept on smiling, because he knew, of course he knew, that there's no point finding the hat if you didn't give it back after.

I said, "Do you have beer or fags in this office?"

"Do you really think this is the time?"

"Bottles of beer, packs of fags," I replied sharply. *"Weapons."*

Earle's face was a grey shadow in the darkness. I was grateful I couldn't see his expression. "Catering department," he said. "You can try office drawers."

"Good. This place must have some sort of warding, protective spells, yes? I mean, if the Aldermen work here..."

"Some, yes. Wards against evil, hostile intent, that kind of thing."

"Will they fire automatically?"

"The second anything steps across the threshold. I don't think they can stop the death of cities; our insurance doesn't cover it."

"Mr Earle! Was that a moment of light-hearted humour?"

"No."

"Oh. 'Course not. My mistake. I don't suppose anyone here knows what the spleen does?"

Silence in the darkness, then a polite cough, Oda's voice. "I do. But for the sake of keeping you focused on Mr Pinner, I'm not going to tell you."

"Terrific. Mr Earle?"

"Yes, Mr Swift?"

"You Aldermen lot do whatever it is you do when forces of primal evil are about to obliterate you and your ... I nearly said loved ones, but you get the idea ..."

"Where are you going?"

"Fags and bottles of beer," I replied. "Oda?"

"I'm coming with you," her voice drifted from the darkness. "Just in case."

"It's nice to have certainty in life. These wards ..."

From somewhere below, there was a crack, a crash, distant, far-off, almost embarrassed to have its effect ruined by the weight of cold winter air between us and it. The Aldermen all at once turned their faces towards the window, and, since this was strange behaviour for anything that wasn't a pigeon, we followed their gaze as well.

In the darkness of the city outside, a single red light came on, somewhere on the other side of Aldermanbury Square. Then another, then another, a line of little red lights, here embedded in the walls, here stuck on above the street signs, here in the tops of pavement bollards. A spreading line of bright scarlet rippled down from across the other side of the square, shimmered in the double red parking lines on the streets, reflected off the red warnings on the signs, bounced and reflected off the darkened windows of the lurking buildings around, and then more. The light crawled out of its sources, spilt across the square, seeped between the legs of the hoodies—how many spectres could one guy summon?!—illuminated the empty nothings in their hoods, the cracks of nothingness between their loose, grey clothes, and still spread.

It shimmered up the side of the tower, spilt through the windows of Harlun and Phelps and kept growing and rising, a bright, unremitting crimson light that made our head hurt, a photographer's lamp amplified to the point where the eyes ached to see it. The red light ran up through the whole height of the tower, crawled out of the walls, the floors, the ceiling; everywhere there was a surface to shine, it shone red. When the Aldermen moved, they seemed to trail scarlet behind them, as if the light were a thin solid, or a floating fog, rather than a thing of insubstantial energy, and it occurred to us with the slow shuffling pace of a thought slightly shy to have been caught late to the party, that this same all-pervading light was the same blood-red of the dragon's cross, and that, looked at from the right angle, the office of Harlun and Phelps might well make a strong starting line from which you could draw the same cross on the very streets of London.

By the bright blood glow, I turned to Earle. "I gotta hand it to you..."

But he raised a hand, commanding me to silence. "*Domine dirige nos,*" he breathed, and the Aldermen chanted it in reply. "*Domine dirige nos.*"

Then, "They're inside. They're coming up the stairs. Spectres and . . . and something else."

Earle had never met the death of cities.

"He bleeds paper. You can't kill him," I said quickly, "not while the curse is still doing its thing, but you can slow him down. Protective wards, incantations, general big explosive effects. I need a way out of here, I need to get the hat to Ngwenya..."

Earle nodded briskly. "Seventh floor, there's a jump, but if you're smart..."

"Oda!"

She was by my side, face lit up dark, night-time blood in the all-pervasive redness.

"Earle..." I began.

"Run, Mister Mayor," he breathed. "We will slow them, distract them, fight them where we can. Run. Get the hat to your traffic warden. Damnation on you, sorcerer, burn in hell—*run!*"

We ran.

Blood dripped scatty and unsure behind us, forming diamond-shaped splatters on the thin carpet. The lifts were dead, no point even trying, the stairs were concrete and grey. Oda had a torch, a gun, I had my torch from my jacket pocket. But I didn't want to risk summoning a light. What little mortal strength we had now, we were not going to waste, not while there was still a chance that we might survive the night. The white light from our torches was gobbled up in an instant by the all-pervasive ruby glow, spilling from every inch of wall and floor. I could see it stretch and part around my feet as we ran/tumbled down the stairs, gasping for breath, heart pounding in our ears, scared, scared, just the anxiety, just scared, just nothing, just feeling, just mortal things for mortals to worry about, just run!

Eighteenth floor; what kind of penis-obsessed architect builds so high anyway?! (Land prices, think land prices, think running...)

Sixteenth floor, fifteenth, couldn't breathe, just keep on falling and gravity should do the rest, fourteenth floor and a sign caught my eye—"Oda!"

"What?"

"Catering."

"But..."

"Come on!"

I dragged her through the fire-exit doors onto the fourteenth floor, pushed her at the nearest line of boring plywood desks. "Fags, Sellotape! Every cigarette you can find!"

Scowling, she started to rummage through drawers. I hurried down the corridor to a pair of white double doors with a round glass window set in each one, pushed them back, lurched into a kitchen of stainless steel and giant tubs for suspicious soups made mostly of floating carrot to boil in, started tearing open everything on the shelves. We nearly screamed our frustration—what kind of big office didn't have some hidden cache of booze?!

Big cartons of Perrier, fizzy water, lemonade, fruity fizzy water, water with added vitamins, water with added volcano, fruit juice made mostly out of sugar, fruit juice made mostly out of crushed ginger, yoghurt drinks, "power" drinks, protein drinks, more water, carbonated, decarbonated, hydrated, dehydrated, mix and match in one cup and see if your head explodes...

"Matthew!" Oda's voice drifted through the doors.

"What?"

"They're coming!"

"Get in here!"

She came through the double doors to the kitchen without complaint, carrying a depressingly small armful of cigarette packets and a roll of Sellotape. "Beer," I muttered, "gotta find beers, where are they?"

"I saw a face...a not-face...an empty-face at the door."

"Beer bottles!" I dragged open another stainless-steel cupboard door, dragged down sacks of flour, great packets of gelatin, opened another and there it was! Tucked away discreetly at the back, the shelf of expensive green glass. I dragged them down by the armful, started to fumble at the tops.

"Sorcerer!"

Oda's voice from my left; I turned and there were two of them by the door, bobbing along to the silent beat, empty nothingnesses inside their hoods, penknives in hand. I raised my hands towards them, pushing my blood-soaked palms out in front of me. "Oda, light the cigarettes, empty the bottles, put the fags in them still burning, got it?"

She grabbed the fallen bottles I'd been working at, and started fumbling in her pocket for her knife, trying to get the lids off. The spectres shuffled towards me, bobbing from the hips down to their unheard rhythms, swinging their shoulders as if to say, "you think you're hard enough?" So they swaggered towards me, arrogant noth-ingnesses in a tracksuit, and I held up my hands towards them and felt the crosses carved into my skin, and I said:

"'It is apparent to me that you, being a...thing...aged ten or over namely, (a) have acted, since the commencement date, in an anti-social manner, that is to say, in a manner that caused or was likely to cause harassment, alarm or distress to one or more persons not of the same household as yourself and (b) that this order is necessary..."

The air thickened around my fingers; blood oozed down my palm, to my wrist, splattered onto the floor. The spectres kept coming.

"'...to protect persons in the local government area in which the harassment, alarm or bloody major distress is caused or is likely to be caused from further anti-social acts by yourself; and as the relevant authority—' Oda hurry up!..."

Thick light began to shimmer off my skin, and spill down my arms onto the floor. As the spectres neared, they began to slow, arms sliding through the air like vengeful t'ai chi gurus, each movement reduced to a crawl; but still coming—

"'...for the purpose of determining whether the condition men-tioned in subsection (1)(a) above is fulfilled, the court shall disregard any act of the defendant which he shows was reasonable in the cir-cumstances. The prohibitions that may be imposed— 'Oda! Faster!"

The spectres were a few feet from me, moving now so slow, caught full fast in the enchantment and I screamed the words of the spell, felt the power run through my arms, burn at the ends of my fingertips: a new spell, a young spell, and still not strong enough. I let it fill my lungs, my blood, lift me almost off my feet with the force of it, feed-ing it everything I had: "'...prohibitions that may be imposed by an anti-social behaviour order are those necessary for the purpose of protecting from further anti-social acts by the defendant (a) persons in the local government area; and (b) persons in any adjoining local government area specified in the application for the order..."

One of the spectres raised its knife; in slow motion, the weapon screeched and hissed and spat furious angry sparks as it moved through the air as slow and gentle as a freak wave on a starlit night—I pushed back against it with everything I had, saw it slow still further, but still coming, poured out the spell with every last drop of air I had in my lungs, bellowed it at the empty hood of the spectre, "'An anti-social behaviour order shall have effect for a period (not less than two years) specified in the order or until further order. Subject to subsection (9) below, the applicant or the defendant may apply by complaint to the court which made an anti-social behaviour order for it to be varied or discharged by a further order—' *Oda!!*"

Something was pushed into my hand, moving quickly through the air that had thickened to porridge between me and the spectre. It was a green beer bottle, the sides sticky with the drink just poured out. A single cigarette smoked dully inside, dark mist crawling out from the top. We nearly laughed, and drawing back our arm, thrust the bottle as hard as we could into the slowly drifting face of the spectre, shrieking with the attack, "Hey, man! Like *total* respect!"

The spell I had been casting broke. The spectre should really have screamed, but what it was was already shrivelling down inside the bottle, vanishing into the mist of the smoking cigarette, behind the foggy cage of the glass. Its clothes crumpled into a messy heap on the floor; the knife fell through empty air to break its own blade on the pale tiles. I snatched the bottle back as the hood shrivelled into itself, planted my thumb firmly across the opening and snatched Sellotape from Oda's hand, sealing the bottle and tearing the strip free with my teeth.

The other spectre, freed from the spell I had been weaving, lurched towards me, but I snatched another bottle from Oda's hands and waved it, roaring, "Come on, then! Another nothing for eternity!"

The other spectre retreated a few paces; we stepped sharply after it, it moved too late, tried to put the knife between our ribs; but we had the bottle with its tantalising smoke, and jammed it into the empty middle of that vacant hood, sucking it down until nothing but a pile of baggy clothes remained, and another foggy beer bottle.

Oda stuttered, looking at the sad clothes on the floor, "Just like..."

"Yes. Just like that."

"That was an ASBO you just..."

"Yeah. I know. That's why it didn't really work. Bottles!"

She handed me four, put another one in my coat pocket, kept two to herself, held in either hand. "This will kill spectres?"

"Contain them. The invocation of an ASBO will slow them down as well, if there's more than one of them, but, like you saw, it's not a perfect spell. And if the cigarettes burn down before the bottle is filled, they won't work either. But it should be enough to get us to the seventh floor."

"I can't..."

"You push the bottle into their faces, and if it doesn't work, tell them, 'respect'. Say it like you mean it."

"I can't just do ma—"

"You can."

"I can't! I'm not some..."

"It's a simple binding, nothing more than a piece of sympathetic magic. You want to live?"

"And not be damned!"

"Well, you're gonna have to pick one or the other. *Come on!*"

I dragged her, or maybe she dragged me, or maybe we just got in each other's way, out of the kitchen, across the dull office floor turned the colour of blood, or crosses, or dragon's eyes, or maybe just a tasteless brothel-red, to the stairway. And there it was, the beat in the stair, echoing up the concrete walls: *dumdumdumdumDUH dumdumdumdumDUH dumdumdumdum*...

"Another stair?" I gasped.

"Sure, because I know—"

"It's not really a question!"

There was another staircase, tucked in at the opposite end of the office floor.

sshssshsssCHA sshssshsssCHA sshssshsssCHA . . .

"Where now?"

"Down, gotta get down . . ."

"Do you even know where this Ngwenya woman is?"

"Sure I do," I muttered. "The death of cities is about to kill the Midnight Mayor; that's the last defence the city's got, the last thing that's gonna stop us all burning. Of course I know where Ngwenya is!"

"Jedi spidey-senses?"

"Obscure mystic forces."

"The spectres are *here*, Swift! Mr Pinner is *here*; do you really think we can just walk this one down?"

"Right," I scowled, dragging her back. "*Fine.*"

Red light, spinning chairs, dull desks, silent sleeping computers, big glass windows behind the doors of the executive cubicles, plywood doors, plaster walls. "Do you suppose there's those big vents like there are in American thrillers?" I asked hopefully.

Oda grunted in reply, her eyes still fixed on the stairwell door through which was coming the sound of:

sshssshsssCHA sshssshsssCHA

dumdumdumDUH dumdumdumDUH dumdumdumDUH

"OK." I looked down at the floor. Our hands were shaking, we hadn't even noticed this time, the edge of our vision seemed to be going off on its own business.

"I can see them coming!" hissed Oda, scrambling back from the doorway at a sight on the stairs. "They're nearly here!"

"How many bottles do we have?"

"Maybe six? Can they hold more than one spectre?"

"What do you think?"

"I'm thinking that life was not made to be easily lived."

"I was thinking something ruder than that, but yeah, you've got the basic gist."

I could see shadows moving behind the door; taste them. And something else, something that made the fingers of our right hand curl in disgust and fear. "Back into the office," I hissed. "There."

Oda obeyed, kicking back a plywood door to reveal an office garnished on a theme of golf: clubs, pictures, trophies and all. The far wall was nothing but glass, slightly curved outwards, looking down on the dark/red soak of the city. I ran my hands over the window, felt the cold glass, pressed my nose up against it, ran my tongue over it, tasted the dull dirt. "This'll do," I muttered.

"For what?" she hissed.

"You still got your penknife?"

She handed it over; I wrenched through the blades until I found the pointed end of a four-head screwdriver. Turned the point towards the glass.

And a voice from the door said, and there was no hiding the anger, "Give me back my hat, sorcerer!"

I glanced over my shoulder, and there he was, Mr Pinner, and he wasn't smiling, not now. His jacket billowed, his hair stood on end, his face was cold and pale, and behind him the office trembled. The furniture bounced gently on the floor like flowers in a breeze, the computer screens cracked, the chairs spun giddy on their axis, the files on the shelves split open, the paper started to tumble out, a few sheets at first, then more, dozens, hundreds, endless walls of paper spilling out into the room, caught in a whirlwind, blasting and screaming in the air behind him, filling the doorway with nothing but an A4 snowstorm.

"Give me back my . . ." he began, and I drove the end of the screwdriver as hard as I could into the glass.

It went *thunk*. I drew it back slowly. A tiny white scar, no bigger than the end of a child's finger, appeared on the glass. Then a little fault line shimmered out from the edge, divided, spread a bit further, split, divided again, moved again, split, divided, spread. It took no more than a few seconds, but watching each spreading fibre through the glass was like waiting for a glacier to move down a mountain.

Behind me, Mr Pinner shrieked his fury and rage, raised his hands and seemed to throw his whole weight towards us. The paper whirlwind burst around him, shrouded him in a second, filled the room with a thousand screaming edges of white, razored sheets that cut and tore and slashed. I pressed my palm against the scar in the glass and pushed, throwing the weight of my arm, my shoulder, everything, jumping, lifting my feet off the floor to push against the glass and it shattered with a roar, splintered into a thousand thousand shards that burst outwards around me.

And that was nothing. *Nothing;* in the offices above, below, on either side, everywhere, the little cracks had spread to run their course. The glass burst and shattered, spilling out into the crimson night, and from every office tumbled a whirlwind of paper, spiralling and floating out on the cold air. I grabbed Oda as the glass began to fall, pulling her down until we were both crouching almost to the floor and, kicking aside the last clinging remnants of glass still hanging off the blasted steel frame of the office, I pulled her over the edge, into the night.

Not far, as luck and sensible precaution would have it. As we fell, we twisted, turned; I grabbed at the frame and swung with my legs, and she, clever, strong Oda who was so very good at killing things that should have killed her, swung as well, pulling me as much as I pushed her through the shallow fall from our broken office window down and through the shattered window of the office below. Outside, the glass and paper fell like hail and snow in a gale, splattering and spilling down to the street below. We landed on a floor covered in twisted files and warped plastic, Oda pulling my head down as the computer on the desk above us popped and flared in angry, futile explosion at the indignity of its circumstances. And then she was dragging me to the window again and already halfway out, lowering herself down over the shattered steel edge where carpet met open air, and swinging her legs down to the floor below. I looked down; it was much easier to do now there wasn't a window to stop me craning my head. It was a long way. I wheezed, "Oda, I can't..."

"Ngwenya dead with a bullet in her brain!" she snarled back, already in the darkened office below. "I swear to God, Swift, I swear by all that is sacred, by all that is holy, I shall put a bullet in her brain and it will be your fault, the sin on your head, burn in hell, Matthew Swift! Now *come on!*"

I looked up and there was Mr Pinner, standing on the edge of the office above, looking straight down at me, like Harlun and Phelps was nothing more than an open dolls' house, and we no more than its occupants. We snarled, stretched our fingers to the air, felt for a fistful of glass spinning by and hurled it furiously back at him. He ducked away, but a fat spinning shard of glass tore his cheek, right across his eye, and from the whitened centre I saw slide another sliver of paper, which he pulled carelessly from his skin and threw away.

We scrambled down, flopping like a dying fish from one window to the other, Oda catching us at the bottom of each drop and throwing us, speed more than strength her advantage, into the room below before we had a chance to fall.

We went down three floors in this clumsy way, before enough glass remained on the floor below to make the jump impossible, and I crawled onto my knees and gasped, "Just a moment, please, just a..."

"No time!"

Oda grabbed me by the arm, dragged us through the office floor to the nearest stairwell, and there it was still playing, *dub-dub...de-dum! Dub-dub...de-dum!*

Tenth floor, ninth, it was getting louder, getting nearer, and above me I could hear doors being blasted back, the roar of paper, smell paper as it started to fill the stairwell, spinning up and down like a tornado in the middle of the stairwell to tear and batter at us. Eighth, seventh; Oda kicked the door back and there it was, just waiting on the other side. The spectre raised its knife and I wasn't close enough, I was still in the stairwell. She'd led the way and it was there, going to tear her apart. Instinctively she raised her hands and in one of them was a bottle that had once held beer. She plunged it deep into the spectre's hood, not thinking, too fast to breathe; and all at once the spectre started to crumple, sucked into the hot smoking interior of the bottle. I caught her arm as her fingers began to let go, held the bottle in place, kept pushing it into the hood until the creature's clothes were nothing but a pile on the floor; then stuck my thumb over the lip, slipped Sellotape over the hole. Oda was just standing, staring, not moving, mouth hanging open. I grabbed her by the shoulder, dragged her into the office; we hurt, every part hurt; pulled her past the desks and the computers and the water coolers and all the samey sames of any office anywhere, tangling our feet in the fallen tracksuit of the spectre as we went.

We looked for signs, markings, anything to tell us the truth of this wonderful exit Earle had spoken about; and there it was, fire muster point, in big white letters on a green board. We rushed towards it, pushed the door open, stepped into a corridor that was bare except for a few recycling bins left forlornly on the concrete floor, ran to the end, saw a door, a handle, a sign warning of alarm, and there it was, burning blood-red on the door: the twin crosses, on fire, emitting too much light to look directly at them. I covered my eyes with my sleeve, slammed down on the door release with my elbow, kicked it open and looked out onto a dark rooftop on a cloudless night.

There weren't any stairs down. Just a rooftop, sloping at a shallow angle, red tiles, old-fashioned chimney stack, new-fashioned TV antennae and satellite aerials, and this door, leading onto it from Harlun and Phelps. The roof was part of some old guild building, leading down from here to there, wherever there was.

There, rather than here. I pulled Oda out of the door, stepped past the uneven angle onto the sloping roof, slid, caught at the tiles, felt them hard and sharp beneath my fingers, slid a few steps and pressed myself flat, belly-down onto the slope. Oda was beside me, breathing even faster than us. We were . . . our eyes were . . . and our hands were doing some other business, and we'd slipped because there was blood beneath our feet, and it was our blood, what had Oda said? What was a spleen good for anyway?

My bag was still on my back.

The hat was still in the bag. I looked up, saw Harlun and Phelps lit up like a giant crimson warning against careless playing with matches, and half-imagined that somewhere in its depths, I could hear screaming. Aldermen fighting, Aldermen dying, while we snuck away in the night.

"We have to get away," I hissed at Oda. "Come on! We have to find Ngwenya."

Oda's head was turned back towards the red tower, her eyes wide. "They're..." she began.

"We can't kill him! We can't stop Pinner without undoing this spell! We have to move! Oda! You have to help me!"

She half-turned, stared straight at us, and in her face was a look of such hollow nothingness that for a moment I thought I saw the empty hood of the spectre, not the flesh of a woman at all. "Damnation," she whispered. *"Damnation."*

"We can undo it!"

"Not this."

"Oda! Listen to me, I need your help, we need to get to Ngwenya, I know where she'll be, you have to help me! *Oda!*"

Our shout seemed to shake her for a moment, and there was something still there, hard old psycho-bitch, tough as tar. She turned her head up to the top of the roof and started to climb, scrambling over the old red tiles to the chimney stack and dragging me up behind her. My hand slipped in her fingers, blood sliding over skin between us; she caught me by the wrist and pulled, dragging me up to the top of the roof and looking down. On the other side of the slope, the roof dropped down into darkness, promising at something else: a flatter roof, another building, just below. We slid down the other side, tiles bumping and banging uncomfortably beneath us, reached the gutter, crawled over it, the old black metal creaking uncomfortably, jumped the little foot or so between us and the next building, landed on a roof of stagnant dirty water, old pigeon poo, silent, rusted vents and cracking grey concrete.

"London Bridge," I hissed. "We have to get to London Bridge."

Behind us, Harlun and Phelps was a burning crimson brightness, the whole tower lit up with it, and there was someone in the door, the same one we'd jumped out of, hands in pockets, looking at us, just looking.

Oda had seem him too, and didn't seem to be able to take her eyes away. I shook her, and still she didn't turn. We slapped her, hard, across the cheek, and her hand instinctively rose into a fist, that stopped its swing an inch from our nose.

"Listen!" we hissed. "She cast the curse on London Bridge, she summoned him on London Bridge, it's where it has to end; we have to get there!"

She crawled to the edge of the roof, looked down. Below us were concrete tiles, a walkway, a hangover from the days when architects had big dreams and only limited budgets, part of an overhead network that stretched from the northern reaches of the Barbican on the Goswell Road to the southern face of Moorgate and London Wall. In the 1960s, it would have seemed like science fiction; today, almost no one knew the walkways even existed. Oda slithered off the edge of the roof down the short drop onto the tiles, which thudded and echoed heavily, the mortar never even laid. I crawled after her, flopped, fell, landed on my toes and fell onto my knees, banging my hands against the stones.

Oda picked me up by the armpits, pulled me away from the burning-blood building behind; and there they were, those friendly mystic yellow lines on the floor that would always lead you somewhere you never expected to be. I pointed away from them: "There! Moorgate — there!"

We ran, as graceful as a burst beetroot. Concrete flags, lights

coming on around us, the area of darkness fading as we fled from
Harlun and Phelps, dead container plants, old cigarette packets tumbling in the street, blood between our fingers. There were stairs down
from the highwalks, strange dark concrete stairs smelling of piss and
old thin mould, running down the square back of a black-glassed slab
of a building, moulded out of the old walls of a domed pub; the street
below, Moorgate, all yellow-orange neon glow and sleepy shops selling chocolate, coffee and suits. An Underground stop, but the trains
wouldn't be running; a bus stop, but it was waiting for night buses, for
twenty-four-hour routes, both of which by their very natures were
destined never to quite turn up when you needed them.

Not a car in sight, not a cab, not a truck, the city was as dead as a
street could be, the utter silence of an empty road that should have
been heaving, that lived to heave, roadworks and traffic jams. We
could half-close our eyes and there they were; the shadows ran to our
feet, tumbled up from the pavements and between the cracks in the
tarmac, remembering the daylight when they buzzed and shuffled
and heaved and pressed against each other in the busy need to get
from A to B as quickly as possible, important business, important
things to do in the city, the smell of traffic and the juddering of builder's tools into the earth. Silence in the city is terrifying, beautiful, a
reminder of just how small man is in the streets he built. We ran down
the middle of the road, letting the shadows trail us, feeding on some
of their memories, recollections of rush hour and busy, busy, busy,
feet slapping dully on the white hazard lines in the middle of the too-
narrow street for all the traffic of day, and Oda followed, stumbling
like a deranged zombie, eyes fixed on nothing at all, legs moving simply because they didn't know what else to do with themselves.

The traffic lights between Moorgate and London Wall flickered
red to green and back again as we approached, signalling invisible
drivers to go about their business; to one side of the junction, a dig-
ger had dug a fat hole in the earth, revealing plastic pipes and ancient,
dirt-encrusted black neighbours running through the ground, marked

out by a sign thanking us for our patience while these vital works were undertaken. The bright burning redness of Harlun and Phelps was going out; I could see the scarlet overwash of the light fading, as the wards that had ignited within the building also died; for what reason, I didn't know, couldn't guess, didn't want to guess. The street narrowed further as we crossed the traffic lights, tall, gloomy buildings with high imperial windows turned dark in the night, blocking out all but the thinnest pathway of sky overhead. Banks, their names written up in a different language and script above every door; ordinary money wasn't their trade, not pounds and pennies like we were used to. The figures they dealt with had more zeros in them than most mortals had vocabulary to describe. Alleys winding off the side, a reminder of a time when the streets had sprung up contrarily, to their own devising, so much for urban planning, can't stop us building here, can't make it right, this is *our* city. Pubs, leather sofas, brass taps, low dark tables covered with stained green towels; a telephone box down one alley, defaced with white letters on one wall:

VE ME BA

A building overhead, cherubs carved into the gutters; another where Greek maidens in drooping robes held up the roofs; and here, if you looked, a tiny dragon in black iron placed as a weathervane on top of a domed tower, looking south-west across the city with two eyes set above a jaw open in perpetual fury. These were buildings made to demonstrate imperial glory, grandeur, wealth as power, great slabs of yellow stone fretted with ornaments across the roofs, forcing the passer-by in the street to crane their head right up to appreciate the skill of the mason's work.

Lothbury, the great cliff walls of the Bank of England, a palace fit for an arrogant Pharaoh, guarded by bare-breasted Britannias and huge iron doors; another wall too high for any mortal to see over, another street too narrow for the traffic that flowed through it during the day. To one side the stone wall built to celebrate wealth and glory, to the other a length of black reflective glass built by people who knew that real wealth was fickle, and could be more sensibly contained. I could see the should-be-roundabout ahead where so many things met; Cheapside, Poultry, Moorgate, Bank, Thread-needle Street, King William Street, the Merchants' Exchange, Mansion House; the richest junction in all England, full of old names and uneven glittering prosperity. Statues of stern-faced old dead men looked down on the narrow twisting of joining streets; a clock ticked in an illuminated plastic frame for no one to see, shop windows were still lit up bright and cold to show you the suits on offer, the range of cufflinks, the finest whiskies that they had to sell.

I ran out into the middle of the junction, heard Oda a few steps behind me, felt something move, looked up to my left, saw a shadow on the walls of the Bank of England, raised my hands, and heard a roar of air. I looked to my right, and too late saw the gates of the steps down to Bank station burst open, heard the roar come up from inside it—not just air but feet and footsteps and trains and escalators and beeps and tickets and shouts and cries and commands and everything all at once, the great rumble of the Underground—put my hands over my head and threw myself on the ground.

Around me, across the whole junction, the gates of the subway stairs blew upwards, outwards, spinning broken metal across the streets, and up came the roaring, a trapped unheard din of music players, announcements, warnings, cars overhead and trains below, printing machines and tapping keys, in a blast of air so hot and so dirty it looked like ash bursting from the volcano, spilling and spiralling up from under the street and around the streets and from every exit all at once, turning the cold orange-sodium night black and hot in an instant of furious shrieking ash. I looked behind me, saw Oda crawling away from the nearest subway on her hands and knees, hair smoking from the blast, face burnt, ears bleeding, she had been too close, even closer than me. I scampered on hands and knees towards her, caught her in my arms and dragged her away from the spinning,

writhing wall of furious darkness that tumbled and spat hot fury out
of the subways, rising up to block out the sky overhead. I couldn't see
the streets beyond this wall of blackness, couldn't see through the
volume of dirt and dust piling up from the subway's open mouths,
forming an arena wall around the junction. I shook Oda gently,
hissed, "You OK?" and felt the warmth in my breath snatched away,
my tongue turn to dirty dry meat in my mouth at the effort of speaking through the storm.

She nodded numbly. "Break it," she whispered. "Break it!"

I felt for my bag, felt the bulk of the hat inside it again, patted it
like a crucifix for comfort, looked around our narrowing circle of
burning darkness for tools, felt...stones rumbling, sleeping stones
being disturbed just a little way off...and saw *him*. He walked
through the screaming roaring shattering sound and the burning suffocating filth from beneath the streets like it was sunlight in a dappled
forest. Utterly clean, utterly untouched by it. He had his umbrella,
which he leant on slightly as he stopped to stare at us. He looked...
not entirely his usual self, but he still managed to muster a smile.

Mr Pinner said, as the storm belched all around us, "End of the
line."

I raised a trembling hand towards him and stuttered, "Uh-uh.
Blackwall."

For a moment, doubt flickered on Mr Pinner's face. I turned my hand,
pointed it in the general direction of where I thought the street called
Poultry was. "Midnight Mayor," I added, seeing his confusion. "*Dub.*"

He understood, but just a bit too late. I felt a rumbling, heard the
rattling of an old, badly kept engine, saw a pair of headlights breaking
through the dark, pulled Oda into my chest; and we didn't quite have
it in us to look away. For anyone else, we would have — not for this.

The bus came rattling through the storm like it was just another
futile traffic-calming measure on a road built for racing; it was a night
bus, it didn't believe in slowing down, not for anything. A double-
decker, its walls were red, its glass was scratched, its wheels were

smoking, its driver was just a shadow lost in the darkness of the compartment. On the front was its number and destination—the number 15, heading for Blackwall, and pity the creature that tried to stop it getting there. Mr Pinner was standing between it and its destination. Night buses don't believe in braking unless it's absolutely, entirely, and without a doubt necessary. This bus didn't brake. I watch it slam into him too fast to really tell what happened; we felt almost disappointed—there should have been the slow-motion crumpling of the health and safety ads you got at the cinemas, a twisting of limbs into unfortunate places, a slow swinging back of his neck as his spine crumpled, a shattering of bones as his legs, then his waist went under the bus, a snap as his upper body was thrown against the wide red front. There was none of that; one second, bus driving towards man, next second, bus driving *over* where man should have been. It occurred to us that all this might have been like the health and safety videos, if Mr Pinner had a spine to snap.

The number 15 rolled on, vanished again through the whirling black storm, which itself began to crumple and sink, the sound and the dirt sucked back in like an obscene drawing of breath by a pair of dying lungs, dragged back down through the open gates of the subway stairs, sucked beneath the streets. A figure lay in the middle of the road, as flat and thin as a piece of paper.

It began to twitch.

I grabbed Oda by the wrist, started to run, pulled her past the not-dead thing slowly rising back up from the black tarmac. Down towards King William Street, past a church, all red brick and spike, the long narrow streets snaking towards Cannon Street and Monument; shut coffee shops and the twisted remnants of an escape exit from Bank station. Lombard Street, St Swithin's Lane, Abchurch Lane; I could see the junction of Monument right ahead. In an electronics store on one corner, cameras were watching us and projecting onto a dozen TV screens where our image got bigger and bigger as we ran towards it.

There was something behind us. I could hear it, a great angry rumble on the air. I risked a glance back and there it was, filling the street, higher than any houses, turning the night sodium-bright with reflected glory as it tumbled up into the sky. It didn't have any shape that I could call a creature or give a name to; it was just a tidal wave, a storm surge, a great falling mass of paper, thousands and thousands of pieces of paper, receipts, bills, demands, flyers, bank notes, envelopes, letters, cheques, invoices, statements, ads, maps, leaflets. And at their heart, somewhere lost in the tumbling weight of it, Mr Pinner, hands held up to the sky, the papers pouring out of his flesh, tumbling upwards and outwards, over the roofs of the buildings and down the street towards us, thicker than the snow of a falling avalanche.

Oda had seen it too, was now overtaking me as she ran towards Monument; we weren't going to get there, neither of us. We were going to drown first, going to be torn apart, suffocated, crushed. It was thirty feet behind us, twenty, rumbling like some great rusted locomotive down the street behind us; ten feet. I grabbed Oda, pulled her close to me, and held up my burnt hand to the storm.

Domine dirige nos.

(What a stupid way to die.)

Blood dribbled off my fingertips. I saw a big red drop run down to the joint between wrist and arm, reach the curve of that line, drool for an uneasy second, and fall.

Domine dirige nos.

And as it fell, it changed. The deep red of my blood started to burn, shine, shimmer, ignite; it wasn't a falling liquid, but a falling twisting bubble of energy, turning, in the blink of an eye, the thickness of a piece of paper, if thickness was time, to a bright burning electric blue.

Then the blood dribbling from our side also ignited, furious blue, and the blood in our veins, and the blood in our eyes, and the blood that had seeped into the twin crosses carved into our hand. They caught fire, bursting back to their natural state of glorious electric fury; and I let it burn, boil inside, spill out of my wounds and mouth and eyes. Of all the ways to die, I was willing to let this be the one that did the job. We were going to burn, going to catch fire, going to explode with pure blue electricity, beautiful as a bomb, rolling fire through the sky, beautiful and wondrous and defiant!

And the papers spinning towards us, hitting the rising blue tempest of our fire, ignited, shrivelled, turned to ash, grey thin ash billowing in the fury at our feet; going to burn, beautiful burning, going to set the sky on fire, going to burn going to...

...I could see nothing except the blue tumbling fire which still seemed in some way to stem from the burning twin crosses blazing on my right hand; the paper, the streets, the sky, everything was lost within this cocoon, going to burn going to burn skin cracking blue fire in eyes, mouth, nose, ears, tongue, burning screaming delight going to...

A hand reached through the fire. It was paper-white. It was attached to a sleeve. The sleeve was pinstriped. It reached calmly through the flames without a second of hesitation, grabbed Oda by the throat, pulled her free from my arms and with the easy strength of a hydraulic ram, threw her aside. She vanished into the fires, and somewhere beyond that, into the storm, the street, the stones, the whatever lay beyond our burning brightness. We screamed, raised our hands up and let the fires burst from every part of us, blazed electric fury dragged up from the streets, breathed the gas from the shattered pipes, sucked the water up from under the cement, the glass out of the windows, the scrabbling from the telephones, the chittering from the radio waves. We took it all, pushed it all towards that paper-pale hand fumbling in the fire and let it burst, fire and fury and light and electricity and sound and lightning and digital screaming and glass and stone and dirt and heat and shadows—how many shadows could one city hold?—we threw them into it as well, sucked them up from the streets and let them rage, scream through the air towards Mr Pinner, too thick to see, closing our eyes against their weight, crumpling down into the middle of the street, hiding our head in our hands as they screamed up from all around, too many to comprehend; too thick, too heavy, too much of too much. Open your eyes and understand it, and you know why the dragons were mad; too much of too much couldn't stop it, couldn't do it, too much of too much, *burn!*

Something dragged us forwards, like the sucking in of air to a fire. Then, the fire being sated with what it could eat, it threw us backwards, twisting and turning us on the air and throwing us across the street, blasting stones and glass and electric fire and paper, so much paper, throwing it into the sky and then dropping it back down. We fell into the gutter, the shock of it knocking the fires out in our blood, sending us reeling into some dull, stupid part of our mortal skull, little mortal frail flesh trembling at the blast, and it was all I could do to tuck our chin into our legs and shield our face from the shockwave as it rippled down the street, shattering every brick and pane of glass that had survived the storm, blasting spinning paper along the road and into the sky, suffocating heat in the cold night air.

And slowly, it too settled.

I opened my eyes, peered out between my red bloody fingertips. Mr Pinner stood in the middle of the street, paper falling gently all around. His hair was dishevelled, his coat torn, his skin dripping small receipts and lines of ticker tape. He wasn't alone. His head was turned upwards to the thing that had grown out of the darkness behind him, his eyes fixed on the twin points of red madness that stared back down at him. I heard him start to laugh, but he didn't take his eyes from the creature. "Is this it?" he chuckled. "Is this the best your city has?"

The thing, standing as high as the street, its wings bent back uncomfortably to make space for the buildings, put its head on one side and looked down at him. To call it a dragon was...

...an efficient way to describe something we did not wish to comprehend.

"I am the death of cities!" roared Mr Pinner, opening his torn arms to the beast. "I am your undoing, the breaking of the legends, the stories and the *shadows*! Your city is damned by its own people, condemned out of the mouths of your own! Betrayal and vengeance! You cannot harm me!"

I crawled to my feet. Bits of me that shouldn't have made the sounds they did made sounds. My heart was a steady, dull *dedum* in my chest—too steady, too dull, as if it had run out of the strength to race. I called out, "Mr Pinner?"

He half-turned, saw me, smiled. "Mr Mayor!" he called out merrily. "Do you keep a pet dragon?"

"No," I replied with a sigh. "It keeps me." I turned my head up to the black shape of the shadow-beast, skirted my eyes over the edge of its mad own, couldn't look, couldn't bear to look, to risk infinite falling into a red void. I looked just past it and said, "Fido! Walkies!"

Mr Pinner spun back round, raised his hands up towards the beast. It opened its jaws and fell, spinning darkness and scarlet endless falling, down on top of him.

London is a dragon.

New York is probably King Kong.

It's just a way for mortals to understand something too big for the brain.

On the other hand, Mr Pinner did have a point.

What good is a city against its nemesis?

We turned our face away from the darkness in King William Street, and as the paper tumbled gently from the sky, hobbled towards Monument. Behind us we heard . . . sounds not fit for the human ear, sounds we could not explain, comprehend, had not the vocabulary to describe. We call them sounds only because the human brain cannot find another way by which to understand them, did not have the means to grasp, without going insane, the clash between the dragon and the man in the pinstripe suit. Had we been just blue electric angels, just ourself in the wires, we would have known then how to speak of it. But I could not have spoken of the sound without going insane, so will say simply and true — that in King William Street that night, a dragon summoned from the stuff of the city met the creature summoned to destroy it.

And the creature was going to win.

Buying time; we'd seen *Terminator*, we knew the value of buying time.

We hobbled past Monument as the paper fell, saw our face reflected a hundred times in the window of the electronics store, heard the thud of our footsteps echoing off the glass front of the chemist and the window of the sushi bar, stumbled above the top of a stair leading down to Cannon Street, snaking away below us. Tucked away to the left, a discreet nothing bursting into sight, was the spike of the Monument itself, golden flame sat dull and silent on its top, scaffolding around its base to support the old monument to another time when the death of cities had come to London, another burning, another loss. Office block to the right, symbols carved into the stone — an all-seeing eye, a pair of compasses, a thing that by a different light might have been a swastika, hangovers from a day when London liked to flaunt its mysteries.

A dropping away of buildings.

Neon-filled darkness to either side.

A broad street widening out into a bridge, an empty nothing over water; on the far side, railway bridges, glassy reflective buildings set all at odd angles: Hay's Wharf and Tower Bridge to the east, Southwark to the west, Southwark Cathedral poking up above the offices and pubs, the *Golden Hinde* sitting in its dry dock, bow just pointing out over the water, the curve of the London Eye sticking up over the edge of the tallest building, the numberless clock on Waterloo Bridge, the white blade of the Millennium Bridge, the tower of Tate Modern. Please, dear God, please any higher power which may or may not be watching over us, this is the moment to do your thing, please...

London is a dragon.

Protector of the city.

Light, life, fire.

London Bridge in the small hours of a winter morning.

No traffic, no buses, no taxis, no lorries. Just an empty street, lit from above by a long line of silent, sad lamps, and by red floodlights illuminating the sides of the bridge. Railings cut off the pavements from the road. I staggered down the side of the left-hand lane, clutching my satchel to my side, gasping and reaching out for the railings to carry my weight. Someone had filled my eyes with empty honeycomb, thick, solid, airy, sticky, all these things at once and none of them natural; the pain that should have been in every part of my skin was just a distant prickling of pins and needles, too much blood between our fingers, some bastard shot us! Too much blood...

Where was Oda?

Where was Earle?

Where were the Aldermen?

Digested from the inside out.

Poor Loren alone in her room in Camden.

Vera dead and turned to paint.

And Nair had screamed, just like little Mo had screamed, just like all those dead men had screamed when they were still human to do it.

Give me back my hat.

Light, life, fire.

Protector of the city.

A dragon's pet.

There was a woman standing alone in the middle of the bridge.

She was looking east, towards the place a sunrise might pretend to be in a few hours or so.

Her hands were turned towards the river, her face towards the sky.

She was breathing in the river air. That beautiful, calming, relaxing, cooling river air, sorcerer's balm after a hard day with the voltages; time and stillness and movement all rolled into one breath on the bridge.

The palms of her hands were girly pink, the outsides deep, dark brown. Her hair was woven in plaits so tight it must have hurt, had no choice but to hurt.

We staggered towards her.

She didn't notice.

Her eyes were closed, her heart beating in time to the running of the water below the bridge.

Ten paces, five, three, two.

We stopped a step away from her, leant against the side of the bridge, gasping for breath.

Penny Ngwenya didn't move, didn't blink, just stood on the bridge and smiled at the smell of the river.

I said, "Miss?"

Nothing.

"Miss?!"

Nothing.

I fumbled in my satchel, pulled out the traffic warden's hat, smearing its surface with my bloody fingertips. "Miss Ngwenya?"

A flicker on her face. Her head half-turned, her eyes half-opened, distant, but still there, looking at me, even if she didn't entirely see.

I held up the hat. "Penny Ngwenya?"

Her eyes went to the hat in my blood-covered hands. Her fingers twitched, her mouth opened to let out a little, sliding breath.

I reached out with one shaking hand, took her hand in mine, pressed the hat into her fingers, closed them, unresisting, over the black fabric. "I brought you back your hat," I said.

A moment.

A pause.

She didn't seem to understand.

Her eyes fell slowly down to thing in her hand. "My . . . hat?"

"Yes. I heard you lost it. I brought it back."

"Do I know you?" she asked, turning it over in her fingers, looking at the yellow "Penny" written inside.

"No," I replied. "My name's Matthew."

"You...you look..." she began, voice a million miles away, eyes fixed on the hat.

"I happened to be passing," I said carefully. "No trouble."

"We...haven't met, have we?"

"No," I replied. "Just strangers." And then, because up seemed to be wanting to give down a try, and down was feeling flexible enough just this once to let up have its way, I slid down against the side of the bridge, burying my fingers into the cold concrete in case sideways wanted to try the same trick on me. I saw the edges of my vision start to cave.

"Jesus!" exclaimed Penny, dropping down with me, trying to hold me up. "You've...you've been..."

"It's fine," I muttered. "It's fine, just fine, it'll be...I had to bring you back your hat, you see?"

"You've been fucking shot!"

"Yeah, I noticed."

"Don't move, OK? You'll just make it worse, I'll...I'll call an ambulance."

Her attention had for a moment been taken from the hat, but as she reached into her pocket for her mobile phone, her eyes skated across the fabric again and she froze, mouth slightly open, staring at the little, old-fashioned, ugly black dome.

"Where did you...?" she stumbled.

"I heard it was important to you. I thought, since I was in the area, I could bring it back."

"Why would you do that?"

"It's your hat. It seemed the least I could do."

"But..."

She had the hat in one hand, was fumbling for the phone with her other.

A voice said, "Get away from him."

She looked up.

So did I.

A thing that might have once been Mr Pinner stood in the middle of the road. His suit was a raggedy painted thing of badly torn paper trailing down from the thin, uneven ripples of his flesh. His neck was bent in and then sharply out again, like a crumpled old Christmas cracker, his trousers were wrapped up tight in old receipts and bits of soggy newspaper. A thousand cuts had been torn in his flesh, from which dribbled little pieces of paper falling away into the street. One eye had been slashed straight through and was now oozing blue biro ink down his cheek. When he spoke, his voice was a distorted, lumpy thing.

He said again, "Get away from him. Penny. You can't trust him."

She stuttered, "Who are you? I don't know you."

"I'm Mr Pinner," he replied. "I'm here to help you. I'm a friend. *He's* out to use you, Penny. He wants to hurt you."

"But... he gave me back my hat..."

"Don't you wonder how he got it? A little prick on a bicycle stole your hat!" Mr Pinner was shouting; I had never seen that before. "A little arrogant cocksure prick stole your hat and pedalled away laughing and you really think some random stranger would go to any effort at all to bring it back, that he cares, that it matters anything to him? There's no reason for him to help you: just another fucker in the street, another guy you can't trust, another harmless man who at the slightest word is going to hit, or stab, or shout, or spit, or do all the things these pricks do because they can, because they're fucking strangers and you can't trust them! *Get away from him!*"

Penny looked down uncertainly at me.

Mr Pinner blurted, "You think he just *found* your hat, Penny? There are eight million people in this city! You are tiny, you are *nothing* to them, an infinitely small part of a great machine too big to ever be understood; people don't care! You can walk down the same street a million times and never see the same faces, never be recognised, never be appreciated, smiled at, laughed with, loved, *known*, because you're just a nothing to them, another person who happens to live in the city, getting in their fucking way, so why should he bother? Why would anyone ever fucking bother with you?

"You've seen it, Penny Ngwenya, stood on the edge of the hill and looked down on the city and known you can just lift up your toes and fall for ever, tumble for ever into the void and no one will ever notice, no one will ever even know! Cretin! Maggot! Scum! Stupid kids in their fucking hoods, stupid fuckers pissing in the street! He's part of it! He's come here tonight to hurt you! He's part of the fall, one of the men who laugh when your back is turned, part of the insanity!

"Give me the hat, Penny. Give it to me, and we can end this. Just like you wanted to, we can end this tonight, just give me the hat..."

Penny half-rose, turned towards Mr Pinner. I grabbed her hand as she stood, pulled her back towards me; she jolted at our touch, as if surprised to find us still there.

"There's no such things as strangers, Penny Ngwenya. Not in the city. Just other Londoners. Not strangers at all."

She looked at me with a pair of perfect oval eyes in a perfect oval face.

She smiled, and carefully pried her fingers away from mine, wiping the blood off casually on her trousers as she rose.

She stood up, straightened, and turned towards Mr Pinner, who held out his arms towards her, paper frame twitching and shuddering as if short of breath.

She raised the hat in her hands, turned it, dome up towards the sky.

Mr Pinner smiled.

She lifted the hat towards him, and then past him, up in a long, careful arc, and without a word, put it down on her head, twisting it into a familiar, comfortable position.

She let out a sigh, closed her eyes, seemed to relax over every inch of her body.

Mr Pinner made a little sound. It was somewhere between a choke and the rustle of old crumpled paper.

Penny looked up, stared Mr Pinner straight in the eye and smiled.

She said, "You weirdo psychopath. Fuck right off out of here before I call the fucking police, I mean *Jesus*."

Mr Pinner whimpered. He staggered away from her a few paces, his arms falling limp to his sides. "But I...I..." he stammered.

"Seriously, I'm not shitting around. I mean, where do you get off with this crap?"

"I meant...I meant it for...I only wanted to..." he gabbled. Paper drifted from the tears in his arm, popped out of his left ear, dribbled down his right nostril in thin pale strands.

"Look, I'm calling the police, seriously," she said, reaching into her pocket and pulling out a mobile phone. "You can do all the shouting and spitting you fucking want; I've got community support officer training and I've had it up to *here* with weirdo psychopaths thinking they can get away with it. I mean, look at you! You wanna go to jail, arsehole? You wanna? Because I swear that this is the last time some testicle of a male mouths off at me! Look! Dialling!"

She dialled 999, held the phone to her ear.

Mr Pinner held out his hands imploringly. His thumb started to unravel, long white sheets spilling down from his fingers like a mummy's bandages. "Please," he whimpered, "I only wanted to help, I was...I was..."

Paper tumbled down from underneath his tattered trouser, spun in the river breeze.

"Yeah, police and ambulance please. Yeah? Yes, that's the number. Penny Ngwenya. Yes."

Mr Pinner's eyes fell on me, blue biro ink dribbling out of the tear glands. "I'll...I'm...I'll..." he croaked, but his mouth was filling with fat reams of paper, choking on it. His jacket had come undone to let out files and sheets that tumbled from his thinning chest like it was skin shaven from a corpse.

"You still here?" she asked, holding one hand over the receiver of her phone.

Mr Pinner tried to speak, couldn't, his jaw was melting away into spinning thin shards. His shoulders dribbled down his back, his legs crumpled and began to give way, revealing thin tubes of cardboard, that bent and twisted beneath the little remaining weight of documentation on his torso.

"Hi, yeah, London Bridge. The middle of the actual bridge. There's this guy...looks hurt...yeah, this other guy's been mouthing off at me, but..." Penny's eyes rolled over the skeletal paper remains of Mr Pinner. "...but I don't think it's gonna be a problem. Yeah. Ambulance. Yeah."

"I...I...ah..." gasped Mr Pinner, and then there wasn't a throat left to gasp with, a body left to gasp.

Bits of limp paper drifted by me.

I caught a few in my bloody fingertips.

...buy now and save £25 on the initial...

A water meter fitted to your system can greatly reduce...

...ISA investment profit projection of...

—GIRLS GIRLS GIRLS GIRLS—

The last piece of paper to fall from Mr Pinner's body was half the size of a sheet of A4, covered in small formal text. It said:

Penalty Charge Notice
Road Traffic Act 1991 (as amended)
(Sections 48, 66, 75, 77, Schedule 3 and Schedule 6)

Notice No.: 0215911   Date: 03-10-2009

Time: 15.19

The Motor Vehicle with
registration number: L602 BIM

Make: Volvo   Colour: Green

was seen in: Dudden Hill Lane

By Parking Attendent no.: 11092

Who had reasonable cause to believe that the following
parking contravention had occurred...

I let the paper go, watched it drift out over the edge of the bridge,
spin into the air, fall down into the darkness above the river. Penny,
standing on the edge of the pavement, lowered her phone and said
carefully, "That guy just turned into paper."

"Yeah," I sighed. "How about that?"

"Um..." she began.

"The city is a dragon, Penny Ngwenya. A great big, mad, insane,
dark, brooding, furious, wild, rushing, fiery, beautiful dragon. Do
you know what the spleen does?"

"No, I..."

"No," I sighed. "Me neither."

And then, because it seemed like the right and most sensible thing
to do, I closed my eyes, put my head down on the pavement, and let
the gentle rustling of the river below me and the whispering of paper
falling through the air sing me into an endlessly falling darkness.

Epilogue: The Sorcerer's Apprentice

In which all things end, and something new and unexpected begins.

The Lord said, "Let there be light."

And lo, mankind decided to capture said light, put it in a neon tube, install it in all hospitals everywhere, and leave it on at unwholesome hours when sensible members of the Homo sapiens line should have been sleeping.

For this reason, rather than because we felt like it, we opened our eyes.

A hospital.

Again.

Life suspended.

Not our favourite place.

A private room; nice. A wristband proclaiming "John Doe". Also nice. A heart monitor that went "ping" without any good reason and with no explanation at random intervals. A woman asleep at the end of the bed. This is the sort of thing soppy single men in need of mothering dream about.

I said carefully, "Oda?"

The woman stirred slowly, looked up, said, "Who's Oda?"

Next to the woman was a traffic warden's hat.

An Alderman came to visit.

I didn't recognise her, but the big black coat and hard expression were a giveaway.

She said, "Ms Dees. I'd offer to shake hands, but maybe when you're not wired up to machines that go 'ping'?"

I said, "Where's Mr Earle?"

"Mr Earle...did not make it. We're having a memorial service tomorrow afternoon. I'll have some flowers sent in your name. Don't worry about the cost. We'll settle these things when you're feeling better."

"Did many..."

"Aldermen died; Aldermen lived. The details are unimportant," she replied.

"Kemsley?" I asked. "Did Kemsley..."

"Mr Kemsley is in a stable condition. He has been moved from Elizabeth Garrett. He is scheduled for major reconstructive surgery to...iron out...some of the consequences of his encounter with Mr Pinner, just as soon as his body is strong enough to survive the procedure. You need not concern yourself with Mr Kemsley either."

"What should I concern myself with?" I asked carefully.

"At the moment, very little!" she replied. "The city is saved, Mr Pinner is gone, the Midnight Mayor lives. I'd say that was deserving of a Christmas bonus, yes? There is only one question outstanding."

"Well?" I asked.

"The city is saved. But for how long?"

I shrugged, feeling stitches pull. "A while?" I suggested.

"While an untrained sorceress wanders the streets?"

"You mean Penny?"

"If we are being so *informal* about the woman who summoned the death of cities to our streets, then yes, Ms Ngwenya."

"You know she's sat in the corridor outside eating takeaway curry, right?"

"I know," she said. "The Aldermen are watching."

"Ms Dees?" we asked carefully. "Do you know what the spleen does?"

"Part of the immune system," she replied calmly. "Stores blood reserves, breaks down old blood cells from the body. Why do you want to know? You've still got one, I believe."

"We just wished to understand you a little better," we told her. "That's all."

She smiled, leant forward across the bed until her face was a few inches from mine. "Mister Mayor," she said, "everything changes, sooner or later. Especially the city. You look after yourself, Mr Mayor. I'm sure we'll have plenty of time to discuss these things later."

And she left.

The next day I got a bunch of flowers, too big to put anywhere except against the opposite wall, in a wide wicker basket.

Three weeks later, I got the bill.

There were other things that needed to be done.

Blood is hell to shift from clothes that aren't soaked immediately.

The hospital declared my old clothes a write-off and graced me with a set of surgeon's slacks that made surprisingly comfortable pyjamas.

On my release, I bought a new pair of shoes.

I also indulged in a few nights at hotels. Pampering has its place.

Sometimes, when I was trying to go to sleep, the twin crosses on my right hand ached.

We got used to it.

There was a phone call that had to be made.

I didn't think about it until it happened, at 10 p.m. on a raining Tuesday night. I just picked up and dialled without looking at the numbers.

The phone rang, and kept on ringing, until at the last, someone answered.

She said, "Yes?"

"Loren?"

Silence. Then, "Who is this?"

"Matthew. It's Matthew."

Silence.

"Loren?"

"Goodbye, Matthew."

She hung up.

We didn't call again.

There was supper with Sinclair.

It was polite, pointless, and pompous.

We felt better for having had it.

We never say no to free food.

There was Oda.

Her hair had been burnt off, one side of her face was crinkled and withered. She said she was only there because the Aldermen had asked her. One hand was wrapped in bandages, thicker than the skin they protected. The skin drooped over her right eye like the skin of an old prune. She wouldn't look at us, wouldn't talk to us, wouldn't say a word, except one. When we stopped her at the elevator, said, "Oda..." she looked up at us and replied, *"Damnation,"* and walked into the lift, and didn't look back.

Time passed.

It's something time is good at doing.

Impersonal, passive, just rolling along like the river, too big to notice the bits of paper that get dragged along with the tide.

There was one thing left to do. Not for the Midnight Mayor, not even for us and our fears or desires. One thing I had to do, and get it done with.

I went back to London Bridge.

Walked to the middle, drooped my arms over the edge of the railing, felt the stitches pull in my side and didn't care. Breathed beautiful river air, let it swim through my body like liquid diamond, purifying all that it touched. I don't know how long I waited there; but it wasn't long.

Penny Ngwenya draped her arms over the edge of the bridge beside me, and said, "Hello, sorcerer."

"Hello, sorceress," I replied. "How are you feeling today?"

She shrugged. "OK, I guess."

We watched the river in silence. Finally she said, "A woman called Ms Dees talked to me today."

"Really? What did she say?"

"She offered me a two-week away-break, all expenses paid, job guaranteed when I came back. Just walked up and said, 'Take it, and it'll be OK.'"

"What did you say?"

"It's in Scotland."

"Scotland can be very pretty, when it's not raining."

"It's in the *countryside* — and when does it not rain in Scotland?"

I sighed. "Don't take it," I said. "Ms Dees will ship you up to Scotland and you'll never come back. She'll make sure you never come back, never return to a city ever again. It's part of her job."

"OK."

Silence a while longer. Then she said, very quietly, "The... they tell me I nearly destroyed the city."

"How tactful of them."

"The Aldermen."

"I know. I recognised their lack of tact."

"They tell me I'm a threat. A danger. That for me, good people have died."

I thought about it. "People have died," I said finally. "'Good'... who knows? But yes, people have died. And yes, you dunnit. I'm sorry to tell you, but you dunnit fair and square. You stood on this bridge and cursed the city, damned it to burn and suffer for what it had done to you, called forth the death of cities to plague the people within. He was your vengeance, your curse. And you were utterly and completely innocent of it. You couldn't help it. You're a sorceress. Sorry. Kinda stuffed on that front."

Silence.

Then, "Should I go?"

"Go? Where?"

"Like...Scotland, like the lady said?"

"Seems a little hard on Scotland."

"If I did this, if I somehow..."

"You know you did. If you didn't know it, feel it in your belly, hear the shadows tell you and the river whisper it, if you couldn't feel it in your blood and bones, you'd be shouting a lot more abuse right now. You know what you are. You just didn't have anyone to explain it at the time."

She nodded slowly, eyes fixed on the water. "What should I do? I...I didn't mean..."

"There are other sorcerers," I said. "They can train you, help you get a control and, say, *not* summon primal forces of darkness and death—something you should keep an eye out for, by the way. You could try Fleming, in Edinburgh, she's excellent, or Graham, in Newcastle. Or, how's your French? There are some top-of-the-line sorcerers practising in Paris right now—Aod is a sweetheart; I mean, the flavour of the magic there is very different, much more stylised, I guess, not the same sodium stuff of London. But it's a nice city and you can learn some useful skills there."

Silence. Then, "I don't think I want to go to any of these places."

"There's others," I said. "If you don't want to stick too close to London after all this, I get it. There's some excellent practitioners in Hong Kong, and English is widely used round there anyway..."

"No," she said firmly. "That's not it. This is...this city is my home. This is where I want to be."

"You did almost wipe it out in a splurge of unconscious magical destruction," I pointed out. "I mean, others might find that a bit, you know, threatening."

She looked up sharply and said, "Do you?"

"Me? Well, no..."

"Who's good in London?"

"You really want to stay?"

"Yes."

"The Aldermen...?"

"You said I can be trained. If not, then it's kinda hard on Hong Kong."

She had a very stubborn chin when she needed one.

I sighed. "Look, sorcerers in London...there was this thing... there's not many...I mean..."

"Do you know any good sorcerers in the city?"

"No. I don't."

"Do you have an apprentice?"

"No."

"Can you teach?"

"No."

"Why not?"

"Penny, I'm not just...I mean, obviously not just...But there's things about who I am..."

"Are you a murderer?"

"No."

"A paedophile?"

"No!"

"You expect other people to do your washing-up?"

"What? No!"

"Secretly married with two kids you beat up whenever you go home?"

"No!"

"Then what's the problem?"

"Well, for a start...I'm the Midnight Mayor!"

"Which means?"

I hesitated. "I'm still not entirely clear on that," I said. "Protector of the city is a vague job description at the best of times, but that's not the point. We are not willing to...I'm not going to take the risk, OK?"

"Of teaching me? Am I that dangerous?"

"It's not you, it's me."

She grunted. "Heard that before."

"Penny!" we snapped. "Listen! We are not merely a sorcerer! We are more! Brighter, faster, we are me and I am us, and we... we burn the things we touch. We burn because of the beauty in the burning, because life is precious, extraordinary, and we would live it as if we were on fire with the brightness of it. Life is magic. We live to prove this true. It is a fire that mortals cannot sustain. I will burn, one day. My skin will crack and my blood will fall and when it does it will be blue electric fire and all that is human and mortal in me will dissolve in fire and speed and fury and delight and not even notice that it has died though I am senseless and alone. I cannot teach you. I will not have you share this fate, capisce?"

She thought about this a long hard moment, then said, "Well, bugger you with a pineapple."

"Beg pardon?"

"I said..."

"I got the idea."

"Way I see it," she snapped, "is, if you are this protector of the city, and I am, basically, a walking bomb waiting to burst, then isn't it your job as fucking protector to stop all threats from wandering the streets? Now, I'm going to wander your streets, Matthew Swift, because they made me who I am, because they defined me and what I believe in and how I think and feel and travel. And if I happen to go apeshit while doing it, then up yours, protector. You'll have failed, all because you were scared *you* might hurt *me*. When I was going to destroy this city for... for so many fucking things... you gave me back my hat. You could have killed me, and you got *shot* giving me back my hat. And you really think you're going to hurt me? Christ! Get a shrink already!"

We stared at her in horror. "But we..."

"Don't give a shit!"

"I can't..."

"Seriously! Look at my face! From now on I am going to be a difficult bitch until I get my way, and you, Matthew Swift, are standing right between me and my intended plan of being one kick-arse sorceress who can totally go out there and get her shit done. So either help me, or get out of my way, and the only way you're getting out of my way, Mr Mayor, is by helping me. It's your choice."

"It's not really a *choice*."

"Then it should be very easy to make."

I looked her up and down slowly by the neon lights of London Bridge. I looked up at the reflected sodium glow in the night-time sky, down at the river rippling below. I heard the rumble of traffic, the squawking of seagulls made fat on chips, smelt coffee and exhaust fumes and the distant rumbling of London Bridge station. I ran my fingers over the twin crosses scarred into the palm of my right hand, rubbed the back of my head, stretched from my nose to my toes, let out a long sigh of pure Thames air. Thought of mad eyes in a night-time dragon, of the songs that the telephones used to sing, and the shape of a traffic warden's hat.

I said, "If we do this..."

"Yeah?"

"...promise me you won't give up the day job?"

She shrugged. "Too late. Already quit. When do we start?"

I sighed, turned on the spot to look at the city, stretching out all around, the lit-up wonders in the night, Tower Bridge, the London Assembly (which would always and for ever be known as Ken's Bollock), Hay's Wharf, HMS *Belfast*, Southwark Cathedral, the *Golden Hinde*, Southwark Bridge, Millennium Bridge, Tate Modern, Blackfriars, St Paul's Cathedral, the Old Bailey, the Monument, a great golden flame frozen for ever on top of a stone pillar, reminding the city of the last time it nearly died...

...nearly being the operative word...

I started to smile.

"Life," we said, "is magic."